Cursed with a poor se~~~~~~~~~~~~~~
propensity to read, **An**~~~~~~~~~~
her childhood lost in b~~~~~~~~~~~~~
Literature followed by ~~~~~~~~~~~~~
didn't lead directly to her perfect job—writing
romance for Mills & Boon—but she has no
regrets in taking the scenic route. She lives in
London: a city where getting lost can be a joy.

Karin Baine lives in Northern Ireland with
her husband, two sons and her out-of-control
notebook collection. Her mother and her
grandmother's vast collection of books inspired
her love of reading and her dream of becoming
a Mills & Boon author. Now she can tell people
she has a *proper* job! You can follow Karin on X,
@karinbaine1, or visit her website for the latest
news—karinbaine.com.

Also by Annie Claydon

Country Fling with the City Surgeon
Winning Over the Off-Limits Doctor
Neurosurgeon's IVF Mix-Up Miracle
The GP's Seaside Reunion

Also by Karin Baine

Midwife's One-Night Baby Surprise
Nurse's New Year with the Billionaire
Tempted by Her Off-Limits Boss

Christmas North and South miniseries

Festive Fling with the Surgeon

Discover more at millsandboon.co.uk.

THE DOCTOR'S ITALIAN ESCAPE

ANNIE CLAYDON

SPANISH DOC TO HEAL HER

KARIN BAINE

MILLS & BOON

All rights reserved including the right of reproduction in whole or in part in any form. This edition is published by arrangement with Harlequin Enterprises ULC.

This is a work of fiction. Names, characters, places, locations and incidents are purely fictional and bear no relationship to any real life individuals, living or dead, or to any actual places, business establishments, locations, events or incidents. Any resemblance is entirely coincidental.

Without limiting the author's and publisher's exclusive rights, any unauthorized use of this publication to train generative artificial intelligence (AI) technologies is expressly prohibited. HarperCollins also exercise their rights under Article 4(3) of the Digital Single Market Directive 2019/790 and expressly reserve this publication from the text and data mining exception.

® and TM are trademarks owned and used by the trademark owner and/or its licensee. Trademarks marked with ® are registered with the United Kingdom Patent Office and/or the Office for Harmonisation in the Internal Market and in other countries.

First published in Great Britain 2025
by Mills & Boon, an imprint of HarperCollins*Publishers* Ltd,
1 London Bridge Street, London, SE1 9GF

www.harpercollins.co.uk

HarperCollins*Publishers* Macken House, 39/40 Mayor Street Upper, Dublin 1, D01 C9W8, Ireland

The Doctor's Italian Escape © 2025 Annie Claydon

Spanish Doc to Heal Her © 2025 Karin Baine

ISBN: 978-0-263-32509-6

06/25

This book contains FSC™ certified paper and other controlled sources to ensure responsible forest management.

For more information visit www.harpercollins.co.uk/green.

Printed and Bound in the UK using 100% Renewable Electricity at CPI Group (UK) Ltd, Croydon, CR0 4YY

THE DOCTOR'S ITALIAN ESCAPE

ANNIE CLAYDON

MILLS & BOON

CHAPTER ONE

Seven o'clock in the morning. Dr Joe Dixon swallowed the last gulp from his reusable coffee cup and turned his face up towards the morning sun, which slanted across the pavement. People were already up and out, making the most of what promised to be a fine Saturday morning, and he could take a moment or two before finding his keys and opening the doors of the community medical clinic.

People-watching had always been something of a hobby of his. When he was a kid he'd watched the confusing hierarchy of people whose job it was to shape his future, with increasing diligence. He'd practically made a study of them, keeping coded notes and lists for future reference. The social workers and children's rights officers who probably wouldn't bend the rules to make things happen, and those who might. Those who might be persuaded to smile and talk to him and those who wouldn't be getting too involved...

Things were different now and he'd taken his own life in hand—along with the lives of others—he watched his patients as assiduously as he'd once wished he might be watched. He'd rejected London, taking his revenge for the string of abandonments that the city had meted out to him, and come to Rome. People-watching had served him well here, too, allowing him to settle into his role as a trauma doctor at the English-speaking hospital in Rome and then pour all of his free time and money into setting up a free clinic, which served those who were dealing with the long-term effects of life-changing illness or injury.

And on this fine morning people-watching was sending a pleasurable tingle up his spine. Dr Bel Trueman, whose smile currently decorated the list of recent arrivals that was pinned up on the doctors' noticeboard, had seen his own notice asking for volunteers to help at the clinic and used the email address printed at the bottom. Joe had replied, thanking her for her interest and saying he'd be at the clinic from eight in the morning on Saturday. She was welcome to pop in at any time that was convenient and he'd show her around. And now she'd just turned the corner at the end of the street, a full hour early, and everyone else had suddenly become invisible.

Joe leaned against the front door of the clinic watching her carefully, which probably wasn't strictly necessary because the days when his future was controlled by others were long gone. He'd seen her at the hospital, even been introduced briefly, before they both had to hurry in different directions, and she'd seemed no different from the other doctors who were working in the Trauma Unit. Focused and professional, wearing the uniform of scrubs under a crisp white coat. But now she seemed to have a lot more in common with the gradually awakening life on the streets.

If she hadn't spent time in Italy before, then she was a quick learner. In London a white shirt and skinny jeans could be as neutral as anyone wanted them to be, but here in Rome, women were more likely to treat any outfit as a fashion statement. The way her shirt was folded and tucked at the waist made Bel look as if she'd be at home on a catwalk, and her soft leather pumps and matching tan handbag completed the ensemble. Her dark curls, which looked casual but were probably the result of a determined encounter with a hairdryer this morning, made it clear that she didn't consider the weekend an appropriate time for the more severe tied-back style he'd seen at the hospital.

Gorgeous. She looked gorgeous, and if Joe had been the kind of man to fall for a virtual stranger then he'd be falling right now for Bel. Instead, he watched her carefully, returning her smile when she caught sight of him.

'*Salve.*' The one word betrayed a fluency that Joe could only envy. After three years in Rome, his Italian was good but still marked him out as English here at the clinic, where Italian was usually spoken.

He nodded in reply. 'You're early.'

Bel shrugged, indicating the coffee shop across the street. 'Not really. I have a book with me and I can be as late as you like.'

Don't!

Don't offer to buy the coffee, and join her beneath the flapping sunshades, in an effort to get to know Bel on a personal level. Joe had tried to get to know foster families and carers too many times, and even the couple who'd taken him in when he was ten and given him the stability of a real family hadn't been able to rub that instinct out. He couldn't think of anything urgent he needed to do before the clinic opened at ten o'clock, but he was sure to find something to keep him busy.

He turned, unlocking the door. 'I'll see you later, then?'

Her smile made *later* seem far too far away. 'Anything wrong with now?'

'Nothing at all. Thanks for coming...'

Joe motioned Bel inside, while he drew up the shutters over the windows. When he joined her, she was looking around the reception area with obvious approval.

'This is nice. Welcoming...' Her fingers skimmed the leaf of a large flowering plant on the reception desk. 'Not so scarily antiseptic as the hospital.'

'We do different things. Our patients are in a different stage of recovery from those we see in the Trauma Unit.'

Bel nodded. 'That's why I volunteered. I want to see what happens to people after they leave the hospital and what challenges they face. I'm hoping it'll make me a better doctor.'

Joe reckoned it probably would. No one spent their free time volunteering at a place like this unless they wanted more for their patients. 'We're not short on challenges.'

Red rag to a bull. Bel's dark eyes flashed as she looked up at him. Her perfect proportions had made her seem taller at a distance, but now he towered over her. It gave him the oddest feeling of wanting to protect her, although Bel's confident manner made it very clear that she could protect herself.

'It's exactly what I want. Everyone's a volunteer here?'

'Yes, apart from Maria, our receptionist. She's here every evening during the week, and on Saturdays.'

She nodded. 'What made you set this place up?'

'I volunteered with a similar clinic, back in London. When I came to Rome...' He shrugged. 'There are exactly the same kinds of needs here, and I'm passionate about my job.' Joe reminded himself, in case he was tempted to forget, that his job was the one and only thing he dared to be passionate about.

Bel nodded. 'You're a Londoner? Which part?'

Joe had moved too many times to lay claim to any part of the city as home, apart from the small house in Chelsea where his adoptive parents had lived. He was ten when they'd first fostered him and they were in their fifties, but they'd seen straight through his bravado, and had given him his first taste of what it was like to be part of a family. When they'd died, four years ago, Chelsea had been added to the list of places he didn't go back to.

'I moved around a lot. I was a Chelsea Football Club supporter.'

She grinned. 'What a coincidence—I grew up in Chelsea. My mum and dad still live there.'

If that was an invitation to share, Joe would pass on it. Bel's accent betrayed traces of the more prosperous side of the borough, and he guessed that she'd grown up in a different world from the one he had. He changed the subject.

'Have you worked in Italy before?'

'No, but I've always wanted to. My mother's Italian, and we used to come here for holidays. The job at the hospital is a real opportunity for me but it doesn't give me the chance to use my Italian. I hear that the clinic's mostly Italian speaking?'

'Yes, that's right. We've recruited as many local doctors and therapists as we can, and they've become the backbone of our work here. Unlike the hospital, we cater mostly to local people, not visitors and tourists. I've passed my language exams to practise here, but sometimes my accent leaves a bit to be desired.'

She grinned up at him, and Joe's heart inexplicably missed a beat. Bel reached into her handbag, pulling out a sheaf of paper and handed it to him. 'My curriculum vitae.'

Generally, if Joe could get a volunteer who'd already gone through the rigorous screening and interview process that the hospital put its employees through, he skipped the CV part of the process. But when he went to hand the papers back to her, Bel frowned at him. Maybe she was keen to prove that prosperous Chelsea hadn't played its part in getting her this far in her career.

'Thanks, I'll take a look at it later if I may. Perhaps I can show you around?'

She nodded. 'Yes, I'd like that.'

Bel took some time looking at the photographs of the clinic's volunteers in the reception area, and then they moved on to the first-floor consulting rooms and the cramped office that Joe shared with anyone who wanted somewhere quiet for paperwork. Then back downstairs again, to the semi-basement, where there were more consulting rooms, an art therapy room and a gym.

'This is the largest part of the clinic—the building's on a slope so at the back the basement becomes the ground floor...' He stopped to switch on the light at the top of the staircase and Bel hurried ahead of him, disappearing past the curve in the stairs, obviously eager to explore. The light flickered, and he heard Bel call out to him, a note of urgent command in her voice.

'Joe! Switch the light off!'

Automatically he flipped the light back off again, hurrying downstairs to find out what the matter was. Then he saw it...

She was standing on the last stair but one, looking down at a dark pool of water that extended along the corridor and seemed to be coming from the open door of the gym. Joe froze in horror. His brainchild. His passion...

'We need to switch the water off. And the electricity.' Bel's voice cut through the shock. She motioned towards a light fitting in the corridor, and he saw water dribbling from it.

He moved. Back upstairs to the utility cupboard, behind Reception. In a daze, he switched off the main electrical supply. The stopcock for the water supply refused to budge at first, but he gingerly applied his strength to it and it turned.

'Has it stopped?' he called down to Bel.

'I think so. Seems to be slowing a bit.'

Joe muttered a curse under his breath. Slowing a bit wasn't enough, the rooms downstairs must already be waterlogged. But there was no time to worry about the heavy weight of what felt almost like grief which had suddenly landed on his shoulders, robbing him of the ability to think straight. He needed to get back downstairs and see what he could salvage from the mess.

He grabbed a torch and made for the stairs. Bel wasn't anywhere in sight but her pumps and soft leather handbag, propped on the bottom step, gave him a clue. When he reached the basement corridor he saw her standing in the gym, her skin-tight jeans rolled up to her calves.

'This is where it's coming from.' She pointed to a dripping hole in the ceiling. 'It's slowed down a lot—it was pouring through before you switched the water off.'

Joe walked over to the hole, feeling his trainers begin to squelch as they absorbed water. He could feel Bel at his side, or rather smell her scent. Delicate and expensive, a stark contrast with the mess around them. He held out his arm, stopping her from going any closer to the mess of plaster on the floor.

'Stay there, I'll go and get a ladder.' He handed her the torch and hurried to fetch the stepladder from the large cupboard in the hall, returning to find Bel had ignored him and was standing right under the hole in the ceiling, shining the torch upwards. When he chivvied her out of the way, she retreated to the rehabilitation steps, sitting down and pulling her feet up out of the water, watching him solemnly.

He *had* to stop thinking about every little move she made, as if that were the most important thing he had to deal with at the moment. Joe climbed the stepladder, shining the torch into the cavity between the ceiling and the floor upstairs. The news wasn't good and it was surprisingly comforting to have someone here, to give it to.

'I can see where the water pipe's burst—it's at one of the joints and it's come apart completely. Some of the water's gone downwards but...' He shone the torch into the cavity, looking carefully at the ceiling joists. 'It looks as if it's travelled across as well, so it'll be dripping down into the other rooms.'

'We should go and look. May as well get that over with,' Bel mused as he climbed back down the ladder.

'Why don't you go home? I'll need to get a plumber in and start getting everything dried out—' The words dried on his lips as Bel got to her feet. Standing on the second, shallow rehab step, she was practically eye to eye with him, her hands on her hips.

'You're going to send the only volunteer in the place home, when you have an emergency to deal with?' She shook her head, as if he was a recalcitrant child. 'What sort of manager *are* you?'

There were a lot of answers to that, but only one that he could give at the moment. 'If you don't mind, staying to help out…'

Bel rolled her eyes, stepping down onto the floor. The top of her head barely reached his shoulder, but it still felt as if she was more than a match for him. 'I don't mind. It's far better than being moved out of the way when there are things to be getting on with.'

Bel could have been a little more tactful. But something about Joe, his delicious bulk and his obvious distress at seeing the damage… Bel had always had a soft spot for a gentle giant.

Joe could stay right where he was, though, in the nice-to-look-at-but-out-of-reach zone. Even if he did have blue eyes that seemed to change with the light, darkening to the colour of the ocean in the shadows of the gym. And even if she did reckon that spending a little more time outside might bleach his light brown hair to a delicious natural shade of blond. That was none of her business, nor were his strong shoulders and the hands which clearly knew exactly how to be tender. She'd made up her mind that she wasn't in the market for a new relationship, and what good were resolutions if you didn't stick to them when the going got tough?

Now was a time for practicality, though. You saw a need and you moved heaven and earth to meet it. And in less than three hours there would be patients knocking on the door. Presumably Joe would have enough volunteers to meet that need, but he didn't have anywhere for them all to go.

Then he smiled at her. Bel had summoned up the nerve to silently challenge him to send her home if he dared and it must have shown on her face, because he held his hands up in a gesture of surrender.

'Offer gratefully accepted. Since your Italian's probably much better than mine, how do you feel about phoning round to find someone who can provide us with dehumidifiers? As cheaply as possible...'

Bel nodded. She could do that, but she wasn't leaving Joe alone down here to face the damage all by himself. That was just plain good manners. 'Okay, let's take a look around, and you can tell me exactly what you're going to need.'

Joe nodded, his jaw setting as if he were steeling himself for the worst. There was an art therapy room next to the gym, which almost broke Bel's heart, with ruined pictures peeling from the walls and other projects soaked and spoiled. He hurried her out of there into two consulting rooms, both of which had soaked carpets and water dripping out of the mattresses on the patient couches. The two smaller rooms at the back of the property were a little more encouraging. There were water stains on the ceilings and the carpets were wet in places, but nothing that wouldn't dry out and be put right easily. Joe opened the windows and a door at the end of the corridor which led out into a walled garden, letting a warm breeze into the chill of the basement.

'I reckon...just give them the size of the four rooms at the front, and let them tell us what they think we'll need. We can compare prices and make a decision.'

Bel nodded. She had a better idea but she'd tell him about that if and when it worked.

He could hear her voice drifting downstairs from the reception area as he mopped the tiled floor of the corridor, trying to make a start on getting as much water out of the place as he could. Bel's tone was warm and conversational but businesslike, and Joe wondered whether he'd be able to deny her anything if she tried those tactics with him. Three-quarters of an hour later he heard her calling him, and walked back up the stairs.

'I've got three quotes.' She was sitting at the reception desk, her phone in front of her. 'You want the good news or the bad news?'

'Bad news first.'

She slid a sheet of paper towards him and he sat down. Just as well—the cost of this was eye-watering...

'Now for the good news.' She handed him a second sheet of paper, clearly unable to resist a slight flourish as she did so. Joe focused his eyes reluctantly onto the page. Even the best news he could imagine wasn't going to get the job done.

'This is...it's much better. Are they a reputable company?'

She tilted the screen of the receptionist's computer around and he saw a very professional-looking website. 'They're the best. Very well regarded—look at the reviews.' She clicked a link, displaying a string of five-star reviews. There *had* to be a catch, surely…

'How did you get such a good quote?'

'A successful company is more likely to be in a position to give a discount on a job that'll enhance its reputation. I went to the three best firms in the city and told them that we're a free clinic, doing important work.' She smiled at him. 'Then I begged a little.'

He doubted that. 'You begged?'

She shrugged. 'Maybe it was more a case of asking nicely. One of them wouldn't give me a discount, and two did. This is the best one, and they said they could send a plumber this morning to fix the pipe.'

'And what's the catch?'

'Don't be such a cynic. There's no catch. I just said that we'd give them a good review if they didn't cut any corners on the job. You can do that, can't you?'

Joe nodded. 'I'll give them the best review I've ever written if they do it for this price. Are you sure this includes everything?'

'Yes, positive. I spoke to the managing director at home…'

'Wait…' Joe held his hand up and she fell silent. 'You know the managing director?'

'No, but he's the one with the authority to do a good deed if he wants to. I spoke to someone at the office and told them that I was sure their boss would see this as an opportunity. Clearly, he did because he rang me back…'

Joe laid the paper down on the desk. Bel had done something that wouldn't have occurred to him, but she'd solved a problem and got the clinic what it needed for a really good price. 'Am I allowed to call him back and thank him? Tell him that I hope I'll be the first person he calls if there's anything I can help him with.'

She shot him a smug look. 'Too bad. I've already assured him that I should be the first person he calls—you can be the second, if you like. But you can speak to him to accept the quote if you like. *Lo sono molto grato...*' She snatched up the sheet of paper and called a number then slid her phone across the desk towards him.

'Yeah, okay, I think I can stretch to thanking someone.' Joe chuckled. He'd thought he was taking on a volunteer and found himself with a whirlwind on his hands. But right now, a whirlwind was exactly what he needed.

CHAPTER TWO

THE VOLUNTEERS WERE starting to arrive now, along with Maria, the receptionist. Joe had decided that the best course of action was to close the clinic for the weekend and offer video appointments which the volunteers could carry out from upstairs and, so far, his plan seemed to be working well. People were used to video appointments after going through lockdown and Maria had told Bel that no one had opted to reschedule so far.

Joe was busy co-ordinating the volunteers and speaking to patients and Bel set to work downstairs, speaking with the contractors when they arrived and doing what she could to clear the gym and the art room, along with the two consulting rooms that were the worst affected. It was hard work, and she had to call for help with the heavy gym equipment, but everyone was pulling together and doing what they could. If she'd been looking for testimonials to the clinic that Joe had created, then this was it. The clinic was obviously important to the people who gave their free time to work here.

He appeared in the doorway to the gym just before noon, and the look on his face said everything. Joe shook the hands of each of the workmen, thanking them, and then he turned to Bel. His smile replaced the weariness from backbreaking work, and she began to see only what had been achieved.

'This is…it's beyond great. Thank you so much.'

She felt a tingle of warmth travelling towards her fingertips. Bel had perfected the art of playing it cool, ever since Rory had broken her heart, and left her reputation in tatters, but Joe was a challenge that she hadn't anticipated.

'Looks a bit better, doesn't it? The plumber's almost done with the water pipe now, and the bits of plaster are almost all out of the carpet.' She gestured towards one of her own contributions to the cleaning-up process.

'It's marvellous. Can I ask one question?'

'Of course.' Bel looked around the room, wondering what had caught his eye.

'Where did you get wellington boots from, in Rome, in the summertime? And the socks to go with them?'

Bel looked down at her blue and white spotted boots. 'That's my secret. I got them when I went out for some LED lights, so that we'd be able to see what we're doing down here. You want a pair?'

He chuckled. 'Far too stylish for me—I couldn't carry them off. Are you thinking of going home any time soon?'

'No, I'm afraid you're stuck with me for the day. Why?'

'How do you feel about doing what you came here for? We've had a walk-in, someone who needs our help. She's summoned up the courage to come and I don't want to turn her away, so I was going to sit down with her and take her through exactly what she wants from us. Or you could, if you want.'

Bel could do with a sitting-down job right now, but she wasn't sure that she was up to this. 'I came here to learn. I don't have a lot of experience with the kind of work that you do here.'

'You can talk to people, can't you? Right now, all we want to do is find out what she wants from her rehabilitation, and what she thinks she's not getting elsewhere. And to reassure her that she's done the right thing in asking for help and that we'll do everything in our power to give her what she needs.'

'I'm…' Bel decided against telling him that she wasn't really dressed for the part. Neither was Joe, and he didn't seem to be worried about that. 'Okay. You'll be there?'

'I'll be there. I'm counting on you not needing me.'

'Everyone has a learning curve.' Bel tried not to sound too breathless about having Joe overseeing hers. 'I expect you to step in if I miss anything, or go beyond the clinic's remit.'

He nodded. 'Received and understood. How do you take your coffee? Maria's going over to the café across the street to get drinks for everyone.'

'I haven't had my morning cappuccino yet…' A takeaway coffee with milk after ten in the morning was generally considered to be something that only tourists asked for.

Joe pulled his phone from his pocket. 'I'll tell Maria. And tender your apologies.'

The woman sitting in Reception was hollow-eyed and her smile seemed to be more for show than an indication of how she really felt. Maria handed Bel a clipboard, which contained a form with the woman's details, gathered up a stack of paper cups from her desk and left them alone.

'Mrs Chiara Albertini?' Bel glanced at the form, holding out her hand to the woman. 'I'm Dr Trueman—Isabella.'

Chiara nodded, silently shaking her hand, and Bel pulled one of the seats around to face her, sitting down. She recognised the way that Chiara seemed to have accepted defeat before they'd even started, because she'd started thinking that way herself with the long succession of lawyers who'd helped her fight Rory's claims about her...

Use the feeling. It's the only thing that makes it all worth it.

'This is hard, isn't it. I guess we're not the first people you've come to.'

Chiara twisted her mouth in an expression of regret, shaking her head.

'That's okay, it sometimes takes a while to find people who can give you exactly what you need. I'm new here as well, and I turned up this morning to find they have a flood in the basement, so today hasn't been going quite as planned...' Bel had lapsed into colloquial Italian now and she glanced at Joe, wondering whether he was keeping up. His brow was slightly furrowed but he said nothing, and Bel decided to take that as an invitation to continue.

'I did my homework before applying to join the team here, and I'm confident that this clinic will be the last place you need to come, even if it's not the first. But if I'm wrong, then here's my personal promise to you. You won't need to go through the process of looking again, because I'll do that for you.'

The beginnings of something ignited in Chiara's eyes. Surprise maybe, but it seemed that there was a little hope there, too. She smiled suddenly, making a subtle gesture, which asked Bel whether she wasn't overstepping the boundaries a little.

Maybe she was, but Bel didn't really care. Joe had put her in this seat, and she had a personal responsibility to her patients. She glanced at him again, and this time he responded.

'That's right. If we don't have the resources to help you, then we'll find someone who does. If we don't believe it's possible to help you, then we'll explain exactly why and give you the name of someone who can give you a second opinion, if you want one.'

Nicely put. Joe's expression had softened suddenly. Clearly, he wasn't quite as keen on throwing his patients in at the deep end as he appeared to be with his volunteers.

'Are we clear on that, then?' she asked Chiara.

'Yes. Would you like to see a copy of my medical notes?' Chiara reached into her handbag, taking out some sheets of paper, folded together. Bel glanced through them.

'Thanks. May I keep these for the file, please? I'd like to hear it in your own words as well, if you don't mind.'

Bel waited patiently as Chiara told her the story. Her traffic accident, and the long stay in hospital. All of her other injuries had healed well, but after intensive therapy her dyspraxia was still a problem for her.

'I'm sure your doctors have already told you that dyspraxia takes different forms. Can you tell me a little more, and maybe some of the practical things that you can't do, which you'd like to?'

Chiara nodded. 'I have difficulties with judging distance and speed. Knowing where I am in relation to the things around me. I can be clumsy and disorganised...' She turned the corners of her mouth down.

'In my experience, people with dyspraxia are often quite well organised. They need to be,' Bel encouraged her gently and Chiara laughed.

'Yes, that's true. I manage well at home now. I keep everything very tidy and in the same place. And my therapist helped me to improve my co-ordination and motor skills.'

'And you're happy with that?'

'Yes. I'm still learning, but it's getting better.'

Bel nodded. 'That's great. So would I be right in saying that your hospital therapist has taught you things which will keep you safe and allow you to be independent? But there's something more now that you want to do?'

'Yes. It's an unimportant thing, really...' Chiara was nervous again now.

'If it's important to you, then it's important to me. Can you tell me about it, please?'

Chiara smiled. 'I used to sew.' She reached hesitantly into her bag, bringing out a wrapped package and cradling it protectively in her lap.

'Would you like to show me?' Bel asked and Chiara carefully removed the plastic and fabric wrappings and produced a piece of embroidery.

Bel caught her breath. 'That's beautiful.' There was colour and movement in the design that made it seem almost alive. 'You made this?'

'Before my injury. I was beginning to sell my pieces at craft fairs, but now I just can't do it any more. I have a little boy, he was born a few months before I had the accident, and I try to help him draw but...my drawing's worse than his. My husband draws with him but…' Chiara's eyes filled with tears.

Bel wanted so much to promise her that the clinic would help, but she honestly didn't know. She aimed her finest imploring look in Joe's direction, but his attention was on Chiara.

'You know that we can't guarantee success?'

Chiara nodded, turning her gaze onto him. 'I know. The thing I can't accept is not even trying.'

'We'll try. I have just the therapist in mind for you, Martina's very highly qualified, with a great deal of experience in helping people with dyspraxia. When her granddaughter was born she showed me some little dresses she'd made for her, so she understands the basics of sewing as well. How does that sound?'

A tear rolled down Chiara's cheek. 'That would be wonderful. Do you think she'd agree to see me?'

'I'm sure she will.' Joe got to his feet. 'Let me go and call her now, and we'll work out a time that suits you both—'

'Any time. I will come any time that she is able to see me. Tell her I would appreciate it so much, please, Dr Dixon. Thank you. And thank you, Dr Isabella.'

Joe grinned. 'We haven't done anything yet. I'm not going to be doing anything at all—it'll be you doing all of the hard work.'

'I'll work. Please, just give me a chance and I'll work hard.'

'Just do what you can, that's all we ask of you. You'll have the therapy that you want and a doctor will be assigned to you, to co-ordinate everything and answer any general health queries you might have. Since Dr Trueman has experience in treating head trauma and brain injuries, then—'

'Yes, of course,' Bel interrupted him. Maybe she shouldn't sound quite so pleased that Joe had obviously found the time to read the CV she'd given him. 'Perhaps we could think about any other things which are important to you and make a list, Chiara?'

Joe smiled at her, nodding in approbation. If a couple of reindeer decked out in jingling bells had just flown past the window it really couldn't have felt any more like Christmas. That wasn't an entirely professional attitude to take either, and Bel decided that it was time to stop trying to prove herself to Joe.

'I'll leave you to it and go and make that call.' He rose from his seat and Bel wondered if he felt two gazes fixed on his back as he left the reception area to go upstairs.

Then Chiara turned away, her eyes full of tears. 'Thank you so much, Dr Isabella.'

'It's my pleasure.' This wasn't the same as her work at the hospital, where success was measured in different and more immediately quantifiable terms, but it was just as rewarding. 'Now, let's make that list, shall we? And I'll also want to know about all the physical symptoms that you're still experiencing…'

The first floor was busy. Joe had rigged up makeshift cubicles so that the volunteers could video call their patients as privately as possible, and he decided that going downstairs would be his best bet if he wanted somewhere quiet to speak to Martina. The dehumidifiers were already set up and working and he walked out into the small walled garden at the back of the clinic to make his call, putting Martina on hold to phone up to Reception and check what time on Monday Chiara would be available for a video call.

Maria brought him his coffee, sniffing in disdain when he suggested that she might like to go home, since she'd already organised what everyone would be doing today and the clinic was officially closed. She was sure she'd find something to do, and he was to sit down for half an hour and take a break or he'd have her to answer to. Joe obligingly sank down onto the garden bench, feeling the muscles in his legs and back pull a little after a morning spent shifting furniture and computers.

This. It had taken a catastrophe for Joe to realise that this was what he'd worked so hard to create. People who refused to go home when he told them to. A separate identity for the clinic which allowed doctors and therapists time to concentrate on what came after hospital therapists had done their job. Chiara had reminded him how important it was to help people regain their sense of self.

The information pack that Joe had emailed to Bel explained all of that very carefully, and she'd clearly read it and put all of the principles it outlined into action. He hadn't needed to intervene and nudge the conversation back on track. She'd been perfect, right from the start. So much so that he was confident that Bel and Chiara would be managing just fine without him.

He closed his eyes, tipping his face towards the late morning sun. The shock of realising that the clinic would have to close for an unspecified period of time was wearing off now. Things were already on their way back to normal and the work was carrying on. He could dare to plan again, maybe even think about making a few improvements when the work of putting everything back together again was undertaken...

He was just considering a more practical flooring material for the gym, since the carpet was obviously ruined and would have to be taken up, when he heard the doors leading into the garden squeak open. Maybe they should do something about that as well... The thought was hastily parked at the back of his mind when he saw Bel.

She had a delicious air of animation about her. Somehow, her lips seemed redder and her dark hair more... Joe couldn't think of a word to describe it. More like the 'after' pictures in the ads for shampoo which demonstrated bounce and shine. Perhaps, in the unsettling experience of seeing the basement full of water, he just hadn't noticed that about her before.

'Happy?' The question seemed to be an important one to her.

'In what respect?' Joe decided not to mention that he was *very* happy to see her.

Bel rolled her eyes, coming to sit down next to him on the bench. 'With my performance.'

Something fell into place. Joe was driven over his work—he knew that. It had a lot to do with not being able to fully trust his relationships with people and turning to something he *could* trust. He'd fallen into the trap of defining Bel by her seemingly effortless grace, but maybe she felt that she had something to prove, too.

'I did look at your CV, even though it's probably not necessary since I've no doubt that the hospital put you through the same recruitment process as everyone else.' Something about that very obvious statement caused a flash of outrage.

'Of course they did.'

Joe resisted the temptation to ask why on earth they wouldn't. 'You've already done more on your first day than we could possibly have expected, if that's what you're wondering. Practically speaking, we'll be able to open again sooner because of the quote you got us. And medically speaking, you listened to Chiara and found out what she wanted, so that I could match her with a therapist straight away. What's not to like?'

That seemed to mollify Bel. 'So I've got the job?'

'It's not a job. You're volunteering.'

'And volunteers are second-best? Is that what this clinic is—a place for second-best people?'

Joe was beginning to like her forthright approach. He knew where he stood with her.

'No. Quite the reverse, in fact. I find that volunteers are often a lot more exacting than people who are being paid for what they do. Maybe passion is more persuasive than money for some people, and they're the people I want for this clinic. I can't expect to take all of their time, but a few hours is precious.'

Finally, she smiled. It seemed like an achievement of some sort, something he could luxuriate in for a moment.

'Right then. That's good.' Bel had been clutching the clipboard to her chest as if it might be needed as either armour or an offensive weapon, but now she proffered it to him as if it were a gift. 'I've made a list of the things that Chiara would like to work on. What happens next— I give this to Martina?'

Finally, an easy question. 'I'll show you how to enter it all on the computer system. Martina's recently retired and she'll be logging in from home before she speaks with

Chiara on Monday.' Joe glanced at the closely written pages. 'Chiara's signed the data protection agreement?'

'Yes, Maria gave it to me when she brought the coffee. We read through it together.'

'Good. And Chiara understands what she can and can't expect from us?'

'Yes, I explained that every brain injury is different, and however hard we try we might not be able to help her regain all that she wants to. She knows that already, and reiterated what she said earlier. The thing she can't live with is not trying.'

Joe smiled, getting to his feet. 'We'll help her try. Actually, Martina will be forcing her to try when the time comes—it's not going to be an easy process. Since the office has been taken over for video conferencing, I'll go and get the laptop. This is as good a place as any to take you through entering everything onto the system.'

'I have mine here…' Bel produced a smart-looking device from her handbag, which appeared to have been carefully packed with anything that might be useful, and Joe smiled.

'Not yet. Before you connect your own devices to the system, we need to have *you* sign a data protection agreement and we'll have our IT guy check on your laptop's security. He's not available for a couple of weeks—he's a volunteer too, and he's on holiday at the moment.'

Bel nodded. 'Of course. Where do you get all of these volunteers from?'

Joe hadn't really thought about it. 'There's no particular strategy in place. I just know what we need and I ask.' Much as Bel had done this morning, only her approach had been a little more thought-out and she'd taken her request right to the top, which Joe very rarely did.

'It takes trust.' She was suddenly thoughtful. 'Expecting the best of people.'

It took audacity in Joe's experience, having the bad manners to ask busy people to give just a little more. Maybe trust on a different level from the emotional trust that Joe had long since decided wasn't for him. He decided that this wasn't a question he came equipped to answer.

'I'll go and get the laptop…'

CHAPTER THREE

Bel's apartment in the centre of Rome was one of a dozen, arranged on two floors around a courtyard. It was quiet, and with a bit of careful planning it remained comfortably cool through the heat of the day and into the evening. But pacing up and down, questioning herself, was making her feel hot and bothered.

She flung herself down onto the sofa, wriggling out of her jeans. Pacing barefoot, the tails of her white shirt brushing the tops of her legs, was a great deal more comfortable but still not making her feel any cooler.

She'd messed up today, badly. Joe was the kind of man that you could like on sight, good at what he did and clearly happiest in his skin when he had a medical problem to deal with. Particularly gorgeous skin, she might add, which was heart-thumpingly consistent with the rest of him. She'd wanted him to like her back and she'd tried too hard to earn his approval.

He was right, she was a doctor with good experience and great references, and that should have been enough. But Rory had stripped away all of her confidence.

It had been a whirlwind romance. Rory had been working in the financial services department of her father's company and they'd met at a company day out. His attentiveness was flattering and when he'd asked her to marry him after only three months, telling Bel that when you knew, you knew, she'd been swept off her feet and accepted his proposal.

It had never occurred to her that he didn't see her at all, and that all he saw was her father's wealth. But even that wasn't enough for Rory. He'd spent her birthday weekend at her parents' house in Chelsea, and when they'd gone back to their own flat he'd seemed dissatisfied with their home, complaining that Michael Trueman's only child should be better supported by her father. She'd even forgiven that careless cruelty—Rory couldn't have known her parents had wanted a bigger family, but that her mother's pregnancy had been difficult and after Bel was born there had been no more children.

It was all so easy to see now, to count the red flags and the hallmarks of emotional abuse. But back then, she'd been blind to it all. She'd blamed herself for Rory's dissatisfaction and fought to keep his love, telling herself that she could be whatever he wanted her to be. He'd started to come home late, leaving her sitting alone waiting for him when they'd arranged to go somewhere together, and she'd made excuses for him.

Then, six months later, the scandal had hit. Rory was accused of making use of private information about her father's company to play the stock market, buying stock just days before a new venture was announced and the share price skyrocketed. It was just good luck, wasn't it? But the words 'insider trading' wouldn't go away, however much Bel believed in Rory's innocence. She'd hung on, refusing to believe her father's lawyers, until they'd presented her with the statement he'd written, implicating her in his money-making venture.

She *hadn't* taken her phone to her father's study, photographed the documents filed away in his desk drawer and then emailed them to Rory. Nor had she drawn up a plan for stock purchases and asked Rory to make them on her behalf, via several different shell companies that had been set up in her name. But it had taken a year to prove her innocence, and that year had taken its toll on Bel. She was no longer the confident young woman who knew she'd been lucky to have a privileged upbringing, but also knew that she'd achieved something on her own. She was someone who could, and probably would, be judged only as the daughter of a rich man. A person who had something to prove.

And now she was worried about what Joe thought of her. She'd tried to prove herself to him, even though he'd told her what she knew already—that her qualifications spoke for themselves. But still she'd put herself on trial, hoping he'd give her the reassurance of pronouncing her innocent. Had she learned nothing?

Pacing wasn't doing any good at all. Bel stopped by the coffee table, picking up her phone and staring at it, as if that might give her some answers. Surprisingly, it did. Her father had always been there when she'd wanted to talk.

He answered almost immediately. 'Hello, sweetheart. How's my favourite doctor?'

'Good. Finding my way around the hospital still.' Just hearing her father's voice made Bel feel a little better. 'What are you and Mum up to?'

'Your mother's gone to her book club cheese and wine

evening, and so Wilf and I are fending for ourselves. He took me out for a run and now we're watching a film on TV, with a bowl of vegetable soup and some rather nice rosemary and garlic bread. All homemade and low in saturated fats, in case you were wondering...'

Her father had suffered a mild heart attack two years ago and that had been a wake-up call, for Bel and her mother at least, if not for him. He'd brushed off his doctor's advice, but Bel had made herself less easy to ignore and now her father had stopped working at weekends and had a much healthier diet. Wilf, the cocker spaniel, had more than enough energy to keep her father fit.

'No, Dad, I wasn't wondering. You're the one in charge of the changes you've made. Although I wouldn't mind knowing how your yearly check-up went.'

'Fine. My cholesterol and blood pressure are both down and Dr Humphries was very pleased with the twenty-four-hour ECG report. He congratulated me on obviously having followed his instructions to the letter.' Her father chuckled. 'I didn't let on about your intervention, he seemed so pleased with himself.'

'Good thought. Send me the ECG report, I'll take a look and let you know exactly what it all means.' Dr Humphries had done all of the right things, but her father didn't respond well to a list of dos and don'ts. He'd built his multi-million-pound business by thinking out of the box and making innovative decisions and Bel had approached him on that level, explaining everything to him and challenging him to take charge of his own health. That, her mother's cooking and the gift of a puppy had done the trick.

'Thanks, will do. How's your day been?'

Bel puffed out a breath. She'd been hoping that the conversation might take her mind off Joe.

'Interesting. I've volunteered to help at a free clinic which helps people in rehab. The next step in the process after we see them at the hospital.'

'You're thinking of expanding your scope of operations? How did that go?'

Dad had a habit of putting things in business terms, and an idea occurred to Bel.

'Actually... Would you mind if I asked your advice on how I might raise some cash?'

Her father chuckled. 'Ask away. That's my area of expertise...'

The beginning of the week in the trauma department of the hospital was busy, as the number of tourists in Italy's capital began to swell. Joe found himself working alongside Bel in A&E and at the outpatient clinic, and mutual respect for each other's skills, combined with having little time to think about anything but work, had allowed them to settle into a more companionable relationship. Bel still took his breath away and her smile never failed to make his heart beat a little faster, but Joe was dealing with it.

On Thursday they both happened to be travelling in the same direction for a minute or two and Bel gifted him with a scintillating smile. 'How are things going?'

'The basement's almost dried out now. It's looking much better than when you last saw it.' Joe decided not to mention the next stage, which was now occupying his thoughts during the evenings spent at the clinic. The insurance would take a while in coming through, and might not cover everything that needed to be done...

'Great. I don't suppose you're free for a coffee some time? It's to do with the clinic...' Someone beckoned to her urgently. 'Sorry. I'm busy with a patient at the moment, but perhaps I could catch you later to make a date?'

Bel hurried away, leaving Joe suddenly hungering for coffee. Since it *was* to do with the clinic and not a social invitation, he'd be justified in making himself free whenever Bel wanted to see him, but tonight was clearly out since Bel was busy and he was about to go off shift.

His phone bleeped, the familiar tone of the hospital's paging system telling him that he wasn't going anywhere just yet. He accepted the case, and made his way to the consulting room indicated on his screen.

Bel was already in attendance, along with an anaesthesiologist, and she left the young woman who was lying on the couch in his care for a moment, giving Joe a querying look.

'When I called for another doctor to assist, I didn't realise they'd be paging you. Shouldn't you be leaving in a minute?'

'Nope. Are you leaving?'

She smiled up at him. 'Nope.'

'Fill me in, then.'

'Lydia Crawford, aged twenty-one, she's a tourist from America. She came off a motorbike and has a displaced ankle fracture and second degree road rash on her left arm. She was in a lot of pain and I called the anaesthesiologist to administer a sedative, since she'll have to go into surgery to have her ankle realigned.'

Joe nodded. The road rash, caused by dragging along stones or asphalt, would need to be cleaned and irrigated, which was a painful process. 'You've decided to deal with both her ankle and her arm at the same time?'

'If we can. It'll be easier on her, I think.'

'Yeah. Which do you want me to take?'

Bel seemed surprised at the idea. 'Won't you be taking the lead? You're the senior doctor.'

He supposed he was. Her CV had told him that he was five years older than she was, and that Bel had only recently completed her six years of specialty training. But he knew full well that it would have equipped her to lead a team in the operating theatre, and Joe had never been inclined to pull rank on younger doctors.

'We don't do that here.' Some did, but Joe didn't. 'We're all doctors, and you know best how to deal with your own patients.'

Bel thought for a moment. 'Okay. I'd like you to concentrate on her leg, please. I'll deal with the road rash on her arm.'

Unusual choice. In Joe's experience, many doctors were all about the higher profile attached to surgical procedures, and would have left the painstaking process of tweezing debris from a patient's arm to whoever came to assist them.

'You're sure?'

Bel nodded. 'I had a tutor who had a particular interest in this kind of injury, and she taught me a lot. I think I can do well for Lydia.'

That put Joe in his place. If he'd been thinking that Bel was trying to please him, then he'd been mistaken. She'd already moved on now, turning to the nurse who was in attendance.

'Will you get Lydia ready for surgery now, please.

Dr Dixon and I will go and speak to the boyfriend, and then scrub up.'

The nurse nodded, and Joe followed Bel out of the consulting room and into the waiting area. She consulted her phone, looking up and scanning the handful of people who were waiting for news of their loved ones.

'Luke Matthews?' Her gaze settled on a young man with sun-bleached hair and a badly scuffed leather jacket. It looked as if he'd come through the accident better than his girlfriend.

'Yes…' He held up his hand, getting to his feet and walking towards Bel. 'I'm waiting for news of Lydia Crawford.'

'Hi, I'm Dr Trueman. Will you come with me, please.' Bel took him to one side, motioning for him to sit down with her. 'Lydia's going to be okay, but I'm afraid she's broken her ankle, and will need a short surgical procedure to realign the bones. She also has some nasty scrapes on her arm, which need to be cleaned and dressed. But she's in good hands and she'll mend.'

Luke nodded. 'Can I see her?'

'Not right now. She was in pain and an anaesthesiologist has sedated her. They're getting her ready for surgery and perhaps you'd like to go and get a drink and something to eat—there's a nice cafeteria here in the hospital. Come back in an hour, and the receptionist will be able to tell you where Lydia is.'

Luke heaved a sigh. 'We've got train tickets for Paris tomorrow. I don't suppose…?'

Bel shook her head. 'We'll be keeping her here overnight and tomorrow at least—her leg's very swollen and we may need to make adjustments to her cast. And, of course, Lydia needs time to recuperate after her surgery.'

'How long will that take? I really wanted us to see Paris together. I'm a Fine Arts major in college…' Luke took Bel's stunned silence as an invitation to elaborate on his theme. 'Lydia really likes that old film where they ride through Rome on a motorcycle, and we thought it would be fun. I *told* her that I should drive—none of this would have happened if she'd listened to me.'

'Luke…' Joe heard a trace of steel in Bel's tone. 'When she first came in, Lydia asked me to call her family, and I've passed their number over to our patient care team. We'll be liaising with them over what comes next, and my advice to them, and to Lydia herself, will be that she doesn't travel until she's well enough, which certainly won't be tomorrow. I dare say she'd appreciate a visit from you, but please concentrate on reassuring her rather than blaming her for spoiling your holiday. Do you understand me?'

'Yes. Okay…thanks, Doctor.' Luke turned the corners of his mouth down, shaking his head, and Bel rose from her seat. As soon as her back was turned, Luke grimaced up at Joe. 'Can you believe that?'

No, not really. Joe was surprised that Bel had let Luke off so lightly but, in all fairness, she didn't have time to give him a more thorough telling-off and it was beyond her remit to call him a selfish idiot.

'Listen to the doctor. Do as she says.' He turned his back on Luke, and followed Bel towards the operating suite.

He caught up with her in the scrub room, where she was clearly taking her frustration out on her own fingers.

'Steady on. It's not worth scrubbing until you're red raw over. What's the film they were trying to recreate?'

Bel relaxed suddenly. 'Haven't you seen *Roman Holiday*? It's an old black and white classic.'

'I don't watch too many films. I'm not a big fan of happy endings. I generally find myself wondering when the other shoe's going to drop.'

'You'd love this one, then. It's very sad at the end.'

'They fall off the scooter?' Joe chuckled.

'No, they…' Bel stopped herself, pressing her lips together. 'I'm not going to tell you. That would spoil it for you if you ever *did* get around to watching it.'

He probably wouldn't. Unhappy endings didn't do much for him either. 'Well, the ending to this particular scooter ride is that I'll be going up to the ward when we're finished here, and letting them know that they're to keep an eye on Luke. He'll be out of there before he knows what's hit him if he doesn't behave himself. They'll be keeping Lydia's parents informed as well, and making sure she gets to speak with them as soon as she can—they're very used to dealing with cases where patients' families are abroad.'

Bel nodded. 'Thanks. That's great. I was expecting they would but it's nice to hear.' She took a paper towel from the dispenser and dried her hands. 'Let's put this young lady back together again, shall we?'

Joe was a dream to work with. Focused and yet always aware of where she was and never straying into her space. They worked side by side, Bel on Lydia's left arm and Joe on Lydia's left leg, communicating with each other by just single words.

Bel stood back to stretch her arms while Joe closed the incision on Lydia's leg. She watched as he expertly stitched the wound and scooted quickly out of the way as he stepped back.

He grinned suddenly. 'Out of my road, Doctor.'

Bel smiled back. 'You stay out of mine, Doctor.'

One moment of eye contact, which seemed to reverberate through her like a caress. Then they were both back to business.

'I'm finished with the ankle. You want me to irrigate?' Joe nodded towards the pieces of grit and debris that remained under Lydia's skin.

'Yes, thanks.' There wasn't too much more to be done now, but having Joe clean the wounds as she went would decrease the amount of time that Lydia needed to be kept under the anaesthetic.

They went back to work, closer now. When Bel judged that all of the debris had been removed she dressed the wound and Joe looked up at the clock.

'Forty minutes. Not bad going.' He glanced at the anaesthetist, who nodded back at him. The procedures had gone like clockwork and Lydia could start to recover now. 'I'll go up to the ward and speak with them, then get Reception to give Luke a call. Maybe remind him that Lydia's the one who needs care and attention right now, not him.'

'Thanks.' Bel smiled up at him. 'Are you going to the clinic when you leave here, or can I buy you that coffee? There's something I want to ask you.' She'd had her doubts when her father had suggested the solution to all of the clinic's problems, but it was too good an offer to turn down. She hoped that Joe would see it that way, too.

'I'm going to give the clinic a miss tonight. Maria called me earlier and there's nothing that I can do there right now. I didn't get any lunch, so was thinking of getting something to eat if you want to join me?'

Bel nodded. 'Yes, I only got to eat half my lunch before I was called away. Something to eat sounds like a good idea.'

Half an hour later, they walked out of the main entrance of the hospital. Bel was wearing a dress today. Retro in tone, with soft, folding skirts that foamed around her legs as she walked, and a fitted bodice. The bright red pattern was an invitation to look at her and her dark hair, swept up in an effortlessly perfect pleat at the back of her head, reminded anyone who cared to look that this was a woman who was more than capable of dealing with any attention that she got. She'd finished the look off with a small red handbag, looped over her arm. Joe's open-necked shirt and trousers felt a little pedestrian next to her style.

'You're going somewhere later on?' It was probably a little too early in their friendship to tell her that she looked nice, and if he plucked up the courage to do so, *nice* wouldn't have covered all he wanted to say. Bel looked fabulous.

'No.' She shot him a querying look and then glanced down at her dress. 'I got up this morning and thought that today could do with some colour.'

She'd succeeded in that. Even here, in Rome, Bel dressed traffic-stoppingly well. And it was clear that she dressed to please herself and not anyone else, which somehow pleased Joe more than he could say. The thought of walking her home in the warm softness of a darkening city sky reared its head and he decided that maybe they shouldn't spend too long over dinner, and part before that became a possibility.

'There's a nice place along here…' He indicated a side road and Bel nodded, following him to the small eatery.

She seemed a little nervous, suddenly. Fair enough, he was inexplicably as nervous as a kitten, and he reminded himself that this was just an impromptu meal for two colleagues who had things to discuss. He chose a table outside, under the shade of a large awning, and Bel deposited her handbag on the table and sat down.

'I have something to propose. An idea for the clinic…' She ignored the menu completely and when the waiter approached them Joe picked up the drinks menu instead and suggested a glass of wine. She nodded, pulling her handbag onto her lap and fiddling with the metal clasp.

'Go on, then. I'm listening.' He felt rather more at ease with listening to ideas and then trying to fashion them into some kind of plan than he did with Bel's dazzling smile.

She took a deep breath. 'It seems to me that the biggest challenge you face right now is keeping the clinic running while you wait for the insurance money to come through.'

Joe nodded. 'Yes. That and the fact that it may not be enough to pay for getting new things where they're needed. We set the place up on a shoestring and a lot of the gym equipment was second-hand, from a place that was closing down.'

'Then…perhaps I can help.' The waiter had brought their drinks and she reached for her glass, her hand trembling slightly as she took a sip of wine. Then she opened her handbag and took out an envelope, proffering it.

He only had a few moments to wonder at the oddness of it all, and then he opened the envelope and saw what was inside. The banker's draft, made out for a substantial amount of cash and originating from a London bank, made his jaw drop.

'What's this, Bel?' He resisted the temptation to ask all of the other questions that had flooded into his mind. How had Bel managed to raise all this in less than a week? Where had it come from? And what on earth was she doing, giving it to the clinic?

It appeared that she wasn't going to answer any of the unspoken queries. 'It's a donation. From a benefactor who'd like to remain anonymous.'

Joe stared again at the banker's draft, picking up his glass in an effort to buy some time to think. This would solve every last one of the clinic's current problems. But it wasn't a few euros added to the box that Maria kept under the reception desk, which might very well be accepted without knowing who the donor was.

'This is very generous. But with a sum like this I have a duty to manage the clinic's finances properly. That means knowing where this money came from.'

Bel twisted her mouth, clearly trying to work out what she did, and didn't, want to say. That wasn't making Joe feel any more confident about this. 'I didn't rob a bank or anything. It's all absolutely above board.'

'I'm not accusing you of anything. But I'm sorry, before I accept this I do need to know.'

She puffed out a breath. 'Dad told me you would. He said anyone worth their salt...' She closed her mouth, obviously feeling she'd said a little too much, and Joe consoled himself with the idea that *someone* thought he was doing the right thing. Maybe not entirely for the right reasons, he had to admit he was curious, but he'd keep that to himself until he knew a bit more.

'My father is Michael Trueman.' For a moment Joe couldn't place the name, other than that it made sense that he and Bel should share a surname. 'Michael Trueman of Trueman Industries. You've heard of them?' She tossed her head in a gesture that indicated he might not have done.

That was false modesty, and cold, hard anger started to swell in his chest. *Everyone* had heard of Trueman Industries and its founder, the man who'd built a multi-million-pound company from nothing but good ideas and hard work. The notion that he needed to re-evaluate everything about Bel made him suddenly feel a little sick. It was the same feeling that had accompanied his dealings with adults when he was a child, and the knowledge that they were likely to make inexplicable decisions about him which he had no control over.

'I've heard of them. You got this from the charity that the company runs?' It was well known that the charity supported organisations that were considered to be innovative in their approach, and Joe liked to think that the clinic was that.

Bel rolled her eyes. 'No, of course not. Charities take their time in making grants to organisations—there's a whole process that needs to be gone through. And anyway, it would look a lot like favouritism if they supported a place where I was volunteering, wouldn't it?'

True. At least Bel hadn't gone that far, but the alternative was just as unpalatable. 'So…what? You called your father and asked him for the money?'

'No, I did not! Who do you think I am? I called my father to find out how he was doing because…well, because he's my father. And he needs to watch his cholesterol levels and I'm not having him sneaking cream cakes just because I'm out of the country. But I also asked him if he had any ideas about what I could do to help the clinic raise some money. Because, believe it or not, that's what he's really good at.'

Bel's cheeks were flushed with anger now, and she drained her glass, signalling to the waiter for another. He came immediately, maybe recognising what Joe had failed to understand. She was a rich girl who could do anything she liked, and she lived in a world that was way beyond his reach or understanding.

'I'm sorry.' The apology did little to mollify her, and Joe wasn't entirely sure he meant it. 'Your father agreed to donate the money. At your request.'

'No! That's not the way we do things, so you needn't start getting angry over that. I'm not some trust fund kid who calls Daddy every time she wants a new toy.'

And he'd thought that he was concealing his own view of this so well. 'What *did* happen, then? This is not idle curiosity, Bel. As director of the clinic I really do need to know.'

Bel took a gulp of her wine. Maybe he should order something to eat, but the waiter seemed to be ignoring him.

'We talked about it. Dad said that the real issue was cash flow—he was assuming you'd be sensible enough to have insurance…?' She raised an eyebrow in query.

'Yes, I like to think I'm sensible enough to have insurance as well.' That sounded combative, but maybe Joe meant it that way. No one was going to write him off just because he wasn't one of the powerful people in this world.

'Right then. So what you need is a bridging loan, and probably something to make up for what the insurance doesn't pay for. We talked about that a bit, and Dad said he liked what I'd said about the clinic, and that he wanted to make a donation. What was I going to say? *No, sorry. It's the answer to all of the clinic's problems, but your money's not good with them.* I doubt he'd take that particularly well—who would?'

'I know this is a kind gesture, Bel, and I appreciate it. But your father doesn't know anything about the clinic. How can he give this much money and know it'll be well used?'

Bel looked as if she was about to explode. 'He took my word for it. He's my father, and he trusts me. Unlike you, obviously.'

Joe picked up his glass, and then put it down again, deciding that wine was only going to escalate things. Then he saw the tear in the corner of Bel's eye. This meant something to her—he wasn't sure what, but she wasn't just angry with him because she wasn't getting her way.

'Can we start this conversation again?'

She calmed suddenly, dabbing at her eye with a napkin. 'Yes. Let's start again. Only let's not talk about the money this time.'

Joe could see her point. The money really wasn't the problem here, which was a lot to say for an amount this generous. *They* were the problem, and that was a much more difficult proposition.

He was attracted to Bel. He could admit that to himself, if not to her. And the very same vulnerabilities, the reasons he couldn't trust anyone in a relationship, were the ones that had made him react so badly to her offer of money.

That might be okay if the money had been for him, but it wasn't, it was for the clinic. He had no right to reject it because of his own hang-ups. And somewhere deep inside he knew that he'd treated Bel unfairly, and that he owed her an explanation.

'Yeah. You're right. Shall we have something to eat?'

She nodded, gesturing to the waiter, who seemed to have magically reappeared from somewhere, and ordered a snacking plate for two. Then she turned her bright, clear gaze onto him. 'Seems we both have some explaining to do.'

CHAPTER FOUR

Bel had wondered how Joe might react to her father's donation, and he'd very successfully managed to push all of her buttons. It wasn't much consolation that she'd clearly managed to push a few of his in return.

But walking away and never speaking to him again wasn't an option. There were the practical considerations—they worked together and how else was the clinic going to get the money at such short notice? And Joe's commitment and the way that he cared about people were values that Bel cared about, too.

He'd clearly readjusted his view of her, though, and that hurt. Maybe people had always thought of her differently because of who her father was, and Bel just hadn't noticed it before.

They'd picked at the snacking plate in silence, which had given Bel the chance to calm down and assess the situation. She and Joe needed to find a way to agree about her father's donation, for the clinic's sake. That was what mattered. Her pride came second to that.

'Don't… Just listen to what I have to say, please.'

'Say whatever you want. I'll listen.'

Bel took a breath. 'I know exactly how lucky I am. My parents were in the position to give me everything, and they had the good sense not to. Mum and Dad have a really nice house, in a lovely part of the world, but… they could live anywhere they wanted and it's not ostentatious. I had every opportunity they could give me. I went to a good school and we travelled as a family during the school holidays, even if Dad usually worked a bit while we were away. But it was always up to me to take advantage of those opportunities. When I went to medical school Dad gave me the cash to buy a reliable second-hand car and I had to go out and find something to get me from one place to another.'

Joe nodded, smiling. The kind of smile that would have been the same whatever she'd said.

'I didn't talk too much about my family, but it was no secret. No one can buy their way through medical school, and I had to work just as hard as everyone else. You know that.'

Maybe she was trying a little too hard to gain his acceptance, but it seemed that Joe's face had softened a little. He opened his mouth to say something and then closed it again, obviously remembering his promise to say nothing. But Bel wanted to hear his reaction.

'Go on. Say it.'

He shrugged. 'Just that…your childhood is a very long way away from my experience. But you should never have to feel ashamed of it, or that what you've achieved on your own is any the less for it.'

'Thank you.' The words slipped out before Bel could stop them.

'Who made you feel like that?' Joe's gaze seemed to slide past all of her defences.

'There was someone… I was serious about him. When

he left me, it became very obvious that he'd only been with me because of who my father was and… He was involved in some fraudulent dealings on the stock market, and when he was caught he said that it was all my idea and I'd actually been the one to steal the insider information he used. He had some so-called proof. He'd used my phone to photograph documents from my dad's desk and then emailed them to himself. There was an enquiry and I had to clear my name. That's why Dad made a personal donation. The trustees of his charity would have held an emergency meeting if he'd asked them, and assessed the clinic's application for funds as a matter of urgency. But he didn't want any suggestion of favouritism or financial irregularity, because he knew how badly that had already affected me.'

'I'm sorry.'

Those two words meant everything. Joe hadn't asked whether she actually *had* been innocent of the insider trading that she'd been accused of. He didn't question anything—he just believed her. Bel had learned just how much of a luxury that was.

'My dad knows how important rehab is—he had a heart attack two years ago. He had all the best medical care, but when he left the hospital he was very lost. His doctor was just telling him to do things without explaining properly. I was a doctor, so I could tell him the thinking behind everything, and let him take a few executive decisions of his own. Mum and I clubbed together and bought him a puppy for Christmas, and he and Wilf adore each other…' She saw Joe grin suddenly. 'What?'

'Sorry. I can't help thinking it's a little incongruous

for Michael Trueman's wife and daughter to have to club together to buy a puppy.'

'No, it isn't! I mean… Mum could pay for a whole platoon of puppies just by wearing the same dress for Christmas that she did last year, but her wardrobe is the one thing that they don't apply the *not ostentatious* policy to. We're lucky enough that money isn't really the point, though. Wilf's a member of *our* family and we wanted to get him for Dad together. And he likes going for walks, which was the main point of it all.'

Joe had left the banker's draft on the table between them, seeming unwilling even to touch it, and Bel had stowed it back into her bag before it blew away in the evening breeze. She took it out, determined to offer it a little better this time.

'My dad personally understands the value of a clinic that helps people with the after-effects of illness or injury, and he trusts me when I tell him that the clinic is a project that deserves his support. There's nothing underhand about it, and I didn't persuade him against his better judgement. We'd both be grateful if you would accept his support for the important work you're doing.'

Joe stared at her. 'I… It's a very generous offer, and made with a graciousness that I don't deserve.'

She'd done her best, but Bel wasn't going to sit here all evening holding a money order while there was food and a remarkably nice glass of wine on the table. 'Go on, then. Deserve it.'

He chuckled. 'You're not going to let me off the hook, are you?'

'You want me to?'

'No, not really. After what you've said, there's a part of me that has to explain why I reacted the way I did.'

And another part of him that didn't want to? Bel ignored the implication because she wanted to hear what was on Joe's mind. She put the banker's draft out of sight, under the heavy snacking plate.

'My childhood was different from yours, although we probably didn't grow up too far away from each other. My adoptive parents lived in a small house on the outskirts of Chelsea and they had to economise to make ends meet. But they had this fierce, uncompromising love that turned my life around.'

'How old were you when you were adopted?'

'Ten. My mother put me into local authority care soon after I was born, but she always refused to give me up for adoption, so I was fostered. As soon as I was old enough to misbehave, I managed to find a few creative ways of making trouble.'

'Wasn't that just a reaction to the situation?'

'Yes, I dare say it was. I didn't want to entertain the thought, but in retrospect I imagine I was pretty transparent. In all fairness, the adults had their hands tied as well because my biological mother wouldn't sign the adoption papers, and she spent a lot of time fighting to prevent me from being adopted.'

Bel nodded. If it was hard to listen to this, how hard must it be to say it? But Joe betrayed no emotion, just a kind of blank acceptance.

'But your adoptive parents got through to you.' If Joe had met their attempts to reach him with the same lack of emotion then that mustn't have been easy.

'Mum made it quite clear to me from the get-go that

however clever I thought I was, however tough, she was ten times cleverer and twenty times tougher. And that nothing I could do would make her give me up. It took a while to get that through my head, but I finally realised that she really meant it. I settled down, stopped playing truant from school and… They were proud when I got into medical school. I used to tell them that they were right to be, it was largely their doing.'

'Your parents sound like really good people. Where are they now?' Bel hadn't missed Joe's use of the past tense when he'd referred to them.

'They were in their fifties when they took me on. They died four years ago.'

'I'm so sorry. You lost them both, together?'

'Within three months. Dad had been fighting cancer and I knew that his consultant didn't expect him to live for much longer. But Mum went first, from sudden cardiac arrest. After the funeral Dad told me he'd had a good life but he was ready to go now. I was with him when he died, and he seemed…peaceful.'

'It must have been very hard for you, though.'

Even that didn't seem to reach him, although he must feel something. 'They were the only people I've ever been able to trust. No one else was around for all that long.'

Bel thought for a moment. There was nothing more she could say, and Joe was shutting down, retreating from the realities of a goodbye that must have torn him apart. Maybe it was better to move on now, since that was what Joe clearly wanted to do.

'So allowing yourself to depend on my father's donation when you've never even met him would be a definite no-no.' She hardly knew Joe as well, but Bel didn't want to say that.

'It would be horribly ungrateful, in the face of an extremely generous offer of help.' Joe pursed his lips, obviously trying to negotiate his way between what he knew and how he felt. 'Don't think for a moment that I don't know I'm being unreasonable.'

'I didn't exactly help things along, did I? What are you expected to think when someone offers you a large amount of money with no explanation about where it came from?'

He shrugged. 'Don't make excuses for me, Bel.'

She couldn't get through to him. He was perceptive and very frank, but it was as if he were talking about a maths problem. He'd survived by keeping his emotions under wraps.

'We're very different, Joe. But I hope you can understand that I want some of the same things you do. The clinic's important.' More important to Joe than she'd thought. He clearly didn't have any family ties, and he'd poured all of his passion into the place. It was the one thing that he trusted enough to care about.

He nodded, sliding the envelope out from underneath the sharing plate. 'Is it too late to accept this?'

'No. What are your conditions? I can't imagine that you don't have some.'

'I'd like to account to your father for every penny we spend.'

'He didn't ask for that, and if he'd wanted it he would have. But I think he'd really appreciate the gesture. He told me that I shouldn't get involved with the financial side of things because…' Because of Rory. He had no place at this table. 'Maybe Dad's being a little over-protective.'

'This has to be between him and me, Bel. There's no reason why you should be involved, and I'd really rather you weren't after what's happened to you.'

Bel felt a little thrill of warmth radiate from her heart. 'I'd like to take some before and after photos for Dad, though.'

Joe nodded. 'Sounds good to me. I'll make sure to take some too, during the week. Done?'

He held out his hand and Bel put hers into his. His touch was tender and this felt more like a lover's tryst than a handshake. 'Done. Anything else?'

He grinned suddenly. 'I get to buy an uptown girl dinner?'

Bel straightened in mock outrage. 'You can buy me dinner. Never, ever, call me an uptown girl again.'

Joe usually worked four days a week at the hospital so that he could spend all day on Friday at the clinic. He'd been busy, seeing patients and organising the clean-up in the basement, and had sat down for an hour to compose a thank-you note to Michael Trueman, enclosing a list that Maria had drawn up of the expenses so far. He'd just read it through for the second time when he saw Bel in the doorway of the office. She had tears in her eyes.

'What's the matter?' He jumped to his feet, wondering guiltily if this was a reaction to anything he'd done.

'Nothing…nothing…' She fanned her face with her hand. 'Happy tears. I just went down to the basement and put my head around the door of one of the consulting rooms.'

Ah. So she'd seen Paolo and Leonardo, both wheelchair users, along with several members of their families and friends. 'They all turned up this morning. They'd decided that now those rooms are dried out they could do a bit of painting. I told them that we didn't expect them to help, but they'd brought enough food to keep them going for about a week and were in no mood to take no for an answer.'

Bel plumped herself down on a stack of boxes and blew her nose. Today she was wearing a filmy leopard-print skirt, with a wide leather belt and gladiator sandals. She looked like a million dollars, but telling her that might prompt an indignant list of how cost effectively she'd put her outfit together. Joe contented himself with just thinking it, and watched as she flipped through photographs on her phone.

'I took some pictures. They're making a really good job of it.'

'Leonardo was a painter before he was injured, falling off a ladder. He promised me he'd keep everyone in order and make sure all of the edges were nice and straight, so I left them to it.'

Bel nodded. 'This one's a good one. Do you want me to send it to you, so you can send it to my dad?' She held out her phone and Joe took it. When he zoomed in on the line between the wall and the ceiling it was reassuringly straight, which meant that he wasn't going to have to explain to the volunteers using the room why they were going to have to put up with a less than professional job.

'I've just finished writing him a note, now.' Joe decided he didn't need to read the email through again, and pressed *send*. 'You send him whichever photographs you think he'll like. We'll keep the business side separate, shall we?'

She nodded, smiling. 'Yes. Thanks.'

The moment was broken by the sound of the clinic's alarm system. Bel jumped, looking around her.

'Basement.' Joe got to his feet, hurrying towards the stairs.

'How do you know?' Bel was right behind him, and it was no surprise that she had questions. Blindly following wasn't her style.

'The alarm console's in Reception. But since no one else is in the building, then I'm taking a guess...' He hurried down the stairs and reached the consulting room only moments before Bel caught up with him.

Paolo was lying on the floor, and Leonardo had already got the other helpers to stand back. He didn't look best pleased when Paolo tried to reach for his upturned wheelchair, telling him to stay put until help arrived.

'Thanks, Leo.' When everyone saw Joe in the doorway, the situation started to defuse a little. 'That's great, everyone—you all did the right thing.'

'All but one of us.' Leonardo was obviously annoyed about something, but Joe reckoned that would keep.

He didn't need to say a word to Bel. She'd already righted the wheelchair and was kneeling down on the other side of Paolo, waiting for Joe to go through the questions and examination that would tell them whether Paolo was unhurt or not.

'Okay. Looks as if you haven't done any damage, but don't brave it out if there's anything that worries you later on.' Joe lowered his voice. 'The next time you want to push yourself, make sure you do it when Max is here.'

Paolo nodded, his face twisted with disappointment. 'There was a bit that someone had missed and I reckoned if I stood I could reach it. I *can* stand, I do it with Max.'

'I know. Max is your therapist and he knows exactly how to do things safely with you. I have to trust you to listen to him. You want to stand for your wedding, and we're doing our best to get you there. You're just working against us by trying things you're not ready for yet, however tempting it is.'

'Sorry, Doctor.' Paolo had already been told not to try things on his own just yet, and he knew why that was. Joe knew it was frustrating, but he had to emphasise Max's advice.

'No harm done. Just think the next time, eh?' He beckoned to Leonardo's wife, who came over to steady the wheelchair, as she'd been shown during her sessions with her husband. Then Bel took up her position, and on his count they lifted Paolo back into the wheelchair.

'Thank you, Isabella. Dr Dixon.' Paolo reached to clasp Joe's hand.

'No problem. I'd go and have a word with Leo if I were you. He doesn't look too happy.'

Paolo nodded, moving over to Leonardo, who threw up his hands in a gesture of exasperation. The two men started to talk, and Leo reached for his friend, resting his hand on his shoulder. He'd taken on a role as unofficial mentor to Paolo, and it was time for Joe to go.

'That's harsh.' Bel had followed him silently, but delivered her assessment of the situation when they re-entered the office.

'Yeah. I know. Paolo has to stay within what he can

do safely though…' Joe shot her a questioning look as she shook her head.

'I meant for you. That you have to be the guy who pulls him up on it.'

Joe shrugged. 'Paolo knows I want him to succeed. Leo understands his frustration, and it was time for me to step back and let him reassure Paolo. We can't always be the nice guys. We encourage our people to help and support each other and I feel that's one of our greatest strengths.'

She nodded. 'So we're the ones who get to read the riot act from time to time, then.'

'Yeah. You can do that, can't you?' There was no question in his mind that Bel could, and that she would if necessary.

'I can do it. Leo and Paolo each seem to have very different goals.'

Joe smiled. Sometimes it took volunteers a little while to notice that, but Bel had immediately seen the people and not the wheelchairs. 'Yeah. Paolo's not going to be able to walk for more than a couple of steps without his wheelchair, and he knows that. But, like a lot of wheelchair users, he can stand a little, and he really wants to make the most of that for his wedding in six months' time. Leo's getting involved with wheelchair sports now so his ambitions are different. He has an entry level sports wheelchair and he's looking to develop his fitness and find out what's right for him. The process isn't the same as in the trauma department of the hospital, where we have one, very well-defined, aim.'

'To do what's medically necessary.' Bel was obviously thinking this through.

'For the most part, yes. You didn't ask Lydia whether she thought that pieces of grit and tarmac in her arm were a good look or not—you knew you had to remove them to prevent infection and help the arm to heal. I dare say she understood that too. Later on, if she has any scarring, then what medical science can do will be all about how she feels and what she wants.'

Bel straightened a little, and Joe recognised the signs. She was about to take issue with him. 'Are you telling me that you think I botched the job, and that I'll leave her with scars?'

'No. It was just a *for instance*. What I meant was that rehab is partly about being able to do the things you have to do, but also about living your best life.' He liked the way that Bel always called his hand on things. Maybe he did play his emotional cards a little too close to his chest at times.

She was still thinking, and Joe could feel another question coming. 'Do you suppose…' She softened it with a smile. 'Are *we* living our best lives?'

Clearly, she'd been thinking about their conversation last night. And he already knew how direct Bel could be. 'I don't know about you, that's for you to decide. I'm not entirely sure about me either, but I feel passionate about the work we do here and at the hospital, and it gives me a lot of satisfaction. I think that's my best life.'

Maybe one element of a best life. Maybe Bel was another part of that life that had always seemed completely beyond him. Joe had always told himself that having one thing that he really wanted was enough.

She was silent, and he wanted to know what she was thinking. 'What do you reckon?'

'I think you're probably right.' Bel seemed as unenthusiastic about the idea as he felt at the moment. Perhaps it was time to move on.

'How's Lydia? Did you see her today?'

'She's…physically doing very well. Luke decided to take the train to Paris this evening, and she was a bit upset about that. She said that it was better to find out what his priorities were sooner rather than later, and I told her I could agree with her wholeheartedly on that score.'

Joe grimaced. Bel hadn't said how close her relationship with the man who'd betrayed her was, but she'd obviously been hurt very badly. 'So she's on her own here?'

'Her mother's going to fly out, and she'll be arriving on Sunday. That's what I popped in to ask you. We were going to go through some cases on Saturday, ready for me to start work with the clinic next week, and I wondered if we could put that off until Sunday. I'd like to go in and see Lydia, and cheer her up a bit if I can. It's no fun being in hospital in a strange city, with no one to visit.'

'Yes, of course. Sunday's better for me too. I need to spend some time on sorting out what we can do for ourselves and what we need to get contractors in for, and that's a lot easier when suppliers and contractors are in the office.'

'Thanks.' Bel smiled at him, her eyes flashing with mischief. 'Are you finished here? I could be persuaded to buy a guy dinner. On the understanding that neither of us has to share any more confessions tonight.'

That was Bel all over. She'd obviously worked out that Joe would be feeling awkward about that, and he guessed she probably did too. So she'd come right out and said it, to defuse the situation.

'I'll leave the thing about being a cat burglar for another time, then?'

She chuckled. 'Yes, please do.'

Maybe he *would* take a chance and spend an evening working on his definition of a best life. 'I'm done here. I think it's about time our volunteer painters went home, and dinner sounds good.'

CHAPTER FIVE

Bel had spent several summers with her parents in Rome, but this felt like the first time she'd really seen the city. Vibrant, new and different every day. At home with the past, able to keep the beautiful things it wanted and let go of those it didn't.

When she'd asked Joe whether he'd seen many of the treasures of Rome, it didn't come as much of a surprise to find that he hadn't. He'd been immersed in his work, and they'd had to wait. He'd told Bel that there was no fun in seeing the sights alone, and she'd taken that as a challenge.

Starting slow, she'd managed to persuade him away from the clinic on time for three Friday evenings in a row. The long queues at the Colosseum meant that exploring the inside was an all-day venture but seeing it from the outside was still an experience in feeling very small in the presence of its imposing bulk.

And then he'd texted her. This was a new development in their relationship—something that had nothing to do with the clinic or the hospital and wasn't a spur-of-the-moment decision. Joe was going to be working late at the clinic on Friday evening, but he was thinking of going to the art gallery in the Palazzo Barberini on Saturday afternoon, and wondered whether she would like to come along.

Bel's immediate reaction was that she wanted to go, but she hesitated. The wording of his text was casual enough, and it was a natural consequence of evenings spent together on an impromptu basis. But this was a plan, and one that involved meeting up for no other reason than the pleasure of each other's company. She was more drawn to the idea of seeing Joe than she was to staring at paintings, and that made it feel even more like a date.

'Don't be ridiculous,' Bel muttered reproachfully to herself. 'It's whatever you decide it is…'

That was enough of an excuse to text back and say she hadn't been to the Galleria Nazionale di Arte Antica in a long time and she'd like to revisit it. Joe spoiled the casual tone of the exchange slightly by texting back almost immediately, saying he'd be leaving the clinic at three, and maybe they could meet at the gallery at half past. Bel put her phone back into her pocket. She could maintain her distance by replying later.

Or she could reply now. She ignored the flutter of apprehension, the tiny voice in the back of her mind which questioned whether it was wise to get this close to Joe, and took her phone from her pocket again, texting him back to tell him that she'd arranged an appointment with Chiara for after lunch at the clinic, so she'd see him there.

It was always a thrill to see Joe after they'd been working apart for a couple of days, and when Bel saw Chiara out he was already waiting for her in Reception. Smiling and relaxed. Gorgeous. The gorgeous part of the equation was awkward, but Joe couldn't help it, and Bel could never stop herself from noticing it.

'Call me if there's anything.' He turned to Maria, who shot him an annoyed look.

'What is there going to be? We have plenty of other people here, we don't need you.'

'No, of course not. But call me if there is...' Joe hurried Bel out of the door before Maria could answer.

There was a reassuring distance between them as they walked along the busy streets towards the Palazzo Barberini.

'You like art?' Bel asked.

He nodded. 'I like people-watching and looking at faces. An art gallery is about the one place you're *allowed* to stop and stare. I used to love the National Portrait Gallery when I was a kid.'

'You went there a lot?' Bel had been to her share of art galleries when she was little, but it generally wasn't her family's first port of call when they went to a new place.

Joe shrugged. 'I'd been there on a school trip and something about the pictures fascinated me. Mum found out that I'd played truant to go back and see them again, and told me we'd make a deal. I went to school during the week and she'd take me to whatever museum or gallery I chose at the weekend. I insisted on looking around on my own so she'd find a bench and pretend to read, although I expect she was keeping a close eye on me.'

It was the first time since their argument over her father's donation that Joe had said one word about his childhood. The thought of a lonely blue-eyed boy, staring up at faces in paintings, tugged at her heart. She should probably let this go, but she couldn't.

'So you haven't entirely given up on London, then?'

Joe shrugged. 'One art gallery isn't really enough to make you want to live in a city. I started to look for jobs overseas after I lost Mum and Dad. London had far too many memories for me, and with them gone none of them felt like good ones. And I do like the sunshine and warm weather.' He gestured towards a rack of brightly coloured scarves outside a shop. 'They look nice. You want to have a look?'

'Give me a bit of credit, Joe. If that's all you want to say about it, that's fine. Don't try to divert my attention with scarves, because it won't work.'

He chuckled. 'Okay. Sorry. London's been well and truly left behind now and we're in Rome. And that's all I want to say. You really *don't* want to look at scarves?'

'No, I don't. Not those, anyway. As you so rightly say, you're in Rome now, and it's time to up your game if you're going to use clothes as a distraction.'

Joe clasped his hand to his chest as if mortally wounded, but he was smiling. Even their bickering seemed to bring them closer, heading unerringly towards territory that was dangerous for both of them. But Joe was showing no inclination towards turning back, and Bel didn't want to either.

Joe always paid his way, but Bel knew he couldn't afford to pay for her as well and they'd fallen into the habit of going halves on everything, even pavement coffees. When he'd bought his entry ticket he handed it over to Bel and she stowed it away in her handbag, along with hers.

As they walked towards the first gallery, she slipped her hand into the crook of his arm, in a silent message that he wouldn't be looking at *these* faces alone. Maybe Joe got that, and maybe not, but he smiled, laying his hand over hers in a signal that this was where she belonged. It was more than just companionship or solace. Bel was becoming used to the ever-present hunger to be closer to Joe and somehow it felt that this *was* where she belonged.

Art took on a new meaning. Bel had never thought of the faces in paintings as timeless, but today they were. Joe stopped in front of a portrait of an unknown woman, regarding it thoughtfully.

'What do you suppose she's thinking?'

Bel stopped to consider the question carefully. 'I'm not quite sure. Maybe she's decided not to give us any clues.' Bel had seen that expression before, in shops and in the street. In hospitals.

Joe nodded, turning the corners of his mouth down. 'Yeah. They're always the most challenging patients, eh?'

The most challenging people. That was one of the things that Bel liked about Joe—he was honest. He didn't just tell her the truth, he went further than that and told her what was on his mind and she had a very good reason to value that. It occurred to her that Joe did too, for different reasons.

'Let's move on, then.' She tugged at his arm and he smiled, walking with her to the next painting. 'Now, I know exactly what's on *her* mind.'

Joe stared at the painting. He seemed to see nothing of the ornate red dress or the carefully arranged fabric that covered the woman's hair, just the stray lock that fell across her forehead and the look in her eyes. 'Yeah, I think I do too. You first…'

* * *

The Palazzo Barberini wasn't just an exhibition space, the whole building was a masterpiece in itself, a baroque palace that was filled with frescoes and soaring pillared walkways. Eager to see everything, but knowing that would take far longer than just a few hours, they pressed on to see the throne room. The huge, empty expanse invited visitors to look up at the painted ceiling and lying on the floor to appreciate it was de rigueur here.

Bel picked her spot and lay down, wondering if Joe would follow. Of course he did. There was no mistaking the intimacy that had grown between them, suffusing every part of the afternoon with delight. Their feet were over a metre apart but their shoulders were pressed together as they stared up at the ceiling.

'I could stay here for ever.' Somehow his hand had found hers, his light touch allowing the gesture to be interpreted whichever way Bel wanted to. Right now, she wanted to interpret it as a promise for a future which was uncertain but would be all the better for having Joe in it.

'Me too. Maybe not *quite* for ever. We'd need cushions for that.'

'Yeah. A long time, though. Or until closing time, whichever comes first.'

'Closing time won't be long enough.' She tapped her forefinger against his, to emphasise the point. If Joe thought that they'd leave this behind when they walked out of the building then Bel hoped that he was wrong.

'You're right. Closing time definitely won't be long enough…'

* * *

Joe couldn't claim innocence over what was happening here. He'd known exactly what he was doing when he'd invited Bel to the Palazzo Barberini, and he'd gone ahead and done it anyway. All of his fears, his inability to trust that any relationship would last, meant that asking Bel on a date was out of the question. But he'd deliberately put himself in the romantic equivalent of harm's way—and when intimacy had unsurprisingly come to find him, he'd stood his ground.

They hadn't spent long enough looking at the ceiling in the throne room, but Joe wasn't sure that he could ever spend too long looking at a ceiling with Bel. He'd scrambled to his feet, pleased to find that she'd been slower than he was and given him the opportunity to help her up, and they moved on. This time he risked holding out his arm for her to take, and when she did, shivers ran down his spine.

They'd continued on their aimless trajectory, wandering through rooms full of art, where they could enjoy the wonderful silences between them as they stared at faces. One day, maybe soon, he could stare into Bel's eyes and see what she was thinking. The idea didn't fill him with as much terror as it should.

They hadn't been here long enough when seven o'clock approached and the palace started to empty out. He and Bel were amongst those who seemed determined to stay until the very last moment.

'Where shall we stop last?' Joe asked. Which moment would they take with them, out into the streets of Rome?

'The Borromini staircase,' Bel replied immediately,

obviously having thought about this and chosen carefully from the treasures on offer here.

'Good thought. That's…' Joe looked around, trying to get his bearings.

'This way.' Bel pulled at his arm, leading him towards the elliptical staircase in the south wing of the building, which would take them back down to the main entrance.

Leaning over the stone balustrade, and looking downwards at the ever smaller oval repeats, clearly made Bel a little light-headed. She moved back suddenly, and Joe laughed. 'Maybe we'll do that when we get to the bottom, and there's nowhere to fall.'

'Yes. I've seen photographs and if we stand in the right place and look upwards it looks like a snail's shell. Seeing it first hand will be better, though…'

Joe nodded. Somehow they both understood that their time here couldn't be captured in just two dimensions. It was a matter of the heart.

Bel started to walk down the staircase and he hung back, waiting for her to complete a half turn before he set foot on the steps. She turned, obviously wondering where he was, and then smiled, matching her pace to his as they both moved downwards. Together and yet apart, drawing closer and then further away, as the oval shape of the stairs guided their separate trajectories.

She stopped halfway down and Joe followed suit, leaning against the stone balustrade that edged the well of the stairs.

'It's beautiful.' She was staring up at him and Joe nodded.

'Shame we can't stay a little longer.' A party of tourists were walking down behind him and Joe stood back to let them pass, watching as they wound their way down. Bel did the same and then they were alone again, in this delicious formal dance, which seemed so much more intimate for the distance between them.

They lingered as long as they could, and then made their way together to the bottom of the stairs. When he reached Bel she was standing in the middle of the stairwell, looking up. Joe was just in time to steady her as she stepped back suddenly, clearly finding the upward view almost as dizzying as the downward one had been.

'Steady...' He murmured the word quietly, and she leaned against him. Just for a moment, so they could both look upwards together. And then the moment was gone, as the door into the main entrance opened and an attendant appeared, clearly intent on chivvying them along before the gallery closed for the evening.

That was probably all for the best. Joe wasn't sure how to let go of this, although he knew he must. They took one last look behind them and then they were outside, walking towards the main gates.

'What next?' Joe regretted the question as soon as he'd asked it. He didn't want to go for coffee or a meal, and talk about everyday things—that felt like a step backwards. And there was no going forward either. It was too soon when he couldn't find any words for what had just happened between them.

Bel's forehead creased in thought, and then she reached into her handbag, taking out their entrance tickets. 'I think I'd like to go home now. But the tickets are for the Galleria Corsini as well. We'd have to go within the next twenty days.'

That was...exactly what Joe wanted too. No need to

talk about this just yet, but there was the promise of more. Another chance for them both to tear themselves away from the past and find a way forward.

'I'd like that.' Bel proffered one of the tickets, and Joe shook his head. 'You keep them safe.'

She nodded, unzipping one of the compartments inside her bag and stowing the tickets carefully away. This was fine. It was all good. Now all he had to do was work out how he was going to be able to tear himself away from Bel.

She appeared to have that under control as well. 'I'll see you on Monday then, at the hospital. Text me when you have some time for the Galleria Corsini.'

'I will. Maybe not next weekend, but the weekend after?' That would give them both a little time to think.

She smiled. 'I'll look forward to it.' Bel reached out as if to shake his hand, and then seemed to think better of it.

A kiss, even on the cheek, was out of the question. Joe caught her hand, his fingertips brushing hers, and she smiled up at him.

'See you later, then…'

Joe nodded. 'You can count on it.' He took a breath and then turned, not wanting Bel to feel that his gaze was still on her as she walked away. But he couldn't help looking back just once, and caught Bel doing the same. Joe raised his hand and she returned his wave.

It was a long walk home, but standing still for long enough to wait for the bus was out of the question. Joe kept up a brisk pace, wondering whether that would help him handle the feeling of excitement that tore at his heart, making it beat faster.

There was no denying it, he'd fallen a little in love with

Bel this afternoon. It wasn't a feeling that Joe had any experience of—his relationships had never included any possibility of love. Mutual attraction, yes. Along with an understanding that there were no strings attached, which allowed a parting that morphed effortlessly back into friendship. Love had always been out of the question.

He'd left London because he couldn't handle the constant reminders of his parents, and come to Rome to distance himself from his grief. That had worked, and he'd built a new life here, compartmentalising the pain of having to part with them. If he fell in love now he had to be sure, and Joe knew that Bel did, too. They both needed a little time.

Still, the promise of a ticket to the Galleria Corsini warmed his heart. He and Bel weren't done with each other yet.

CHAPTER SIX

It had been an odd week. Bel had seen Joe at the hospital, working with him on a number of different cases, but neither of them had mentioned the Palazzo Barberini. It was still there, though, a secret pleasure for them both to keep. Something had changed and, despite all of her fears, all the resolutions that she could do without another relationship, the sweetness of those moments with Joe just wouldn't go away.

Maria's greeting when she turned up at the clinic the following Saturday was a little different from usual. 'Bel, have you heard from Joe this morning?'

'No. Should I have?'

'We were hoping you had. We've been worried about him. He was so very tired yesterday he even snapped at me, although he apologised afterwards.'

'There was an emergency at the hospital on Thursday. We were operating for most of the night, and I stayed and managed to get some sleep afterwards. Joe went home and I wouldn't be surprised if he went on straight to the clinic...' Bel frowned. Joe always worked hard, but he pushed himself to the edge of exhaustion sometimes.

Maria frowned. 'I thought as much. I wish he'd take a day off every now and then, he's not doing himself any good. I've tried to call him but he's not answering his phone. I don't suppose you could go and see what's happening? Max says that he and Aurora will take over the new patients you were going to see this morning.'

Maria had obviously thought about this, and made a few amendments to this morning's schedule. That was fair enough. Bel was worried too. When he wasn't working, Joe's phone never went unanswered.

'Okay. What's his address?'

Maria raised an eyebrow. She knew everything that went on in the clinic and it was impossible that she could have missed that Joe had been leaving with Bel more often than not over the last few weeks. Clearly, she'd seen only their increasing intimacy and underestimated their mutual caution.

'Here…' She consulted her computer screen and wrote down the address. 'You know where that is?' If she suspected anything, then Maria had obviously decided to play along.

'Uh…yes, I think so. Down to the end of the road and turn right. It's somewhere on the left…?'

'Second on the left.' Maria gestured that she should hurry up. 'See if you can talk some sense into him, and call me. I'll call you if he turns up here…'

Joe was probably just tired and had overslept. Bel half expected to bump into him on the fifteen-minute walk to his place, and kept an eye out for him in the busy street, and in the pavement cafés where he might have stopped for coffee. But when she reached the address that Maria had given her and looked up, the curtains covering the folding doors that led out onto the third-floor balcony were closed.

She pressed the bell. No answer. Pressed it again, forgetting to take her thumb off. Still nothing. Bel wondered if anyone else in the block was at home and might let her in.

'What?' She heard his voice from the balcony above, bleary and annoyed, and stepped back so that Joe could see her. He was wearing a pair of loose-fitting sweat shorts and a sleeveless vest that left less to the imagination than usual, and Bel suppressed a smile. She'd been thinking about what his body might look like, and the promises made by the way he filled out his work clothes were more than fulfilled.

'Sorry... I must have overslept.' When he'd seen her, his annoyance had morphed into remorse. He hadn't got to embarrassment yet, and hopefully he wouldn't for another few moments.

'You look terrible.' Bel fired the accusation up at him. That wasn't entirely true, but his face was drawn and his eyes still bleary and a little swollen from sleep.

'Thanks. I'll go get a shower and be at the clinic in half an hour...'

That was an obvious invitation to leave. *'Oh, no, you don't, Joe.'* She muttered the words and he planted his hands on the rail of the balcony, leaning forward.

'What was that?'

'You're not working today.' She saw him shake his head, dismissing the idea, and switched into Italian. 'You want to discuss it? I've got all morning. We can discuss it. Right here and now...'

That did the trick. If Joe's body didn't embarrass him,

and why on earth should it, then the idea of a spirited discussion from his balcony, which his neighbours would not only hear but understand, clearly did. He disappeared for a moment, and she heard the door release buzz.

By the time she'd climbed three flights of stairs, Joe had pulled a sweatshirt over his head and unsuccessfully tried to flatten his hair. If he thought that made him look any less delicious, then that was an unusual lapse in judgement. He led her through into a small, neat kitchen where coffee was brewing in a moka pot on the stove.

'Sorry, I didn't manage to grab any sleep on Thursday night, and yesterday was a busy day at the clinic. I'll be there…' He turned as the moka pot emitted a gurgling sound, seeming a little at a loss. Clearly, he was a little too drowsy to speak and make coffee at the same time.

'And what are you going to do at the clinic? Make mistakes for everyone else to put right?' She nudged him out of the way, turning the heat down under the pot and flipping open the nearest overhead cupboard, which contained a couple of espresso cups. She poured the coffee, handing one to him.

'I'll be okay when I've had coffee…'

'Oh, really?' Bel watched as Joe drank it down. 'You're okay now, are you?'

'And a shower.' He frowned at her. 'I won't be a minute.'

Bel glared back at him. 'I'll wait here, shall I?'

'Go and sit down.' He motioned towards an arch at the far end of the kitchen and turned back towards the door.

She took a seat in the sitting room. Joe's apartment was compact but it was well decorated and very tidy, presumably because he didn't spend enough time here to make much of a mess. It was noisy, though, set on one of the main roads into the centre of the city, and the windows rattled every now and then as a heavy lorry drove past. How he ever managed to sleep was a mystery, and Bel supposed that hitting the pillow with your eyes already closed was something of an advantage.

She took her phone from her handbag and texted Maria to let her know that Joe was okay but very tired, and he could do with the weekend off. Maria texted back almost immediately, saying that everything was under control at the clinic and if she saw Joe there she'd give him a piece of her mind.

Ten minutes later he appeared in the doorway of the sitting room, freshly shaved and showered and wearing a pair of casual trousers with a crisp blue shirt. He smelled sweet and cool, like gelato on a hot day.

'Ready to go?'

'No. Not yet.' She pointed towards the armchair which stood opposite hers, and Joe puffed out a breath and sat down.

'What is this, Bel? I overslept. I'm sorry that you were worried enough to come round and see whether I was okay, and I appreciate it.'

'When was the last time you took a day off? I know you haven't in the last three weeks.'

'There's been a lot to do, keeping the place going while the basement's been out of action…' He pressed his lips together as if the answer didn't satisfy him any more than it did Bel. 'About six months. When the clinic first opened, I was working all the hours just to get it up and running. I knew I couldn't keep that up and so I made a rule for myself, to take Sundays off. Then we started to get really busy...' He shrugged.

'You need some time off, Joe. You can't keep going like this, and you really don't need to. There are people at the clinic who'll step in and take some of the weight.'

Joe shook his head. 'They're all volunteers. I don't like to ask too much of them.'

'I got there at ten this morning. By that time, you'd already been missed and I had nothing to do because Max and Aurora had shared my work out between them. We *are* volunteers and in return for that you need to allow us the right to care about the place enough to step in and help, if that's what we want to do.'

He puffed out a breath, leaning wearily back in his seat. Joe really did need some time off—he didn't seem to have either the will or the strength to fight her.

'I know it's hard to trust other people with something you've built. Especially for you.' There were times when Joe hadn't come too far from the kid who couldn't trust anyone, and letting other people take care of his dreams for a while seemed an impossible thing to ask.

'You're right. Of course.' His eyes flashed a warning, just in case she was rash enough to think that he was going to capitulate entirely. 'I don't like it...'

'No one's asking you to. But if you continue like this, you're going to make a mistake. It's okay to order one too few pots of paint, but what if you make a mistake with a patient?'

'That's not fair, Bel. When have you seen me turning up for work when I'm not fit for purpose? And don't even try to tell me that the other night was the first all-nighter you've ever done.'

'Never. And no, it's not my first all-nighter and it won't be my last. But you *know* you have to take time off—you made that resolution once. Make it again, before…' Bel stopped herself before she got into the tearful phone call from her mother, on the evening her father had collapsed and been taken by ambulance to the cardiac unit of the hospital. 'Before it's out of your hands.'

'As it was with your father?' Joe might be weary, but he still didn't miss much.

'Yes. He says now that slowing down was the best thing he's ever done, but it was a hard way to have to do it.'

He nodded. 'No puppies. And I'm going to call Maria, because… I'm just going to call her.'

'Of course you are. And I wouldn't inflict your lifestyle onto a poor helpless puppy. I'll make some more coffee…'

Bel could hear Joe on the phone, from the kitchen. Maria was obviously giving him a piece of her mind, because the conversation consisted of long silences on Joe's part, peppered by the odd '*Va bene*, Maria.' He managed to get a few questions in about some urgent things that needed to be done today, and Bel took the opportunity to inspect the contents of his refrigerator, which didn't take long at all.

When she carried the coffee through into the sitting room, he brought the conversation to a close and ended the call. Then he puffed out a breath. 'I thought that Maria was going to be far nicer to me than you were…'

Bel chuckled. 'Never underestimate a woman on a mission. I *could* be a great deal sterner, if you want.'

'Don't be. Winning gracefully is an art.' He reached

for his coffee, and downed it in one. 'So...now that I have the whole weekend off, do you have any ideas about what I should do with it?'

'We'll take a walk down to the market, maybe stop for something to eat, and then on to the supermarket. Then I'll cook for you.'

He chuckled. 'You're going to take the comfort food route?'

'No, I'm taking the putting something into your fridge, so that you eat for the next week route. Do you ever cook?'

'I cook. When I have the time.'

'Right then. We've got the time this weekend.'

Maybe this was his best life. If Joe had woken half an hour earlier, he would have gone to the clinic and brushed Maria's objections aside. But Bel wasn't so easy to ignore. There was a vulnerability about her forthright concern for him, and an understanding of his own helplessness in breaking away from the obsessions of his childhood. She got to him, in a way that was sometimes frightening but always held a dash of delight.

Rome was theirs for the day. They could wander wherever they wanted, and if Joe looked at his watch a few times, that was only out of habit. They shopped and then cooked, and he fell asleep on the sofa for an hour. When he awoke and walked through into the kitchen, he found Bel perched on a stool, reading. She laid her book aside and waved his apologies away.

He could feel the stress beginning to lift, floating away in the warmth of the evening air, when they went out to spend an hour watching the world go by. And they talked, about nothing and everything. Bel seemed to sparkle in the lights of the city, and when she left him alone, with a promise that she'd be picking him up early tomorrow, the small apartment felt suddenly lonely. Ignoring the ever-present hum of traffic, Joe fell asleep thinking only of Bel. The woman who'd come for him, ignored all of his protests, and saved him anyway.

CHAPTER SEVEN

Bel had torn herself away from Joe, knowing that last night's sleep hadn't been enough and he needed to sleep again tonight. Wanting to stay with him, and watch over him as he slept, but knowing that she'd never be able to confine herself to just that. Joe was getting under her skin, and however much she tried to stop it, she couldn't.

All the same, she made her preparations for tomorrow, texting her neighbour Costanza to ask if it was all right for her to pop in, and receiving an invitation to keep her company since her young son Nico was in bed and asleep. In exchange for a promise to sit with Nico for an evening next week, and a packet of almond biscuits, Bel received a map and the loan of Costanza's car on Sunday.

She arrived outside Joe's flat bright and early, slipping into a parking spot before anyone else had the chance to take it. When she rang the bell, he appeared on the balcony.

'We're going out?' He grinned down at her, which entirely made up for the fact that he was fully dressed this morning.

'Yes. How did you know?' She'd meant this to be a surprise.

'You're dressed for walking. And holding a map. Do I need to bring a pair of trainers?'

'Yes, you'll need them.' Bel decided that giving away this much was a wise precaution.

Joe disappeared, and Bel looked down at her outfit. A summer dress wouldn't have told him anything, even if she had spent longer than usual choosing it this morning, but she supposed that her rubber-soled canvas pumps might have given the game away. She stowed the map away in the glove compartment of the car, so that he couldn't gain any more clues from it.

When Joe joined her, he looked the same as ever—downright delicious. He got into the car, twisting around to see the child seat in the back.

'This is your car?'

'No, it's my next-door neighbour's. I promised Costanza I'd look after her son while she goes out for the evening, in return. I think I got the best part of the deal. I sit with him when she goes out shopping sometimes, and he's a delight. Nico is autistic and the supermarket tends to put him into sensory overload.'

Joe nodded. 'I guess that being right next door is handy for both of you.'

'Yes, Costanza has her mum and several other trusted friends who'll look after Nico, but sometimes she just needs to pop out for half an hour. She was a tour guide before she had Nico, and she's given me a strict itinerary for this morning.'

'And you're not going to let me in on that yet?'

Bel shot him a smile. 'No. Not yet.'

She parked in the car park that Costanza had suggested, and Joe took the small day pack she'd brought from her shoulder, insisting that he carry it. When they got onto the bus, to take them the rest of the way to the Via Appia Antica, he must have realised where they were going, but said nothing.

'Have you been here before?' Bel asked as they walked past the visitor centre, along a paved route that was more than two thousand years old, and connected Rome to Brindisi.

'Never got around to it.' Joe was obviously pleased that he had now, and set off at a jaunty pace, leaving Bel to run to catch up with him.

The National Park was closed to traffic on Sundays, and if it hadn't been for the other walkers and cyclists it would be easy to imagine that they were travelling out of the city and back in time. They spent a couple of hours exploring, stopping to see villas, basilicas, aqueducts and tombs along the way, and then sat down for a while to rest and enjoy brunch from the backpack, surrounded by rolling countryside.

'This is wonderful.' Joe flopped onto his back on the grass, his eyes closed, letting the sun warm his face. 'It feels like a different world...'

That was exactly as Bel had hoped. She'd wanted to take him away from the everyday for a while, and allow Joe to experience the feeling that there were other worlds, other ways of existing. She felt it too, that here it was possible to see beyond the people and things that had moulded her life.

'There's a lot more to see. This park stretches for more than ten miles.'

'It would be a shame to rush it and miss anything. We'll have to come back.'

Maybe one day soon, along with the local people who brought picnics on a sunny Sunday and were almost as numerous as the tourists who wanted to walk or cycle the Appian Way. Bel nodded.

'What happens to it after it leaves the park? On its way down to Brindisi?' Joe asked, rolling onto his side and propping himself up on one elbow.

'Costanza says it varies. In places it's covered by roads and buildings, and in other places it emerges and you can walk it. She says that in some places they're digging down to find it and bring it back.'

He nodded. 'It's amazing. I can't help thinking of all the toil and suffering that's gone into this place, as well as the magnificence of the achievement.'

All brought together by the passage of the years. There was a lesson here, for both of them, in the peace of this sunny morning but Bel couldn't quite bring it into focus.

'I suppose that's life, isn't it? Never quite one thing or the other.'

'Yeah. I suppose so.'

Instead of exploring any further, they decided to take their time in walking back and taking a second look at the things they'd already seen. But Joe marked their progress on the map that was spread out between them on the grass, smilingly telling Bel that this was for the next time they visited. That was more than enough for one morning.

The park had worked its magic on both of them, and there was suddenly no reason why Bel shouldn't ask Joe in for coffee when she parked Costanza's car back in its regular spot, after stopping to fill the petrol tank. Then she unlocked the door that led to the small courtyard, around which the three-storey block of apartments was arranged. Costanza was in the courtyard, watching Nico play, and Joe hung back, giving Costanza a cheery wave as Bel went to talk to the boy and return the car keys.

'This is nice.' They climbed the steps up to the third-floor walkway, lined with pots of flowering plants and herbs, and Bel stopped outside the sliding doors that led into her sitting room. 'It's hard to believe we're in the centre of the city, here.'

'Yes. The rent's very reasonable, because the landlord's selective about his tenants. No wild parties or subletting...' Bel bit her tongue. She could have just agreed with him, but instead she'd allowed a streak of defensiveness into her response.

Joe chuckled. 'You're not living in any more luxury than you can afford on a doctor's salary, then.' His grin told her that he was teasing, but it still hurt a little.

'No, actually. I'm not. I just took a bit of time in finding somewhere nice to live.'

'Point taken. I should do the same, my apartment's a bit noisy.' He shot her a querying look as Bel huffed at him.

'I'm not making any points, Joe. I don't have to justify everything I do in terms of whether or not my father's helped me out.'

He kept his cool. Maybe Bel should take a leaf from his book and simmer down—her own preoccupations were beginning to show. 'I meant that I'd taken the point with regards to my own lifestyle. What you do is entirely up to you.'

Suddenly everything was okay again. Bel laughed, unlocking the door and sliding it back. Joe stepped inside, then made a show of looking around and shrugging dismissively. The magic of the Via Appia still remained, and they could still look back and see the roads they'd already trodden as different from the road ahead.

'Can't you find somewhere else?' Joe must have a good salary from the hospital, even though he only worked four days a week. Bel suspected that she knew where all of his spare cash had been going.

'I've been thinking about it. The money I'd put aside for a deposit came in handy when we needed to dry the basement out. The clinic couldn't afford all of it.'

'Just as well I managed to get a good price, then.' She reproached him, 'You'd be living on the streets.'

He chuckled. 'Not on the streets. I might have been sleeping under my desk in the office. Or there's actually a small loft living space at the clinic. We did think of raising some cash by doing it up and letting it out, but there's no separate entrance and we couldn't get the relevant permissions. It's done a few of the volunteers a good turn, though. Max stayed there for a while a couple of months back when he split up with his girlfriend.'

'Living above the clinic would be a bad idea though, wouldn't it.' Joe would struggle to take ten minutes off, let alone a whole weekend.

'Yeah. Suppose so.'

She wouldn't put anything past Joe, in his determination to make sure the clinic survived. But maybe now wasn't the time to raise the issue of whether he really should be giving this much, when there were other ways of handling the clinic's problems. Today was supposed to be the time when they could take a short holiday from all of that.

'Are you hungry?' After a morning spent walking in

the open air, Bel reckoned that Joe would be as ready for something to eat as she was.

He nodded. 'Since you insisted on cooking for me yesterday, then today you can drink cocktails or read a book—whatever floats your boat—and let me cook for you.'

'All right.' Watching Joe cook was actually the thing that would really float her boat... 'I think you'll find my fridge is a little better stocked than yours was.'

'Yeah.' He shot her a grin. 'Of course it is...'

Today had been just perfect. Joe was well aware that Bel had put some effort into making it so, but he knew that he'd contributed something too. The chemistry that sparked between them had blossomed into fire, when they'd both allowed it a little time to do so. All it had taken was an unspoken agreement to set aside the past.

That couldn't last. But for now it could be enjoyed, like an exquisite flower that bloomed only for one day. They'd cooked together, and eaten together. And then, with nothing else to do, they'd watched an old black and white movie, chosen from Bel's collection of films.

'That was...predictable.' Joe had taken the liberty of putting his arm on the sofa cushions behind her shoulders, since Bel had taken a similar liberty in moving close during a particularly tense scene, and never moved away again. He'd spent the second half of the film taking more notice of her scent and the warm feel of her body than what was happening on the screen.

'That's why I like old films. You tend to know who the villain is.'

From what she'd told him, Bel knew all about villains.

Although the one who had hurt her had managed to conceal his true nature. Joe was just wondering whether she might have a type, and he could be classified as a villain, when he felt her move against him.

'Thank you for today. I really needed a break, too.'

He felt her lips against his skin as Bel kissed his cheek. She lingered a little too long for that to be a gesture between friends, and Joe's hand shook as he reached up to run his finger gently along her jaw.

They could stop now. Pretend that this was just a show of affection on a lazy Sunday afternoon. If they wanted to, they could stop right now. But then Joe's gaze found hers and it was too late.

All the same, he hesitated. He gave Bel every opportunity to draw back and make coffee, or find another film, or whatever else might defuse the sudden heat between them. But when he ran his thumb gently across her lips in a gesture that might signify an end, even though that was the very last thing on his mind, he felt her hand on his wrist, keeping it right where it was so that she could kiss his fingers.

'Is this a good idea, Bel?' At least there was no longer any question over what was going on between them, and he could ask.

'No, I think it's a terrible idea.' She leaned forward, kissing his cheek again.

'And…so you think we should stop?' Joe caressed her cheek.

'You want to?'

'No. I don't.'

'Neither do I.'

Her admission broke him. He wound his arms around

her, and pulled her close. There was one exquisite moment before their lips met, a chance for Bel to pull away from him, which he knew now that she wouldn't take. Joe kissed her with all the tenderness he could muster, and she responded fiercely. He kissed her again, this time taking all that he wanted, and heard her gasp.

He could feel her flesh burning under his touch. He'd never wanted a woman so much before, never felt that what happened next was a matter of life or death. If he was going to take all that he needed right now, then he had to be sure.

'What would the clinic's biggest donor say if he knew what I was about to do with his daughter?' The question was deliberately intended to pour cold water over their desire, but Joe realised that a bucket of water was little use against a rapidly spreading inferno.

'It's none of his business.' Bel moved away from him, trapping him in the warmth of her gaze. 'Anyway, what do you want more? Me or the clinic?'

Right now, the clinic could fend for itself. But tomorrow things might be different, and Joe wouldn't take what he wanted by giving Bel false promises.

'You won't like my answer...'

She smiled suddenly. 'It's honest and I like that very much. I don't have any promises to give you, Joe, and I know you don't have any for me. But we could spend the rest of the afternoon showing each other that things could...just might...be different.'

'That's something I *can* believe in.'

Her laugh sounded like pure joy. Something not yet tamed by any of the awkward realities of life. Bel pulled away from him, stepping back a couple of feet, her fingers straying to the top button in the line that stretched down the front of her dress.

She was going to let him watch her undress. The thought was exquisite, but there was something he wanted even more. Joe got to his feet, drawing her against him. He knew she must be able to feel his arousal, and she melted against him, letting out a sigh.

They were both ready for what came next, but this was far too precious to rush. He tipped her chin up, and her gaze met his.

'Look at me, Isabella...' He'd never used her full name before, but now it seemed appropriate. More beautiful, and a mark of his respect for her.

'What are you going to do, Joe?'

Making that clear to her was all part of the pleasure. 'I want you to leave the buttons to me. Just let me see your face.'

She smiled, stretching her arms up and wrapping them around his neck. He backed her slowly until the wall stopped them, and then reached for the top button, his hand skimming her breast as he did so. Bel gasped, but never took her gaze from his as he undid the button carefully, sliding his fingers across the skin beneath it.

'There are at least twenty...'

That sounded a lot like a challenge. Joe undid three more, and found the soft, silky material that covered her breasts. His hand could explore a little more now, and he could see from her reaction that it pleased her. She pressed her hips against his, smiling as he struggled to maintain their naked eye contact.

'Are you going to last as long as twenty? There may be more, I'm not sure,' Bel teased him.

'I can if you can.' That sounded a lot like a promise, but it was one he wasn't afraid to give.

Buttons were important. Cheap buttons could ruin an outfit, and changing the buttons on a piece of clothing could lift it from ordinary to exclusive. But Joe could turn them into a countdown of desire.

He wasn't afraid to change the pace, driving her to the very edge and then pulling her back, so they could explore a little more. And he was there for her, sharing his own pleasure as freely as he enjoyed hers. There was an honesty about his lovemaking that released Bel from the fears that Rory had left in her heart.

Finally, he slipped the dress from her shoulders, letting it fall to the floor. 'Bedroom?'

'Yes. Bedroom.'

He kissed her as she propelled him towards her bedroom door. She tugged at his shirt, pulling it over his head, and he finished undressing hurriedly. The time for slow appreciation was gone now, and he lifted her up, laying her back down on the bed.

'You have condoms?' he asked.

'What would you do if I told you *no*?' Bel meant to tease him, but Joe didn't miss a beat, removing her underwear and letting his fingers and tongue stray across her body, moving downwards.

'I have condoms… They're in… Oh!' His hand slipped between her legs before she could finish the sentence.

Joe grinned up at her. 'Too late. Did you think I wouldn't finish what we started?'

Not for one moment. She gave herself up to him, letting him do whatever he wanted. He was focused entirely on her pleasure and their journey here had already told him exactly what turned her on. Her orgasm seemed to have a mind of its own, unstoppable and relentless, leaving her trembling in his arms.

'They're in the second drawer down. By the bed...' She waved her hand towards the bedside cabinet.

'Now?'

Desire was still surging inside her, still pushing her on. 'I want to feel that again. With you, this time.'

He didn't need to be told twice. Joe reached across, flipping the drawer open to fetch the box of condoms. She took him by surprise, rolling him over onto his back, and then he was all hers. Trembling as she took her time over rolling the condom down into place. Gasping as she straddled him, slowly letting him inside her.

'Isabella...'

'I like it when you call me that. Tell me what you want, Joe.'

He took her hand, pressing it to his lips. 'I want to be able to see you. You're so beautiful.'

Weren't those the words that any woman wanted to hear? But Joe really meant them. She felt him swell inside her as she moved, saw his eyes darken with desire. Bel tried to go slow, but there was no denying either of them now. She came first, the orgasm rolling over her like warm water this time, a long and easy road towards completion. Joe must be able to feel its slow pace, because he was clearly holding back and letting it run its course, but Bel knew he couldn't resist her for much longer. She knew just how to move against him and he let out a cry, clamping his hands around her hips, his body arching beneath her. She felt him pulse inside her, and then suddenly they were both reaching for each other. He took her in his arms, and she felt the heat of his skin, the wild beat of his heart.

Their lovemaking seemed to have robbed him of everything but the desire to be close to her. It was the most intoxicating feeling of all and Bel cradled him in her arms, feeling her own body relax along with his.

'You want to sleep now?' They could pull the light bedcovers over themselves and sleep together until the morning.

Joe looked over at the clock which stood on the bedside table. 'I could rest for a while. But it's only five o'clock, we still have the whole evening left.'

Bel supposed she shouldn't take anything for granted. Maybe this was a one-time thing that chemistry had dictated they both needed to do before they could move on. 'We could go out and eat?'

'We could.' Joe didn't sound any more enthusiastic about the proposal than Bel felt. 'Or we could stay here if you want.'

'And play a little more?' Her smile must have given her away, because Joe chuckled.

'Yeah. And play a little more…'

Joe's father hadn't gone into the whys and wherefores of sex all that much, but he'd given him one valuable piece of advice. Always respect a woman. Maybe he'd broken that golden rule this evening—several of the things that he and Bel had done together during the course of the evening didn't seem entirely respectful. But then she'd initiated most of them, and they'd given both of them a great deal of pleasure.

It was a reflection of the relationship that had grown up between them over the last month. They challenged each other, sometimes pushed each other out of their comfort zones. But if that worked for them and was reflected in the way they made love, then wasn't that simple honesty? Joe reckoned that was the greatest mark of respect of all.

He rolled the idea around in his head for a while, staring at the ceiling while she dozed in his arms. It was still early enough for her to throw him out, if she wanted to, and he could walk back to his apartment and sleep alone. When she stirred against him, he realised that he needed to ask.

He phrased the question as carefully as he could. 'What we did together was amazing. Mind-blowing—' She opened her mouth to reply and he laid his finger across her lips. 'I will promise you one thing. I won't speak of this afternoon unless you speak of it first. But I'll always remember it.'

'Have you quite finished?' She poked her finger into his ribs. That was probably a good sign.

'No, not really. I could elaborate…' He kissed her cheek, feeling Bel snuggle against him.

'On how this isn't going to make any difference at all to anything?' He could feel her lips moving against his skin as she spoke, and it was uniquely delicious. 'I don't want to hear it.'

'It made a difference.' Bel had turned his world upside down, and nothing was the same. However hard it was to admit it.

She sat up suddenly, throwing the bedcovers back. 'I rather liked it.'

It was very difficult to have a discussion with a woman

as perfectly beautiful as she was when she was entirely naked. If Joe was ready to give her up to fond memories, then his body, still revelling in satiated pleasure, was undoubtedly sending a different message.

'I liked it. A lot.'

She leaned over to kiss him. 'You don't have to spend time wondering when the other shoe's going to drop, Joe. Whatever happens next is up to you and me, and you can trust me to tell you what I want.'

The years of never being sure of anything but himself had left their mark, but maybe they *could* both learn to live their best lives. Maybe even together, although that seemed like a challenge.

'I meant it when I said that I'd be taking a bit more time off in the future and...' He shrugged. 'We're still busy people. But Sundays could be just for us from now on. And evenings...'

Bel nodded her agreement. 'Public holidays?'

He reached for her, pulling her down next to him. 'Definitely public holidays.'

She kissed him. Joe allowed himself the possessive pleasure of rolling on top of her, in a promise of what was suddenly still possible between them, and she reached up to caress his cheek.

'You have a deal, Joe. Will you stay with me tonight? I'd like you to.'

'I'd love to. I can get up early and walk back over to my place for a change of clothes. After I've made it clear that I'll be seeing you later, of course.'

'I'll look forward to it. In the meantime, I don't suppose you'd like to take me out for pizza, would you? I'm really hungry and it's still only nine o'clock. There's a nice place just around the corner from here.'

Joe chuckled, getting out of bed. 'Pizza would be great, I'm hungry too. Only I may need to shower first.'

'Me too. If we do it together, it'll save water…'

CHAPTER EIGHT

DESPITE ALL THEIR DIFFERENCES, there was one thing that they both agreed on. Neither Bel nor Joe was in love.

Enjoying spending time together was absolutely fine. Honesty was more than fine. It was the thing that held them together. Feeling that they'd turned each other's worlds upside down was good too—it was all part of the best life project. Love was a dangerous commitment, a step too far that neither of them was willing to take. If something went unacknowledged, then wasn't it like a leaf falling in a forest, with no one to see or hear it? How could it exist, let alone change their lives?

That didn't seem to hold Bel back, though. When Joe left the hospital on Monday evening, bound for the clinic, he found that she was walking beside him, her hand in the crook of his elbow.

'This is nice. But don't you want to go home?' During the few hours they'd been apart, a seed of longing for Bel had already begun to grow in his heart. Joe had resolved to ignore it, because there were things he had to do this evening.

'Are you?'

'No, I have a couple of patients to see, and then I need

to check on the new flooring in the gym, and see how that's going.'

'Two patients and looking at a floor won't take long, will it?'

'No, but...' There were probably quite a few other things that would claim his attention and fill the whole evening, but Joe couldn't call them to mind. 'You're not taking me in hand, are you? Because I'm quite capable of organising my time.'

She laughed. 'I wouldn't dream of it. You've held down a job and built a clinic in the last three years. That's an achievement in terms of time management, if ever there was one.'

He stopped walking, looking around the crowded pavement. 'There's a *but* heading my way, I'm sure of it. I just can't see it yet.'

'No, there isn't.' Bel shot him an exasperated look. 'I know you have commitments, Joe. I can walk with you from the hospital to the clinic though, can't I? It's more or less on my way home.'

That was a challenge he hadn't anticipated. It was heart-warming to find that Bel was willing to snatch this time with him as he hurried from one task to another, but it wasn't really fair. And she couldn't disentangle him from the mass of jobs and responsibilities that the clinic provided—only he could do that.

By Wednesday he'd admitted that maybe he'd become a little bogged down in tasks that he could leave to others. On Friday he'd asked Maria whether she might consider coming in at four o'clock instead of six for a while, to oversee the repairs, and she'd jumped at it. She and her husband were planning a trip next spring and she could do with the extra money.

On Saturday Bel had spent the morning at the clinic, and Joe had promised to be at her place shortly after six, when the clinic closed. He'd left at six o'clock sharp, leaving Maria to lock up, and found himself hurrying to meet her. Bel had buzzed him in, and was waiting at the front door for him, ready to fling her arms around his neck.

'That's nice.' He disentangled himself from her kisses. 'What did I do to deserve this?'

'You kept your promise.'

That hadn't been difficult. He'd been thinking about this evening, and the prospect of another Sunday spent with Bel, for the whole week.

'Did you think I wouldn't?'

She shrugged, turning away from him and walking into the kitchen. She'd been preparing something, and a covered dish stood on the top of the cooker, ready to go into the oven. Bel opened the wine cooler, taking out a bottle and showing him the label. Joe nodded without even looking at it, and she fetched a pair of glasses. Her movements seemed somehow jerky, and strange.

'Hey...' He took the bottle-opener from her hand, laying it down. 'That can wait. What's up?'

'I just... I didn't want to expect too much of you.'

'I said I'd be here. Did you think I'd leave you sitting around all evening, wondering when I was going to turn up?' She probably had been, and Joe had to admit that he hadn't given her much reason to expect otherwise. He was still unsure of how a commitment ought to go, and hadn't told her that he'd been aching for some time alone with her.

She dismissed the idea with a wave of her hand. 'That doesn't matter. It didn't happen…'

'It *did*, though.' Joe hazarded a guess. 'Your father?'

She shook her head. 'No, Dad was always busy and he worked long hours. But when I was little he used to go into work early so he could be home in time to read me a story a couple of evenings a week. He probably did a few more hours in his study afterwards, but I always knew he'd be there if he said he would.'

'Who then?'

She turned the corners of her mouth down in a frown. 'It doesn't matter.'

'It obviously matters to you.' Joe took her in his arms. 'And it matters to me, too. We're both in a profession where sometimes we have to work a little late. That makes it all the more important to me that you know this. If I say I'll be here and don't turn up then it really is a matter of life or death.'

'My fiancé.' The word made Joe swallow hard. He'd known that there was *someone* but hadn't realised it had been quite that serious. 'He was always working late, never there when he said he'd be. And I'd always wait for him. When it came out that he'd been involved in fraud, I didn't believe it and I defended him. And when he implicated me…' A tear ran down her cheek.

'You didn't believe that either?'

'It was Dad who made me see it. His office has a card system that logs everyone in and out, and he ran a check on exactly when Rory had been in the building. He hadn't been working late at all, he'd lied to me.'

'Where was he?'

'I have no idea. I'm not sure that I want to know either. There *was* a woman involved in the fraud—she'd apparently turned up at the bank and signed a few things with my name. Dad took me down to his lawyer's office and they went through everything with me. One allegation after another…'

'That must have been very hard.' No wonder Bel couldn't let go of it.

'It was hard for Dad as well. He told me afterwards that he was wondering if I'd ever speak to him again, but he'd reckoned that I had to know the whole truth, in order to defend myself.'

'But you did. Speak to him.'

'It was touch and go at one point. I loved Rory, and he'd manipulated me into thinking that he loved me. But I knew that I couldn't blame Dad for what he'd done and, if anything, it's made us closer.' She turned her gaze up to meet Joe's. 'I can't judge you by it either.'

Joe smiled down at her. 'I don't know. If a little punctuality and letting you know if I really *am* detained at work is enough to get me into your good books…' He winced as Bel planted her hands on his shoulders, pushing him away. 'Okay. I'm hoping you see a little more in me than that.'

'Don't fish for compliments, Joe. Do you imagine that *not* being Rory is enough? That's setting the bar very low.'

He'd always been aware that he didn't have a great deal to offer Bel. He commanded a good salary from the hospital, but most of that went on the clinic and he didn't have much left over to spend on himself or her. Her parents might not live an ostentatious life, but they'd been able to give Bel opportunities that were way beyond Joe's reach.

'Maybe I'm hoping that you do set the bar a little low, so that I can reach it.'

'Did you think that last Sunday was setting the bar low?' She reached forward, hooking her finger around one of the buttons of his shirt. Just one small gesture that set him on fire.

'Last Sunday couldn't have been any more perfect.' Joe forgot about his uncertainties and wound his arm possessively around her waist. 'And to tell you the truth, you're a great cook, and I'm sure that's a very good bottle of wine. Right now, I'd like to set the bar a little higher.'

'How are you going to do that?' She reached up, standing on her toes to kiss him.

Not the way she thought. Joe kissed her again, breaking away from her to pick up the book that was propped upside down on the kitchen counter. Bel always had a book with her, and she'd clearly anticipated his late arrival and provided herself with a little company.

'You're reading Jane Austen?'

Bel shot him a puzzled look. 'Rereading. I've read this one before, but I really like it.'

'How do you feel about going back to the beginning? Reading the first few pages together?' This was somehow more intimate than sex. Letting Bel into a world that he'd always kept for himself.

'That was about the last thing I had in mind for this evening…' She grinned up at him. 'I wouldn't have thought you'd be a Jane Austen fan.'

'I used to read a lot when I was a kid. Mostly anything

I could get my hands on—it's surprising how many things you find you *do* like.'

Bel took the paperback from his hands. 'This means something, doesn't it. I'm just not quite sure what.'

If you were going to romance a girl with a book, then she needed to know what that meant. 'When I went somewhere new I'd wait a while and then ask if I could read one of the books on the shelves. Everyone used to say yes, and I'd work my way through as many as I could. Some places were four book places, others five or six...'

'Ah, I see. So there was *something* you took with you whenever you moved. You didn't tell me that.'

'I haven't told anyone. My parents figured it out, and they started to sit down with me every evening before tea. We'd take turns to read, ten minutes each. Dad used to be really good at doing all of the voices—he had us in fits of laughter when we read *The Moonstone* together.'

'That's such a nice memory. Thank you for sharing it.' Bel reached up, caressing his cheek. 'I haven't read *The Moonstone*, but I do have loads of other books...'

'So you do.' The stacked bookshelf in the sitting room was impossible to miss. 'I'm not very good with sharing, because it gives me something to lose. But I'm sharing this with you, and in return I want you to know that I'll be here when I say I will.'

Bel hesitated, running her fingers across the cover of the paperback. It was a lot to ask of her. A lot for Joe to give. Then suddenly she pressed the book into his hands.

'Dinner can wait. Let's read, Joe.'

He picked up the bottle of wine, and Bel reached for the glasses and the bottle-opener. Then she propelled him through the sitting room and into the bedroom.

* * *

Time had gone so quickly. And yet slowly too, because Bel had been catapulted into a world where everything was new and different. They were like explorers who'd discovered an enchanted forest and—hand in hand for courage—had dared to step inside its scented canopy.

But somehow it was all right. She could make a habit of being this easy and relaxed with someone. Not just any old someone—it had to be Joe.

Last night had been very special, but they still had a way to go and Joe was stepping as carefully as she was. He hadn't taken an invitation to stay the night for granted, and they'd had to walk back to his apartment on Sunday morning to pick up a change of clothes for him. A window in the sitting room had been left ajar to let in some air, and he closed it, shutting out the noise of the traffic. Bel sat down, trying not to look around for some sign that Joe had made a home here.

'Sorry. It's not very welcoming...' Joe seemed to be seeing it for the first time.

'How long have you been here?'

'Since I first arrived in Rome. I thought I'd stay for a couple of months and look around for something nicer, but I never got around to it. I'm not here all that much, and it suits its purpose.'

What purpose would that be? Not having anything that looked too much like home, so that it wouldn't hurt to lose it? Bel decided not to ask.

'My landlord mentioned that an apartment in my block was going to be free soon...'

He smiled. 'Say what you mean, Isabella. You called him and asked, didn't you?'

Bel glared at him. 'I happened to call and he happened to mention. That's as far as I'll go, if you're going to interrogate me about it.'

Joe nodded. 'I imagine the deposit will be a lot more than I'll get back on this place. They don't have any difficulty in finding tenants, do they?'

'No. I put my name down for a place there as soon as I knew I was coming to Italy and I was lucky to get my apartment so quickly. I could put a word in with the landlord though, he might well agree to letting you pay part of the deposit later. His primary concern is getting good tenants, he says that's worth a lot…'

Joe walked over to the sofa, sitting down next to her. When he put his arm around her shoulders, Bel knew she'd probably said too much.

'And this landlord. I don't suppose you happen to know him, do you?'

Bel puffed out a breath. 'He's actually my dad's friend, but he comes to the house a lot when he's in London, so I've known him since I was little. But this is business. He has several apartment blocks in Rome and I pay the going rate for rent.' She felt her spine begin to stiffen defensively.

'I didn't say that you don't. That's not quite the point, though.'

'Well, what *is* the point? Are you saying that I can't ask a family friend about finding a nice place to live?'

'Not for a moment. And you don't have to justify your actions to me.'

Joe always said that, and Bel was just beginning to believe it. But now she'd started the conversation, she couldn't let it go. 'Well, you don't have to justify your actions to me either. But I'm not at all sure that I understand you sometimes, Joe.'

'That's good. Trust me.'

'Is that supposed to be an explanation? Because I don't understand that either.' She frowned at him, pushing him away when he went to kiss her. There were some things that Joe could bat away with just one touch of his fingertips on her skin, but this wasn't one of them.

'Okay. I've just found your hard limit with regard to avoiding the subject. That's good, I'll keep it in mind.'

'Yes, do. It'll save a bit of time in future.' They might not see eye to eye at the moment, but the future was still there, holding them together. 'So what's the problem? You don't want to live in the same apartment block as me?'

He shook his head. 'I wouldn't have to walk so far for a change of clothes. I might not like this place very much, but it serves its purpose. It's close to both the hospital and the clinic, the rent's low and…' He shrugged. 'No one's done me any favours to get me here and I really wouldn't care all that much if I had to leave.'

'And that's still one of your hard limits?' After last night she'd thought it might have softened a little, but then she'd never had to leave a place she called home, nor had she ever worried about not being able to repay a favour if needed. They were privileges she'd just taken for granted.

'Afraid so. I know it must sound as if I'm being unreasonable.'

'Yes, it does if I don't think too much about it. But however much I'd like to deny it, I was born with a different set of rules than you were.'

He leaned forward, and this time Bel allowed him to kiss her. It was well worth the wait...

'That's not a bad thing. My mum and dad did their best to undo those rules, and for a while they did, but then I lost them...' He shook his head. Another hard limit. Joe never betrayed his feelings over his parents' deaths, but leaving London behind and coming here spoke for him.

'You need to do this one on your own, don't you. I get it, Joe. We don't need to do everything all at once.'

He nodded. That was the most she'd get out of him, but it was enough. His response when she kissed him again told her that.

'Are we done? Can I go and get changed now, so we can get on with our day?' They were planning to use their tickets to the Galleria Corsini today.

She closed her fingers around the material of his shirt, hanging on tight. 'No, we're not done. If you can't take any help in finding somewhere, then maybe we'll just have to find a way to stop the clinic from draining your bank account from every spare cent.'

'Okay. Not sure how we're going to manage that...' He gently disentangled her fingers from his shirt, getting to his feet. 'I don't imagine that'll stop you from thinking about it, though.'

Joe never entirely shut her suggestions down. He might reject some of her answers, but he was always open to more. They were on a journey together, where the landscape might change with every turn of the road. That was a challenge to both of them, but there was always some hope of change.

Lending him the money for a deposit was out of the

question. Bel knew he wouldn't accept that. Giving him a way to make the clinic more stable financially—he couldn't turn that down and it would give him a chance to spend some of the money he earned on things that he needed.

There was a way. One that challenged Bel, and put her directly in the firing line for anyone who wanted to judge her. She'd thought about it, though, and by the time Joe arrived at her apartment the following Friday evening she'd decided on what she was going to do.

'You're early. I'll make some coffee before we read, shall I?' She took the book that he'd picked up from the sitting room out of his hands and he grinned.

'Yeah. Coffee will be nice. What did you want to ask me?'

Joe was always one step ahead of her. Bel supposed that was only fair, since she usually knew what was on his mind. 'You could at least wait until I decide to say I have something to ask.'

'Okay. Fair enough.' He usually stayed in the kitchen to talk when she had something to do there, but now he walked back into the sitting room and sprawled on the sofa, tapping his fingers on the cushions in a show of mock impatience.

'All right. You can stop now.' She took the coffee in, setting the pot down on the table in front of the sofa. 'I've got an idea.'

'A two cup one?' Joe had picked up the Italian habit of draining a small espresso cup in one, and he set his empty cup down next to the pot. 'Go on…'

'It strikes me that the clinic needs to have a fighting fund.'

He nodded. 'Yeah, that was always the plan. We're the victims of our own success in that way—the demand for our services has always outstripped our fund-raising capacity.'

'In that case we need to think big, try and raise enough money to cover the clinic's costs for the next year. Something to give you a breathing space.'

He stared at her. 'That sounds…amazing. Is it even possible, though?'

'No, not with a few collecting boxes and a raffle. But we could organise a fund-raising evening. Mum and Dad get asked to that kind of thing all the time—they go if the charity appeals to them. They have champagne and a nice dinner.'

Joe chuckled, clearly not even reckoning this was worth thinking about. 'Sounds like a nice evening out. You do know that there are a lot of things that need doing before we can even contemplate champagne? Maria has to open a window and tell people to push hard on the entrance door…'

'Yes, I'd noticed. We can dispense with the champagne and the dinner. We are what we are. The clinic has different things to offer.'

'I won't disagree with you there. But isn't the whole point of one of these high-class dos that you get a really nice evening out, in return for a donation?'

'Yes, it generally is. Dad always complains that he'd rather just make a donation, he can go out and drink champagne with his friends whenever he likes. But the thing is that it's really all about making contacts. Matching the right people with the right charities, and setting up a support network. I can do that, Joe. I have the contacts because I've grown up in those circles.'

'You're a doctor, Isabella.' Joe frowned. 'That's what you've chosen to be, not someone who can use their contacts for a bit of PR. When you first emailed me and volunteered to help, all I saw was a doctor who was willing to give up a bit of time to help others. That's what I, and everyone else at the clinic, values you for.'

'I appreciate you saying that.' Joe had immediately put his finger on the thing that was difficult for her.

'I mean it. We're not going to compromise on that.'

'It's up to me whether I want to compromise or not, and I'm a pragmatist. There's no point in my recommending specific courses of long-term treatment if the clinic's future isn't assured. And right now, it depends on you for its survival. That was okay when you were starting out, but it can't go on for ever. You owe it to the clinic and everyone who benefits from it to give it a secure future.' Bel frowned. Maybe telling Joe that the clinic needed to function independently of him was a step too far.

He thought for a moment. 'Yeah, I take your point. What you're saying makes a lot of sense, but I just don't know how we're going to get there. Our whole ethos is about helping people be what they want to be. I know you don't want to be valued for your father's money, and I understand a bit better now why that's so important to you.'

'But you're willing to agree to a fund-raising event in principle?'

He puffed out a breath. 'Yes, of course. As long as you promise me one thing.'

'Don't do that. I'm not promising you anything until I know what it is.'

'So making love to me until I can't move is out of the question, then? Too bad,' he teased her and Bel raised an eyebrow. 'I was going to ask you to promise me that you won't be stepping out of your comfort zone. I know that you could set up a glittering evening that attracts really big donors, but that's not what you're all about, and it really doesn't reflect what the clinic's about either.'

'My comfort zone has been widening a bit lately.' That was all down to Joe.

'I very much doubt we'd be having this conversation if that wasn't the case.' His face softened. 'Mine's been widening too. But we still have our limits, and I won't agree to anything that doesn't respect yours. However much money that might raise.'

Bel refilled each of their cups with coffee. She'd been concentrating on what Joe might accept, but he'd made it very clear that this was all about her. He couldn't have said anything nicer, or more encouraging.

'It'll take some ingenuity.'

'You don't think you're up to it?' A smile flickered at the corners of his mouth.

'I didn't say that. I'll have to take a few risks, and you're going to have to trust me, but I promise I'll let you know if I do find myself colliding with my limits.'

He nodded, picking up his coffee. 'Then we're done. Let me know what you have in mind, and what you want me to do.'

'I'll come into the clinic tomorrow and make a list.' Bel downed her own coffee. 'You want to read? Or I could make love to you until you can't move—that sounds like a challenge.'

He chuckled. 'I'm the last person to deny you a challenge. Let's do both.'

CHAPTER NINE

BEL HAD TOLD JOE that they had to work fast. The clinic needed money and they couldn't wait for the kind of lead-in times that were normally required to secure a date in the calendars of the rich and famous.

Her strategy involved a combination of word-of-mouth and formal invitations. She'd spent every evening of the following week on the phone, and Joe had left her to it, supplying her with food and drink when she looked as if she was flagging. Her contacts would invite their own contacts personally, and Bel would follow up with one of the colourful invitations for a dress down, early evening event which would allow people to leave early if they had another evening engagement to attend. She'd assured Joe that printing invitations was the one thing they needed to spend money on, and he hadn't told her that he'd paid for them himself.

Last weekend they'd broken their no-work-on-Sunday rule and spent the whole day replying to emails and the RSVP cards she'd included with the invitations, assuring everyone that their presence was all that was needed, and they could pop in and back out again at their own convenience.

Everyone had helped out, volunteers and patients

working together to do whatever they could. The place was clean and tidy, and Maria had made sure that the workmen in the basement had finished on time. Martina had taken charge of the catering, which would consist of various people contributing a plate of party food, which would apparently all come together and make a good spread. Joe had played his part, tidying up the office, which produced a large bag of things that needed to be thrown away and a smaller pile of things he'd thought he'd lost.

He'd found a large box, and put it behind Maria's desk in the reception area, telling her to only accept one bottle of wine from everyone, and placing his own donation in for starters. The *one bottle only* rule had been undermined when Chiara and her husband added three bottles, insisting that one was from their young son, and several other people had taken it as an open invitation to spend as much as they liked on their one bottle.

And now Bel was as nervous as a kitten. She'd dressed up for the occasion, adding a heavy gold bracelet to her plain black dress, which proved the rule that one good piece of jewellery was enough, and she was pacing up and down behind the front door of the clinic.

'Hey, Isabella…' He caught her hand, bringing her to a halt. She smelled gorgeous, but then Bel always did to him, irrespective of the price of her scent.

'You look wonderful. You've already done the most important thing we set out to do. Everyone's shown what this place means to them.' Joe hadn't realised until now how much everyone had wanted to help.

'You didn't know, did you?' She smiled suddenly.

'I didn't have the time to stop and look. I have now.

Whatever happens next, everyone here will succeed or fail together, and that's already more than I could have hoped for at the start.'

'What happens if no one wants to donate?'

He shrugged. 'Then it didn't work. We'll try something else.'

'I could kiss you right now...'

They'd taken care to keep their relationship out of their work lives, which had been relatively easy at the hospital, and more difficult in the family of patients and volunteers here. Joe had been wary of letting anyone know, because he hadn't been able to believe that someone like Bel would stay with him for long. But now was time for this evening to work another of its miracles. He bent, kissing her lightly on the lips.

She reached up, wiping the lipstick from his mouth. Martina and Chiara had abandoned their therapist-patient relationship for the evening and were standing at the other end of the entranceway, waiting to greet their guests, and Joe noticed that they'd both spun around, turning their backs. He wondered whether that was his prompt to kiss her again, because one kiss was never enough.

Bel smiled up at him. 'Everyone knew already...'

The doorbell rang, and she started. Joe had spent a couple of hours with some sandpaper, under Leonardo's watchful eye, and the door didn't stick any more now. Bel flung it open, and suddenly her face was wreathed in smiles.

'Uncle Edo! I'm so happy to see you!' She hugged the man on the doorstep.

'You too, Isabella. How's your father?' Uncle Edo disentangled himself from Bel's arms and stepped inside.

'He's well—he and Mum send their love. Dad wants to know when you'll be coming to London next, he misses your nights together at the opera.'

'Soon…'

'Shall I call him and tell him to insist on a date?'

Uncle Edo chuckled. 'That would be very nice of you, darling. Now, where am I supposed to go?'

'I want you to meet the clinic's founder and director first…' Bel turned, introducing them.

'Delighted to meet you. Isabella's been telling me all about this new home of hers.' Hearing Joe's name, Uncle Edo switched effortlessly to English. 'I'm very interested in finding out first-hand what you do here.'

'Thank you. It's an honour to have you here, sir.' Edoardo Rossi was the fashion designer that every woman in Italy would give her favourite handbag to have on her guest list.

'My pleasure entirely.' Uncle Edo looked round as Chiara stepped forward.

'This is Chiara Albertini. She'd like to take your coat, and explain a little about what we do here.' Bel had taken hold of Chiara's arm, presumably to stop her from curtseying.

'Thank you. Will you indulge me, Chiara, and tell me where you found your dress?'

Chiara reddened furiously. Martina had persuaded her to wear something that she'd made for herself, before her accident, and the simple dress was elevated by a riot of embroidery at the neck and cuffs.

'It's Chiara's own creation. It's beautiful, isn't it?' Chiara was clearly completely lost for words, and Bel came to her rescue.

'Indeed. Quite remarkable.'

'I had a head injury and couldn't sew. But Martina's teaching me how to do it again...' Joe had made it clear to everyone who was helping tonight that no one was expected to tell their own story, they were here solely as hosts, but Chiara seemed anxious to add some more details. 'Now that I've seen how I might be able to do it again, I don't mind wearing some of the dresses I made before. May I take your coat?'

'Thank you.' Chiara helped Uncle Edo out of his coat, putting it carefully over her arm, her fingers running along the collar in clear appreciation of the fine material. His idea of dressing down appeared to be a silk waistcoat, made from a patchwork of riotous colour. 'It seems we have something in common and I'd be fascinated to speak with you a little more.'

Chiara straightened suddenly, beaming at Uncle Edo. Another success for the evening before it had even started. Martina appeared behind her, relieving Chiara of the coat and leaving her to guide Uncle Edo through to the reception area, where there was a gallery of photographs covering all aspects of the clinic's work.

'Edoardo Rossi is your uncle?' Joe murmured to Bel as soon as they were out of earshot.

'No, but I always called him that when I was little. My mother got to know him in Milan, and when we were there on holiday we'd spend a lot of time with him and his wife. When he lost Aunt Beatrice, five years ago, he came and stayed in London with them for several months.'

'Okay. That sounds like family to me, but what do I know? Any other very good friends turning up tonight?'

'I'm hoping for a few. And that some of *their* good

friends will be coming as well…' She shot Joe a mischievous smile as the doorbell rang again.

The evening was going better than Bel had expected. There were informal tours, carried out by volunteers and patients for whoever expressed an interest, and the craft room in the basement had been cleared and food and drink laid out. People had popped in and didn't seem to be in any hurry to pop back out again. The room was full, everyone chatting to each other over a glass of wine, balancing their food on paper plates. Joe was going to have to give the just-in-case speech.

She checked that he still had his notes in his pocket, receiving a grin in answer. Then she tapped a knife against an empty glass and the room fell silent. Joe stepped forward, looking so handsome that surely anyone would give him anything in return for one of the smiles that he'd been giving away for free this evening.

'Ladies and gentlemen. I want to tell you what you've done for us already this evening…'

What? She'd expected he might drop in a few asides, because they hadn't been sure if there would be enough people together at the same time to even give a speech. But he hadn't taken his notes out of his pocket.

'Our belief here is that we can try for what seems impossible. We may not make it, but sometimes it's the journey that's worth our while. Tonight, in filling this room, Isabella has shown us that we *can* achieve the impossible if we set our minds to it.'

A spontaneous burst of applause started in one corner and rippled around the room. Bel was torn between not wanting to encourage him and being captivated by the way he'd brought everyone together so effortlessly.

'We started out wanting to raise funds for the clinic and we still do. Isabella tells me that I must mention that we'll gratefully accept anything that you feel able to give, and we'll put it to good use. She's absolutely right, but… I have to tell you something. What I see when I look at this clinic are volunteers who go above and beyond what I'd ever dare ask of them. I see patients who do the same, and who return to help others in face-to-face encounter groups and internet groups…'

Bel puffed out a breath. Everything that Joe had said was right, but he might have stressed the part about raising funds a bit more.

'Isabella has brought you here tonight, asking you to accept us as we are. And you came, and have given us your valuable time. I've personally answered a lot of hard questions, which have made me think about the issues as you see them. *This* is what we value, and we thank you for being here to give us that gift.'

He grinned as an enthusiastic round of applause, from both helpers and guests, rose in the air.

'Smart man.' Uncle Edo leaned across, whispering to her in English. 'I'd be very surprised if he hasn't just doubled a few of the cheques that'll be written on the way out…'

'He's not being smart at all—it's what he believes.' It was what Bel believed as well and she couldn't help liking that Joe had said it, even if it wasn't what she'd written.

Uncle Edo nodded. 'You're the smart one, then.'

'We're just…' It was underestimating Uncle Edo to say *friends*. He could see the body language as well as anyone else. 'Don't tell Mum and Dad just yet, eh? I don't want them worrying about me.'

'As you wish. I wouldn't say they have anything to worry about, though. I'm very impressed with him.'

'Hold that thought, Uncle Edo.' Joe was making his way over to her, stopping only to shake a few hands that had been proffered in his direction. 'One of the things that impresses *me* about him is that he'll be expecting me to mention that the speech I wrote for him is still in his pocket.'

Uncle Edo smiled, waiting for Joe to join them and shaking his hand. 'Good speech.'

'*Not* the one I wrote, though.' Bel couldn't help smiling up at him.

'Sorry. I know you spent a lot of time on it and I fully intended to stick to it… But I saw everyone just staring at me, waiting for me to say something, and reckoned that if they'd broken the rules by staying, the least I could do was tell them how I really felt about that. What the clinic means.'

'Bravo.' Uncle Edo had been nodding in agreement with Joe, and now he turned to Bel to see what her answer was.

'Uncle Edo! Could you give me just a couple of minutes to actually *have* this conversation and then I'll tell you all about it?'

'Of course.' Uncle Edo held his hands up in an expression of surrender and Bel rolled her eyes. He was one of the kindest men she knew, but surrender really wasn't his style.

But at least she had Joe to herself now. She turned to face him.

'You were absolutely right. You may have cost us a bit just then, but we agreed we wouldn't pretend that we were anything other than exactly what we are. And you put it all very nicely.'

'So we're not going to have a full and frank discussion about it?' Joe looked slightly disappointed at the thought.

'No, I'm kicking myself at not having written something like that in the first place. I'd have included something to indicate that it was *you* who gave the clinic its values.'

'I would have mentioned that it was *you* who made me look beyond my assumptions. Since you have family here, I thought it was better not to. It's up to you to decide when and if you want to tell them about me.'

'Uncle Edo's already guessed, but he knows how to keep a secret. You're aware of the fact that his new collections surprise even the most well-informed fashion correspondents?'

Joe looked at her blankly. 'No, I wasn't. But I know now.' His hand found hers and gave it a surreptitious squeeze. And then they both jumped as a loud crash sounded from the drinks table.

In the moment of silence that followed, Bel heard a wail of anguish, and Chiara's voice, repeating the word *sorry*. She turned to see Chiara picking herself up from the floor next to the overturned drinks table, and the ever-watchful Martina making her way determinedly towards her. Joe had moved too, squeezing through the press of surprised people to reach Chiara, who had begun to cry.

'It's okay.' He murmured the words, quickly wrapping a napkin around the blood that was running down

Chiara's arm. 'Don't worry about this—it doesn't matter. Come with me and let me take a look at your arm.'

Chiara shook her head and Joe put his arm around her shoulders, firmly refusing to take no for an answer. Martina was comforting her too, telling her that it wasn't clumsiness but all a part of her compromised ability to judge distance and position and the two of them guided her away from the mess and out of the room.

Then something marvellous happened. The wife of one of Rome's leading industrialists took off her stylish jacket, handing it to her husband, and rolled up the sleeves of her silk blouse. She started to pick up some of the bottles that had rolled onto the floor, and another of the guests stacked them carefully out of harm's way. One of the volunteers had fetched a large packet of paper towels from a cupboard, laying them down on the new non-slip rubber flooring to soak up the spilt wine. Everyone began to work together to clear up the mess and Leonardo appeared from nowhere, directing operations and warning people away from the broken glass until gloves and brushes and pans could be fetched from the cleaning cupboard.

Bel climbed onto a chair, raising her voice. 'If our guests would like to move through into the garden while we clear up…'

Several of the guests drifted out of the room, but most of them ignored her. Uncle Edo was on the phone, and impatiently beckoned her down from her perch.

'This is… I wish they wouldn't…' Bel grimaced as he put his phone back into his pocket.

'What do you expect? You make people a part of the

family and then you tell them they can't help? Go and let Filippo in, will you?'

'You're going home?' Filippo was Uncle Edo's chauffeur.

'Of course not. Just let him in, please.'

There was no arguing with Uncle Edo when he was in a mood to insist and it seemed that everything was under control here, even if no one was doing what they were supposed to. Bel heaved a sigh and went upstairs, pulling the door open to find that Filippo was already on the doorstep and carrying two crates of champagne, one stacked on top of the other.

'What?' Bel stared at him.

'You know your uncle never goes anywhere unprepared, Miss Trueman.' Filippo gave her a cheery smile. 'Where do you want it, Mr Rossi?'

'Put it down here, thank you.' Uncle Edo appeared at the top of the stairs. 'And will you fetch the other ones, please.'

Filippo deposited the crates in the hallway and made his way back outside again. Bel turned to face Uncle Edo.

'What's all this?'

'I thought you might run out, so I brought a few extras just in case. I underestimated you—there was plenty for everyone, but I didn't expect that half of it would end up on the floor.'

'Chiara couldn't help it. She has difficulty in judging distances…'

Uncle Edo waved her explanations away. 'Whatever. I'm sure no one will refuse a glass of this.'

No, they probably wouldn't—it was a very fine vintage. 'They might all be leaving any minute now.' She'd already seen one of their guests walking into the small room behind the reception area to find his coat.

'You lose a few, maybe. You keep the ones you really wanted in the first place.' Uncle Edo smiled genially at the man as he emerged, his coat over his arm. 'Thank you for coming, Claudio. I look forward to seeing you again soon.'

'Yes.' Bel smiled at him. 'Thank you so much and… sorry for the unexpected turn of events.'

'Don't apologise, Isabella,' Uncle Edo whispered as their guest left. 'It wasn't Chiara's fault and if he doesn't want to drink my champagne that's his loss. Don't you want to see what your partner is doing?' He used the Italian word that implied a dance partner rather than a business partner.

Actually, no. It had never occurred to Bel that Joe wouldn't be dealing perfectly well with Chiara's injured pride along with the cut on her arm. It appeared that trusting someone, irrespective of whether they were a dance or a business partner, was finally coming naturally to her.

'He'll be managing. He'd have called me if he needed me.'

'If you say so. I'll ask Filippo to carry the boxes downstairs and we'll put the bottles on ice in the garden, ready for a toast when everyone's finished clearing up.' Filippo appeared right on cue with another two crates. 'Filippo, you brought the ice packs?'

'Yes, Mr Rossi, I packed them around the crates so the champagne's already cool.'

'Very good. Thank you. Out of the way, please, Isabella…'

CHAPTER TEN

Since everyone was clearly managing without her, Bel allowed herself to join Joe in the downstairs consulting room. Chiara was sitting with Martina on the examination couch and seemed to be recovering from the shock of her miscalculation.

'Hey.' Joe grinned at her. 'What's happening out there?'

That was Joe all over. His first concern was always for his patients, and he'd acted on those unswerving values. Martina could have dealt with the cut on Chiara's arm, but Joe knew that his place as director of the clinic was with the most vulnerable person in the room.

'They haven't left, Joe. Some of them have insisted on helping clear up—I couldn't stop them. Uncle Edo came prepared, with four crates of emergency champagne in the boot of his car, and his chauffeur's setting up in the garden as we speak.'

He chuckled. 'You've got everything under control, then?'

'Me? No, I have *nothing* under control. Everyone else seems to have everything under control.'

'That's the way you've been telling me to work for the past few weeks. If you set things up in the right way, then that gives people the ability to help. How are you finding it, by the way?'

'More annoying than I thought it would be.' Bel realised that she'd automatically slipped into English to speak with Joe, and that Chiara was looking at her nervously. 'Sorry, Chiara...' She repeated everything she'd told Joe in Italian.

'So... I haven't spoilt everything?' Chiara asked.

'You heard what Bel said—you haven't spoilt a thing. If I asked a little too much of you when I encouraged you to help, then that's my fault.' Martina had clearly already given Chiara that message and Joe nodded.

'My fault, actually. I'm the one who's supposed to be in charge here.' His grin clearly questioned whether he was in charge of anything at the moment.

'If we're going to disagree over whose fault it was, I'd be disappointed if you all overlooked me. *I* organised the evening...' Bel added, and Chiara finally smiled.

'I was the one who knocked the table over.'

'You have a disability, Chiara. Accidents happen and we owed it to you to take better care of you. I can only apologise to you that we didn't.' Joe firmly put an end to the conversation. 'How do you feel about joining Mr Rossi in the garden for a moment? Just to show you're okay.'

Bel nodded. 'I'm sure he'd like that.'

Chiara hesitated shyly and Joe nodded. 'Later maybe. Stay here with Martina, and I'll go and show my face for a couple of minutes.'

A firm knock sounded on the door and he turned, opening it. Uncle Edo was carrying two paper cups with what looked suspiciously like champagne in them. He grinned round at Chiara. 'You have a visitor.'

Chiara sat up straight, beckoning Uncle Edo inside.

'How are you? I hope you do not have blood on your beautiful dress... And that you are not hurt, of course.'

'No, it was a small cut, and Dr Dixon stopped the bleeding before I even knew about it. My dress and I are both well, thank you, Mr Rossi.'

'I'm so pleased. In that case, might I persuade you to join me in a little champagne?'

Chiara shook her head. Uncle Edo handed the champagne to Bel and she passed it on to Martina, who took a sip, nodding in appreciation.

'What about some hot chocolate, Uncle Edo?' Bel suggested.

'Even better. Thank you, Isabella. May we go to the garden now and find a seat where we can talk, Chiara?'

'Yes!' Chiara slid down from the couch and took Uncle Edo's arm.

'Is he always like this?' Joe murmured as he followed Bel into the small kitchen on the first floor.

'No, he's usually worse, but he promised me he wouldn't interfere when I asked him to come.' Bel reached up for two cups from the cupboard, while Joe got milk from the fridge. 'Now you have an idea of how the Italian side of my family behaves, do you have second thoughts about me?'

He curled his arm around her waist. 'Not for a moment. A little constructive interference from friendly uncles is something I missed out on, so I'm very grateful for it now. Just as I'm incredibly grateful to you for your constructive interference in my life, even if I sometimes don't appear to be.'

Another surprise, in an evening full of them. This was the best, though. 'Are you saying that you'll do exactly as I tell you in future?'

'Of course not. Do you really want a man who doesn't put up a fight?'

'No. That would become boring...' She kissed him, and he smiled.

'That's what makes *my* evening complete, Isabella. But we need to make the hot chocolate and then get ourselves downstairs to thank each and every one of our guests personally for staying...'

The evening was supposed to run from five until seven o'clock, but no one seemed disposed to leave and the mix of patients, volunteers and guests were still out in the garden chatting at nine o'clock. Uncle Edo offered Chiara and Martina a lift home at ten, and volunteers and patients who were car-pooling started to pull on their coats as well. Joe and Bel said goodbye to the last of their guests, and when he closed the door behind them Bel fell into his arms, hugging him with relief.

'You want to go and see what's in the donations box?' He was holding her tightly, clearly as overwhelmed by the evening as she was.

'You know...actually, I'm not even sure that I care.'

'Me neither. I think we collected more than money tonight. Our people had a chance to reach out and speak about the things they've faced. And they were listened to.'

Bel nodded, snuggling against him. There *was* more at stake tonight—it was important to raise some money to ease the financial burden that the clinic placed on Joe. She enjoyed the warmth of his arms for one moment longer, and then moved away.

'We'll look. At least we won't be wondering all night, eh?'

There were some five and ten euro notes in there, presumably from those who'd taken the sound of broken glass as a cue to leave. But there were cheques as well, along with an envelope with her name on it in Uncle Edo's precise handwriting. Bel read his note, while Joe counted the cash and made a list of the amounts donated by cheque.

'Joe, read this!' She handed over the note and he scanned it. 'I told him that he wasn't to donate anything, we just needed him to be there, to lend some social prestige...'

Joe read the note. 'Six front row seats for his autumn show in Milan. Chiara to be his special guest...' He grinned. 'She'll love that. The other five seats can be auctioned off in support of the clinic. And... What's he saying in the final paragraph?'

'Fashion houses often alter clothing for very important or influential customers. Each of these six seats includes one piece of clothing from the collection, whatever the person chooses and made individually for them.' Explaining the Italian words still didn't seem to give Joe any idea of what it all meant. 'Do you *know* how valuable a gift this is?'

He shook his head. 'From the look on your face, I don't think my guess would cover it.'

'It's worth... I don't know what it's worth, to be honest. You can't buy a seat at one of Uncle Edo's shows, they're by invitation only, and for serious fashion experts with a few film stars for good measure. The front seats are the most coveted, of course.'

His brow darkened. Joe wasn't going to turn this down, was he?

'Will Chiara be all right?'

'Yes, she'll be fine. I've been in the past, but I've been too busy for the last couple of years. My mother *always* goes, though, and I'll ask her to look after Chiara, we don't need to worry about her...' Bel thought for a moment. 'You don't mind, do you? I didn't ask Uncle Edo to do this.'

Joe shook his head slowly. 'I'm a bit out of my depth with it but... How could I mind, when he's been so generous?'

'I meant do you mind that this is my family?'

He leaned over, kissing her. 'You're beautiful, a great doctor, and you have a true heart. I have no idea why you choose to spend your time with me, Isabella. But I'm very thankful that you do.'

'Don't underestimate yourself, Joe.' Bel returned his smile. 'Although if you could be a little quicker in totting up those donations, I'd be even *more* impressed with you.'

Joe nodded, rechecking the figures he'd jotted down and showing her the total. 'This will be more than enough to cover the rent and Maria's salary for the next year *and* give us a fighting fund for contingencies. That's a huge step forward. We can both concentrate on being doctors now, and I don't have to worry about whether we'll make next month's bills.'

Bel nodded. 'You deserve that, Joe. Are you going to

think about putting some of your own salary aside to get a decent place to live now?'

'Yeah. I have to admit that'll be a relief as well.'

Nothing came without a price. Joe had the most beautiful woman in the world in his bed—or rather she had him in hers, because Bel's preference for the quiet of her own apartment was more than reasonable. The clinic's short-term future was secure, and he could start to consider how he might build on that. He was waiting for the other shoe to drop.

But maybe it was enough that it didn't drop on Sunday morning, when he and Bel went back to finish clearing up after the party and found that several of the volunteers had had the same idea. The work went much quicker than he'd expected, and he settled down in his office to start writing the personal notes of thanks to everyone who had come last night.

Sunday afternoon was theirs, to eat and talk and make love. Bel's yellow and white baseball boots hit the floor with a very satisfying thump, which didn't bother him at all.

He kissed her goodbye as the sun rose on Monday morning, making his way home and then on to the hospital. Her smile as they passed each other in the corridor on their way to different patients seemed a little subdued, but she was clearly busy. He was busy too. A patient with multiple injuries had just been brought in and he'd be operating on her this afternoon. But when Bel's name popped up on his phone as being free to assist, Joe couldn't help feeling a trickle of extra warmth in his veins.

She attended the short briefing session before lunch, and Joe stayed until everyone else had left, knowing that Bel would wait. She was sitting, nursing a cup of tea and lost in her thoughts.

'Penny for them?'

She glanced up at him. The troubled look in her dark eyes sent a shiver down his spine.

'Have you seen your email?'

'No.' Joe fished his phone from his pocket, stabbing at the screen with one thumb. There was a string of new emails, the subject lines all different but *clinic* and *volunteering* featured in all of them. He dismissed the urge to open a few of them and closed the door, coming to sit down opposite Bel.

'What's going on?'

She took her phone from her pocket, opening a picture of what looked like a newspaper clipping. 'See for yourself. This was on the doctors' noticeboard this morning. I haven't looked anywhere else, but it's clearly on its way around the hospital.'

Joe shook his head. 'I don't want to see for myself, I want to hear it from you.'

The ghost of a smile hovered on her lips, but she didn't reply. Joe reached forward, clasping her hands between his. 'Tell me, Isabella. What's the matter?'

'It's… I'm being silly…'

'Let's dispense with the disclaimers, shall we? I'm going to take a guess and say that you're *not* being silly, and that whatever this is it's *not* nothing. I'd love to be able to give it the time it deserves, but we have a long procedure ahead of us and we need to get our heads straight and have something to eat before we scrub up. So please just tell me.'

Bel grinned suddenly. 'Don't pull your punches, Joe. I can take it.'

'Well, go on then. Tell me.' He heard tenderness creeping into his tone.

She heaved a sigh. 'Somehow, the gossip columns got wind of what we were up to on Saturday. I don't know how that happened, but I suppose I should have thought of it. We never made any secret of what we were doing and there are people whose job it is to keep tabs on what people like Uncle Edo are doing, and send photographers along.'

'Okay. So...what? He was photographed going into the clinic?' That didn't sound particularly salacious to Joe, but he wasn't acquainted with the complexities of dealing with the paparazzi.

'There's one of me greeting him on the doorstep, and another one of me answering the door to Filippo. They must have looked the clinic up on the internet and put together a story. *"Struggling free clinic runs out of champagne for Rome's rich and famous..."* Someone found it and they've pasted it up on the noticeboard, next to your appeal for volunteers.'

Joe frowned. 'That explains my inbox. I'll grant you that's annoying because it rather misses the point, but I'm assuming that's not what's bugging you.'

Bel shook her head. 'You updated your website and added my name to your volunteers list...'

'Yeah. You said that was okay at the time.'

'Yes, it was. I'm a doctor, and my name's on a lot of

things in that capacity. But Uncle Edo's a close family friend and…' She shrugged.

'They put two and two together and named you as Isabella Trueman, daughter of Michael Trueman. Friend of Edoardo Rossi. I know you're not ashamed of your father or your friends, but that's not all there is to you.'

'I hope not.' Bel pressed her lips together. There was something more…

"Has anyone here been giving you a hard time?' Joe wondered whether it was appropriate for him to fly to her defence and demand an apology. He really wanted to, but Bel might decide she wanted to do that for herself.

'You know Dr Kemp in Urgent Care?'

'Vaguely. Young guy, a bit full of himself. Spends a lot of time schmoozing the registrar.'

'That's him. When I first arrived here he was too busy to give me the time of day, but this morning he came rushing up to me and started to congratulate me on what I'd been doing at the clinic. He told me that he had a few contacts and that he'd be happy to work with me on expanding the clinic's fundraising efforts and raising its profile.'

Joe could see how that must have hurt Bel. She was still bruised from her fiancé's behaviour. 'I hope you told him that we don't need a social secretary.'

'I said that he should email you, since you dealt with all of the volunteering. He didn't much like that, and said he'd prefer to send his details to me so that I could explain things to you and give you my recommendation.' She frowned. 'Which was a bit of an insult to you, I thought.'

Joe shrugged it off. If Dr Kemp didn't want to deal with him that was just fine. 'So what's your recommendation?'

Bel gave the offer a moment's consideration, which was more than it actually deserved. 'That's not what the clinic's all about.'

'Agreed. I'll write and tell him that. If he approaches you again—'

'I'll deal with it, Joe.'

He narrowed his eyes. 'So you're *not* going to give me the opportunity of defending you. I reckoned not.'

She smiled, reaching forward to caress his cheek. 'You get the job of making me strong. So I can defend myself.'

'Okay. I can hack that. I'll give all of these other emails to Maria to answer, saying that we'll be back to them within the week. There may be genuine volunteers there who just hadn't heard of us, but I think we need to weed out all of the sightseers.'

'The clinic does *need* volunteers, Joe.'

'Yes, it does. It needs people who are dedicated to helping our patients, not those who are attracted by the prospect of someone rich and famous walking through the door. It subverts everything we believe in, and it's an insult to the people who took us as we were and helped us on Saturday.'

'Maybe I should stay away for a little while.'

'No, Bel, don't do that, please. I saw the clinic in a different way on Saturday. It's a place of safety for everyone…' Joe struggled for the right words and finally said what he really wanted to say. 'I need you, Bel. And I will protect you.'

A tear ran down her cheek. Maybe it was what she'd been waiting to hear. 'Just keep telling me that, Joe.'

'As many times as you want me to.' He looked at his watch. 'Are we agreed? I need you to be there this afternoon as well.'

'To make me feel better?' Bel was teasing him now, and that was a very good sign.

'No, the general idea is to make my patient feel better.'

Bel got to her feet. 'In that case… Would you like me to get you a sandwich and something to drink from the cafeteria?'

'Would you? I'd like to take another look over these X-rays.'

'I'll be back in ten. We'll look at them while we eat.' Bel slung her bag over her shoulder, suddenly purposeful.

Joe had a feeling that he'd just witnessed the dropping of the second shoe, and it hadn't actually been so bad. Bel had been upset, but they'd worked things through together. Maybe he should take that as a lesson for the future.

Joe always made her feel better. They talked, sometimes they argued, but in the end they always saw eye to eye, always seemed to find a common purpose. And right now, that common purpose was in the operating theatre.

'She has a lot of injuries,' Bel noted as they finished scrubbing up together. Taken alone, none of them were life-threatening, but six broken bones and numerous lacerations of varying degree and type were devastating when taken together.

'Yeah. I heard that the fire department had to practically dismantle the car, it was right on top of her. And she's been weakened by shock and blood loss as well, so we need to keep a close eye on her. We have a good team, though.'

Joe was a good lead surgeon. He made sure that everyone knew exactly what they were doing, and his quiet, confident manner pulled them together as a team. Nurses, doctors and anaesthetists all liked working with him.

He'd identified the worst injury as the open, displaced fracture in their patient's leg. They would need to pin the bone, which had broken into three pieces, and then close the deep wound that had been made where one of the pieces had pierced the skin. It was concentrated, precise work, and operating with Joe always brought out the best in her.

'I think we can close now.' He was finally satisfied that the pieces of bone would heal correctly.

'Agreed.' Bel's one word confirmed his decision and he nodded.

'Guys…' Sofia, the anaesthetist, spoke suddenly, a shrill note of urgency in her tone, and Joe looked up at her. 'I think…'

One of the nurses let out a yelp, and Joe moved suddenly. He was quick enough to remove Sofia's hand from the gas flow control valve and wind his arm around her waist, catching her before she hit the floor.

'Tim, I don't think she's fainted. Keep an eye on her breathing…' Sofia was slumped against him, and he unceremoniously transferred her weight to the waiting arms of one of the nurses. 'Amy, I need an anaesthetist on the phone, now. Everyone else, stand back and take a breath.' Joe sat down in the anaesthetist's chair, his gaze on the screens that monitored their patient.

'I've got Dr Meyer on the line.' Amy spoke up and Joe nodded.

'Thanks, will you put him on speaker…? Richard, I'm standing in for our anaesthetist, who's just been taken ill.'

'So I gather. We're getting a replacement sorted for you, I'll have someone down there as soon as I can. In the meantime, the big blue and white machine is the one you want, Joe…' Richard Meyer's dry sense of humour lightened the tension a little.

'Good to know, thanks. The patient's stable and I think our best option is to continue. You're logged into my monitor?'

Bel hadn't even been aware that the anaesthetic machines were networked. But Joe seemed to know just as much about everyone else's jobs in Theatre as he did his own.

'Yes. Everything looks fine.'

'Good. Tim, is Sofia coming round?'

'No, but her breathing's okay and I've called for a gurney.' Sofia was lying on the floor in the recovery position and Tim had been monitoring her.

'Good. Make sure she's being seen by a doctor and then scrub back in. We'll be needing you.'

Joe quickly went through what everyone needed to do to cover for their missing colleagues, receiving acknowledgements from each member of the team.

'Right then. Let's show 'em what we're made of…'

He'd turned a potential crisis into a short pause for breath. Bel stepped forward, ready to start work again.

It took another three hours to knit a broken body back together again. When their patient was finally wheeled through into the recovery room there was a palpable sense of achievement.

'First time I've ever seen that happen,' the scrub nurse remarked. Student nurses and doctors fainted all the time in Theatre, but no one had heard of an anaesthesiologist passing out. 'Maybe Sofia's not well.'

'We'll see.' Joe had obviously been concerned for Sofia, but he didn't seem to want to pass an opinion. 'You all deserve a pat on the back for rallying round.'

'Any of that champagne left over from the weekend, Bel?' Amy chuckled and Bel saw Joe stiffen.

'Afraid not. It was a tough job drinking it, but somebody had to do it. Next time we'll be sure to invite you to give us a hand.' Bel saw Joe relax again. The sting of that newspaper article seemed like an inconsequential pinprick here, where life and death were the only things that really mattered.

'No, don't do that.' Amy shot her an expression of mock horror. 'I'd be telling operating theatre jokes.' She turned the corners of her mouth down, and everyone laughed.

'Interesting, though. I often wonder how people are going to get on after they leave here,' Tim mused.

'Well, drop in for coffee and find out. Everyone knows where we are now.' Bel grinned at Joe.

'Yes, we should,' Amy agreed. 'Did you raise the cash you needed?'

'Bel did a fine job. We'll be able to keep going for a while now, thanks to her.' The pride in Joe's voice sent tingles down her spine.

'Nice one. How's it feel to be rescued by the heroine of the hour then, Joe?' Amy teased him.

* * *

'How *does* it feel then? Being rescued?' Bel nudged Joe as they walked together out of the hospital.

'Better than I thought. Fewer bruises and I have no signs of altitude sickness. How does it feel to be the heroine of the hour?'

'That's better than I thought, too. Thanks for setting me straight.'

He chuckled. 'Any time. Although I think you set yourself straight, didn't you?'

It was difficult to tell. Maybe they'd just done it together, and the priorities of the operating theatre had finished the job. 'Did you get to speak to Sofia?'

He nodded. 'Yeah, she was feeling much better, but she was out for a while. They've arranged for some tests for epilepsy and she'll be seeing a specialist. I have to admit that was the first thing that occurred to me—it just didn't seem like a fainting fit.'

'They're obviously taking it seriously, then. But epilepsy isn't good news for someone working in an operating theatre.'

'We'll have to wait and see. I knew a nurse back in London whose epilepsy was controlled and she'd returned to work in Theatre after two years. Sofia's great with patients and she's a good doctor, and if the hospital needs to modify her role to support her they're obliged to do that.'

'You're always so committed to making things work for people, Joe. Helping them live their best lives.'

He put his arm around her shoulders, pulling her in

close as they walked. 'You asked me once whether I thought we were living our best lives.'

A little thrill ran down her spine. 'And what do you reckon?'

'This is my best life. Right here, right now. I want to hold on to it.'

'I do too. We'll do it together, shall we?' It felt like a promise. One that Bel intended to keep.

CHAPTER ELEVEN

So much had happened in the last three months. Bel had come to Italy to reclaim the peace that she'd lost in London, and Rome had brought her so much more than she'd expected. The proud history and the vibrant streets were still as she remembered them from her childhood, and now she had the added pleasure of living and working here, in a job she loved. But the best thing about Rome had been Joe. The Englishman who'd grown up just a few miles away from her, but who she'd travelled more than a thousand miles to find.

The eve of her thirty-second birthday fell on a Friday, and Joe had taken the day off from the clinic. He'd booked lunch at a small restaurant in the Piazza Navona, and laid a wrapped parcel on the table when they sat down.

'Since you're going back to London for your birthday, I'd better give this to you now.'

Bel caught her breath. She knew that Joe must have dipped into the money he was putting aside each week for the deposit on a new apartment in order to afford the restaurant, but telling him that a present was far too much would dent his pride. She closed her eyes, letting her fingers explore the shape of the parcel.

'It's a book, isn't it.' And so carefully wrapped, the green marbled paper obviously handmade. 'I'm not going to open it yet. I just want to appreciate it for a while.' She wanted to make this moment last.

He chuckled, obviously pleased that she'd noticed the care he'd taken. Bel had never had to think about what she might spend her last penny on, and Joe's decision to spend his limited funds on a present for her said far more than anything he could possibly buy her.

'Okay. You think you can last out until coffee?'

Bel smiled back at him. 'I'm not sure… I'll have to now you've said it. I wish I wasn't going home now. That I could spend this weekend with you.'

He shook his head, frowning at the idea. 'We'll have plenty of weekends together. This one's special and you should spend it with your family. That's a gift you shouldn't refuse.'

He could so easily have persuaded her to stay here in Rome, but he'd been generous in that respect, too. Joe hadn't had enough family birthdays and it seemed important to him that Bel should have hers.

Lunch had been far too good to rush, angel-hair pasta with a delicious seafood sauce, followed by creamy panna cotta. But as soon as Joe signalled the waiter and ordered coffee, Bel picked up her present, carefully peeling the sticky tape back.

'Joe! It's beautiful—wherever did you get this?' The leather-bound copy of *The Moonstone* was showing its age a little. The gold lettering on the spine was slightly worn and when Bel opened it, the gilded edge of the pages had rubbed off in places. But that only showed that it had been read, which made it seem even more precious.

'I had to phone around a few second-hand booksellers in London to find a copy in decent condition. Look at the inside of the front cover…' His mouth turned down in a sudden expression of nerves about the gift.

Bel flipped back to the front of the volume, and caught her breath. Its first owner had written their name in the top left-hand corner, along with the date. The second had followed suit and then the third… Halfway down there were three names bearing the same surname, where the book had obviously been passed from one member of a family to another.

'Joe! This is wonderful. All of the people who've looked after this book and read it before me.' Bel read through the names, which spanned almost a hundred years. The first were written in copperplate script using a fountain pen, and later ones in more modern handwriting styles with a ballpoint.

He was grinning now, and proffering a pen. Bel took it gingerly. 'Perhaps I need to practise first.'

'Just write your name. Your own handwriting's good enough—that's what everyone else has done.'

The waiter brought the coffee and Bel snatched the book up, hugging it to her chest, well out of the way of any potential spills. Joe chuckled, moving both cups across the table towards him, and Bel cleared a space on the table in front of her. He seemed to be enjoying this impromptu ritual as much as she was, and he watched her carefully as she wrote.

Isabella Trueman. Bel decided that she should be the first to institute a new trend and wrote *Rome*, before adding the date. The moment was caught now, preserved, like all the other moments when this book had gained a new owner.

'You want to read the first few pages over coffee?' he asked and Bel shook her head.

'We have to read it together, don't we?'

'Not necessarily. I can read one book, you read another. I've never had a three-book romance before.' He seemed to like the idea of breaking his own record.

'Well, I'm not going to rush it. So if you want to get to four you'll just have to stay around for a while longer.' The silent, implicit promise was enough and she'd savour each page.

They'd spent a few hours in the piazza, the small shops and street performers quite enough to hold their attention for a while. Then they'd fetched her suitcase from her apartment and boarded the train for the airport. Joe stopped at the departure gate, kissing her.

'I'll give your regards to London.' Bel smiled up at him.

He shrugged. Joe had moved on from London, and its treasures seemed to mean nothing to him. 'You can if you want.' He bent to kiss her again. '*Arrivederci*, Isabella.'

They didn't speak Italian when they were alone together, and somehow the words meant something. Joe had made a home here in Rome. A home that included her. Ten books, twenty or thirty even, suddenly seemed well within their grasp.

'*Arrivederci*, Joe...' She'd see him again soon.

The weekend had been wonderful. Her parents had both remarked on how well she was looking, and Bel had privately given Joe the credit for that. She wouldn't have any trouble in persuading them to come and visit her in Rome, and when they did they'd know that she'd finally made the right decision when it came to choice of partner. There was no rush and she'd take that at whatever pace Joe felt comfortable with.

They'd heard all about the clinic from Uncle Edo, although he'd kept his promise and not mentioned that Joe was more to her than just its founder and director. Her father had questioned her closely about how it was run over after-dinner brandy on Friday evening, but her mother had silenced him on Saturday morning, waving her finger at him and declaring that today there was no time for business. There were presents—a silk shirt from her mother and a new travelling bag from her father—and a party in the evening, under the sparkling lights of the large patio at the back of the house. Sunday was for sleeping in, and then taking Wilf for a long walk with her father, while her mother prepared a late lunch.

And then... Monday. Bel was flying back to Rome in the evening, and as soon as they'd finished breakfast her father had beckoned her into his study and waved her towards one of the leather-bound seats that stood around the fireplace.

'What's this, Dad?' The large, airy study was for business only, and her mother usually only ever crossed the threshold to haul him out of it, telling him he'd spent long enough in here and there were other things to do.

'There's something I want to discuss with you.' Her father batted away Bel's questions about his health, telling her that his heart was functioning perfectly well and that he intended keeping it that way. 'This is about *you*,

Bel. And the trust I established for you when you went to medical school.'

'That was a long time ago.' Bel had forgotten all about the small trust that her father had set up, which was intended to give her enough to make a start when she began work.

'Yes. You told me that you had a lot more studying to do after you qualified as a doctor and you didn't need it yet. And then...' Her father waved his hand.

'Then I met Rory. And things went a bit pear-shaped for a while.' When Bel had first met Rory she'd thought her only future was with him. And after that she hadn't been able to contemplate a future of any kind, she'd been too bound up in trying to clear herself of the charges levelled against her.

Her father smiled. 'So you're saying his name now, are you?'

Since she'd been with Joe, *his* was the only name that made her feel anything. 'I've been leaving all of that behind me, Dad. You said I'd eventually get to that point and it turns out that you were right.'

'Then this *is* the right time.' Her father smiled, walking over to his desk to fetch a document holder, which he handed to her. 'I intended to give this to you on your thirtieth birthday, but we were all making decisions about how to get from one day to the next and it would have just been another thing you had to think about.'

Bel nodded. That birthday had been one she'd rather forget, coming right in the middle of the enquiry into her own part in Rory's fraudulent dealings. 'You were right. I was already panicking about you paying for the legal help I needed, because I didn't want to look like some rich kid who was above the rules. I think that anything else would have sent me right over the edge.'

'I know. But the trust is still there and I've been adding to it a bit over the years. In response to various changes.'

Bel shot him a reproachful look and he shrugged.

'You're my only child, Isabella. What else am I supposed to do with it?'

'You and Mum have always been so sure about me making my own way in life. And you were right, I really appreciate the chance you gave me to do so.'

'Move with the times, darling. You've carved out a place for yourself and you're someone who can do a lot of good in the world—someone who *wants* to do a lot of good in the world. Your mother and I are very proud of you and this is something to help you on your way with that.'

Bel opened the file and took out the typed balance sheet which lay on top of the papers and documents inside. There had been regular additions over the years, including a large one at about the time she'd told her parents she wanted to get married, and another when it had looked as if the charges against her could become a criminal matter, which might result in her name being removed from the medical register. A third, very substantial, sum had been added a few weeks ago, presumably after Uncle Edo had reported back on the work being done at the clinic. This was the kind of money that her father usually dealt in, and which her parents had always protected her from.

'Dad! What on earth were you thinking? This isn't just something to help me on my way…'

* * *

A three-book affair. Joe's relationships usually only ran to a few Sunday newspapers, if he was lucky. Three books had always been way beyond his comfort zone.

And yet somehow, this time it wasn't. When Bel returned from London the bookmark between the pages of *The Moonstone* showed that she'd already made a start. And by the time they'd reached the weekend she was a third of the way through, and Joe was contemplating whether another book might be an appropriate gift, or if he should leave it to Bel to choose her own reading matter.

'I've got something to discuss with you.' They'd got up late on Sunday morning and Bel was making breakfast. Joe had turned his hand to sandwiches for later, to sustain them on their ongoing exploration of the Via Appia.

'Yeah?' He looked up at her. Bel was particularly beautiful this morning, and he guessed that he might be under the influence of having missed her last weekend, and over the course of a busy week. Allowing himself to miss someone was new, too. 'Shall we do it in the open air, while we walk?'

She nodded, her brow puckering in an uncertain frown. Maybe it was more urgent than that. He turned, reaching out to caress her cheek.

'It won't wait that long? Is something bothering you?'

'It'll wait.' Bel seemed to come to a decision. 'It's nothing bad, and talking as we walk is a much better idea.'

The day began to move forward again. A slow, relaxed progress that made breakfast something to be savoured and the bus ride to the Via Appia time well spent. They took a short cut to the point on the road they'd reached the last time, and resumed their slow pace along the cobbles. His rucksack was a little lighter this time, since it contained only their lunch. Bel had thrown his clothes from yesterday into the washing machine this morning, and he'd left them behind to finish drying with hers. One more step along a road that Joe had never thought he would take.

'What's this thing that you want to discuss, then?' He turned his face up to a clear sky, feeling the warmth of the sun on his skin.

'My father dropped a bit of a bombshell on me when I went home. Apparently, I have a trust fund...'

'Yeah? I thought that was against his rules.'

Bel's laugh in response sounded a little nervous. 'He set it up when I first went to medical school. It was a few thousand, just to help me on my way when I needed it. I knew he'd done it, but I'd forgotten all about it. Apparently, he hasn't and he's been adding to it.'

A few thousand sounded like admirable restraint. Even if that now ran to a few hundred thousand, Joe couldn't imagine that it would be enough to change Bel's life. She was just reacting to the idea of a trust fund, but she should look at it as an opportunity to take on new challenges, as and when they presented themselves. The idea left him surprisingly unconcerned.

'We've been through this before, Bel. I know you've been hurt by the way that others have seen your father's wealth, but this is a good thing, isn't it? That you feel ready to accept whatever he's set aside for you.'

She smiled. 'I hoped you might see it that way. And yes, it's a very good thing. He'd planned on making the trust available to me when I was thirty but at that point we were still working through all of the problems with my ex. We've both managed to leave that behind now.'

'I'm glad to hear it. And you don't need to gain my approval, or even mention it to me. It's not my business, and I'm over the shock of finding myself in a relationship with someone whose father could buy her a whole hospital for Christmas if he wanted.'

'That's... Don't joke about it, Joe.'

There was something very confronting about the way that Bel seemed to be taking a stupid joke so literally. 'I didn't mean an actual hospital.'

'No, it's not quite as much as that. But he's given me enough that... I can either do nothing for the rest of my life, or I can do something significant. Something that makes a real difference.'

'And which do you plan to go for?' Joe reckoned he knew the answer to that question. Her father probably did as well, and that was why he'd chosen this particular time to tell Bel about the trust.

She rolled her eyes. 'You mean die of boredom, or do what I've always wanted to do? Take a guess, Joe.'

'Just checking. This is your father's understanding of the situation as well?'

'Yes, of course it is. You don't suppose he'd offer me cash if he thought I'd see that as an opportunity to throw away everything I've worked for, do you?'

'That's not the impression I have of him. Can we sit down for a minute?' Joe could feel changes coming, and he reminded himself that change wasn't always a bad thing. It wouldn't be a bad thing for Bel—it sounded as if she'd just been given a significant opportunity. That meant that whatever happened next mustn't be a bad thing for him.

They left the road, finding a secluded spot to sit on the grass. Bel produced several folded sheets of paper from her bag and handed them to him, telling Joe that she wanted him to read them through when he again mentioned it was really none of his business.

'This...it's not just money, is it. There's a whole investment and property portfolio here.'

Bel nodded. 'The idea is that whatever I decide to do is self-sustaining. There's cash to set up a project, and an income to keep it going. Or I could use another financial model. It's not all about medical choices, it's about commercial choices as well. I don't really understand all of the options right now. Dad said that he can help me.'

Something cold closed around Joe's heart. This was a once-in-a-lifetime opportunity. More than that, it was an opportunity that was only ever offered to the very rich. Bel had to take it.

'So you'll be going back to London?'

'For a little while. Not for good—nothing needs to change between us.'

Everything needed to change. For a woman who'd had every opportunity that life could offer her, Bel just wasn't thinking big enough. She'd realise that soon enough and that one city couldn't contain all of the possibilities that her father had just made available to her.

Joe had thought this equation through already. He'd left London because he couldn't deal with the memories of loss and the grief after his parents died. Rome had allowed him to function again, beyond the obvious necessities of work and sleep, and he'd set up the clinic knowing that it was his last chance. Poured everything he had into it, not just financially but emotionally.

He and Bel had reached for the 'best life' that they both wanted. But maybe Joe had been foolish to believe that it would be any different from the other promises he'd been made every time he'd gone to a new family. Maybe he should have trusted his experience a little better, and realised that Bel would ultimately leave, in just the same way that everyone else had.

If he followed her now, he'd sooner or later want to build something else of his own. And the next time her opportunities were too good to miss, his world would come crashing down again. No relationship could withstand that and it was better for both of them if he lost her now, rather than holding on and trying to believe that there could be any other ending for them. The thought was like a physical blow, leaving him almost stunned at its force.

Or—maybe it wasn't quite as straightforward as that. Bel wouldn't just leave him behind, so he'd have to find a way to make her go. That thought hurt even more, although, of all people, Joe should know how to deal with the loss of having to move on.

A sudden quiet settled on him. He knew what happened next, he'd done it enough times before. He'd keep the part of him that he could truly call his own sheltered from the storms of having to say goodbye. Joe would walk away, so numb that he could hardly feel anything.

CHAPTER TWELVE

Bel had chosen her moment to tell Joe about the trust, and maybe that had been wise. He seemed to be taking all of this surprisingly well. There was no reason why the clinic couldn't benefit from the trust. He might draw the line at that, but Bel reckoned that they could come to an agreement that would work for everyone. And he seemed to be totally on board with the idea that she'd be in control of a very large amount of money.

'It'll work, Joe. It's a lot of money and I'd have to give up my job at the hospital. But I can put myself on a similar salary to what I earn there, so in practice nothing much is going to change. I just get to work on something that…' She wanted it to be something that she and Joe could build together, more than anything. Her dad might urge caution in that respect, for obvious reasons, but he could build in as many safeguards as he liked because she trusted Joe. She needed his strength and expertise to help her.

'*We* could work on something that matters. I wouldn't for one moment ask you to give up the clinic, but between us we could do a lot more than I can do alone.'

He shook his head. 'It's a nice thought, and thank

you for trusting me with it. How long have we known each other?'

'If that's the way you feel...' Bel thought for a moment. 'We could know each other for a while longer. None of these decisions need to be made straight away.'

'You do need to make some decisions. And they're too important to make if you're starting out with conditions. Like having to be in any one particular place.'

He was so cool. Almost cold. And frighteningly assured.

'Joe, this isn't a way for my dad to get me back to London. Mum and Dad would obviously like that, but I'm thirty-two years old. I'm allowed to work wherever I want to work, it's not as if they don't have the capacity to visit as often as they like.'

'I know. But I can't—I won't—tie you down.'

Suddenly Bel knew as well. He'd already said goodbye to her. Joe had closed down, the same way he'd learned to close down every time that he lost something. Some*one*. He wouldn't talk about her and he'd do his best not to think about her.

'Can't we talk about it? You could stay here and find someone to run the clinic. Join me when you can?' That was a last-ditch attempt to save their relationship, and Bel knew that Joe could never agree to it.

'The clinic is what I have, Bel. I've built it from nothing and... It may not be much in comparison with what you're able to build now. But it's my achievement, the thing I feel most proud of.'

She'd been so wrong to trust him. Rory had acted out of greed and self-interest, and Joe... His motives were very different, his painful childhood had taught him lessons that he couldn't forget now. And he wanted her to leave and take the opportunities that he'd never had. Maybe she should respect him for that, but she couldn't because it all boiled down to one thing. Her trust in Rory had been misplaced and her trust in Joe had, too.

'I see that. I should never have asked you to give the clinic up, I know how much it means to you.' Still, she couldn't walk away from him. If she kept a dialogue going then there was a chance that they might find a way through this. 'Can we go back now? I don't want to walk any more.'

'Of course.' He got to his feet, holding out his hand to help her up. Bel took it automatically, and wished she hadn't. The touch of his fingers was almost too much to bear.

They walked back to the bus stop in silence, and thankfully there was only a five-minute wait. She wanted to scream, throw something at him. Anything, to break through the reserve that protected his heart from pain. Somehow, she managed to find something to say, pointing out things along the way, and Joe replied every time. It was torment by polite conversation, but it was better than nothing at all.

Her heart started to beat a little faster as he followed her up to her apartment. Perhaps she was wrong. Maybe he was still here and he'd save her after all. They'd argue, shout a little, perhaps even break a little china in the process, but they'd work something out. Then Joe dashed all of her hopes.

'If it's going to be awkward at work, I can speak to HR and swap to the night shift for a while.'

Bel shook her head. 'No, it's okay. I'm nearly at the

end of my three-month probationary period and the hospital's due to send me a new contract but they haven't yet, so I'm well within my rights to leave immediately. You know there's a waiting list for doctors who want to transfer to the trauma department?'

Joe's look of surprise was an agonising reminder that he still had some emotion left. Just none for her any more. 'I didn't, actually.'

'They told me that when I joined. They won't have any trouble in getting a replacement for me.'

'Someone to do your job. Not a replacement.' His face softened fleetingly, but then he was back to the practicalities. 'I'll just take my clothes, then...'

'You could leave them here. I won't be going anywhere for a few weeks, there are things to be sorted out.' That was about as close as Bel could get to begging, when she was just as angry as she was heartbroken.

He hesitated but shook his head. 'We said that we couldn't make each other any promises, when we started out. I hope that you can understand why I won't be back, and that we can part as friends.'

Friends? They'd been doctors, lovers, people who aired their differences by quarrelling loudly and often... Anything that involved a bit of passion. She and Joe had never been just friends. But it seemed that was all they were left with.

'Of course.'

He nodded stiffly. 'Thank you. I appreciate it.'

Joe hurried to collect his things, stuffing them into his backpack as he made for the front door. Bel didn't move. She wasn't going to help him go by opening and then closing the door. He'd have to do that all by himself.

But he didn't look back. When Bel ran to the window she saw him walking away quickly, his gait purposeful.

She was done with him. Joe had let her down, just when she needed him the most, and she couldn't forgive him for that. It would hurt for a while and then she'd be free of him, just as she was free of Rory. The only problem with that was that she knew in her heart that she could never stop loving Joe.

Moving on was a great deal more difficult than it had been when he was a child. Then he hadn't had to actually do anything, he'd just followed the instructions of the adults around him. Joe had been able to allow numbness to carry him through the transition between one set of welcoming faces and another, and concentrated on finding out whether he'd be allowed to take a book from a new set of shelves and read it. Now it was more as if his whole body was shutting down. He couldn't breathe, and his heart felt as if it had been torn from his chest.

He kept walking. Straight past his apartment, because although Bel hadn't spent a great deal of time there, his main attachment to it was that it did hold some memories of her. Past the hospital, because he didn't want to contemplate the thought that she'd have to turn up there at some point, to tell them that she wouldn't be signing a new contract. The places they'd been together were no-go areas for the time being, but maybe that would change.

He had to go somewhere. Leaving might be the same, something that ran through his life like an unbreakable thread, but when he was a kid there had always been a new place to go, with food on the table and a bed to sleep in. This time he had to fend for himself.

Joe stopped at a café, ordering pizza slices and hot chocolate. Now that his stomach was full, he needed to find a bed for the night. He started to walk again, and found himself outside the clinic. Here, there were other memories, which might soften the shock of losing Bel.

He climbed the stairs to his office and stared at the blank screen of his laptop for an hour. Then he went downstairs and polished Maria's desk, reckoning that if nothing else could come of the evening, at least she might notice and be pleased with the gesture. He cleaned the kitchen and looked for any minor specks of dust in the consulting rooms which might claim his attention for a few minutes, then fell asleep on the sofa in the reception area. Waking early, with the impression of sound and colour still in his mind from dreams he couldn't remember, he made his way to work.

Bel had spent a week locked in her apartment, going out only when she needed to buy food. She'd cried a lot and raged at Joe, but still she'd waited for his call. When it didn't come, she'd called her father, asking when they could start work on plans for the trust, knowing that 'now' was always his preferred option. She'd packed her bags at the weekend and flown back to London, ready to start work on Monday morning.

One thing about her parents' house in Chelsea was that she had no opportunity to dwell on her feelings. There were papers to read and discussions with lawyers and accountants to fill her time. She'd never realised that the process of working out how to spend money could be so complicated.

The Moonstone lay on her bedside table, reminding

her that she and Joe had only ever managed to finish one book together. She'd abandoned this story, although she couldn't put the book away on a shelf. It was a reminder. That she'd loved Joe, and even if he'd let her go, they'd had something real.

But the stress of hidden emotion was exhausting. She'd spent Sunday morning in her pyjamas, unable to sleep but not ready to get dressed and go downstairs yet.

'Not feeling well?' Her father appeared in her bedroom doorway.

'I'm fine, Dad. Just a bit tired, this last week's been a bit full-on.'

He nodded. 'Well, you need to get up now. We have a meeting.'

'On Sunday? What about lunch?' Sunday lunch was sacrosanct, and Dad would be catching the sharp side of Mum's tongue if he broke that particular rule.

'It was your mother's idea. Get dressed, we're going in thirty minutes.'

'Where?'

'The Hidden Door.' Her father smiled. 'It's important.'

It must be. The Hidden Door was probably the most exclusive restaurant in London, situated behind a popular Chelsea eatery, where people went to see and be seen. In contrast, The Hidden Door was where you went if you wanted to eat out in the knowledge that you wouldn't be seen, and its hand-picked clientele was selected from the ranks of the very rich and the very famous.

'What am I wearing, Dad?' Bel called after her father.

'Clothes, I imagine. Not my territory...ask your mother...'

She heard his voice from the other end of the hallway, and then Wilf's excited yelp as he whistled to him to come and play catch in the garden while Bel showered and dressed.

Her father was waiting in the car exactly thirty minutes later, and Bel's mother shooed her out of the front door. There wasn't a great deal of time to wonder what all the rush was about or who they'd be meeting, and ten minutes later they drew into an undercover driveway behind the main restaurant. A parking valet collected the car keys and opened what looked like a service doorway, which led to a small foyer.

'Mr Trueman. How nice to see you. We have table four ready for you.' The concierge guided them into the dining room, where six tables were carefully arranged to afford space and privacy to each party of diners. A waiter pulled out a chair for Bel and she sat down.

'This table's set for two. Who are we meeting?'

'I'm meeting with you.' Her father dismissed the waiter with a twitch of his finger. 'Or I suppose we could say that you're meeting with me.'

'Couldn't we have done that at home? In the kitchen?'

'I don't have as good a selection of wine. And I haven't been here for ages, I hear they have a new menu.'

'Dad, you're not steamrollering some business contact of yours into submission, this is me you're talking to. Why did you haul me out of bed and bring me all the way down here?'

Her father nodded. 'Because the outcome of the conversation we're about to have may affect your trust. And you're my daughter and I wanted to treat you to a nice lunch.'

'Okay. Better. Are we going to have a glass of wine, then? You choose it...'

Her father beckoned to their waiter, ignoring the wine list and ordering a whole bottle of one of his favourite vintages. Things were obviously getting serious.

'I'm going to put my cards on the table, Isabella. Your mother heard a noise and found you crying in your sleep earlier this week. She sat with you and sang a lullaby and you quietened down a bit. Do you remember that?'

Bel shook her head, feeling herself flush with embarrassment. 'No, I... It must have been a dream, Dad. I'm sorry, I know that would have worried her and I wish that hadn't happened. Let's go, I'll explain everything to her.'

Her father laid his hand on hers. 'You mean you'll come out with a whole string of excuses and try to convince her that everything's all right? That's not going to wash, I'm afraid, because the things that worry a parent the most are those that their child won't tell them about. She called Edoardo the next day, and it took her ten minutes to break him down. He said that it was rare to see a couple so made for each other.'

'When I accepted the donation for the clinic from you...there was nothing going on between me and Joe then.' Bel pressed her lips together miserably.

'I appreciate you telling me that, but it wouldn't have mattered if there was. The money I sent to the clinic was an investment in people's futures, and the updates and photographs I've received have given me a great deal of pleasure. He seems to be a good man.'

'He is, Dad. A really good man...' The waiter approached with the wine, and her father took the bottle from him before he could begin with the ritual of displaying the label and pouring a mouthful for him to taste.

'Thank you, Sam, that's splendid. May we have a few minutes, please?'

'Of course, Mr Trueman. Call me when you're ready to order.'

Her father turned his gaze back onto Bel as he poured the wine. 'Why don't you tell me all about it, Isabella? Maybe I can help and maybe not. But I *can* listen.'

It had all come tumbling out. The way that the clinic was helping people in ways that Bel hadn't even thought about before. How much she'd learned, and how committed Joe was to his patients. Her father listened quietly, stopping her only to order a mixed plate of starters.

'But you haven't included the clinic in your plans for the future.' Dad was being tactful. What he really meant was that Joe wasn't included in her plans.

'It's complicated.'

'Of course it is. When is it not?' Her father leaned back in his seat. 'But it sounds to me as if you love him. Is that the word you're afraid to say?'

She couldn't even say it now. Even though it was the only thing that made any sense to Bel. 'Dad… Can the trust wait?'

'Of course. It'll be there whenever you want it, that was always my intention. You don't owe it your attention if you have other things to do.'

A weight seemed to lift from her shoulders. 'I think I do have other things right now.'

Her father nodded. He was always at his most focused when there was something to be done. 'In that case, I recommend a square meal for starters. You've hardly been eating this last week. Shall I order…?'

Joe had lost track of the days, because suddenly the nights had become so much more important. That was when he could bring Bel back to him, even though the memories always involved a sense of heartbreaking loss.

He'd kept going, though, because that was all he knew how to do. On Friday, Maria brought him to a screeching halt.

'Where's Bel? She's not sick, is she?'

For all Joe knew, she might be. She could be here still, in Italy, or she could already have flown back to London. That was one of the hardest parts. He'd always known more or less where Bel was, and when he might see her again. But now he was adrift. Becalmed on a lonely sea, without any idea which way he should go to reach his next destination.

'She's going back to London. There was…an opportunity there for her that she couldn't miss.' *That* was better. He'd acknowledged for the first time that Bel was gone, and maybe now he could move on.

'An *opportunity*? And so she just dropped everything and left?' Maria was bristling with disapproval now.

'It was…' He couldn't allow Maria to think that Bel was at fault. 'There really wasn't any choice about it. I told her that, and that she should go.'

'Joe!' Maria frowned angrily at him.

'What? You think I should have lied to her? Asked her to stay when it was in her own best interests to go?' However much the truth had cost him, he'd had to face it.

'And what do you suppose a woman does when you ask her to stay?'

Joe shrugged. He'd never been in that position before.

'She makes up her own mind.' Maria supplied him with the answer. 'But when you tell her to go, you give her no choice. She goes.'

Joe hadn't thought of it in quite that way before. But he wasn't going to argue—it at least put the responsibility squarely onto his shoulders. 'I suppose so...'

Maria puffed out an exasperated breath. Clearly, she wasn't done with him yet. 'What are you doing on Sunday?'

That was a *very* sore point. He imagined that Maria probably knew that, and didn't care. 'I'll think of something.'

'Right, then. You're coming to lunch. Both my daughters are coming as well as my son and his family, but we'll make room. We can't have you moping.'

Joe wasn't aware he *had* been moping. Not in public, at least. What he did in his own time was his business. 'Don't think I don't appreciate the invitation. I'm okay about it all though...'

'You want my son to have to come and fetch you?' That was an obvious threat, since Maria's son was an officer of the Polizia di Stato. 'He could arrest you if you don't show up.'

Joe held up his hands in surrender. 'Thanks, Maria. I'll look forward to it.'

Lunch had been a long and slightly riotous affair. Maria's husband, her son and his wife and her two daughters had all made him welcome, treating him as if he were a part of the family and expecting him to pile in and help with whatever needed to be done to get lunch on the two different tables that had been pushed together under a large sunshade in the garden.

But the one clear image in Joe's head as he took the bus back to his apartment was Maria's grandson. He was only six, but had solemnly shaken Joe's hand, along with the older men, when he'd been getting ready to leave. Then he'd stretched his arms up, demanding a hug.

'*Arrivederci*, Joe.' His words were the same as everyone else's. The same as the ones he'd exchanged with Bel at the airport, when he'd seen her off on her birthday weekend. He was just a child but he already knew how to say goodbye without turning it into loss.

The sun was going down, and that was one more ending. Tomorrow might just be a new beginning, though.

CHAPTER THIRTEEN

IT HAD BEEN three weeks now. Joe had missed Bel for every waking moment, but he'd been busy. He'd moved forward with a determination that had almost frightened him at times, and now he was almost done.

But his last move was made for him. As he opened up the clinic on a bright Friday morning, he heard a car draw up. He recognised it before he remembered whose it was, and then saw Costanza in the driving seat. She tumbled out, her face tight with stress.

'Dr Dixon...'

No one ever called him that unless they needed his help. 'Is everything all right, Costanza?'

'My boy, Nico. He's hurt himself and... I know this is not what you are here for, but can you help, please? The hospital is so busy...'

Particularly in the early morning, when urgent care centres all over the city would still be dealing with the fallout from the night before. It was an environment that would challenge anyone, but an autistic child would find the noise and the people unbearable.

'How is he hurt, Costanza?' If taking Nico to the hospital was the only option, then perhaps Joe could accompany them, and ease their way a little.

'He fell and cut himself. Bel says that it will need to be cleaned and perhaps a couple of stitches…'

Bel. She was still here? Joe dismissed the thought. He knew that Bel wouldn't have stayed in Rome for another three weeks when there was something for her to be doing in London. Maybe Costanza had phoned her.

Now wasn't the time to wonder about that. 'Bring him in, Costanza. No one else will be here for another couple of hours and we'll find somewhere he's happy with and take things at his pace.'

'Thank you. Thank you so much…' Costanza turned, beckoning towards the back seat of the car. And suddenly, it was as if a meteor had just appeared in the sky and was heading straight for him. Joe froze as the car door opened and Bel got out, her face twisted with the same agony that he felt.

'I'm so sorry, Joe. I didn't want…' She turned, and Joe saw little Nico behind her. He was pulling at his T-shirt and wore a pair of headphones to distract him from the early-morning activity of the city, but he allowed Bel to lay her hand on his shoulder, guiding him out of the car. His arm was bandaged in an obvious attempt to stop the bleeding, but Bel wouldn't have had what was needed to clean and stitch the wound at home and her decision to come here first, before trying the hospital, was the right one.

He had to breathe. Focus on the child. 'It's okay. Bring him in.' He stood back from the door, letting Costanza and Bel shepherd Nico inside.

They took their time. Bel had suggested that Nico might feel more at ease in the garden and Costanza had agreed. The boy had chosen a shaded corner, and Bel had fetched a seat for him, with one for Costanza and another for Joe. Blood was beginning to seep through the bandage, and Joe hurried to fetch the things he'd need from the clinic's first aid cupboard, arranging them on a tray.

'Joe...' He turned to see Bel standing behind him, once more in an agony of embarrassment.

'It's okay.' It really wasn't but it was all he could think of to say. 'Nico first.'

She nodded. 'Maybe we can talk?'

Joe wasn't sure if he was ready to talk just yet. But that could wait as well. 'Wash your hands, I'll be needing your help...'

When Bel followed him back to the garden the effortless synchronicity kicked in, almost knocking him sideways. Muscle memory, maybe. An echo of the concentrated focus of the operating theatre. Or maybe something more. But there were no words needed, they each knew exactly what to do, and the gash on Nico's arm was cleaned and stitched with the minimum of fuss.

'Well done, Nico.' The boy looked up at him and gave him a nod. 'Your arm will heal very well.'

'Will you look at it again?'

'Yes, I'll come to your home in one week and look at it.' Bel had been explaining what was going on to Nico every step of the way, but maybe she wouldn't be around to monitor the wound.

'Okay. That's all right.'

Joe smiled. Once they'd settled him and he'd begun to feel safe, Nico had been a much better patient than some adults, uncomplaining and co-operative.

'Thank you, Nico. It was very nice to meet you.'

Costanza was smiling now. 'Thank you so much. We so appreciate your time. What will this cost?'

'This is a free clinic.'

'But I can pay...' Costanza reached for her handbag, clearly determined to give Joe something, but Bel laid her hand on her friend's arm.

'Perhaps you and Nico can make some biscuits and bring them here. Would you like that, Nico?'

Nico nodded and got to his feet, clearly ready to go home and make biscuits right now.

'Tomorrow, Nico. We'll make biscuits tomorrow.' Costanza gathered up their things and shook Joe's hand warmly. 'Thank you again, Joe.'

'My pleasure...'

Suddenly the haze of uncertainty descended on him again. And then Joe remembered what Maria had told him. Essentially, if you ask a woman to stay, she'll make up her own mind.

He turned to Bel, his heart lurching in a mixture of terror and joy. Now was the time, and he had to grasp it. She was fidgeting uncertainly, but that only increased his resolve.

'Please stay.'

She nodded, and sat down in the seat he'd been occupying. Bel said her goodbyes to Nico and Costanza, and left Joe to accompany them through to the front door. He waited for them to get settled in the car, and waved as they drove away.

Suddenly he couldn't breathe. He had no idea why Bel was back here in Rome. He wasn't ready yet...

Too bad. Bel was here and that was all that mattered. If he had to go into this situation unprepared, then so be it.

* * *

Bel hadn't wanted to just turn up on Joe's doorstep again. He'd retreated from her, doggedly and uncomplainingly, and ever since she'd flown back to Italy three days ago she'd been pondering the best way to approach him. Then Costanza had banged on the door of her apartment, holding Nico in her arms. One look at the blood dripping from the gash on his arm had told her that the boy needed more than just a plaster, and Bel hadn't been able to think of a better place to bring him.

Joe had been here, as he always was, and he'd been so good with Nico. Talking *to* him, rather than straight over his head, making sure that he understood what was going on. Nico had responded to that, and so had Costanza. And there was still something there between her and Joe. So strong that it made her heart break all over again, into too many pieces to just pick them all up and leave.

When he came back out into the garden his face was unreadable. But Joe was still there, she could see it in his eyes. He hadn't retreated behind the wall of polite rejection that had sent her away from here and back to London. That was something, at least. Maybe everything.

She got to her feet. 'Joe, I... I went to London. I'm back now. This isn't the right time for me to start thinking about what to do with the trust. I'm staying here, in Rome.'

Genuine surprise showed on his face. And something of the warmth that she so badly wanted from him. 'What does your father think about that?'

'He agrees with me. The trust was only ever meant to facilitate things that I wanted to do, not to take my life over. It'll wait.'

'Okay.' Joe was clearly trying to choose his words carefully. 'You're coming back to the hospital? The clinic?'

'No. My job at the hospital is probably filled, and I don't care about the clinic...' That wasn't true. 'I mean that's not what I came back for. I came back for *you*, Joe. I know you told me to leave, but you were wrong. And I was wrong to listen to you, so I'm going to correct that error of judgement.' She folded her arms defiantly. That probably wasn't the best way to tell him what she'd been meaning to say, but it was a relief to just say it, without beating about the bush.

He smiled suddenly. 'Someone told me that if you tell a woman to leave—'

'Forget whatever anyone's told you, Joe. Listen to me. Now.'

His lip curled. The thrill of battle ignited in his eyes. That gave her courage, because she was here to finally fight for what she wanted. 'All right, let's talk about now. You turn your back on the opportunity of a lifetime and show up here. No job. Do you even have a place to live?'

'My apartment's on a six-month lease. And what was I going to do, tell Costanza to deal with Nico on her own?'

'That's *not* what I meant, Isabella. Of course you should have brought Nico here. But you have a family and opportunities. Don't ever think that doesn't matter in life.'

He needed to hear this in words of one syllable. That was okay, Bel could do that. 'I know how much you've lost, Joe. And I know that the only home and opportunities you have are the ones you've made for yourself. But I need you to understand that my family and my opportunities will always wait for me. Right now, I need to be here and tell you that I love you.'

She'd finally said it. Moved past her fear of betrayal and trusted him. It felt like a release, even though she didn't dare hope that Joe could tell her that he loved her. Bel knew that he did, but it would take work before he was able to say it.

He reached forward, taking her hand. 'Come upstairs.'
'Where?'
'Just come upstairs. Please, Isabella.'

She never had been able to resist those blue eyes of his. Particularly when they were full of warmth and gazing at her. And he'd called her *Isabella*. That must mean something, even if it was all that Joe could do to articulate his feelings. Bel followed him up to the reception area, and then up the flight of stairs to the first floor. He walked through the largest of the consulting rooms, opening a door that Bel had always imagined led to a cupboard.

He was halfway up the narrow steps when she realised where they were going. 'Why are you bringing me up to the attic?'

'Nice view.' He turned, smiling as Bel rolled her eyes. Nothing had been talked about or settled, but the chemistry between them was there still. Bubbling and fizzing through her veins, telling her that everything was going to be all right if she just hung in there.

He opened a door at the top of the stairs and they stepped into a long, low space filled with boxes and dust, and partitioned off at one end. He'd told her that there was a living space up here, which wasn't used. Bel picked her way past the crates, and Joe led her through the door in the partition.

It was clean and bright, but that was about all you could say for it. Boxes were stacked in one corner and there was a sofa and a table. An arch led through to a small kitchen and there was another door, which probably led to a bathroom.

'Are you living here, Joe?'

'I moved in last week.' Joe looked around. 'It's not much at the moment, but it could be nice. I could knock a few holes in the partition and build another one further down if I need more room.'

'What happened with your apartment?'

'I gave it up. Now that we know we can keep the clinic running for more than just a month at a time, it became a possibility.'

Bel nodded. Joe could never have taken the risk of losing his home and why should he? He'd already ploughed most of the rest of his salary into the clinic. She walked over to the double doors at one end of the space, opening them. The back of the clinic faced the old part of the city, and the view really was spectacular, with terracotta roofs and ornate domes stretching out into the morning mist.

'And are you spending every waking moment working?' That had always been a reason for him not to move in here.

'No. I've been spending time on a lot of different things. Missing you…'

'Then this place could be really good for you, Joe. It'll give you a chance to get back on your feet financially.' At least he'd missed her, although he seemed to have forgotten what she'd said downstairs. That she loved him. It was okay. Maybe Joe needed a bit of time to process, and as long as he didn't send her away, she'd tell him every day until he believed her.

She heard his footsteps, moving across the room towards her. When she turned, he seemed very close. 'Isabella, I didn't ask you up here to talk about that. I wanted to make it clear to you that what you see right now is all I have.' He fell to one knee.

'Joe...' She tugged at his shoulder, but he wouldn't move.

'I love you, Isabella. I have nothing to offer you, other than that.'

'You have everything to offer me, Joe. All of the things I really need.' She bent, trying to get him back onto his feet again, but Joe was too solid. He wound his arm around her waist, and she sank down onto his knee.

'I didn't just let you go. I drove you away.' He hushed her when she started to disagree. 'I know what I did. I couldn't bear to lose you and so I just switched off, the way I've always done when I feel I'm losing something. I promise that I'll never do that again, because I intend to fight for you.'

She could feel tears on her cheeks. Bel wiped them away. 'That's good to hear. Because I intend to fight for you, too.' Maybe he'd kiss her now. She was aching to feel his kiss on her lips...

He smiled. 'Will you marry me?'

'Yes!' She flung her arms around his neck, holding him tight. 'When?'

He chuckled. 'As soon as we have a place to live and I can afford a nice ring for you. In the meantime...' Joe reached for the neck of his shirt, pulling at a piece of synthetic surgical thread which was threaded through a ring. There was no stone, but the gold love knot was just perfect on its own. Simple and solid, yet beautiful.

'It's gorgeous, Joe. I don't want another ring. I want this one.' She held out her hand so that he could slip the ring onto her finger. He pulled at the thread, but it didn't give. He slipped the ring onto her finger anyway.

'You'll have to strangle me to get away now.' He chuckled and Bel kissed him.

'I'm not going anywhere, Joe. Neither are you.'

'I can promise you that.' He kissed her, effortlessly capturing her in that familiar world where the only thing that mattered was that he was holding her, safe and warm in his arms.

'Did you hear the front door?' She kissed him again. There was no need to stop.

'Yeah.' Joe kissed her back.

'Perhaps we should…' One last kiss. Bel couldn't resist that.

'In a minute…'

They couldn't get enough of each other. Couldn't turn away from the happiness that enveloped them both. But Bel could hear footsteps on the stairs and then a voice.

'Joe! Are you up? Someone's opened the shutters downstairs.'

'That was me, Maria,' he called back. 'I'll be down in ten minutes…'

Bel heard Maria's footsteps go back down the stairs. 'Maybe eleven?'

'Twelve would be better.' He kissed her as if they had all the time in the world. 'I have patients this morning. Will you be at your apartment? I can be there at around lunchtime.'

'No, I'll be here. I'm sure I can make myself useful.'

'If you're off the premises I won't be tempted to come looking for you…'

'I told you that I wasn't going anywhere, Joe. This is who we are. We work hard and then we play well. I'm not going to be the kind of fiancée who hangs around waiting for you. You'd better get used to that.'

He grinned. 'I can get used to it. I didn't expect anything different…' Bel went to stand and he closed his fingers around her arm. 'Wait… Wait a moment. Take the ring off…'

'No! Get a pair of scissors if you can't break the thread. How long have you had it around your neck?'

'Ever since I bought it, four days ago. I was planning on coming to London as soon as I got paid in two weeks' time, but I knew what I wanted and I got some cash back on the deposit from my old apartment. The ring was a reminder that I wasn't going to give up on you, however long it took to prove myself.'

'You don't have to prove yourself to me, Joe. I know who you are, and I love you.'

'I love you, too.' His kiss left her in no doubt about that.

But it was time to go. He led her through into the kitchen, finding a pair of scissors and snipping the thread around his neck, his mouth quirking in a mock grimace. 'You can step away now. If you want to.'

'I'm never going to do that, Joe. Let's go downstairs and get on with the rest of our lives, shall we?'

CHAPTER FOURTEEN

Eighteen months later

A LOT HAD happened in the last eighteen months. But it had happened to them both together.

Joe had insisted she call her parents to share their news with them. Her mother had asked when they could visit, and Bel had relayed Joe's answer, telling them to come as soon as they liked. The next day, they'd been waiting for Bel and Joe in the hospital reception area, having already checked in to a nearby hotel.

Bel had wondered what her mother might say about the rooftop living space at the clinic, but clearly, she already liked Joe well enough to describe it as cosy and romantic, rather than cramped. Joe had taken them both on a tour of the clinic, and her father had nodded quietly, obviously much impressed by his work.

Bel had used the three months left on the lease of her apartment to clean and paint the attic and create a home for them up amongst the rooftops. The hospital had taken her back, and she and Joe had continued their work there and at the clinic.

Their first visit to London had been tough. They'd taken a week off work and Bel had booked them into a hotel, because there were things they needed to do alone before going on to stay with her parents at the weekend. Joe had taken her to see the house he'd lived in with his parents, and then to the bank to unlock a safety deposit box that was full of photographs and mementos. It had been hard for him, but he'd sorted through everything, numb at first and then gripped by the grief he'd suppressed for so long. She'd held him as he wept, going through the pain of leaving the past behind to start a new life.

After a long evening spent with her father, bouncing ideas back and forth, they'd found ways of making the clinic self-supporting without compromising its core values. They'd worked, just as her father said they would, and now the clinic's future was assured on a permanent basis.

They'd worked hard during the week, but Sundays were still sacrosanct. Their time, to nourish their own relationship. And after a year it had been time to move on. They'd been so happy in their apartment amongst the rooftops of Rome, but there were new challenges and new places to beckon them on.

The clinic was expanding, into new and bigger premises. And Bel and Joe had found a villa that they loved, just outside Rome. They'd carefully packed the framed photographs of his parents, which Bel had added to over the months they'd been here. Her own photographs from when she was a child. Joe and her dad, laughing over something in a pavement café. A photo that her mum had taken of her and Joe, against the skyline of Rome. When Joe had expressed his regret over leaving their apartment, and promised that the first thing he'd do at the new house would be to find a place for their growing collection of family pictures, Bel had known that he was finally free.

They'd both needed to build a life together themselves, and her father had given in gracefully, offering them advice and support but letting them pay their own way. The wedding of Bel's dreams had been carefully put together with friends and family, and finally the November day had come.

'What's Dad doing with Joe?' Bel leaned out of her bedroom window, shivering in the cool breeze as she tried to see what was going on in the stone-built outhouse at the end of the garden, which was currently being converted into a home office.

'Advice on how to be a good husband, I expect.' Her mother was carefully removing a spot, which was invisible to the naked eye, from Bel's wedding shoes.

'How much advice does he need, Mum? Joe's got everything under control already.'

'I'm sure he'll think of something.' Her mother propelled her away from the window and closed it. 'He's taking his duties very seriously, you know.'

Both of her parents had. Since Joe had no family of his own, her father had diffidently wondered whether he might be considered as best man, leaving Bel's mother to give her away. Bel had loved the idea, and when she'd asked Joe he'd been touched that her father would do such a thing.

'Look! They're coming inside. He mustn't see you, darling.'

'I'm not wearing my dress yet, Mum. Joe's seen me in my pyjamas already this morning.'

Her mother frowned. 'But your hair... I've just brushed it out.'

'He's seen my hair before as well. It's okay, Mum, really. This is what I chose, an informal wedding. Let's just take a few breaths and relax, shall we?' Bel moved her hands up and then down again to indicate the tempo of slow, relaxing breaths, and her mother smiled.

'You're so serene, Isabella. Everything's just the way you want it.'

Bel hugged her mother. 'Yes, it is. And I can't thank you and Dad enough, for going with the flow and letting us do things in our own way. It means so much to us both that you've supported us in that.'

'It's been our privilege, darling. I don't know quite how you turned out so level-headed, I expect it was your father's doing, but we couldn't be more proud of you. And Joe too, he's the son we were never able to have. I'm going to go downstairs and make some coffee, and Joe can bring yours up to you.'

'Thanks, Mum. Only may I have tea...?'

Five minutes later, Joe appeared in the doorway of their bedroom, grinning broadly. 'Your mum's in fine form. Very relaxed.'

'Just don't drop any of your coffee on my shoes...' Bel pushed the shoes out of sight, under the bed, as a concession to her mother.

'I can stay? There's something I need to talk to you about.'

'Yes.' Bel flopped down onto the bed, and Joe sat down next to her, handing her the cup of herbal tea.

'Hey. Married, eh?' He nudged her shoulder with his and she smiled.

'Married. I can't wait, Joe.'

He chuckled. 'Me neither. Your dad wants to give us a present.'

'He does? But they've already given us all that beautiful crockery.'

'Something more. He said that one day we might want to move back to London.'

Bel puffed out a breath. 'But we love this house! And… London?' Joe had made his peace with London, but it was still the place he'd left to make a new life.

'London's a good place to live. And when the baby comes…'

'He knows about the baby?' Bel's hand moved protectively to her tummy.

'No, and I didn't tell him. But wouldn't you like to be nearer to your mum? Just a few streets away, maybe? A house that's a bit smaller than your mum and dad's, and needs some work? Think of all the shopping trips with your mum, while your dad and I babysit.'

That would be… Bel wasn't going to even think about it, it would so easily turn into a dream for the future.

'Do you really want that, Joe? Our home is here, isn't it?'

'My home is with you and our baby, Isabella. We'd have to keep this house, because we'll need somewhere to stay when we come back to Rome. I don't want to give the clinic up, or our plans to expand and open a few more, and there will still be grapes to pick in the garden and improvements to make…' Joe's smile made it all sound so tempting.

'Stop it, Joe. You're all I need, and this last eighteen months…you've made me so happy.'

'You've made *me* happy. Now that we know what we can do for ourselves, maybe it's time to widen our horizons a bit. When I was offered that teaching post back in London, they said that they understood I had commitments here, and that their offer was open-ended. And maybe it's time for you to start talking with your dad about the trust again.'

'But...' Bel heaved a sigh. 'Can we risk it? When we already have so much more than we'd ever thought possible.'

He took her hand, his thumb straying to the love knot on her finger. That had never been replaced, and never would be. 'Remember all of those promises we made to each other? We've kept them, and we've grown into the life that we wanted. I think it's time to do more now, because we both have more to do. You want to vote on it?'

Bel chuckled. 'I love you so much, Joe. My vote's for London.'

'Mine is too. We don't need a tie-break, but just out of interest...'

'The baby's going to love London too. And our house here in Italy.'

He grinned at her. 'Looks like it's unanimous. You want to tell your dad that we're accepting his offer, or shall I?'

'We'll tell him together.' Today was meant to be the day for them to cement all of their dreams. But suddenly there were new dreams as well.

Chiara had joined her mother, helping with the long row of tiny buttons at the back of Bel's wedding dress. Uncle Edo had done her proud with a simple knee-length creation, textured with white embroidery on the bodice and cuffs, which Chiara had helped to design and stitch.

The assembly room at the local town hall was full to the brim with family and friends, along with staff and patients from the clinic. As Bel and her mother entered she saw Joe and her father both jump to their feet, and a murmur of excitement ran around the guests. The bridal march started to play, and Bel squeezed her mother's hand. 'Ready, Mum?'

'Are *you* ready?'

Joe was waiting for her, the smile on his face the only thing that she could see. Bel was more ready than she'd ever been for anything. She started forward, her mother hurrying to catch up with her.

And then...it was like a series of wedding photographs, all taken through the lens of her own eyes and engraved on her mind. The way Joe spoke his vows, loud and clear for everyone to hear, although the look on his face told Bel that they were for her alone. Her dad hugging his new son-in-law and shaking his hand. Her mother's scream of delight when they told her that they'd be seeing her in London after the honeymoon, to take a look at a new house. The blizzard of confetti and the open fire outside the village hall, which beckoned the guests in to the feast that her parents had organised. Dancing and laughter and, most of all, the love that shone in Joe's eyes.

Then it was time to go. Joe helped her into the white woollen coat that Uncle Edo had made to go with her dress and keep her warm on their journey. A good half of the guests had decided to accompany the wedding party in seeing them off, while the other half stayed behind to keep the party going for their fellow guests' return. Joe helped Bel into the back seat of their car and Chiara's husband drove them to the assembly point, taking the car on to the spot they'd agreed on, a few kilometres along the road.

They stood together on the cobbles of the Via Appia.

Lanterns were lit in the gathering dusk and her parents presented one to each of them, to light their way. A cheer went up as Joe kissed her.

'It's a long road, Isabella.'

'The longer the better. We'll walk it together.'

'Always.' He kissed her again, prompting another cheer.

Other walkers and cyclists had stopped to watch, and as Bel took Joe's arm and they started to walk the sound of wild applause followed them.

Their gazes were already set on the shadowed shape of the horizon up ahead. 'Our first steps, Isabella,' Joe murmured. 'Do you know how much I love you?'

'Yes, I do.' He'd never left her in any doubt of it, and come what may he told her every day about all that was in his heart. 'Do you know how much I love you, Joe?'

'I feel it every day.'

An evening star rose in the sky as they walked. Setting off on a journey that so many had made along this road. One that would last them a lifetime.

* * * * *

*If you enjoyed this story,
check out these other great reads from
Annie Claydon*

The GP's Seaside Reunion
Neurosurgeon's IVF Mix-Up Miracle
Winning Over the Off-Limits Doctor
Country Fling with the City Surgeon

All available now!

SPANISH DOC TO HEAL HER

KARIN BAINE

MILLS & BOON

For Mum & Dad xx

CHAPTER ONE

Inés de la Fuente wasn't used to the sun any more. Despite her Spanish heritage, and her formative years spent living in the Costa Blanca, she'd spent the better part of a decade in London.

But it wasn't the heat, the bright glare of the sun, or even the dreaded mosquitos which were making her feel queasy about returning home to the town of Solara Vista. As she walked down the street towards the familiar family medical practice, it was the prospect of working here causing her anxiety.

Although she'd stayed in contact with her mother these past years, it had mostly been by text, with the occasional call. Actually being here was a whole different ball game. A world she thought she'd never come back to. Never wanted to come back to. Except circumstances had taken over.

She'd arrived late last night and had an awkward reunion with her mother before retiring to her old bedroom. Today was going to be a test, but she'd been through much worse recently and survived. Now she just wanted to get on with this new chapter of her life until she knew what the next one held.

Inés took a deep breath, pushed the button and waited for the intercom static to sound.

'It's me, Mama,' Inés announced herself before her mother had a chance to launch into her spiel about clinic opening times. She knew she was early. By an entire day. Because she had nowhere else to go, unable to face rattling around the family villa on her own with only the ghosts of the past to keep her company. She would rather keep busy, and start earning money. The more she managed to put away, the quicker she'd be able to move on.

The door buzzed and she pushed her way inside. Although the place had apparently been dragged into the twenty-first century, it still had that recognisable clean smell which took her right back to her not-so-happy youth.

Bright and airy, with a light turquoise and white theme, there was no trace of the old dark red walls and brass light fittings which resembled a haunted house and made her shudder even to think about. Perhaps her father had finally decided to move on from the past after all. It gave her a pang in her chest to not have been a part of that and perhaps witness a change from the intimidating man who'd dominated her life. Though she didn't regret leaving when she had. Even if she'd swapped one emotional prison for another…

Inés's father, though a brilliant doctor, had been an unrelenting parent. Strict, unyielding and determined that his daughter would follow him into medicine, on his terms. That meant there was no life for her beyond study, or joining the family business. Too suffocating for a teenage girl who had wanted a life of her own. She'd known that once she enrolled in medical school her future was mapped out for her and she'd be under his control for ever, just like her mother.

Although she had been interested in being a doctor, she had wanted her freedom and secretly applied to study in London. Her act of rebellion was the only way she could ever have the independence she longed for, though it meant leaving it until the last minute to tell them of her intentions, incurring the wrath of both of her parents. Her father, disappointed and angry that she'd disobeyed his plans for her future, had raged at her. Her mother had wept and wailed, and begged her to stay. But for once in her life, Inés had taken control and bravely moved abroad to the unknown.

Naive, lonely and a prime target for a man like Marty who had slowly taken her independence away from her again. She hadn't realised until it was too late that she'd been manipulated and gaslit for years into staying with him. He'd fed into that feeling that she had no one in her life, encouraging her to keep her distance from her family, never repairing the wounds. Until she was completely reliant on him.

It was ironic that the state of her father's health had given her the chance to start again. Though she hadn't known the extent of his illness until recently because of their estrangement, leaving Marty had also given her the courage to reach out to her mother. Her plea for Inés's help had given her somewhere to go. For now.

'Inés!' Her mother jumped up from behind the reception desk and ran over to swamp her in a hug.

'Mama.' Inés accepted her awkwardly, still not at the stage where she was ready to show any affection. After all, her mother hadn't backed her even when she'd finally stood up to her father and told him she wanted to live her own life. Instead, her mother had pleaded with her to, 'Just fall in line', and do as she was told in order to keep the peace. However, Inés wasn't like her mother and wasn't content to sacrifice her independence simply to keep her father happy and hadn't seen why she should.

Perhaps if Inés had had some support she wouldn't have left the country altogether, but in that moment, she hadn't seen any other choice. She'd needed to get as far away as she could from her father's influence.

Looking back, she'd likely thought that she would get her relationship back with her parents once life had settled down for her. Marty had changed that. He'd been instrumental in making the estrangement permanent. Allegedly for Inés's benefit, telling her she didn't need that kind of toxicity in her life. Now she could see it was just another way of manipulating her. Making sure she had no one to turn to other than him and ensuring that she couldn't leave him. Thankfully, she'd come to her senses eventually and made her escape, regardless of not having any support.

'What are you doing here? I thought you weren't starting until tomorrow.' Even though she'd lived here for decades, Marie de la Fuente still hadn't lost her English accent. She'd met Inés's father on a girly holiday and stayed, leaving behind her job and family in London to set up home with the handsome Spaniard who'd captured her heart. Completely dependent on him. Stuck.

A story Inés knew all too well.

'I thought I should get acquainted with the place as soon as possible.' Not quite the truth. It was hard being here when the clinic had been the main source of the conflict between her and her father. When he'd expected her to devote her life to it and didn't care what she might have wanted. But it was worse at home, where they'd had most of their rows. A place she'd come to despise because of the 'my house, my rules' adage which had been quoted ad nauseum. Where she wasn't allowed to have a voice, or an opinion, of her own. Where her father was king. Or a dictator, depending on whose point of view you listened to.

'Your father is delighted you're finally here.'

'It's only temporary,' she reminded her mother. Not wanting either of her parents to get carried away by the idea it was going to be a permanent arrangement. For now, it suited both parties for her to be here, but that would change and she wasn't committing herself to anything. That much hadn't changed in ten years.

'How is Father anyway?' Inés thought she should ask since it was partly the reason she was here. Her mother's plea for help at the practice had simply happened to coincide with her break up and subsequent homelessness.

'Not good.' Her mother sighed and seemed to visibly age before her eyes, although she hadn't really physically changed in the ten years since Inés had seen her face to face. Perhaps there were a few grey hairs and more wrinkles around the eyes, but still the same woman Inés had inherited her blue eyes and freckled nose from. It was only her thick dark hair and olive complexion which harked back to Inés's Spanish heritage. Along with her accent. Thanks to her mother, she spoke perfect English, but she was always going to stand out in London. As much as she did here. Never quite fitting into either world.

'I'm genuinely sorry to hear that.' Despite their issues, Inés didn't wish ill health on him. He was still her father after all.

She'd been shocked to find out how seriously ill he was. And riddled with guilt. So much time had passed between them, yet she'd held on to that anger towards him over the past. Now, faced with the prospect of losing him completely from her life, she was conflicted about how she felt. Perhaps if she'd broken free of Marty's control earlier, she might have reconciled with her parents. Had some sort of relationship with them. But now there wasn't much time for that to happen. There was a kind of grief in knowing that which she was still trying to work through.

'We're both so glad you came. Maybe you could visit him later?'

Inés held her hopeful mother's gaze and responded with a frown. 'I'm not ready to do that.'

Her mother nodded. 'In your own time. Although I don't think he has much left...'

'So, where am I going to be working from?' Inés changed the subject before she was drawn into a possible row. She knew how seriously ill her father was, dealing with stage four heart failure. After a previous heart bypass twenty years ago, he'd finally run out of lives, his age and failing health ruling out any further medical intervention. His time was limited, but coming back to work here was totally different from Inés facing him again.

It hadn't been the altruistic move her parents likely thought it was. Nor was it entirely down to an attack of conscience and a wish for a reconciliation before he died.

After coming to the realisation she needed to get away from Marty, and finally making the break, her mother's call to help out with the practice had seemed serendipitous. Only time would tell if it had been a good move for her personally.

'You can have your father's office. Ángelo is next door.'

'Ah, yes. Ángelo. I'd forgotten about him.' The sainted doctor who worked alongside her parents at the practice and who apparently could do no wrong. Inés had heard a lot about him over the years. The man who'd done everything she wouldn't and made her parents happy into the bargain. Not only replacing her in their affections, and in the practice, but also the substitute who joined them for holidays and Sunday dinners. Their surrogate son who didn't appear to have a life of his own.

Not that she was bitter. She'd been glad to get away from it all at the time, but now she was back at square one. Having left her home and her job, she was reliant on her family again and that didn't sit well with her. Especially when she'd had her taste of independence. Before Marty had done his best to steal it from her again.

Her mother led her to her father's office, which had also had a makeover since the last time she'd been here. Inés wondered if the bright modern decor had been Ángelo's idea and how he'd managed to exert any influence when she hadn't even managed to take control of her own life.

'He should be in soon. Always early, stays late. He's been our anchor. I don't know how we ever managed without him,' her mother gushed.

Inés smiled with gritted teeth. 'Why did you only

come to me when Father is nearing the end? How have you coped until now?'

She'd known her father was ill, but not to what extent. It had taken her some time to get over her break up. Counselling, trying to find somewhere to stay and avoiding Marty, might have been easier if her mother had asked her to come here sooner. Though she probably wouldn't have been ready for another layer of trauma so soon after she'd made the escape. She wasn't sure she was ready for it now.

'You know your father, he kept working until he physically couldn't. Even though he'd had his own diagnosis. I didn't want you to think we were emotionally blackmailing you into coming back, but we got to a point where we needed your help. We've had temporary staff in to cover his absence, but the patients need some stability. Ángelo has worked day and night and taken on some of the load, but he can't do everything on his own.'

Inés imagined he'd tried. Though she'd never seen, or spoken, to the famous Ángelo, she already held some resentment when he seemed to go out of his way to get into her father's good books. Something which she'd never managed to do.

'Well, I'm hoping to start right now if possible.' She just wanted to do the job she was here for and hopefully the time away from her life in London would help her figure out what she was going to do next. Especially since she'd left her job.

'That's fine with me. We don't want to let any of our patients down. I'm sure they'll feel reassured that another de la Fuente is in residence.' Her mother took her hand and Inés resisted snatching it away. She still loved her mother, but it would take a while for them to heal.

Inés still held some resentment that she'd never stood up for her, but her mother had never stood up for herself either when it came to her father.

'Now is as good a time as any.' Inés set the same rucksack she'd arrived with last night on to the desk. Although today it contained her water bottle and some snacks to get her through the day, her few belongings stashed into one drawer back at the villa.

'Is that really the only luggage you have?' Her mother looked aghast once more at the battered bag she shrugged off her shoulders. It was difficult for Inés to explain why she hadn't brought much with her without going into the details of her break up and she didn't want her parents to know her new life hadn't been everything she'd wanted after all.

'I travel light. Besides, I don't know how long I'm going to be here for yet.' She'd had a home and a life in London, but in the end, all she'd wanted was her freedom. Nothing else had mattered and she hadn't wanted any reminders. So she'd left Marty's place with a few personal items and bought some overpriced toiletries at the airport on the way out to Spain. Not a lot to show for ten years.

By the way her mother flinched at the last part of her comment she knew there was an expectation that Inés would stay as long as she was needed. Except she wasn't going to be railroaded. She'd somehow found the strength to leave Marty and his controlling ways and she was determined to break that pattern once and for all.

'I was hoping—'

'Let's just take one day at a time.' She knew exactly what her mother was hoping for, but she wasn't making any promises or commitment. That way if she felt the need to move on, if she couldn't cope being back in this environment, she could move on somewhere else.

For now, she was just happy to have a job and somewhere to stay.

One thing she could be sure of was a steady stream of patients. Despite everything, her father was a good doctor. Plus, being a bilingual practice made them popular with the expat community and tourists who suddenly found themselves in need of medical treatment.

'Hey, Marie, sorry I'm a bit late this morning. The traffic was almost at a standstill.'

A tall figure appeared in the office doorway, taking off a cycle helmet.

Muy guapo!

With a mop of dark unruly hair and deep brown eyes, not to mention the very tight cycling shorts he was wearing leaving very little to the imagination, he was fit in all senses of the word.

How unfortunate that her libido was apparently Spanish and drawn to her fellow country man. Even more unfortunate when she realised who it was.

'Inés, this is Ángelo.' Her mother made the introduction, but judging by his dark glare he had already guessed her identity. It seemed her reputation preceded her. Though she wasn't exactly sure what she'd done to earn his wrath already.

Despite her own misgivings about her new colleague, Inés held out her hand and flashed the biggest smile she could muster. 'It's nice to meet you.'

'I've heard a lot about you,' he responded, pumping her hand once before releasing her. The glower suggesting not everything he'd been told showered her in glory.

It was to be expected, she supposed. According to her father she was the ungrateful daughter who'd shunned the family practice along with her family. Ángelo was the hero who'd swooped in and gratefully taken her place. In her parents' business, as well as their personal lives.

'Likewise,' she said equally coolly and with the same hint of disdain.

'I suppose we should open the doors. Inés is going to start straight away, so it should ease some of the pressure on you, Ángelo.' Efficient as ever, her mother checked her watch. Keen to open the surgery dead on time.

It never ceased to make her wonder how such a strong woman got involved with a controlling man such as her father, who pretty much dictated their life. Then again, Inés had fallen victim to the same kind of toxic relationship. Love made people do stupid things. Exactly why she'd made the decision to forget relationships, focus on work and try to make a life for herself again. Loving meant having to hand over control and she wasn't prepared to do that ever again.

'I'll get changed,' he said, drawing Inés's attention to his taut thighs once more.

She thought it was probably a good idea before he gave some poor patient a heart attack just looking at him.

'Then perhaps you could show Inés how things work around here,' her mother said cheerfully, as though he'd solved all of their problems simply by turning up.

Inés was sure she probably could've figured out the

computer system for herself, but she was doing her best to be as amiable as possible and kept her mouth shut.

'Oh, yes, you wouldn't have a clue about how things work around here.' However, Ángelo didn't appear as eager to facilitate a harmonious working environment.

'It's a bit hard to be involved when you live in a different country,' she said through gritted teeth.

Her mother watched the exchange like a spectator at a verbal tennis match, but said nothing. Probably because she wanted to bury her head in the sand as usual and pretend nothing was happening. Though it was pretty clear to Inés already that she and Dr Caballero were not going to get along.

Still, she wasn't going to let that get to her. There was no way she was going to let Ángelo walk all over her. She'd shed two toxic men in her life and she wasn't afraid to stand up for herself any more.

Ángelo changed quickly into his shirt and tie, swapping his shorts for long trousers, so he looked more professional. He hadn't expected to see the prodigal daughter so soon. But here she was and apparently not pleased to see him working here. Tough. He'd been here for her parents when she hadn't and he wasn't going anywhere simply because she'd come back.

This job was his life and he'd worked hard to get here. Once he was sure he was financially stable he hoped to have the family he'd always dreamed about. Until now he hadn't been able to commit to anyone, knowing he couldn't provide a stable home, and he wasn't prepared to settle for anything less. Family was everything to him. Something which his *abuela* had drummed into him after his mother had walked out on him and his brothers, leaving them with their abusive, drunken father.

His grandmother had helped raise them and if it hadn't been for her support they would have starved. After his father lost his job and money was tight, he turned to alcohol, further depleting their income and causing the arguments between his parents. Yet his *abuela* wouldn't hear a bad word about her son, their father. He was family and that was all that mattered. A motto which Ángelo had carried with him and stayed to look after his father when his drinking had caught up with him. Despite his father's violent temper, and his brothers moving out one by one, Ángelo had cared for his father until his death. He didn't want to earn the same bad name his mother had for abandoning her family.

Now he was trying to make a life for himself again and he wasn't going to let a beautiful stranger take that away from him.

Marie and Juan de la Fuente had been good to him. They'd become like a substitute family to him, not only giving him a job, but inviting him into their lives, sharing meals and holidays that he would otherwise have spent alone. He knew Inés was back to help because her father was ill, but for him, that didn't negate the decade she'd apparently spent without giving them a second thought. They were good people and he didn't want to see them get hurt at such a vulnerable time in their lives. He felt very protective over the couple who had taken him in and given him a future to look forward to and he wasn't going to let Inés spoil that.

However, she was another doctor on board and he

could use an extra pair of hands to help with the patient list.

Her office door was open, but he knocked anyway.

'Come in.' She glanced up from the desk and her stunning blue eyes swept over him, appearing to give his new work attire her approval. Despite his pre-formed bad opinion of someone who hadn't visited her parents for ten years, he took some pleasure in knowing that she liked what she saw. Even if her appreciative look was fleeting.

'I thought I'd give you a rundown of the software we use here.' It would be churlish of him to leave her to figure out the system for herself, not to mention detrimental to the clinic. He got the feeling she was too stubborn to ask him for help even if she needed it. At least this way he had a clear conscience. Whatever his personal feelings for this woman who'd obviously broken her parents' hearts, they were going to have to work together and continue the clinic's success.

'Thanks.' She kicked back on her swivel chair so she moved away from the computer screen, leaving him some space to lean in and show her the set up.

'This is where you'll find the patient files and this is the appointment system.' It was difficult to concentrate when all he could smell was her floral scent and feel her warm breath on the back of his neck.

He stepped back, putting some much-needed distance between them so he could breathe without filling his lungs with her. It was a distraction he hadn't planned on and wasn't particularly happy about. 'I'm sure you can take it from here.'

'Thanks,' she said curtly.

'We have a few of our frequent fliers as we call them. Patients who come regularly because of their chronic illnesses. I can handle them and I think we've one or two emergency appointments with tourists who might need medical certificates before they're able to fly. Will you be okay to take them?'

She narrowed her eyes at him. 'I'm sure I can manage.'

This new working arrangement was seriously going to test them both and Ángelo knew he wasn't going to be the one to break first. He'd worked too hard to let a virtual stranger walk in and take over. Especially when she didn't have a good track record of sticking around.

CHAPTER TWO

'I'll just check with Dr Caballero and see what the recommended wait is before you can fly back home, Mrs Armitage.' Inés had managed her patient list well so far, with nothing she wasn't used to dealing with in the practice she'd worked at in London.

However, she wasn't completely au fait with the rules and regulations around tourists flying after a medical emergency such as Mrs Armitage's broken arm. She was sure she'd come to learn in time, but for now she was going to have to bite the bullet and consult Ángelo on this one. As the practice manager, her mother had been great at helping her with paperwork, but this was one she was going to need a second opinion on. Unfortunately.

She knocked on his office door.

'Come in. Ah, Inés, how are you getting on?' Alone, he was clearly finishing up his paperwork for the day, but turned to greet her.

She forced herself to appear amicable since she needed his assistance. 'Good. I'm with my last patient of the day now. I just needed your advice, if that's okay?'

'Of course.' He directed her to a seat usually reserved for patients.

'Patient has suffered a broken arm and needs a fit-to-fly letter. I'm just not sure on the timings yet.' She had to swallow her pride and wait for the gloating.

Surprisingly, it didn't come. 'Sure. It's usually recommended that the patient doesn't fly for forty-eight hours after having a plaster cast put on. If they're flying before this, they'll need the cast cut in half to leave room for swelling and expansion at high altitude, to avoid deep vein thrombosis. I've got some info on that sort of thing that might come in handy in the future. We get a lot of tourists needing that kind of advice. Alcohol and sun can lead to a lot of broken bones out here.'

'I'm not sure that's what happened to this particular patient, but thank you.'

Ángelo rummaged in his desk drawer and presented her with a folder. 'Some light reading for you.'

The hefty weight took her two hands to hold. 'I've nothing else to do anyway, so I'll have a look through this tonight. Thanks.'

'No problem,' he said, turning back to his own work.

Inés couldn't quite figure him out. He'd definitely been put out by her arrival, yet seemed happy to help. Perhaps he was just professional. All she did know was that she needed to be on her guard around him.

Once she'd typed out the letter Mrs Armitage needed to secure her place on a flight home, she began to pack up her things. Including the paperwork Ángelo had given her to swot up for her next tourist emergency.

Her mother appeared in the doorway. 'Are you ready to go?'

'Yes. I can't wait for dinner. I'm starved.' A slight exaggeration since Ángelo had kindly ordered food in for lunch, but she'd worked up an appetite none the less.

It was nice to be back into the swing of working again, not worrying about what she was going home to. Although she was wary about being back in the family home, at least she was safe in the knowledge that her father wasn't there.

'I'm just waiting for Ángelo to put his bike in the back of the car, then we can be on our way.' Her mother dropped the bombshell, then flitted away again to do one last tidy around of the reception area.

Any good feelings she'd been beginning to have towards her co-worker quickly fell away. 'Why is Ángelo coming?'

Her mother stopped cleaning the plastic chairs long enough to frown at her. 'He comes for dinner most nights. Especially since your father got sick. We both enjoy the company.'

'Don't you think that's weird?'

'Don't be silly, Inés. He's a nice boy. Just a bit…lonely, I think. And the house has been very quiet since you left.'

'Well, I'm back now. Doesn't he have any family of his own to have dinner with?' She didn't see the appeal of spending nights with her ageing parents after working with them all day. Unless he was up to something untoward and trying to worm his way in. He certainly seemed to be doing his best to replace her.

Perhaps that was why she was feeling so resentful towards Ángelo, when she hardly knew him. He'd been able to make her parents happy when she'd never managed to do anything other than disappoint them.

She just wished she'd had the support that they seemed to have given Ángelo. Inés had tried her best when it came to studying and trying to please them. But anything less than one hundred per cent was deemed a failure in her father's eyes. His exacting high standards had seemed impossible to meet and it was that feeling of failure which had put her off the idea of joining the family business. Knowing she would never be seen as an equal in the practice. That had been the beginning of her rebellion, of choosing her own path. As far away from her parents' impossible expectations as possible.

She'd needed breathing room, space to figure out who she was and what she wanted. It was ironic that becoming a doctor was what she'd wanted after all, but on her own terms.

Perhaps, if they'd given her that space, she might never have left at all. In fact, far from not wanting a relationship, she found she was envious that Ángelo had slotted easily into the life she was supposed to have had.

Inés felt slightly regretful that things had been left to fester for so long between her and her parents. If they'd all made a better effort to resolve their problems, they could have all benefited from some family support.

'I don't think his parents are still alive, but I think he has a couple of brothers somewhere.'

'Maybe he should have a family reunion of his own then,' Inés muttered.

'Don't be mean. You just need to get to know him better. He's a lovely boy.'

Inés smiled sweetly and resisted correcting her mother. Ángelo was not a boy, he was most definitely a man.

'I'll have to take your word for that,' she said, following her mother out to her car like a truculent teen.

Ángelo was already there, ensconced in the passenger seat, leaving her to squeeze into the back seat, folding herself in like a pretzel around the bike he'd deposited there.

'Sorry. I'm just so used to jumping in the front lately. Do you want me to swap places with you?' Ángelo began to unbuckle his seatbelt.

'It's okay. I wouldn't want to put you to any trouble.' Inés caught his gaze in the rearview mirror and batted her eyelashes which were more real than her smile.

Ángelo and her mother made small talk the whole way back to the house. Leaving Inés feeling like an outsider. Just as she had at school and later when she'd moved to England. Not part of any little cliques and very much isolated. That ingrained need to study and be the best had travelled with her to England. It seemed even away from her father's influence, that work ethic remained and her focus had been on becoming a doctor. She'd seen the difference her father had made in people's everyday lives and she'd been drawn to general practice. Something familiar in her new world.

With little money, and no family around her for support, she'd worked odd jobs where she could and shared student accommodation until graduation. Even as a junior doctor, she'd shared a house with several colleagues, though the long working hours and conflicting shifts meant she'd never really got close to anyone. Relationships had been scarce and brief. Not everyone shared her work, eat, sleep, repeat, routine. And drinking and partying with every other twenty-somethings would have distracted her from her ultimate goal of becoming the kind of doctor her parents should have been proud of. As a result, she'd become a bit of a loner. Albeit a great doctor.

That self-imposed isolation was probably what had made her an easy target for a man like Marty. A mature, successful surgeon, who'd shown a considerable interest in her in the time they'd both worked in the same hospital, had been hard for her to resist. In hindsight, perhaps she'd been looking for the approval of an older man because of her difficult relationship with her family. Marty had certainly given her that. At first.

To get her to go out with him, he'd love bombed her with gifts and kind words. Flattered and craving that connection with someone who seemed to appreciate her, she'd been easily won over. Expensive restaurants, luxury weekend breaks away and an incredibly romantic partner made falling for him inevitable. After that, things had moved quickly and it wasn't long before they'd begun living together in his apartment.

Given her family circumstances, Marty hadn't had to worry about friends or family getting involved in their personal business and he'd kept it that way. Quickly becoming her world. She hadn't noticed his subtle manipulation at first. He'd had a way of making her feel as though she was on a pedestal at times, so she'd ignored any little niggles. Like convincing her that things needed to be done his way for it to be right. Cooking, cleaning, even what she wore, all had to be to his requirements. Subtly taking away her autonomy until she questioned every decision she made outside of work. Gaslighting her into believing she wasn't capable of doing anything for herself.

It was a wonder he'd let her keep working, though

she supposed that was so that she kept bringing an income into the house. Which, of course, he took control of, too, telling her that he was happy to deal with the financial matters of the household. Taking the burden of worrying about bills away from her. Her wages going straight into his account, inevitably making it harder for her to break free.

It was an even bigger mystery how she, a very competent GP, could be so easily led in her personal life. Though she supposed her childhood, dominated by a similar character, made it easier for her to continue that pattern. Especially when Marty kept telling her her parents couldn't have loved her to treat her the way they had. Encouraging her to keep her distance when her mother had occasionally reached out to her, telling her he was the only person she needed in her life. That he was the only one who truly loved her. Stealing away any chance to ever repair her relationship with her family. One more thing he took away from her.

In the end, it was talk of marriage and children which finally woke her up to the reality of her situation. She'd treated a patient who'd obviously been very badly beaten by her partner, but she'd insisted on covering for him, saying her injuries had been her own fault and refusing to point the finger at her scowling husband hovering nearby. Regardless that there were young children in the household who clearly needed protecting, too.

When Marty had told her it was time they started a family, she knew that level of commitment would have meant being trapped in the relationship for ever. No doubt he would have got her to stop working, going out in public altogether, once he knew she was officially his. Then there were the children...

The anxious faces of her patient's young offspring had haunted her. She didn't want to inflict that restrictive upbringing she'd endured on to another generation. Certainly not with a man whose temper had a tendency to flare up at the smallest perceived inconvenience. Someone she couldn't be one hundred per cent sure wouldn't put her in the same position as the woman she'd treated.

She'd waited until he'd gone to work, packed her bags and moved out. Telling him in a voice message she wasn't coming back and spending the next weeks dodging his calls, and ranting messages. Until her mother had got in touch and offered her a way out from it all.

She shuddered at the thought of her lucky escape. The reception she'd received from her mother made her wonder if Marty had simply fed into her teenage sense of injustice which had taken her to England. Perhaps if he'd let her work through her issues without adding to that feeling that her parents didn't love her, she might have seen her actions, and theirs, with a different level of maturity and understanding. That guilt and shame that she'd been manipulated into severing ties with her family until it was too late, making her question if she even deserved their love and support now. She'd left them to deal with her father's illness alone and she should be grateful they'd had Ángelo here.

Inés hoped being back in Spain was going to make a difference to everyone. Not only was she getting to know her mother again, but she had free will for the first time in years. She was earning her own money and could leave any time she chose. Putting up with Ángelo was a small price to pay.

Once they had arrived at the villa, Inés left him to wrangle the bike back out of the car and walked on inside behind her mother. She hadn't really taken time to look around when she'd arrived, but now she could see nothing had really changed here. It was both comforting and haunting. Familiar, yet frightening. Good and bad memories so inextricably linked to these surroundings.

As the automatic gates closed behind them, she was reminded of how isolated the property was. The outside locked away from sight. It was a beautiful villa and her parents had worked hard for it, but she'd felt trapped here. She took a stroll around the small pool which had been her one source of freedom. Even if her father had curtailed the time she spent there and made sure she washed down the area around it every time she used it.

The blue tiles at the bottom of the water glinted in the sun, teasing her and making her want to jump in for old times' sake. She hadn't gone swimming since leaving Spain and she wondered if anyone still used the pool. It was clean and well maintained and the floral-cushioned sun loungers were still dotted around for those who preferred sun worshipping. No doubt Ángelo made use of the place as he seemed to be everywhere else.

'It's a lovely garden. Sometimes your father would barbecue out here, but I suppose you know all of that.' Ángelo sounded behind her and she fought hard not to roll her eyes.

'I can't say he ever barbecued anything for me. It would have caused too much mess and smoke. At least, that's what he used to tell me. But I guess people change.' She just wasn't sure how much. It made her think about what she had missed in the intervening years. If her father had mellowed, if he'd been remorseful about what had happened between them. It made it even more sad that they hadn't resolved their differences earlier.

Inés turned and walked into the villa, the cool tiles and neutral colours so abundant in Spanish properties, a world away from her centrally heated flat with plush carpets and vibrant decor. Though she supposed that wasn't hers any more either. Not that it ever had been. Marty had always made sure to remind her it was his flat and he was simply letting her stay. So she lived in constant fear that he could kick her out at any moment if she upset him. Ironic when he'd made it so hard for her to leave.

Being back now felt very much like when she'd first left home, with nothing to her name. Except those ten years she'd spent working and building a life now seemed a waste of time and effort.

She went to her old room to deposit her bag. It hadn't changed either. Her old black and white arty prints still hanging on the wall and the same crocheted cover on the bed which she'd spent many nights crying her frustration into.

A smile played on her lips as she lifted her old jewellery box from the top of her dresser. Upon opening, the ballerina inside spun around on one wonky foot as the music played. She poked her finger into the contents, uncovering the treasures of her teenage years. A badge she'd won in a school quiz, plastic pink hoop earrings she bought herself the first, and only, time she went shopping with school mates—her father quickly put a stop to that. He didn't like her wasting money on petty trinkets, nor hanging around with people who were a bad influence on her. She trailed her finger over the tiny gold cross pendant she had got for her eighteenth birthday.

Not that she'd been allowed a big party like all of her peers to celebrate her birthday. Her father had insisted they simply had one at home. A regular dinner with a small birthday cake for dessert. She'd been crushed, wanting to dress up and party like every other eighteen-year-old. But Father had insisted she didn't need any of that to mark her adulthood. No, she just needed to work at the family practice. So began his plans for her to move into the family business, marking out her future for her without letting her have any say.

She closed the lid on the jewellery box. Everything in the house was tainted by her father's need for control.

Now he was fighting for his own life, his presence noticeably absent in the home she'd come to despise, she wasn't sure how to feel. She didn't wish him to suffer, but when it came to any feelings deeper than sympathy for his plight, she was just kind of…numb. That could change, of course, depending on what happened next, but her emotions were currently adrift. Out of her reach. And she wasn't sure she really wanted to catch up with them in the near future when she'd already been through so much.

Walking back into the kitchen didn't help improve her mood.

'What way do you want these peppers sliced, Marie?' Ángelo asked, ensconced at the kitchen worktop, apron covering his work clothes.

'Just dice them, please, Ángelo.' Her mother was in her element at the hob, stirring pots and setting out dishes. A cosy domestic scene which made her feel ill.

'Anything I can do?' If this hadn't been the cuckoo in her parents' nest, she might have been impressed by a man helping to prepare dinner. Goodness knew neither her father, nor Marty, had ever lifted a finger in the kitchen. Only complained when the food hadn't been quite right, or things weren't as spotless as they'd wanted.

Ángelo seemed comfortable in his role as sous chef. As though it was something he often did. Her mother certainly seemed happy with the arrangement. It made her yearn for the chance to have the same ease with her parents. Made her question how he'd achieved it when she hadn't. If she simply hadn't been good enough for them as she'd always suspected. And if there was any chance of ever having this sort of relationship with them given the circumstances of her father's health and the fact that Ángelo had been here for them when she hadn't.

'Sit. Sit. Ángelo and I have everything in hand.' Her mother dismissed her offer of help with a wave of her hand and carried on cooking. Making Inés feel as though she was a visitor, not an actual member of the family.

'What's on the menu?' She did her best to try to be included. If she was staying here for the foreseeable future and this was an ongoing arrangement, she was going to have to get used to the way they did things. Or somehow find a way to be a part of it.

'Just some tapas. It's quick and easy after a day at work.' Inés's mother began dishing out the food and Ángelo retrieved a bottle of white wine from the fridge.

Inés supposed having company at home stopped her mother dwelling too much on what was happening with her father. She knew what it was to feel alone in the world, lost and frightened. No doubt everything her mother was feeling right now.

'It's nice tonight. Why don't we take this outside?' Without waiting for a response, Ángelo headed out towards the patio, leaving Inés and her mother to carry the earthenware tapas dishes out to the table.

He ducked back inside to grab some wine glasses and cutlery and they made a makeshift dinner table in the garden. Inés had to admit it was nice to be able to sit outside at this time of the evening, feeling the heat of the sun on her skin. If it wasn't for her terminally ill father, her broken relationship with her parents and a stranger suddenly immersed in her life, this might've felt like a holiday. Certainly the closest she'd come to one in ten years.

Marty had been a workaholic and expected her to be the same. If she had had any free time, he always found something to keep her busy. At the beginning of the relationship she'd been happy to do the housework, to look after her man. It had made her feel as though she had created a life away from Spain when she was responsible for running her own house. After a while it became obvious that Marty thought that all domestic chores were her department, regardless that she had a career, too. He wanted a little woman at home to look after him, and in retrospect, he didn't do anything for her in return.

There was no divvying up of jobs. He didn't take out the bins or dry the dishes. He simply expected her to take care of it all and if she didn't do it, or things weren't done to his standard, then she'd never hear the end of it. It had been easier simply to do everything rather than listen to him lecture her about the 'traditional' role he expected her to fulfil in his life. No doubt taking over from the mother who had pandered to her only son's every whim and made him into the little emperor he'd become. In hindsight, it hadn't been only her father's footsteps she'd followed in, but her mother's, too.

Inés took a sip of wine, closed her eyes, and let the sun caress her skin. Yes, this was a taste of the freedom she'd been searching for. It was ironic she'd found it at the place she'd run from a decade ago.

'You look as though you need some sun,' her mother said with a tut, forcing her to open her eyes.

'And more wine.' Ángelo reached across the table to top up her glass.

'Perhaps you should have taken a day or two to settle in before you started work.' Her mother was staring at her with a frown and Inés worried she could see right into her soul and everything she'd been dealing with prior to flying out.

When she'd asked Inés if it was possible she could fill in for her father at the clinic for a while, she'd agreed, saying she needed a change and wanted to help. She hadn't mentioned Marty, a break up, or anything which would've caused worry or curiosity.

The same reason she wouldn't admit to being tired now.

Inés didn't want sympathy, pity or criticism for getting into such a toxic relationship and staying so long. She especially didn't want it from Mr Perfect who couldn't seem to do any wrong. Who seemed to have his life completely together and was making her irrationally jealous because she'd failed at doing just that.

'I'm fine. Just soaking up some much-needed vitamin D,' she assured them.

'How did you get on today?' Her mother began cutting into the tortilla, the smell of which was making Inés's mouth water.

It was a long time since she'd had home cooking, or any decent Spanish food. She'd become accustomed to British stodgy comfort food, but in the sun it was good to have something so familiar.

'Good. I need to brush up on the tourist side of things, but Ángelo gave me some info to read on that.' She helped herself to a slice of the potato and egg omelette which her mother had flavoured with peppers and onion.

'It won't be long until you're in the swing of things.' Ángelo passed her the other dishes and she added chunks of jamon and cheese, and some anchovies, to her plate.

Inés knew from experience that, even though these little dishes didn't look like much on their own, they were deceptively filling. It was a good way to end the day with a drink in company and a full belly. Even if that company was another man she had reason to be wary of. At least Marty and her father had taught her not to be taken in by a handsome face and a charm offensive.

A companionable silence fell between the trio as they ate and drank, winding down after the day. It was her mother who broke the spell and reminded her why she was really here.

'So...how long do you think you'll be here for, Inés?'

'I don't really know. Why? Do you need the room

back?' She was attempting humour, but going by Ángelo's judgy look she'd fallen flat.

Her mother, too, looked aghast. 'No. Of course not. You know you're welcome to stay here as long as you want. You always have been.'

Now she felt bad and the omelette her mother had lovingly prepared now weighed heavily in her stomach. 'I know. I don't want to get into all of that now.'

She stared pointedly at Ángelo in the hope her mother would get the hint that she didn't want to discuss their personal business in front of him. Her parents might be comfortable around him, but she hardly knew him and had no desire to change that either.

'I think your mother just wants to know you're not going to disappear again, when this is already a very trying time for her.' Ángelo's sudden, and unwarranted, contribution to the conversation left Inés seething.

Clearly, he'd been told something of her past and her estrangement from her parents. Not enough, however, to realise that he was out of order and had no idea what he was talking about.

'It's a very difficult time for all of us. I'm an adult and if, and when, I'm ready to leave I'll discuss it with you, Mama. We both know there were reasons why I left, but I'm willing to set those aside for now to help out. I'm here for you and the practice.' Not Ángelo. Her personal life was not his business and she didn't owe him anything. Certainly not an explanation, or her schedule.

'I'm sure Ángelo didn't mean anything, Inés. We're grateful that you're here. For however long we have you. I'm sure your father will be content knowing the practice is in safe hands.' Her mother was doing her best to keep the peace as she always had. Though it had always seemed a cop out to Inés, never fully supporting her daughter. Even now she was defending Ángelo's attitude.

She took a deep breath and reminded herself she had nowhere else to go, so she'd have to simply hold her tongue. And her temper.

'Actually, I think today has caught up with me. I'm going to have an early night. Leave the dishes and I'll do them in the morning.' She feigned a yawn and excused herself from the table before anyone had the chance to say goodnight.

Tomorrow she'd be better prepared for Ángelo's jibes. She might even tell him exactly why she'd left and knock her parents off the pedestal he seemed to have placed them on, once and for ever.

'I'm sorry. I didn't mean to upset Inés.' Despite their clash of personalities, Ángelo hadn't intended to bring the evening to such an abrupt end.

He couldn't seem to help himself looking out for Marie and Juan when they'd been so good to him. From what he'd seen and heard, they'd been hurt by their daughter's departure ten years ago. More so by her reluctance to maintain any sort of relationship. He hated to think of them going through that pain again. Especially given Juan's health at present.

However, he had to remember that Juan was Inés's father. She'd come back to help and she did deserve his compassion. Regardless that they seemed to rub each other up the other way. Something they would have to get over when they were going to be working together for the foreseeable future.

Ángelo resolved to apologise. Tomorrow. After she'd cooled off, and he'd given her some space from his bout of foot in mouth. Clearly something had gone on in the family which he hadn't been privy to. And as close as he was, he wasn't part of it. It was no wonder Inés seemed to resent his presence. He'd got too comfortable, but her sudden reappearance had reminded them both that these were her parents, not his. His were long gone and had never been as supportive as Marie and Juan.

'She'll be all right. My daughter has always had a bit of a temper. That's why she and Juan used to clash. Too much like one another,' Marie sighed, finishing her glass of wine.

'She's entitled to feel how she feels when a stranger interferes in her personal life. It's none of my business and I shouldn't have commented at all. I'll apologise tomorrow.' He didn't like the idea of dismissing how she felt. How he'd made her feel.

Growing up with violence, physical and emotional abuse, he knew what it was like to have your feelings dismissed. He would never forgive himself for hurting anyone. When his mother had left him and his brothers when he was only seven years old, his father had beaten him for crying. Told him to man up. The same sentiment coming from his *abuela* who'd told him his mother wasn't worth his tears since she'd abandoned her family. Something which was all important to her. It had been his *abuela's* influence which had driven him to stay with his abusive father long after the rest of the family had moved out, looking after his only parent until he passed away.

Ángelo knew he was the one in the wrong here and,

given that Inés hadn't bitten back as she had earlier in the clinic, he knew he'd hurt her. A matter he hoped to make amends for—perhaps they could call a truce to make things easier for them at work. He knew what a toxic environment felt like and didn't want to be responsible for cultivating one now. They both wanted to make the practice a success in her father's absence.

As far as he could tell, both of their futures depended on it. Although she hadn't mentioned a life away from here, he got the impression she'd left the one she'd had in London for good. Only time would tell if she intended to stay here for any length of time, but for now she didn't seem to have any other place to go when she'd avoided her parents up until now.

'I should probably get home too.' He finished the last crumbs of jamon and cheese, washing them down with the rest of his wine. Glad he only had a short bike ride home.

'Thanks for your help tonight, Ángelo.' Marie got up to see him out. 'And please, don't let Inés get under your skin.'

All he could do was offer a weak smile in response because he had a feeling she already had.

CHAPTER THREE

Inés took her stethoscope off after sounding her patient's heart and finding nothing out of the ordinary which would be causing her sudden fatigue. 'I think we should run some blood tests and make sure there's not something more going on other than running after two small children, Mrs Ramirez.'

She let the young woman rebutton her blouse and began ordering the tests she wanted run. Her mother, as well as being the practice manager, had taken a phlebotomy course and was qualified to take the bloods for her. No doubt a cost-effective initiative her father had implemented in Inés's absence, but she was proud her mother had added to her skill set over the years.

'Do I need to worry?' A frown furrowed Mrs Ramirez's forehead, but Inés didn't like to pre-empt a diagnosis until she had all of the facts at hand.

'Your heart sounds perfectly fine and I haven't seen anything to give me great concern. However, I want to investigate a bit more. Any headaches? Nausea?' She printed off some patient labels and added them to the vials for her mother to fill and send off to the lab for analysis this afternoon before she left. With her father nearing his last days, her mother spent as much time as she could by his side and did her best to complete her work early in the day. They had a temp in as and when she was needed, with an unwritten agreement that she would be filling in full time at some point.

'I have been feeling a bit off colour, but I just put that down to lack of sleep.' Although it wasn't unheard of for new mums to be exhausted, there was something about Mrs Ramirez's pale complexion which was making Inés think there might be more to it.

'Okay, we'll get these bloods done and I'll call you back in for another appointment. We'll take it from there.' Inés got up to see her out and pass on the details of the tests she wanted to her mother.

Mrs Ramirez stood to leave, then reached out to grip the corner of the desk, suddenly swaying.

'Mrs Ramirez?' Inés reached out too late as the woman's eyes appeared to roll back in her head and she collapsed on the floor.

Inés rushed to her side immediately and tried to rouse her. 'Elena? Can you hear me? Open your eyes for me.'

She checked the woman's pulse—it was faint and her breathing laboured. Inés immediately moved her into the recovery position and ran to the door.

'Ángelo? I need help in here!' she yelled so he would hear her through his closed door, not wanting to leave her patient.

Immediately, he and her mother came running to see what was wrong.

'Mama, can you call for an ambulance? Mrs Ramirez was complaining of fatigue, got up to leave and just passed out. I think she hit her head on the desk on her way down.' Guilt weighed heavily on her shoulders that she hadn't been able to catch her patient before she sustained the injury. Especially now that a pool of blood was gradually staining the floor scarlet.

Her mother hurried off to call for help and Ángelo immediately got down on the floor beside Mrs Ramirez, with Inés taking position on the other side of her.

'Mrs Ramirez? It's Dr Caballero. Can you hear me?' The woman remained unresponsive.

'I don't like that tinge to her lips.' Inés noticed the sudden blue appearance, the cyanosis possibly indicating low oxygen content in the blood. She checked Mrs Ramirez's pulse, listened to her heart and realised she'd gone into cardiac arrest.

When she told Ángelo, he immediately ran out of the room and grabbed the defibrillator off the wall in the reception area. Inés set to work opening the woman's blouse so they had access to her chest and began CPR, only stopping briefly once Ángelo had placed the sticky pads on to the woman's torso and the robotic voice of the defibrillator told her to stop chest compressions in order for the machine to analyse the heart's rhythm.

'Stand clear.' Ángelo issued the instruction they'd both been taught when using a defibrillator to make sure no one was touching the patient.

'Shock advised. Charging. Stand clear,' the machine instructed and both doctors had to wait until it told them they could push the shock button to deliver the first shock.

Once Ángelo pressed the red button and the machine had done its job, it was Inés's turn and she restarted CPR. After a couple of minutes, the machine re-analysed and suggested a second shock. Sometimes one shock was all that was needed to bring someone back to responsive and breathing, but not in this case. Inés started chest compressions again, with Ángelo watching their patient for a response.

'Wait. I think we've got her back.' He put a hand out to stop Inés and put his head down to listen for signs of life.

Inés checked the woman's pulse. It was faint, but it was there. 'Thank goodness.'

She hadn't realised she'd voiced her relief aloud and wondered if it would make her seem unprofessional when Ángelo seemed so calm about the event. He made no comment as they moved Mrs Ramirez into the recovery position and they were able to finally sit back and breathe.

The paramedics rushed in and Inés gave them her patient's details, along with a debrief of their resuscitation efforts. It was a scenario she'd been part of a few times, but it was the first time in years that she'd felt as though she had any support. Marty had kept her so isolated, so afraid to reach out to anyone and incur his wrath, she'd all but distanced everyone she worked with up until now.

By the time the paramedics were wheeling Mrs Ramirez out to the ambulance, Ángelo had disappeared. It left Inés a little deflated after all of the drama to suddenly find herself on her own again. She flopped down in the chair at her desk. This was the part she missed about being in a relationship. Not having anyone to discuss her day with and process what had happened. Though it was a small price to pay for her freedom, she supposed.

There was a knock on her office door.

'Come in.' She was surprised to see Ángelo appear carrying a tray of coffees and pastries.

'I thought you might need this.' He unloaded the coffees on to her desk and sat in the patient chair to join her.

Up until their last encounter she would rather have boiled her own head in the coffee maker than sit with him, but she needed the company right now.

'Thanks.' She accepted his offering in the nature it had been intended. Graciously.

With adrenalin still pumping through her body, she wasn't sure she needed the caffeine hit, but she did need time to process what had happened. Work her way through events in her head and reassure herself she'd done everything she could. Although they'd brought Mrs Ramirez back, Inés would replay the drama on a loop as she always did until she was sure the woman was going to be okay.

'I just wanted to make sure you were okay. That was a crazy afternoon.' Ángelo passed her one of the little pastries, fitting a whole one into his mouth. He had quite the appetite from what she'd seen so far. It was remarkable how slim he was considering, but she supposed the cycling helped him burn off the calories. She would have to take up swimming again if she continued to eat so well. Marty had always watched what she ate, ready to criticise if he thought she'd gained as much as a pound. For her own health, he'd told her. But, like everything in hindsight, she could see now it was just another way of controlling her.

Following Ángelo's lead, she wolfed down the sweet treat, enjoying it guilt free for once.

'Yes. Thanks for your help.'

'I think you were doing fine on your own, but we're a team here. We have to work together.' He offered her a warming smile which eroded some of those defences she'd recently built to defend herself. She couldn't take another man riding in and trying to take control her life again.

'I know. I think I've got used to doing things on my own, but I appreciate the back up.' If it had been Marty assisting her, he would have criticised everything she'd done. Probably taken over completely, then spent this debrief telling her how she should have done things, completely undermining her confidence, and making her believe she couldn't do her job properly. As her superior when she'd worked in the hospital, he'd double-checked her every diagnosis and treatment. And she'd accepted that intimation that she couldn't be trusted to get things right, even when she had an exemplary record, because she'd been so used to her father's criticism.

However, Marty had continued to undermine her even when it came to their personal relationship. He'd made her start doubting herself and in the end it had been proved she couldn't trust her own judgement. Otherwise she would never have ended up living with a replica of her father.

She shuddered, knowing how close she'd come to being trapped in that toxic relationship permanently. With no job, no income, there would have been no escape.

Although she was living back home for now, she still had free will and some money coming in. As far as she could tell Ángelo didn't present a threat to any of that. Perhaps she should give him the benefit of the doubt that they'd simply got off on the wrong foot and there wasn't any more to it than that. It would be nice simply to get on with life without living in that constant fear that someone was trying to hurt her.

Ángelo cleared his throat as though he was about to say something, then took a sip of coffee, delaying the moment. As though the words were sticking in his craw.

'About last night… I was out of order. I shouldn't have said anything about your relationship with your parents. It's none of my business.'

Inés could tell it had taken a lot for him to say that. He was clearly very protective of her parents, which was odd in itself, but he wasn't too proud to apologise. A novelty for her. She couldn't remember the last time a man in her life had said sorry for anything. People like her father, and Marty, usually saw it as a sign of weakness. Since Ángelo was making an effort to thaw working relations between them, she thought she should, too. Especially when they had been able to work so well together as a team in an emergency. It would make life easier here at least, even if things at home were tricky.

'It's not, but I think my parents have given you only half of the story.'

Ángelo shook his head. 'It's between you and your parents. I had no business interfering.'

No, he didn't, but she didn't want to go on working here with him thinking the worst of her.

'I can tell you and my father get on well, but he was a very different man when I was growing up.'

Ángelo shifted uncomfortably in his seat as though he didn't want to hear any more which might tarnish the image of the man he seemed to know.

Inés continued regardless. 'I'm sure you've seen for yourself that he runs the show here. He's in charge.

Mama falls into line. Well, he expected that at home, too. From both of us. He was controlling. To the point of suffocation.'

She thought she saw a flash of something in Ángelo's eyes. His jaw tightened and his lips drew into a thin line. She was saying things he likely didn't want to hear, but she was done being seen as the bad, ungrateful daughter. If they were going to have any kind of working relationship, she needed him to understand why she'd been away for so long. Even if she didn't tell him the personal circumstances which had forced her back.

If she hadn't been going through such a rough time in her relationship with Marty and needing a way out, she couldn't be one hundred per cent sure she would have returned, regardless of her father's health, or her mother's pleas. She liked to think that perhaps she would have felt enough compassion, but after everything that had happened growing up she simply couldn't be certain.

Her parents hadn't shown her much consideration growing up. They'd only seemed to care about what they wanted. So her feelings, her plans, weren't deemed important. Making that break so she could have some control in her life again had seemed so final, for her own sake. Now, she wondered if she'd just needed a little space. If it hadn't been for Marty's interference, perhaps she might have salvaged her relationship with her family sooner.

'I know he's very single minded, stubborn even. I suppose that's how he made such a success of his practice.' Ángelo was diplomatic in his response, not denying her truth, but making his own observations.

Still, Inés wanted to say her piece just this once, then

she'd hopefully never have to explain herself to him, or anybody else, again. 'It's also why we were never allowed to run our own lives. He had to control us too. Make sure everything was up to his standard, whether it was telling my mother how to run the house properly, or forcing his daughter to study even in the school holidays. It didn't earn me many friends. Which he preferred. He saw a teenage girl's social life as a distraction, unimportant. I may have disagreed.'

She attempted some levity, only drawing a nod of Ángelo's head in response. There didn't seem any point in going into the details of the arguments and punishments resulting from that difference of opinion. It wasn't the only thing they'd clashed on. Where her mother had decided it was easier to simply go along with her father's wishes and play the subservient role, Inés had tried to make her voice known. To no avail. In the end, she was the child, he was the adult and she'd had to capitulate. At least until she became of age and had the means to leave.

'I'm sure it wasn't an easy time. Although I didn't know him back then, I do think your father has mellowed over the years. Perhaps he regretted his actions?' Ángelo was trying his best to put a spin on the matter, but Inés still bore the psychological scars from her father's behaviour and, even if he had changed, she wasn't sure she could forgive him. If she hadn't have grown up in that very toxic, controlling environment, there was every chance she wouldn't have ended up with someone like Marty. There might have been a chance for her to be happy.

'Well, if he does, he's never expressed it.'

'Perhaps he would if you visited him…'

Inés narrowed her eyes at him. So much for not interfering in business that wasn't his.

Ángelo held his hands up. 'It's merely a suggestion. It would give you both closure before it's too late. Family is family, no matter what.'

Inés couldn't bring herself to believe that. There might not be anything she could do about who her family was, but that didn't mean she had to put up with it. She supposed that's what had formed this unease between her and Ángelo from the start if he was loyal to a fault.

'Sometimes you have to do what's right for you. No matter how selfish that might seem to outsiders.'

Ángelo didn't argue or agree, but she got the impression this was a subject they would never see eye to eye on. Nor did they have to, as long as they respected one another's opinion. It wasn't as though she was going to be here for ever anyway.

Ángelo understood her stance, even if he didn't agree with it. It was the same attitude his brothers had taken once they were old enough to leave home. Family didn't appear to mean anything when they couldn't even be bothered to stay in touch with him. Regardless that he'd looked after their father right until his dying day. Putting up with the verbal and physical abuse even into adulthood, even though it went unappreciated.

Even his mother, whom he'd tried to reach out to, had been more interested in the new life she'd made for herself away from her family and hadn't seemed all that interested in getting to know him again. It had been hard to take when he'd been willing to forgive her, but she'd eventually severed all contact.

He'd heard later that she'd passed away and he'd grieved for the woman he'd barely known, along with the mother/son relationship which had never recovered. Still, he had a clear conscience because he knew he'd tried and he wasn't sure he could say the same for his brothers. Perhaps that was part of the reason he was so keen for Inés to make amends with her father, so she didn't have any regrets later in life either.

Inés seemed conflicted about her own family and little wonder. He could see why she was resentful of her father if he had been so unyielding in her youth, but the fact that she was back, helping out, suggested all wasn't lost. Though, in future, he knew now it was a subject he would do better to tiptoe around. Clearly he didn't know all of the details and she was still hurting from whatever had happened between her and her parents in the past.

It made him think of his brothers and their shared childhood. Perhaps those painful memories had prevented them from staying in touch, too, if they were keen to put it all behind them. Both circumstances made him sad for the families which had been torn apart by bad feeling, and difficult upbringings. More than anything he wanted the kind of family around him that his *abuela* had tried to convince him he could have. Made him believe that if he stayed with his father through thick and thin, that he'd love him back. Show him some of the affection he'd so desperately craved. Now all he could do was hope some day he'd find that with a family of his own.

He'd thought he'd found that with Camila, his ex. Only to find he wasn't enough to keep her happy either. Money causing problems again when she didn't think he could provide her with the kind of lifestyle she wanted. Since she'd left him, he'd been too guarded to get into another committed relationship. He'd kept things casual, only prepared to get involved in a serious relationship once he knew he was financially stable. So his family wouldn't be torn apart by the same problems he'd endured growing up.

The first step had been taking this job at Juan's practice. With Inés here, working as hard as he was, he hoped that his position was safe for a while.

'Well, I know both of your parents are glad to have you here. As am I.' It was true.

More and more he'd felt as though he was holding things together here with Juan's health in rapid decline. Although he wasn't afraid of hard work, and hoped to one day run a practice of his own, it was good to have someone else here putting in the hours. He and Inés might have had their differences, but when it had come down to it, they'd been able to work together to save a patient's life. He couldn't ask for much more. Except perhaps for a guarantee she'd be staying on a more permanent arrangement. He was beginning to enjoy having her around and that probably wasn't a good idea when she didn't seem to have a long-term plan for being here.

If he'd gone on first appearances, he never would've thought this beautiful, smart, sassy lady would have asked him for help in any circumstances. The first thing she'd done when Mrs Ramirez had collapsed had been to shout for assistance. That wasn't a sign of weakness. It was the mark of a good doctor who put the welfare of her patient first instead of her feelings. He'd worked with a lot of people over the years whose ego wouldn't let them ask for help, much to the detriment of those they'd been treating. Inés was exactly the kind of person he wanted working beside him in a medical emergency.

'I hope so,' she said with a sad sort of half-smile, as though she didn't quite believe him.

Ángelo could see she was wary and even had some inkling now as to why she'd been so defensive since her arrival. Clearly, she and her parents had parted acrimoniously and it was natural that she would hesitate to get close to them again. After all, whatever had happened between them had caused her to leave the country to get away from them. The fact that she was here meant that she hadn't slammed the door completely shut on her relationship with her family. Ángelo hoped for all of their sakes that they could find some peace before Juan passed away. Only time would tell what would happen after that.

Inés had shared some very personal information with him, blunting some of the spikiness she'd used so far to defend herself. Although Ángelo appreciated that she was trying to forge some sort of bond to better their working relationship, he wasn't ready to open up the same way. He wasn't sure he ever would be.

He preferred to keep what had happened during his childhood private. Other than his brothers, no one else knew about that time in his life now his father and grandmother had passed away. If anyone ever had reason to run away from home, it had likely been him, but he hadn't. He'd stayed and been a good son to his abusive father until the very end.

It wasn't a story he intended to use to garner sympathy, or, indeed, criticism for staying too long in that terrible environment. Nor to justify where he was in his life today—single and without a family until he could afford to sufficiently provide for one. It was simply his life and was no one else's business but his. Part of the reason he'd realised why he needed to back off from interfering in Inés's personal life. He certainly wouldn't have appreciated the same in return. Going forward, they both needed to keep their private lives separate from their work. Then he wouldn't be open to having her tell him how he should be living his life either.

'I think we both got off on the wrong foot, but I appreciate you being here, Inés. I'm hoping we can start over, because I'm really looking forward to working with you.' He held out his hand, hoping she would agree to wipe the slate clean.

Having a young, compassionate doctor would bring a whole new dynamic to the practice. As Inés shook his hand he saw her really smile for the first time since she'd arrived. Those stunning blue eyes sparkled and something he saw there seemed to squeeze his heart, stop the breath leaving his lungs. He'd witnessed a glimpse of the person behind the tough exterior she'd built around herself.

A sensitive woman who'd been hurt and who was afraid of letting anyone close again. He recognised the pain and wondered if that was the reason he'd been so resistant to her in the first place. Despite everything, he admired her spirit and they had a lot in common. Damn it, he liked her. And more than anything, he was worried it was going to get in the way of everything he'd been working towards.

Perhaps it would have been safer to remain on opposing sides of the battlefield instead.

CHAPTER FOUR

Inés had declined her mother's offer of a lift to work, having decided to walk and enjoy the cooler morning temperatures before the heat became stifling. She was still trying to get used to permanent sunshine after enduring ten years of murky British weather.

'I'm trying to be strong, Ángelo, but he's just not the man he was.'

Inés walked in just in time to see her mother breaking down in tears, her presence unnoticed as Ángelo gathered her weeping parent into his arms.

'I know, Marie, but he has you. And you have me and Inés. We'll get through this.' He gave her mother a hug and met Inés's eyes.

She mouthed a thank you and he responded with a tip of his head towards her. It was good of him to give her mother the comfort Inés couldn't quite bring herself to give yet. He was compassionate, more than she'd ever seen in her father. Something invaluable to her mother as well as his patients, she imagined.

She supposed she should be grateful he'd been here for her parents through all of this when she hadn't been able to. Apart from her emotional issues where her parents were concerned, Marty would never have let her take off to a foreign country without him for an unspecified amount of time. Regardless of the fact her father was dying, he wouldn't have let her have that kind of freedom from his influence. Marty wanted to be her whole world. So she didn't want, or need, anything or anyone else. Making her totally reliant on him.

Looking back, she wondered if part of the reason she'd been estranged from her parents for so long had been because of Marty, too. He'd encouraged the separation, told her she didn't need them in her life. Which meant he'd been able to isolate her even more. Have more control over her.

It made her angry to think that she had been so easily manipulated. She needed this time and space to think properly and decide for herself what she wanted, who or what she didn't need in her life. Marty was at the top of that list.

She walked on through to her office, affording her mother and Ángelo some privacy. Feeling as though she'd intruded, even though it was her family. It wasn't that she didn't feel anything towards her parents, but she was conflicted. And wary. She didn't want to jump feet first into the situation, her emotions firmly wrapped up in the moment, only to leave herself vulnerable. First, she needed to work through those emotions for herself. Without any outside interference.

As if on cue, Ángelo appeared in the doorway of her office. 'Sorry if that was a little awkward. Your mother was upset about your father.'

'Has something happened?' The blood seemed to freeze in her veins at the thought her father's condition must have worsened for her mother to have been so upset.

Despite the circumstances, it was difficult for her to support either of her parents after everything she'd been through. The thought, however, that this could be the end was confronting. She still wasn't ready to see her father, not only for her sake but for his. There was no way of knowing how she'd react being faced with him again, or whatever old feelings it would bring to the fore. She didn't feel capable of pretending nothing had happened, but neither did she want to vent her anger towards him when he wasn't strong enough to hear it.

If this was the end, she'd lost the chance not only to build bridges, but to even say goodbye.

Ángelo must have seen the panic in her eyes as he rubbed her arm reassuringly. 'He hasn't got any worse. Your mother just gets a bit upset after seeing him.'

Inés was grateful for the reassurance bringing her heart rate back to an acceptable level. 'Of course. I'm glad she has someone to turn to. I'm just not ready to be that shoulder she needs right now, so thank you, Ángelo.'

'Without sounding as though I'm getting involved in your personal business again, do you think you'll visit your father before it's too late?' It wasn't the accusatory tone he'd used with her previously on the subject of her relationship with her parents. Ángelo was talking to her with the same tenderness he'd showed her mother and she appreciated his concern.

Inés shrugged. 'At some point. When I'm ready to face him, I suppose. In time I could come to forgive him, but I'll never forget.'

'But there might not be that much time left,' Ángelo reminded her.

Nevertheless, Inés wasn't going to be rushed into a decision. This time she wanted to dictate what happened next in her life without another man's interference.

'I know, but that's between me and my conscience. Now, is there anything else I can do for you?' Inés switched her computer on to let him know she was ready to start work and that this conversation was done.

While she appreciated everything he'd done for her parents and that family meant a lot to him, she wasn't going to justify her actions any more. She'd shared a lot of very personal information with him that she hadn't told anyone before, yet she knew nothing about him before he'd come to the family practice. He might be a friend and confidant to her mother, but he was just a work colleague to her.

'No. That's all right. I suppose we should get ready for the day ahead.' Ángelo turned on his heels and the sound of his office door closing soon followed.

Inés smiled to herself, feeling as though she'd got the upper hand for once. From now on she was going to do things on her own terms and Ángelo was just going to have to get used to it.

'I'll see you again next week to make sure the medication agrees with you, Mr Morris.' Ángelo saw his patient to the door. An English tourist who'd decided to stay on holiday indefinitely, only to find he was allergic to mosquito bites.

It had been a busy day with little time in between appointments to chat. The only conversation he'd really had with Inés was when she informed him that their cardiac patient was recovering well in hospital thanks to their intervention. It was probably for the best that his interaction with Inés was kept to a minimum for now in case he said anything else to irritate her.

He was doing his best not to antagonise her by interfering, but he so wanted her to find peace with her family before she might come to regret it. By coming all this way, helping out at the clinic, he could tell that their relationship wasn't completely beyond repair. For her sake, as well as her mother and father's, he hoped they could build some bridges. At least she still had a family. What was left of his had gone their own ways and, try as he might, he couldn't get his brothers to be a part of his life. He missed them. He missed being part of a family and he wouldn't wish that on Inés, or anyone else.

Suddenly the quiet of his office was interrupted by the sound of shouting and screaming outside, followed by Marie bursting in through the door.

'You need to come quick. There's been a fire in the building down the street. You and Inés are needed.' She'd apparently relayed the message to Inés, too, who had grabbed her medical bag and met him in the hall.

At least he knew from here they would set aside their differences and come together for whatever had unfolded outside.

The area they were in looked like a residential area, but it was a mixture of private businesses, like dentists and solicitors. However, at the end of the street there was a small family-run grocery shop packed to the rafters with all manner of foods and essentials. To Ángelo's horror, it was this small detached building which had smoke billowing out of the door and windows.

'It's the Garcias' place,' he told Inés, unsure if she had ventured into the shop yet, though it was an everyday stop for most people in the area. Him included. It was easier to grab something to eat from the local store on the way home from work rather than venturing to the big supermarkets, even if it cost a little more. He'd come to know the couple who ran the business, along with their children and knew how hard they worked to make a living. This would surely devastate them.

'You know them?' Inés hurried down the street alongside him as the other residents and business owners emerged, likely as worried for their own properties as the one on fire.

'Everyone here does. Your mother said they've been here for years.' Though obviously they must have moved in some time after Inés had moved to England since she didn't appear to know them.

Thankfully when they reached the bottom of the street, Mr and Mrs Garcia were already outside, covered in soot and coughing.

'Has someone phoned the fire brigade and the paramedics?' Ángelo asked a gathering crowd.

Once he'd been assured the emergency services were on their way, he and Inés were able to focus on the injuries the middle-aged couple had sustained.

'I'm Inés. I'm a doctor. Can you tell me where it hurts?' Inés got down on to the ground beside Mrs Garcia to check her over and Ángelo focused on Mr Garcia who was coughing heavily.

'My hands. I tried to put the fire out myself.' Mrs

Garcia held up her hands which were red raw and Inés immediately started to dress the burns. She carefully cleaned the wounds and applied a sterile dressing with gauze and tape to hold it in place.

Ángelo focused his attention on the male patient, seeing that Inés had everything in hand next to him.

'Can't. Breathe.' Mr Garcia's reddened eyes were wide with fear as he fought for breath.

'It's the smoke in your lungs. Don't panic. The paramedics will be here soon and we'll get you some oxygen.' Ángelo tried to calm him down so he could make a proper assessment.

The smoke he'd inhaled would irritate his lungs, causing swelling, and could block oxygen from entering the bloodstream. However, panicking was going to make his symptoms worse, as understandable as it was after being through such a traumatic event.

Ángelo tested his pulse, which was beating frantically under his touch. Beneath the soot and smoke, Mr Garcia's skin was pale and clammy. A cold sweat breaking out all over.

'Inés, I think he's going into shock...' Ángelo was able to grab the patient before he fell back on to the ground and injured himself further.

Inés came to assist Ángelo to gently lower Mr Garcia's head on to the ground.

'Mr Garcia, we need you to keep your eyes open for us until the ambulance gets here. Look, your wife is beside you.' She did her best to keep him responsive, talking to him continuously.

Ángelo pulled over an upturned bin and lifted the patient's legs on to it, improving the blood supply to his vital organs.

Inés loosened Mr Garcia's clothing to ensure it wasn't constricting blood flow. 'He's cold, Ángelo.'

If shock wasn't treated immediately and effectively, it could lead to permanent organ damage, or even death. Not something he wanted to happen to anyone he knew, nor in front of other residents.

'Has anyone got a blanket, or a coat? Anything?' he shouted to the rubberneckers around them. With no response, Ángelo pulled off his shirt and draped it over the patient. The best he could do for now and hopefully enough to keep him warm until help arrived.

'Very innovative.' Inés glanced at him, making him very aware that he was now topless. He saw the half-smile tugging at her mouth and wished he'd thought to wear an undershirt this morning.

Thankfully the blare of the ambulance sirens sounded nearby, taking the focus off his partial nudity.

'Just hold in there for us, Mr Garcia,' he told the man, whose breathing was becoming more and more laboured.

At least the paramedics would be able to get him on oxygen and administer pain relief on the way to the hospital.

'You'll have to go with your husband to the hospital, Mrs Garcia, to have those burns assessed. Try to keep him awake. Just talk to him,' Inés coached her patient. Even though she'd dressed the wounds, there was always a chance of complications and the couple needed hospital treatment.

Ángelo met with the attending paramedics to relay events and the treatment they'd administered so far.

Then he stood back and let them take over. Inés came to stand next to him as they watched the couple being transferred into the back of the ambulance. By now the fire brigade had arrived and were moving people out of the area so they could tackle the blaze. The air was thick with smoke, making his eyes and throat burn. When he turned to look at Inés he could see that her eyes were red and streaming, too.

'Let's get back to the clinic and get cleaned up. We've done our bit.' He reached out to take her hand. A subconscious gesture to show solidarity for what they'd just been through together. He hadn't expected her to take it and follow him back into the clinic.

As odd as it may have appeared as they walked hand in hand up the street, Ángelo still topless, and both smudged with dirt and soot, it felt natural. Comfortable. A few days ago he would never have imagined even being civil to one another. Now, Inés was a part of his working day, as well as his relationship with her parents. He'd spent so long building his career, focused on financial stability, that he'd forgotten how nice it was to let someone else help pick up the slack. To give his hand a reassuring squeeze and remind him he wasn't on his own.

He was beginning to wonder why he was still waiting to find that special someone when he had the rest of his life in order.

Inés was emotionally drained, yet her body was thrumming with the energy burst which always accompanied any medical drama. It would be some time before she came down from the adrenalin high. Not helped by the fact Ángelo had her hand clasped tightly in his.

She hadn't resisted when he'd reached out to her, keen to have that comfort from the only person who knew how she felt in moments like this. How every interaction, no matter the outcome, reserved a place in her heart as well as her head. Something Marty never seemed to understand when the only thing that mattered to him was how good he looked at his job. More interested in praise and plaudits than saving lives. Although she'd only been here for a matter of days, she could tell Ángelo was more invested in his patients than his ego. A refreshing change in her orbit.

Both she and Ángelo went into the treatment room to clean up, standing side by side at the sink, splashing water over their faces.

'Sorry,' she said, as she splashed some water on to his chest. Then she was forced to apologise once she realised she was trying to wipe it off with her hand. Essentially pawing at his chest like a member of a hen party at a male strip show.

'It's okay.' He seemed amused by seeing her flustered. A condition she was having trouble controlling when he was so close and half-naked.

All of that exercise seemed to be doing wonders for his physique when he was so taut beneath her fingertips. It didn't hurt that he had that little smattering of dark hair outlining his pectoral muscles either.

He washed his hands and Inés watched, mesmerised at every flex of the muscles in his strong arms. There was just something about him that made her want those arms wrapped around her, protecting her. Though she knew it would be a long time before she got close to any man again, Ángelo was beginning to make her believe that not all of them were out to hurt her. So far she'd seen nothing but good intentions from Ángelo, even if she'd been resentful of his presence here at first.

Before she could get too carried away singing his praises, that scared inner voice of the woman who'd been hurt too many times reminded her that she couldn't trust her judgement where men were concerned. She'd thought that Marty was kind and generous and she'd fallen for his good looks, too. This wasn't the time for making more of the same mistakes and she would have to keep reminding herself why she was here. It certainly wasn't to be blinded by another handsome man.

'Look at the state of you two. I found some old clothes of mine and Juan's in the cupboard you can change into.' Inés's mother bustled into the room and handed over the folded clothes she'd been carrying.

'Thanks, Mama.' Inés took them gratefully, doing her best not to baulk at the garish patterns.

'How are the Garcias? I hope they're going to be okay,' Mrs de la Fuente fretted.

'They've inhaled a lot of smoke and suffered burns, but with hospital treatment they should make a full recovery.' Ángelo did his best to put her mother's mind at rest even though things hadn't been straightforward.

'I'm sure they have you to thank for that,' her mother effused.

'I'm just glad Inés was there, too. She's been invaluable these past few days.' Ángelo's words, along with her mother's smile, gave Inés a warm glow inside.

It had been a long time since she'd felt appreciated

and it was an unfamiliar, yet welcome, feeling. One of Marty's tricks to keep her under his control had been to undermine her at any given opportunity. Whittling away at her self-confidence so she felt even more reliant on him. It had taken her to leave the country before she'd realised just how he'd been able to manipulate her. Ángelo didn't appear to be threatened by her at all in a professional capacity. Seeming content to share the spotlight with her, with no need to put her down for the sake of his own ego. Comfortable enough in his own skin that he didn't see the need to exert any control or influence over her.

Perhaps that's what she found attractive about him. Not the lean body, deep brown eyes, or dark wavy hair.

'Well, I'll let you two get changed and I'll get the place closed up.' Her mother made a swift exit, leaving them standing awkwardly together.

'I'm not sure it's your style.' Inés held up the nineties-style paisley patterned shirt which was a far cry from Ángelo's usual conservative wardrobe.

He held it up and inspected it with a tilt of his head. 'I don't know. A life-or-death situation can give you a different perspective on the world. Perhaps it's time I lived a little dangerously.'

Inés watched as he shrugged it on, envious of the silky fabric caressing his muscular torso.

'Your turn,' he said, nodding at the chiffon pink shirt she was holding.

Ángelo was teasing her, daring her, and Inés wanted to show she was up to any challenge these days. There was no more being afraid to do what she wanted. Right now she wanted him to watch her the way she'd been watching him. To see that spark of desire she'd felt when he'd taken her hand and stripped off his shirt.

Maintaining eye contact, she undid her blouse. Button by button. Inch by inch. Saw his eyes darken and his smile falter. For once she felt as though she had power and it was a potent aphrodisiac.

She let her top fall to the floor, revealing her lacy white bra to his gaze. Then she pulled the chiffon monstrosity over her head and let it fall over her body.

Ángelo took a step forward and she held her breath, waiting for him to touch her. He reached out and took hold of the ribbon hanging loosely at her throat and tied it into a bow.

'Beautiful,' he said, his voice unusually gravelly.

'If you're a fan of hideous eighties fashion…'

'I wasn't talking about the blouse…'

Inés's pulse leapt, a silent squeal emanating inside her as he looked at her with such a hunger. It felt good to be wanted, to be seen as a prize, instead of something to be subjugated.

'You two look good. Go on, I'll lock up. It's been a long day for both of you.' Inés's mother arrived before anything other than lingering looks had time to manifest.

Probably for the best. Inés didn't know how long she'd be here for, but she needed her job. A foolish fling with a co-worker wasn't going to help set her life back on the right track. All it would do would be to cause her more complications she didn't need.

'I need a drink.' Ángelo backed away with a sigh of what Inés hoped was regret as her mother put a stop to whatever had been happening between them, and disappeared again.

'Me, too.' Anything to drown out the hormones which were making themselves very vocal about how fit they thought Ángelo suddenly was.

'There's a bar down the end of the street if you want to call in? It's always hard to wind down after something like that happens. The fire, I mean.' Ángelo didn't seem his usual cool, calm, collected self. Although he wasn't exactly asking her out on a date, even the suggestion was clearly out of his comfort zone.

Hers, too.

Marty had never permitted her to socialise with her work colleagues when they'd met up outside work for drinks, or birthday dinners. It seemed ridiculous now that she'd capitulated to that, but she hadn't wanted to upset him and it had been easier to turn down all invitations rather than have a row after the event. In the end, people had stopped asking her to join them so it no longer represented a problem.

'Why not?' Simply doing something spontaneous like going for a drink with a colleague felt empowering. It also gave her a boost thinking that Marty would've hated it.

She tried not to read too much into the fact Ángelo had even asked her out.

CHAPTER FIVE

'Are you sure you want to go in here?' Ángelo eyed the small bar warily. It wasn't one he frequented. Run by a British expat, it was usually full of drunken tourists watching the football. He preferred quiet, authentic Spanish establishments which served tapas with their drinks instead of greasy fry ups.

Inés gave him the side eye. 'I've spent ten years living in England. I'm used to this. I like the atmosphere in a good old British pub. Let's face it, that's what it is. They've just relocated it to the sun.'

He screwed up his face. It wasn't his favourite place in the world. The locals didn't always get along with the expat community since not many of them made an effort to integrate into their new surroundings. Some had been here twenty years or more and never even learned the language, relying on the fact that most Spanish spoke some English.

Though he supposed he shouldn't be too critical when that was part of the reason their practice was so successful.

Inés looked so excited by the idea he didn't want to disappoint her either. She hadn't had an easy time since arriving and he supposed one night out wasn't going to kill him.

He sighed, resigning himself to an evening with drunken tourists. 'If this is what you want…'

'It is.' Inés batted her long, dark eyelashes at him and he was putty in her hands.

Ángelo increasingly found himself wanting to please her, to put that gorgeous smile on her face which had been in scarce supply since her arrival.

The pub clientele had already spilled out on to the outside balcony, all deep in high-spirited conversation, clutching their drinks. They had to push through the crowd to reach the bar.

'What can I get you?' the smiley blonde lady behind the bar greeted them.

'A beer, please,' Inés shouted over his shoulder.

'Make that two,' he added.

'No problem. Take a seat and I'll bring them over.' The barmaid directed them to a little table in the corner of the bar which wasn't currently occupied and they sat down before anyone else spotted it.

'Are you really uncomfortable in here?' Inés asked as they had time to take in the decor which was covered in Union Jack flags and English football shirts. 'It just reminds me of when I first moved to England and that sense of freedom I felt. I partied a bit too much in the beginning, before studies, among other things, took all my focus. It's been a while since I've been able to let my hair down the way I want, but we can go somewhere else if you'd rather?'

It was sweet of her to be concerned for him, but he

wasn't bothered in the slightest. Glad to be sitting here chilling out with Inés.

'It's fine, but next time I'm taking you somewhere you can get back in touch with your roots,' he teased. Then he realised he'd promised another night out together. Thankfully she didn't look horrified by the suggestion, even though he hadn't been aware he was already thinking that far ahead.

'Hey, I'm half-English, you know.' Inés nudged him playfully.

'I know, but when was the last time you listened to some Spanish guitar, or danced a flamenco?'

She looked thoughtful. 'I can't remember. You might have a point…'

'That's quite a list of things we need to re-acquaint you with that we're building. I hope you're sticking around long enough to do everything.' It was wishful thinking on his part. Especially when he appeared to be making plans for them to hang out together in the future.

He found himself wanting to give her reasons to stay, not looking forward to the day when she decided to move on. Not only had she proven herself as an excellent doctor, but he liked being in her company. Unlike when he'd been with his ex, Camila, he didn't feel as though he had to prove himself in any way. Though, he reminded himself, Inés was not a potential future partner. As long as he remembered that she was worth her weight in gold at the practice and any romantic inclinations he might have could send her running, he should hopefully manage to avoid temptation.

'Two beers.' Thankfully their drinks arrived before he, or Inés, was forced to make any commitment.

He handed over payment, but the blonde stared at the two of them. 'Are you on your way to an eighties party or something?'

'It was bad taste day at work,' Inés joked, sending the barmaid away with a bemused expression.

Ángelo loved the way she wasn't self-conscious about going out like this. Not everyone would be happy about being seen in public with their make-up washed off, wearing their mother's old clothes. It showed she was comfortable not only in herself, but around him. Things between them had definitely mellowed since their first meeting.

'So where do you usually go, if you don't come here after work?' Inés asked, taking a sip from her beer.

'I'm not one for going out much.'

'Not at all?'

He shook his head. 'Not really. Not since I started working here. I've been so focused on work I haven't really left time for socialising.'

'You don't have a significant other?'

'Not at the minute. Not for some time, actually.'

'Bad break up?' She looked at him sympathetically.

He thought back to the last woman he'd been seeing and couldn't even remember her name—it had been such a long time ago and nothing more than a casual arrangement. Camila's rejection had made him wary of giving his heart to anyone again. He'd been willing to devote himself to her for ever, but she'd found him wanting. Not rich, or successful enough, for her to consider being with long term. Since then he made sure not to tie himself down, or make promises of a happy ever after to anyone. Including himself. At least, not until he had all of the building blocks in place for the foundation of his perfect, happy family.

'Not particularly. Relationships just haven't been my focus.'

'You're not interested in marriage and children?'

'On the contrary. Which is why I didn't want anything serious until I had a steady job and financial security. I won't settle down unless I know I can provide for my family. Both financially and emotionally.' Perhaps now that he had both he might actually open up his life and share it with someone.

He'd been so caught up in work he'd put his love life on the back burner and he wondered if his growing attraction to Inés was simply a symptom of that. She was the only woman in his life at present and he needed to expand his horizons beyond the clinic. By her own admission she wasn't making any promises about sticking around and if he was going to go all in with someone he wanted to be sure they weren't going to leave him the way everyone else in his life had.

'Very sensible.' There was a twinkle in her eye as she took another swig from her bottle and he was sure she was teasing him.

'Well, I know what it's like to grow up in an unstable environment.' He washed down the hint of bitterness which had begun to swell inside him. It wasn't that he blamed anyone for the circumstances he'd grown up in, but he didn't wish it for his own family.

'I'm sorry. You never talk much about your family.'

Ángelo shrugged. He hadn't meant to either, but with a drop of alcohol, and his defences down, it was easy to open up to Inés. Particularly because she'd already shared a little of her family circumstances with him, so he didn't feel so vulnerable opening up a little bit to a listening ear.

'My mother left when I was very young. Father did his best to raise me and my brothers, but he had his own demons with alcohol.' He tipped his bottle with a sardonic grin. Thankfully he'd never had any real vices. Likely because he'd seen the damage it could do to a person and those around them.

'I'm sorry. I guess I imagined you had the perfect family because you were so keen for me to reconcile with mine.'

Ángelo flinched at the reminder he'd butted in where he had no business interfering, when he didn't have all the facts. And because he hadn't known Inés at all at the time he'd tried to tell her how she should be behaving towards her parents. He knew from experience not everyone reacted the same way as he did to certain situations, especially where family was involved.

'I can't apologise enough for that. It was something ingrained in me from my *abuela*. My father wasn't really capable of raising three sons on his own, so she picked up a lot of the slack. According to her, family was everything. No matter what happened. She despised my mother for leaving, but she had to put up with a lot. My father could get very violent when he'd had too much to drink. Which was often.'

'I'm so sorry, Ángelo. I had no idea.' Inés reached out and took his hand, giving him a sympathetic squeeze.

Normally he would have shrugged off any outward display of pity, not believing he'd suffered any more than most growing up in difficult circumstances. Yet, he was glad of her touch. Her comfort. The connection they were making. He let her hold on to him as long as she wanted.

'It's not something I usually share with people.' In truth, he had no idea why he was even telling her now, other than the knowledge that it would give her a greater understanding of the person he was, perhaps.

'Well, thank you for trusting me.' She held eye contact and gave his hand an extra squeeze, but didn't let go. 'Did he...was he violent with you?'

It was a probing, personal question that set his teeth on edge and made his jaw tighten. He didn't want to besmirch his family name, this was his father they were talking about. But he also knew Inés wasn't merely wanting gossip. She cared. For the first time in his life he found himself wanting to tell that story. Acknowledging that it had happened and he'd got through it. It hadn't been easy, but it had made him the man he was today.

He simply nodded, not going into detail. It was enough for Inés to gasp, her hand leaving his to cover her mouth. Inexplicably, he felt tears burning the back of his eyes. It was alien and disturbing. He wasn't someone who tended to feel sorry for himself, or dwell on the past. It was all about the future for him and the family he hoped to have some day.

Perhaps it was this feeling of vulnerability which was making him emotional. Seeing himself through Inés's eyes as the young boy being beaten by his drunken father. It could even be the fact that for the first time someone was really seeing him beyond the successful doctor he'd become. Getting to know the real Ángelo that he kept hidden from most people. Even her parents didn't know about his past.

He waited for the look of horror, the sympathetic noises and being told what a brave boy he'd been. Instead, Inés shocked him completely, turning and pulling him into a bear hug. He didn't remember ever being squeezed so hard, as though she was trying to make him feel all the love and compassion he'd never had growing up from his parents.

He revelled in it. In the comfort she provided, and the feel of her in his arms. With his head buried in her hair, he could smell the smoke from the fire mixed in with her strawberry-scented shampoo. A reminder of their day and everything they'd been through together so far in such a short space of time. When his body began to react to her soft curves against him, however, he was forced to pull away. Embarrassed that he was responding inappropriately to her gesture.

Inés didn't let the awkward silence persist for too long. Though he might have preferred it to the alternative.

'What about your mother?'

Ángelo shook his head. 'I contacted her after my father died, but she didn't want to be reminded of the life she'd had with us. She moved shortly after that and didn't pass on a forwarding address so I lost touch again. I heard later she'd died.'

'And your brothers? Are you still in contact with them?'

Ángelo hadn't meant to go down this particular rabbit hole with her, but it was too late now. Inés seemed genuinely interested, caring about him and the relationships he'd lost, too. If he refused to answer her questions, it would only make things difficult between them again when he was just getting used to having her around.

'No. I've tried, but they have their own lives and don't feel as though they have any ties here any more. As soon as they were old enough they left home and never looked back.' It had been difficult for him in so many ways. At times he envied them their freedom, but it also felt like a punishment that his family had gradually been taken away from him.

'You stayed with your father?'

He knew it probably sounded ridiculous given the circumstances, but he still didn't regret it. 'I cared for him right until the end. My brothers couldn't understand why I stayed. Sometimes I don't either, but he was my only family left. I was all he had and I wasn't going to simply walk away.'

'It's not easy to make that call and sever that connection when you've been conditioned to play a certain role for so long.' As she took a swig of beer, he got the impression they weren't just talking about him any more.

He supposed that sense of duty to family at all costs his *abuela* had instilled in him meant he'd put up with a lot of bad behaviour he didn't need to. If he'd done what Inés and his brothers had done and walked away, prioritised himself instead of someone who'd never cared for him, he could have had a different life. He might still have his brothers in his life. Maybe even a wife and children of his own. Perhaps that was the family he should have been concentrating on instead of the toxic one he'd clung on to for too long.

'But you did. You broke away and started a new life. That's incredibly brave.' They clearly had different backgrounds and attitudes, but he understood what it took to make those big decisions. After all, she'd moved away from everything she'd ever known to a different country. She hadn't taken the easy way out either.

Inés's expression turned into something inscrutable. Dark. As though he'd said something really offensive. She even opened her mouth as if to say something, but took another sip of beer instead. He hadn't meant to upset her, he'd been complimenting her, not intending to patronise. But before he could apologise for whatever faux pas he'd made, the barmaid came over and set a sheet of paper and a pen on their table.

'You've picked a good night. The karaoke's starting in a minute. Write down your request and the microphone is all yours.'

Just when Ángelo thought things couldn't get any worse…

Inés was grateful for the distraction. She couldn't bear Ángelo praising her bravery, knowing that she'd walked straight into another controlling relationship. Without the interruption she might have told him about Marty and what that new life became over the last ten years. She didn't want to let him keep believing she was some strong, courageous warrior woman, when she'd been anything but that. Neither did she want him to look at her differently once he realised she was actually weak and pathetic enough to hand control of her life to another man.

She supposed she had eventually found the courage to walk away from him, too, and now she just wanted to put it all behind her. A night out would hopefully help her do that.

She was grateful he'd been able to open up to her

about his past, no matter how painful that must have been for him. It was no wonder he couldn't reconcile himself with her estrangement from her family, when he'd tried to so hard to keep his together. Though it sounded psychologically damaging to him having stayed at home. It seemed their parents' behaviour had deeply affected them both. They could both do with a night out, cutting loose.

'I'll get us another drink.' She scribbled their names down on the sheet and handed it back before Ángelo realised what she was up to.

'Two tequila shots, please.' Inés had to shout to be heard as the karaoke started and the place was filled with the sound of tuneless screeching from a middle-aged woman who'd clearly had one too many glasses of sangria.

'Tequila?' Ángelo's eyebrows shot up as she brought the drinks back to the table.

A group of young women got up next and gave a clearly well-rehearsed routine which got the whole crowd singing along.

'I think you're going to need it.' Inés clinked her glass to his and threw her head back to swallow the fiery liquid.

'Next up we have Inés and Ángelo,' the MC announced and everyone in the bar began clapping.

Everyone except Ángelo, who was looking at her with abject horror. 'You didn't.'

'I did,' she said with a grin.

Although she wasn't an introvert, on the rare occasions she had been out with her colleagues, before Marty put a stop to it, she'd enjoyed karaoke nights. It had given her a sense of liberation just to get up and make a fool of herself without the fear of recriminations. Marty would've been horrified if he'd witnessed her strutting herself on stage after a couple of wines. This didn't have the same space to move as the bars they'd frequented in London, but it meant a smaller audience to their attempt to sing.

She reckoned Ángelo needed to sample a little of that freedom and break out of his comfort zone for a while. He didn't seem to have a life beyond work and she knew how that felt. Even if he appeared to have isolated himself, rather than because he had a controlling partner. The scars from their pasts had a lot to answer for when they were still letting what had happened prevent them from moving forward.

The barmaid produced two microphones. Inés grabbed one, but Ángelo knocked his drink back before he accepted the other one.

'I can't believe you've betrayed me like this, Inés.' He was frowning at her, but he was taking part regardless and that made her happy.

She had chosen a cheesy eighties duet for them to sing and Ángelo was staring at the screen intently, waiting for the words to appear. It was a song she knew by heart. Mostly because of the repetitive lyrics reminiscent of the era.

Inés blew him a kiss and launched into the opening line. She was convinced she might have to sing his part to when he kept giving her the side eye and shaking his head. For all she knew he might not be familiar with the song. Then he suddenly launched into his verse and surprised her with his fabulous rendition. Inés smiled at him as they harmonised the chorus together and by the time the instrumental bridge came, they'd settled into the song. Ángelo even twirled her around the floor.

Back in his arms, having him sing words of love and being together for ever, it was easy to believe they were a couple. Even for Inés. But all too soon the song came to an end and they broke apart to the sound of applause.

Inés was buzzing from the thrill of the whole thing by the time they sat down. Ángelo grabbed another two beers before he joined her and she waited for a scolding.

'Well, that was unexpected,' he simply said with a laugh.

It wasn't until he smiled at her that she realised she'd been waiting for a negative reaction. That tension back in her body that she used to experience when she'd done something to annoy Marty. He would've been furious if she'd ever dared to pull such a stunt on him, but Ángelo took it in good humour. Letting her relax and enjoy the rest of her drink without worrying about the consequences of her actions.

Clearly taking control of everything wasn't as important to him as it had been to every other man in her life.

'Admit it, you had fun.' She knew she had.

'It wasn't as awful as I imagined,' he conceded.

'And you can sing.' It had been a revelation, along with the fact that he was capable of loosening up.

'Usually just in the shower.'

Now he'd planted the image of him naked under water, Inés couldn't seem to shake it out of her head. The more time she spent with him, the more he seemed to linger in her thoughts. Now she'd seen him half-naked it was even easier to have inappropriate thoughts about him, even if nothing could come of it. She wasn't in the market for a relationship when she was simply trying to get back on her feet. It would be a while before she would ever trust a man not to try to take over her life again.

Ángelo had already made it clear that he was hoping for a relationship and a family in his future, but she wasn't ready to think that far ahead. So she certainly wasn't looking to start something with her colleague who had as much family baggage as she had.

'I hope I'm getting a percentage of your future earnings for discovering your talent.' Inés tried to cleanse her dirty mind by bringing some levity to the occasion.

Except Ángelo's hearty chuckle only added to his appeal. The warm sound reaching deep inside her to tug at parts of her she'd deemed out of bounds.

'I wouldn't give up your day job. I'm certainly not. I think I'll retire at the top, thanks.' He raised his bottle in toast. Inés clinked hers to it.

'This isn't a regular occurrence for you, then?'

Ángelo nearly spat out his drink. 'No. It's been a while since I did any socialising. Not since I joined your father's practice anyway. It hasn't been a priority for me.'

Inés knew the feeling. It was nice, though, just to be able to have a drink with a colleague without fear of reprisals. Perhaps they could do a bit more of it. She might even make some new friends along the way so Ángelo wasn't her sole go-to for company. If she'd learned anything, it was not to rely too heavily on one person. Then they couldn't take advantage of her.

'It's been a while for me, too. Socialising, I mean.' She felt her cheeks flush at the thought he could've misinterpreted her comment for something more personal. Though it had been a while since she'd shared her bed either.

Given Ángelo's apparent focus on his career, she got the impression his love life hadn't been a priority for him. Perhaps that was part of the attraction, knowing that he didn't represent a threat. Ángelo was safe, because he wasn't interested in her, or a relationship.

Yet she was sure every now and then he looked at her with something more than a simple curiosity. Especially when they'd been dancing together and singing about loving each other for ever. The romantic in her wondered what that would be like, but the realist reminded her she'd fallen victim to those fantasies before. Only to find herself trapped with no say in her own life.

It was probably better to keep her thoughts, and her relationship with Ángelo, strictly at work.

'I should probably go home. It's getting late.' She drained her beer in a hurry, even though she would have preferred to take her time over it. It had been too long since she'd enjoyed a night out like this and it was ironic that she wanted to leave because she was in danger of having too much fun. She didn't want it to become a habit. At least not with Ángelo.

'I'll walk you home.' He finished his beer and stood up.

'No. You don't have to. It's not that far.' This wasn't the plan. She was supposed to be putting some distance between them, not finding a way for them to be alone together.

He frowned at her. 'There is no way I'm leaving you to walk back alone, in the dark. Your parents would never forgive me.'

Although he was half joking, Inés knew he was right. Neither of them would ever hear the end of it if her mother found out she'd walked back on her own. Not in a controlling way, but in an 'I'm an over-protective Mama' way. It didn't matter that she was almost thirty years old, or that she'd spent ten years living in London. Here, she was still her mother's baby and she'd been entrusted to Ángelo's care. Neither she, nor Ángelo, were going to take on her wrath for the sake of a five-minute walk.

Resigned, she followed him, only pausing to wave a farewell to the blonde behind the bar.

'Gracias,' she called across the room before another singer had a chance to take the mic.

'Hope we see you next week!'

Inés resisted the urge to tell her this was a one-off. Probably because deep down she was hoping there would be a second non-date. Despite her vow to herself that she wouldn't get too attached to life here in Spain, still trying to maintain some emotional distance from her parents, it did have its attractions. As dangerous as her ponderings were, she wondered what it might be like if she stayed. Being around Ángelo, and the connection they'd made, had her starting to believe that not everyone was like Marty. That some day she might be ready to share her life with someone else. She just had to be one hundred per cent sure that the next time she opened her heart up to anyone else, that they wouldn't take advantage of her.

They'd just made it to the bottom of the steps, dodging around the inebriated clientele congregated around the entrance, when they heard a high-pitched squeal behind them. Inés turned around to see a dishevelled woman in her twenties lying in a heap on the pavement at the bottom of the steps.

'Oww!' The injured party was rubbing at her ankle, one of her sparkly high heels lying broken nearby.

'Ángelo?' Inés touched him lightly on the arm to alert him to the situation, doing her best to ignore the warmth of his skin beneath her fingertips. Every time they made physical contact she felt as though an electric charge was running through her body. Not the ideal scenario when she worked so closely with him. She was in danger of short-circuiting one of these days. Especially when he already seemed to be playing havoc with her hormones.

'Are you okay?' They both turned back to offer their assistance, with Ángelo addressing the casualty since Inés's thoughts had been preoccupied elsewhere.

'My heel snapped and I slid down the last few steps. I think I've twisted my ankle.' The young English woman didn't look too distressed though she was wincing. Judging by the smell of alcohol wafting from her, Inés suspected the pain was somewhat dulled by the cocktails they'd witnessed her party drinking inside the bar.

'What have you done, you daft mare?' One of her friends staggered out with her drink in hand, less than sympathetic to her plight.

'I'm having a lie down...what does it look like?'

Before the pair exchanged any more words, Inés and Ángelo moved to her side and tried to help her up.

'Can you walk on that foot?' Inés asked, encouraging her to try to put some weight on it to assess the damage.

A yelp of pain as the woman limped into Ángelo's arms soon told a story. Though her injury seemed quickly forgotten as she got up close and personal with Ángelo. '*Hola*, Handsome.'

He gave an embarrassed smile and Inés was surprised by the surge of jealousy she felt at another woman showing an interest in him. It was only natural, he was a good-looking man after all. But they'd grown so close, so quickly, she was already hating the thought of him being with anyone else. If she was going to be sticking around for any length of time, she was definitely going to have to get over that idea she had any claim on him. Inés certainly wouldn't appreciate it if Ángelo became possessive over her. At least, that's what she tried to convince herself.

'We should get you back inside.' Inés took charge, lifting one of the woman's arms from around Ángelo's shoulders on to her own.

Between them they provided support on either side of the woman and took the steps slowly so they didn't all end up in a heap.

'Patient incoming!' the very helpful friend yelled, clearing a path through the bar so they could deposit their new friend on to a seat.

'Have you got a first-aid kit?' Ángelo asked the blonde barmaid who was clearly surprised to see them back so soon.

'I'm not sure what we have in it,' she said as she placed the small, green box on to the table.

'Thanks.' Ángelo flashed that megawatt smile that brought him yet another blushing admirer.

'I think you've cut yourself.' Inés directed everyone's attention back to the young woman's injuries which she could see now included her arms and legs. The skin grazed and broken where she'd scraped against the steps.

'Ach, it's just a scratch.' Their patient shrugged off Inés's concern, focusing on Ángelo who was feeling around her ankle.

'Can you rotate your ankle for me?' he asked, as Inés set about cleaning the abrasions with some antiseptic wipes.

The woman sucked in a sharp breath, then affected a babyish tone. 'It hurts.'

'But you can move it so I don't think anything is broken. It's likely just a sprain. I'll strap it up for now, but if there is any bruising or swelling I'd suggest you get it checked out at the hospital.' Ángelo took a bandage out of the first-aid kit and began to wind it around the foot.

'I'd advise wearing flat shoes for the rest of your trip, too.' Inés finished cleaning away the blood and grime from the superficial cuts and grazes, glad there were no serious injuries.

'Yeah. Alcohol and high heels don't mix well.' Ángelo gave her a knowing smile and her heart did a somersault.

It was nice to have the back up and Inés realised she'd been so busy trying to keep herself protected that she was missing out on the best part of being in a medical practice. Working alongside fellow medical professionals had been the best part of her life for a long time. The one place she'd felt able to be herself, even if Marty had curtailed the idea of her socialising beyond the work environment. Ángelo was content to facilitate both where Inés was concerned. Happy to co-operate on medical matters and go out for a drink, without ever telling her what to do.

It was nice not having to be on edge all of the time. Simply free to exist.

Ángelo was everything she needed right now.

CHAPTER SIX

THEY PATCHED UP the young woman as best they could, but she seemed determined to carry on drinking regardless of her injuries. Ángelo and Inés left her with her bandaged foot propped on a stool and a microphone in her hand.

No matter how good he was at his job, Ángelo couldn't get rid of the feeling he'd got himself into a terrible mess where his personal life was concerned. Entirely because he'd had such a good time tonight in Inés's company. In a way he'd been glad when she'd decided to end it. Before they had too much to drink and he was tempted to throw caution to the wind and act on the attraction he felt towards her. One which had been steadily growing. Even more so now that he'd seen this carefree side of her which had encouraged him to shake loose for a while, too.

He'd almost forgotten how to have fun in his pursuit of stability in his life. Something he'd have to rediscover if he ever hoped to find himself a long-term partner. It was all well and good having a secure financial status, but he was going to have to have some kind of social life happening if he was ever going to meet someone.

Someone other than Inés.

As much as he liked her, getting involved wouldn't be a sensible idea. Apart from being a co-worker, and daughter of the people he was closest to, she wasn't in the right head space to be what he was looking for. What he needed.

Except there was no way his conscience, or her mother, would let her walk home alone.

'The lighting isn't the best here. Until you're used to the place there's a chance you could slip and break an ankle. Also, it's prime territory for muggers.' The uneven footway wasn't fit for pedestrians. Especially those who'd been drinking.

Inés shuddered. He hadn't meant to scare her, but warn her of the danger. The place had likely changed since she'd last been here and, if she was ever to come this way again on her own, he wanted her to be prepared.

'And you're going to protect me?'

'If I have to,' he said through gritted teeth, knowing if anyone dared lay a finger on her, he'd defend her. She had a way of making him feel protective towards her and he had to be careful not to overstep in case she saw him as just another dominating male. The truth was, he kind of felt responsible for her. She was the daughter of good friends, a colleague, and someone he'd apparently come to see as a confidant.

'I see you're also going to save me from any out-of-control vehicles, too.' She nodded towards his position beside her, on the outside, so anything coming would hit him first.

It hadn't been a conscious choice. Simply a natural instinct to safeguard her.

'If I have to.' He used the same jokey tone to hide his

genuine concern for her safety. Ángelo had the feeling she wouldn't appreciate it.

'You're too good to me. Thanks, by the way, for getting up and singing with me. I know I put you on the spot.'

'You didn't leave me much choice.' He narrowed his eyes at her. 'It would have been excruciating to have to watch and listen to you doing a duet on your own.'

She gave him a playful slap on the arm. 'Hey, we can't all have perfect pitch. Though I do make up for it in enthusiasm.'

Inés launched into another hearty chorus of their party piece, uncaring about showing herself up in front of passing traffic. He loved that sense of freedom she had. It was infectious and soon he found himself joining in. The two of them walking along in the dark, singing like any other couple who'd had a fun night out together.

They even recreated their impromptu dance, where Ángelo spun her around before taking her in his arms for a waltz. Her smile was as broad as his, even though he knew he was in dangerous territory. Especially when the singing ended, but they hadn't moved out of their dance hold, staring at one another while they clung together.

It would have been easy to lean in and kiss her. He wanted to. She was looking at him as though she was waiting for it. But he knew once he did there'd be no going back. It wasn't something they could simply forget about when they worked together every day. It would always be more than just a kiss and he wasn't sure if either of them wanted that right now.

He reluctantly released her and kept on walking, trying not to pay any heed to the intensity of the moment which had just passed between them.

'They call this Cat Bridge, you know,' he said as they crossed over the strip of wasteland below them which at one time had housed the water system for the area but had since been abandoned to local wildlife.

'Oh? Why's that?' Inés moved along with the change between them. She probably realised they'd been venturing on to dangerous ground, too.

'A lot of stray and wild cats have taken it over. The locals leave out food and water for them. Your mother included.' He knew it encouraged the felines around the property, but he was glad that they were being looked after in some form.

'I'm sure my father loves that.'

'He doesn't know.' It was dawning on Ángelo now just how dominating Juan could be. He'd always taken it for granted that since it was his practice, he made the rules. With the information he'd gleaned from Inés he could see now how her mother deferred to him about everything. Secretly feeding stray cats was likely her one small act of rebellion. She wasn't as different from her daughter as she thought. That feisty spirit there in both of the de la Fuente women.

He knew what it was like to be stuck. Regardless that he'd voluntarily stayed with his father. In a way he'd felt indebted to the man for sticking around after his mother had left. Even if he hadn't been the greatest father. Love was a powerful motivator. He supposed it was the same for Inés's mother. No matter what happened, she couldn't bring herself to leave the man she loved. Inés had been braver than both of them.

'This is me.' Inés stopped outside the gates of her parents' villa.

Ángelo had been too wrapped up in his own thoughts to realise they'd reached their destination all too soon.

'You can let your mother know I got you home safely.'

Inés turned and clicked a button on her key fob to open the electric gates. 'You could come in and tell her yourself.'

Ángelo checked his watch. He doubted Marie was still awake and he was worried that if he accepted the invitation to accompany Inés inside, his vow not to kiss her might be tested. 'It's late. I wouldn't want to disturb her.'

Inés nodded. 'Well, thanks for a good night. I can't remember the last time I had so much fun.'

The twinkle in her eyes under the moonlight and the wide smile said she was being genuine. He felt exactly the same. If this had been a first date it would've been perfect. With a second definitely on the cards. That's what was making it so hard to walk away now. It wasn't every day he met someone he had such a great connection with. What a shame that nothing could come of it.

'Nor me. Thanks, Inés.' He leaned forward to give her a peck on the cheek. A brief kiss goodnight. Polite and respectful. A simple gesture of his gratitude for her company.

At least, that was how it started.

The second his lips touched her skin he was electrified. Zapped to life, the touch of her awakening parts of him that had lain dormant for too long. He was sure Inés felt it, too, as he watched her eyes flutter shut and she tilted her chin up towards him. Her full lips inviting him to taste her. Inside him, a silent groan heralded the last of his restraint snapping.

The alcohol he'd consumed, combined with the good time they'd had together, was starting to make him think this was a good idea. That one little kiss wasn't the end of the world. Merely the natural conclusion of a pleasant night out together.

He moved his mouth the short distance to cover hers and when she opened up to meet him, he was lost. With his defences well and truly breached, he unleashed the desire he'd been holding back since their first clash in the clinic. The passion awakened inside him by her touch, her taste, only making him want more.

He pulled her close, deepening the kiss, her soft body crushed against the hardness of his. The little groans of delight coming from Inés, spurring him on in his pursuit. Mouths clashing, tongues teasing, they engaged in the kiss together with a passion he hadn't expected. It was only supposed to have been a goodnight peck, not foreplay. Yet this was exactly what it felt like. A promise of more to come and something he would've been very keen to explore.

When the electronic gates began to close, deciding that they'd taken too long, it was a wake-up call he probably needed.

'I should go.' He pulled away, trying to remember if there were security cameras. It would be a hard job explaining this to Marie and convincing her they weren't involved in some passionate love affair. Even if one mind-blowing kiss was trying to convince him it wouldn't be such a bad idea.

Inés took a wobbly step back, looking almost as dazed

as he felt. 'Yeah. Um…goodnight. We should do this again some time. Or not.'

She backed into the still-closed gates and Ángelo had to suppress a smile, seeing that she'd been as knocked sideways by the kiss as he had.

'Probably not,' he said with more than a hint of sadness. As fun as it had been, he didn't want to risk his future at the practice by getting involved with Inés. Especially when she didn't know how long she was going to be sticking around for. He had a feeling that he'd get in too deep, too quickly, judging by the effect one kiss had on him. It was better to put a stop to things now before things went any further and ruined the life he was trying to build for himself.

'Yes. You're right. Better just to leave things as they are.' She was flustered now, pressing and pressing the button on the fob in a hurry to get the gates open again.

Ángelo hated that things had ended this way after such a good night. Now she couldn't seem to get away fast enough.

He waited until she disappeared into the villa and watched the gates slowly close between them again. The barrier he apparently needed between them at all times. Next time he went out for a drink and an impromptu karaoke session he should probably do it alone, or with a woman who wasn't a work colleague. If he was ready to get back on the dating scene he needed to set his sights on someone uncomplicated, someone who didn't have a lot of emotional baggage with the people who ran his work place. Preferably with someone who wanted the same things as he did. From everything he'd learned about Inés, he didn't think family was on her list of priorities. A red flag he needed to take heed of when he was setting up his life so he could have one of his own.

'Inés? Is that you?' Her mother peered out from her bedroom, no doubt disturbed by the sound of the electric gates clanging open and closed.

'Yes. Sorry if I woke you. Ángelo and I just stopped for a couple of drinks and got caught up in a medical emergency.' Inés was struggling to keep her voice calm when her head was in the clouds after kissing Ángelo. She felt as though she was floating on air and it was difficult to come back down to earth so quickly. Regardless that their passionate embrace had ended so abruptly.

'You two seem to be getting on well.' Her mother walked down towards the lounge to greet her, then made her way to the adjoining kitchen to pour herself a glass of water.

'We're a good team when it comes to work,' she admitted, hoping her flushed cheeks wouldn't give away the effect he really had on her.

'I know he's glad to have you on board as much as we are.' Her mother cleared her throat and took a sip of water. 'We haven't really had a chance to talk since you came back.'

'Well, there's been a lot to deal with.' She wasn't sure she was ready to have this talk. It was easier in some ways just to get on with her workload and put the past behind her, rather than deal with it head on. She didn't want any more arguments to arise when she had nowhere else to go.

'I just wanted to thank you for coming back. I know things haven't been easy between us.'

Inés shifted uncomfortably at the understatement, but held her tongue. Clearly, her mother wanted to get something off her chest.

'It must have taken a lot for you to come back and it has made me think hard about what happened. In hindsight, I can see that I didn't support you enough. I'm aware how difficult your father can be and I found life was easier simply to let him get his own way. It wasn't fair to expect you to do the same.

'You're stronger than I ever was and I'm so proud of you, Inés. I just hope that you can forgive me and hopefully give me a chance to repair the damage.' It was obvious her mother had been doing some soul searching and it was more than Inés had ever expected to hear from either of her parents. The admission reached deep inside her heart to that place where she'd been holding out some hope of having a family again.

Though she didn't know if she would ever find the same sense of closure with her father, Inés found herself wanting to let go of the resentment she'd held towards her mother for so long. Life with Marty had taught her how much she needed someone in her life she could turn to. Someone she could trust.

'It's okay, Mama. I know what it's like to love someone who takes over your life so much you can't even think for yourself any more. My life in England wasn't as rosy as you might think. I ended up living with a man who tried to control everything I did. It's given me some understanding of what you went through. But I've left Marty and I'm here now. Hopefully, we can move on together.' Inés made the first step forward and opened her arms.

Her mother hugged her tight, as though afraid she'd never see her again. 'I hope so. I'm just glad you got out and made your way back home.'

Inés couldn't promise her that she would be here for ever, but hopefully they would have each other again for some time to come. She went to bed with her heart feeling very full for once.

Inés didn't know how she was going to look Ángelo in the eye this morning. Things last night had been…unexpected and left her dealing with all sorts of jumbled emotions. Not only had she had a much-needed heart-to-heart with her mother, but she'd had that kiss with Ángelo to think about all night. She hadn't realised how much one night out could have such an impact on her. Now she had to see him every day knowing the passion which had sparked so easily to life between them.

It was clear he regretted it the moment it had happened, but she couldn't say the same. That kiss had awakened something inside her that she couldn't seem to shut down again. So many thoughts had been running through her head since. Including how much time she'd wasted being with Marty. She didn't want to repeat past mistakes by being blinded by a handsome man showing her affection and attention. In her experience it didn't last.

It would be nice to be able to let herself get swept away in the romantic fantasy of being with Ángelo without worrying about the consequences, but life with Marty had been so stifling she couldn't take that risk. Ángelo was handsome, kind, successful and wanted to settle down. All the qualities anyone could need in a man. Everything she'd thought Marty was in the beginning, too.

There was no room in her life for any sort of relationship at present, even a casual one. Especially with Ángelo. She was only back in Spain because of her parents and getting involved with her father's employee would only complicate matters between them. Things were messy enough and she didn't need to be distracted by a pretty face and a pair of strong lips.

That was part of the problem now. By kissing her like that, Ángelo had made her wonder if she'd been missing out on that level of passion. Or if it was something only Ángelo could whip up inside her. It was probably just hormones and her sense of freedom which had made their encounter all the more exhilarating, and nothing more. Kissing someone who wasn't Marty felt as though her liberation was complete. Because she'd wanted to, not felt as though she had to. She was no longer bound to a life she didn't want, or couldn't escape.

Inés hadn't had a lot of experience with men before Marty. One or two short-lived flings, but she didn't remember ever getting carried away in the moment the way she had with Ángelo. If it felt like that every time a man touched her, perhaps she was missing out by remaining single after all. She just had to remember to be careful she didn't end up with another control freak again, or get involved with someone she knew she couldn't be with. Either way, she'd be the one who'd end up getting hurt.

Though she was sure her mother would be over the moon with the idea of her being with Ángelo. Her mother was clearly fond of him and she'd made no secret of the fact she wanted Inés to stay in Spain. Especially now that their mother/daughter relationship was beginning to heal. She'd already had to fend off a thousand questions this morning over breakfast about her night out with Ángelo. Though she had known better than to give anything away other than the fact they'd had a drink and a chat. If her mother had any hint of the kiss they'd shared outside the house, she'd already be making plans for the wedding.

Thank goodness one of them had their feet firmly on the ground. Though she had no idea why Ángelo had kissed her in the first place if he wasn't interested in her that way. Most likely it had been drink fuelled. A lot of bad decisions were made under the influence of alcohol. She'd first kissed Marty at a bar after working a late shift together at the hospital and that hadn't turned out so well in the end…

All she did know was that Ángelo had got her all hot and bothered, then dropped her like a stale churro. She'd have been better off not knowing what it felt like being in his arms, or being kissed so passionately.

'Morning.' He passed by without a second glance, telling her all she needed to know about how he felt about their night together. Embarrassed.

'I hear you two had fun last night.' Inés's mother, unaware of any awkward tension between the pair, addressed them both as they passed through reception.

It stopped Ángelo in his tracks long enough to glare at Inés. She could only hope her wide-eyed, innocent expression conveyed to him the fact she hadn't told her mother anything about the kiss they'd shared.

'It was just a drink, Mama…' Inés did her best to play

it down and let Ángelo know she hadn't spilled any of the juicy details.

'I think we needed it to decompress after a difficult day at work.' Ángelo offered her mother a smile as he helped to try to diffuse the situation.

Though her mother seemed determined to blow things up again.

'Inés seemed to have enjoyed it. She was certainly in a good mood this morning.' The mischief in her mother's eyes said she knew it had been more than alcohol which had Inés stumbling in late in a daze.

Inés gave an exaggerated tut and rolled her eyes at her mother, which proved effective when she walked away without pursuing the matter any further.

'Sorry about that,' Inés apologised to Ángelo for her mother's insistence on bringing up what was clearly a moment he wanted to forget. Even if it wasn't proving so easy for her.

'It's all right. I suppose it takes her mind off your father for a while thinking there's some great romance going on under her nose.' His smile this time didn't quite reach his eyes, suggesting that he hadn't been able to brush off the matter as easily as he would have her believe.

Clearly, kissing Inés wasn't something he wanted to be reminded of. Never mind the insinuation that there would ever be anything more than that between them.

It gave Inés a sinking feeling in the pit of her stomach, but she told herself she would've felt the same way if anyone rejected her. Trying to convince herself it didn't hurt more because it was Ángelo who was doing the rejecting after a kiss which had rendered her a puddle of hormones.

'I know, right? As if.' Inés did her best to laugh off any hint of romance between them, trying to convince herself as much as Ángelo that she hadn't read too much into the kiss.

They were left staring at one another in awkward silence and it occurred to her that she might have been better off letting him walk past her as he'd intended.

'We had a good talk last night and I think we managed to clear the air. One down, one to go,' Inés joked, though she wasn't looking forward to the particular conversation she needed to have with her father.

'I'm so happy for you both.' Ángelo pulled her into an unexpected embrace. As though he'd been as anxious for them to resolve their differences as her mother clearly had.

Inés tensed, afraid that if she let herself get too comfortable in his arms, she'd never want to leave. He slowly released her and she took a step back.

'I should probably get on with some work—' Ángelo said, looking concerned that he'd encouraged physical contact with her again.

'What have you got planned for today?' Inés stumbled over his excuse to leave with some small talk.

'Work,' he repeated.

'Oh, yeah. Me, too.' She nodded, hoping at some point either the ground would swallow her up, or there would be another crisis somewhere to divert their attention away from this exchange.

Goodness knew how they were going to keep working together when she couldn't seem to let go of what had happened last night.

'Oh, I was going to go and see your father this afternoon,' he added, as an afterthought, clearly not recognising how much his dismissal of their kiss had hurt her.

'Okay.' She wasn't sure what he expected her to say to that.

Well done? Good for you?

'You could go, too. I'm sure he'd like to see you, Inés. It might be easier for you if I was there with you when you saw him. I mean, I'd let you talk privately. I could just be there for moral support.'

Although she appreciated he was doing his best to facilitate a mediation between her and her father, it wasn't something she wanted to think about right now. 'I'm not getting into this again, Ángelo. I know you have family issues, but they're very different to mine. Please leave it alone.'

The frustration she'd been feeling not only about the change in dynamic between them, combined with his continued attempts to reconcile her with her father, manifested in her raising her voice at him. She wasn't proud of it, but neither was she going to stand back and let another man try to dictate her actions.

He held up his hands. 'I just thought since you'd made up with your mother that you'd welcome the chance with your father, too. That it might have been easier if I went with you. Sorry if I read the situation wrong. My bad.'

Her rage only increased as he walked away, but this time it was directed at herself. It wasn't Ángelo's fault he didn't want her, any more than he was to blame for her strained relationship with her father. She was beginning to think it was her own guilt which was making her defensive when it came to any conversation around her father.

He was dying and she felt that obligation to see him before he passed away. It was her own personal issues that were stopping her. Along with that anxiety that he wouldn't have changed and might still try to dominate her in some way. Ridiculous, she supposed, given her age and the time which had passed between them. She just didn't want to revert back to that submissive version of herself that she'd only just shaken off.

At some point she knew she would have to visit him. Before it was too late and she spent the rest of her life feeling guilty. She didn't want to give him that power over her again.

'How are you today?' Ángelo took a seat by Juan's bedside, careful to avoid the wires and machines monitoring his vital signs.

'Still dying,' he replied without a trace of humour. This was the man he'd come to know over the years. Straight to the point, not bothered whose feelings he might hurt.

Ángelo supposed at this point of his life he had every right to say exactly what he thought without any regard for anyone else. Though he was beginning to see the kind of father he'd likely been to Inés and understood her reluctance to get close to him again.

Ángelo's visit had been a last-minute decision, for various reasons. Not only had it been some time since he'd stopped by, but it had been a good excuse to get away from the clinic for a while. His decision to ask Inés along might have been misjudged, but he'd thought it was the nudge she'd needed to take that final leap.

She certainly seemed pleased to have a relationship with her mother again and he was sure by seeing her father she would get that same sense of closure. Even though suggesting that he accompany her had negated the idea of putting some space between them after last night and he'd managed to get Inés's back up at the same time.

He hadn't meant to push her into doing something she hadn't wanted to do, but he just wanted to see her happy. It was more of an olive branch after the way he'd acted post-kiss. As though in some way being with her when she visited the parent she'd been estranged from for a decade would make up for him kissing her, then telling her to forget it had ever happened. Now he'd managed to rile her twice over.

She seemed to have that effect on him—muddling his thoughts so he made some questionable decisions. Not that it was her fault. He'd been the one who'd instigated the kiss after all. Though her enthusiastic response had eventually been the catalyst for him to end it. He couldn't risk getting carried away any more than he already had been.

Now she probably thought that not only was he some kind of kiss-'em-and-leave-'em playboy, but someone who thought he could still get her to do things she didn't want to do. To some extent making him look like the same kind of control freak she was doing her best to stay away from.

Perhaps this visit was subconsciously some kind

of atonement. Being charitable to her father to make amends for the mess he'd made with his daughter.

'Is there anything else they can give you to make you more comfortable?' It was difficult to know what to say in the circumstances. The man was dying, there was no point in denying that, and nothing he could say could change the inevitable.

Juan, whose usually trim figure was now bloated with fluid, could barely left his head from the pillow to 'tut' at him. 'More painkillers which don't do anything except make me sleep. Not that I can sleep very long with all the noise going on in here. If it's not the man next to me snoring, it's the nurses chatting to one another instead of doing their jobs.'

Ángelo had to suppress a smile that Juan still had the energy to complain even on his deathbed. He didn't envy those looking after him and no doubt hearing the same criticism. It reminded him all too much of the verbal, and sometimes physical, abuse he'd endured when taking care of his own father at the end of his life. At times it was very difficult to take when he was giving everything, sacrificing a life of his own, to look after someone who didn't seem to appreciate him.

He didn't blame Inés for being reluctant to visit, regardless that Juan's acting out was likely because he was scared and in pain. That's what he'd had to tell himself when his own father had been particularly vicious towards him, too. He certainly wouldn't want Inés to suffer the same kind of abuse and perhaps it was best for her own safety and sanity that she did stay away after all.

Not everything was as black and white as he'd once seen it. Having grown close to Inés these past few days, he could understand her position better and his brothers', to an extent. He'd been able to compartmentalise the things his father said and did from the care he'd needed, but that didn't make Ángelo a better person than anyone else. In hindsight now he could see how damaging that time could have been to his brothers if they'd been as affected by what had happened, as Inés clearly had been. He just wished there was some way that they could all find some kind of peace with the past that would allow them all to move on.

'There was a fire yesterday at the Garcia place. Inés and I were at the scene, but I think the couple are going to be okay. Some smoke inhalation and minor burns, but I was glad to have her with me.' He tried to make some small talk, at the same time trying to make Juan feel connected to the practice still and talk up Inés.

'Marie said she was home. I hope she's not giving you too much trouble.'

'Not at all. She's been great to work alongside.' The only trouble he'd had with Inés had been his own doing. Getting too close, too soon, then having to pull back before someone got hurt.

Professionally, she'd been a great addition to the practice and he enjoyed working with her. So much so he'd started to see something blossoming between them that they couldn't afford to nurture.

Juan didn't look impressed. He closed his eyes as though bored with the conversation, though Ángelo knew it was likely the morphine the medical staff had administered for his pain was making him sleepy.

Nevertheless, it didn't make it seem as though he was keen to make up with Inés even if she had turned up here with him, offering her sympathy and apologising for being away for so long.

'Always causing trouble,' he muttered, not opening his eyes.

It was a shame the two hadn't been able to put the past behind them to meet and get to know the people they were now. Before it was too late.

'Inés is an excellent doctor.' Ángelo felt the need to stick up for her in her absence. She hadn't done anything wrong since coming back. In fact, she'd helped out during a very difficult time for them all, when she really didn't have to.

Given the family history, she could very well have declined to come all this way and work at the practice, and no one would have blamed her. Well, except for her father.

'She hasn't come to see me.' This time, Juan sounded more emotional. More human. As though this was the matter that had really been bothering him.

'She's been busy with work. I'm sure she'll come at some point.' Ángelo didn't want to make any false promises, but he had a suspicion that Inés would make an appearance eventually. She was too kind hearted not to see her dying father one last time.

'I'm running out of time. I need to see her.' Juan's voice was weak. Broken. As though that gruff exterior had finally been dismantled and, faced with his own mortality, he'd finally realised what was important. Making peace with his daughter.

'I know,' Ángelo said softly.

Despite the plea, he didn't want to interfere. If he recounted Juan's request to Inés, she might think he was trying to manipulate her. He'd already made that mistake once too often. The decision had to be Inés's to see her father and hopefully she'd make it soon without any outside influence. He didn't want her to live with any regret when it was difficult enough grieving for a parent.

If Inés found some closure with her father, then she might move on and leave him to live his life without the danger of falling for his unsuitable co-worker.

CHAPTER SEVEN

'I'LL DO THE DISHES, Mama. You made dinner.' Although they'd fallen into something of a routine with her mother cooking every night, Inés didn't want to be a burden. Especially when her mother was travelling so often to and from the hospital, trying to spend as much time with her husband as possible. Nor did she want to be treated as though she was a visitor in her own home. However temporary it might be.

'Nonsense. I like to keep busy. You sit down and I'll get you a glass of wine.' Her mother ushered her into the sitting room, ignoring all offers of help. Leaving Inés no choice but to put her feet up.

She would have preferred to keep busy, too. To take her mind off yet another flare up between her and Ángelo this afternoon. It seemed there was a fine line between passion and aggravation. He managed to arouse very strong emotions in her either way. She supposed it was good in a way that she no longer felt the need to hide how she felt. To be afraid of expressing herself in case she suffered the consequences. She knew he wouldn't do anything to harm her, even if he managed to rile her at times.

No doubt he thought he was doing the right thing by

trying to push her and her father back together, but those were big decisions she had to make for herself now. She wasn't going to let anyone tell her what to do any more. Unfortunately for Ángelo, when she was around him she was no longer the timid mouse Marty had made her into, but a tiger lady who wasn't afraid to bite back.

The thought made her smile. She'd come a long way in such a short space of time and he was partly to thank for that when he gave her the space to express herself. No matter how ferociously at times.

The bell sounded at the gate and she rushed towards the front door to let in their visitor, keen to have a distraction. Only to see the gates open at her behest, revealing Ángelo standing there like a mirage. Her pulse immediately kicked up a notch as she remembered being in that very spot with him last night, with his lips on hers.

She gulped and swallowed down the carnal thoughts that sprang to mind, ready to greet him.

'Is Mama expecting you?' Her mother hadn't said anything, but this could be another arrangement she wasn't aware of. Or a misguided attempt at matchmaking, inviting Ángelo over as a post-dinner snack for her.

'No. Sorry. I hope I'm not disturbing you. Your father wants a few things brought up in the morning and I said I'd deliver the message to your mother.'

'No problem.' An unexpected surge of disappointment swelled inside her that he hadn't made a special trip just to see her. Regardless that they hadn't parted on the best of terms this afternoon.

Inés led him into the villa, regardless that he probably knew the place better than she did these days. She tried not to get too caught up in the feeling that he'd replaced her here, especially when he was the one visiting her dying father, too.

'How was he?' she asked, surprising them both. 'I suppose that's a stupid question in the circumstances.'

'He's understandably feeling low, though still alert enough to complain about the staff,' Ángelo said with a curt laugh. 'I'm sure he'd be pleased to know you care.'

Her initial reaction was to refute the allegation, but in the end, she couldn't. No matter how he'd acted, no matter how estranged they'd become, he was still her father and he was dying. She didn't want him to suffer. She simply wished things had been different. That they could have had a better relationship. But she knew wishing for the impossible was a futile exercise when she'd spent years longing for things in her life to be different. The only way change came about was when she made it happen.

She chose not to rise to the comment.

'Ángelo? You should have said you were coming. We could have set a place for you at dinner. There's still some left if you'd like me to heat it up for you?' Her mother bustled into the lounge to greet him, then disappeared into the kitchen just as quickly. Not giving him a chance to refuse the offer.

Inés exchanged a smile with him. 'Looks as though you're staying.'

'Sorry. I didn't mean to spoil your evening.'

'You didn't. At least I'll have someone to talk to, I guess. Mama can't seem to sit down long enough for a conversation.' It wasn't the evening she'd expected to be having, but Inés knew her mother needed to keep busy.

She enjoyed having visitors to fuss over and likely had been at something of a loss when Inés had left home. Ángelo had filled that void for her and now, more than ever, she needed something to keep her busy. Given too long to think, the inevitable loss of her husband would surely sink in and devastate her.

Grief was something Inés would have to deal with, too, but was something she wasn't ready to think about either.

They followed her mother to the kitchen. At least then Inés wouldn't be left trying to make conversation with Ángelo on her own. It never seemed to end well. Either with an argument, or a dizzying kiss. Both of which left her ruminating for hours on their interactions. One scenario leaving more of an impact on her than the other...

'Juan wants you to bring up some clean pyjamas and his razor.' Ángelo took a seat at the breakfast bar and watched as his hostess plated up some dinner for him.

'Still wanting to look his best.' Inés opened a bottle of wine and poured three glasses, before pulling over a tall stool to sit next to him.

'Your father takes great pride in his appearance. I find it a comfort that even now he's trying to make the effort to look his best.' Inés's mother had tears in her eyes as she set down the plates of food for them all to pick from.

It crossed Inés's mind that her father would look considerably different from the last time she'd seen him and, if her mother was finding the change in him difficult, she would have to prepare herself, too. If she decided to go and see him.

'He was tired, but I think he enjoyed the company. It probably gets boring, not to mention lonely, lying in that hospital bed.' Ángelo, who was happily munching away on the sardines and patatas bravas before him, didn't appear to have been making a dig at her. Yet Inés couldn't help but feel guilty that this virtual stranger was providing the support she couldn't bring herself to give. It wouldn't bother her so much if she didn't still care.

'I know he wants to come home, but he's not able to get around unaided now. I'm not capable of lifting him if he has another fall.' Her mother's throwaway comment chilled Inés. It was clear her father had a history of bad falls which she'd known nothing about, but she was sure Ángelo was aware of.

'You'll do yourself more injury if you try to do that again. We both nearly put our backs out the last time we had to lift him in the bathroom. He's in the best place, Marie.' Ángelo squeezed her mother's hand, confirming that there had been more going on than Inés had known.

That guilt that she hadn't been here to help was only overtaken by the shame she felt by the fact she'd been busy trying to keep Marty happy. Even if she'd known at the time she wouldn't have risked upsetting him by suggesting she needed to come home to help look after her father. Thank goodness Ángelo had been here to help. She would have hated to think of her mother having to deal with all of this on her own.

'I know. It's just not easy. I'll put a smile on my face and go and see him in the morning.' Her mother gave a heartbreaking wobbly smile, showing how vulnerable she was beneath the efficient exterior she tried to portray.

Despite everything Inés's father had put them through, it was clear her mother still loved him, and would likely be lost without him.

'Maybe you could take him some of that cheese you bought. It's delicious.' Inés wanted to contribute in some small way, without actually committing herself to anything, and thought perhaps some snacks would cheer him up. Her father had always been fond of his food.

Except her mother shook her head. 'He doesn't have much of an appetite any more. Finds it hard to keep food down.'

Clearly Inés knew nothing about her father any more and it was becoming more apparent to everyone. Including her.

Rather than discuss the matter any further, Marie de la Fuente began tidying up again. Carrying the empty glasses and dishes over to the sink, refusing all offers of assistance. She stood with her back to Inés and Ángelo for several moments and Inés thought she was just trying to compose herself.

Suddenly, she collapsed to the ground, and the glass which had been in her hand smashed all around her.

'Mama?'

'Marie?'

Both Inés and Ángelo immediately rushed over to see her. Although conscious, she was clearly dazed, and her hand was bleeding profusely.

'I just felt a little dizzy.' She tried to get up, but Ángelo placed a gentle hand on her shoulder.

'Stay where you are for now.' He went to fetch a glass of water and Inés began sweeping away the shards of broken glass around her so they could get down to take a better look at her.

'You've cut your hand.' Inés wadded it up with some

paper towels before going in search of the first-aid kit she knew was kept in the bathroom cabinet.

When she came back, her mother was sipping from the glass of water, as Ángelo checked her pulse.

'Your heart's beating a little fast right now. It could just be from the shock of the fall, but I want you to stay where you are for now until we see if it regulates itself again.'

'How are you feeling, Mama? Light headed? Dizzy? Any headache?' Inés, like Ángelo, wanted to get to the bottom of why she'd collapsed.

'A little lightheaded, I suppose. Everything just seemed to be so far away, then my head was spinning and the next thing I knew I was on the floor.' She was pale and suddenly looking her age, sitting there so vulnerable.

'It's no wonder when you're rushing around the way you have been. You need to rest, Mama, and look after yourself for once.' Inés carefully picked the tiny fragments of glass out of the cut across her palm, before cleaning the wound.

'Are you eating properly? You're so busy making sure everyone else is eating, but I'm sure I haven't seen you eat anything more than a nibble of food lately.' It was Ángelo's turn to scold her.

Hopefully, she didn't need anything other than some rest and a proper meal.

'I'm not really hungry. My stomach always seems to be in knots, thinking about Juan.' Goodness knew how she was going to cope when he was gone for good, but Inés was simply grateful that she'd come here when she had. Then she could look after her mother while they were under the same roof.

'You're under a lot of stress, Marie. Even more reason why you should be taking better care of yourself. I'm prescribing a couple of days off work to get some rest. I can take Juan's things to him.' Ángelo's stern, but concerned, tone wasn't one to be argued with.

'I can't ask you to do that and who's going to look after the clinic if I'm not there?' It appeared she wasn't going to go down without a fight.

'You didn't ask me. I offered. We can get agency workers in to help until you're ready to get back on your feet. Isn't that right, Inés?' Ángelo looked to Inés for support and, in this case, she was happy to give it.

'Yes. Mama, you're under too much stress, doing too much. You need to rest. I don't think this needs stitches, but you do need some sleep. We're going to help you to bed and I don't want to hear any complaints.' Inés didn't want to be dishing out tough love, but she needed her mother to comply. The last thing she wanted was another parent ending up in hospital. Especially when they'd just begun repairing their relationship. She didn't want to face the possibility of losing her, too.

Inés finished dressing the cut on her mother's hand and Ángelo checked her heart rate again. Once he was satisfied that she didn't need hospital intervention, he and Inés helped her mother to her feet.

'I suppose it wouldn't hurt to get an early night,' she finally conceded.

'And a lie in. I'll bring you breakfast in bed before I go to work in the morning. I'm going to make sure you do everything your doctor tells you.' Inés smiled at Ángelo, safe in the knowledge they were both in agreement on this matter at least.

Escorting her with an arm each, they walked her mother to her bedroom, then left her to get ready for bed in private. Although Inés promised she'd come and check on her soon to make sure she actually got into bed and wasn't doing office paperwork, or something other than taking it easy.

'I'm sure she'll be okay,' Ángelo reassured her as they left her room. 'She's just been dealing with a lot lately.'

'I know. I think I forget sometimes that she's ten years older than the last time I saw her. I suppose you just think your parents are going to last for ever.' Inés supposed she had thought eventually that they would reconcile and never considered that it would be under these circumstances. When she was going to lose her father sooner rather than later and some day it was going to be her mother, too.

There was no hiding from that fact, try as she might, and she knew if she didn't reconcile with her father now, it could be too late. She might never get that closure she needed if she didn't see him. Even if she wasn't emotionally ready for that confrontation with her past.

'Until they aren't there…' Ángelo seemed to drift off into his own thoughts. He talked so little of his own family, Inés had forgotten he was probably missing them, too.

She headed straight back to the kitchen to grab what was left of the wine. Ángelo took two new glasses from the cupboard and they carried everything into the lounge.

'How long has it been since you lost your father?' Inés

asked as they sat down. She kicked off her shoes and curled her legs under her, getting comfy.

'Five years.' Ángelo poured two generous glasses of red and handed one to her.

'You've been on your own all that time?' Yes, she was prying, but she wanted to know more about him when he was clearly such a big part of her parents' lives and knew so much about hers.

'Pretty much. My brothers don't get in touch very often.'

'Don't you get lonely?' She didn't believe someone as warm and loving as Ángelo obviously was wouldn't have someone beating on the door of the handsome doctor. After all, he'd managed to enchant her after only a few days of getting to know him.

He took a sip of wine and captured her with his intense gaze. 'I'm not a monk, Inés. It's not as though I haven't shared a bed with anyone in five years.'

'Oh.' Inés felt her cheeks flush. She wasn't a prude, but the idea of him casually hooking up with random women to fulfil his carnal needs did make her blush. It also aroused a twinge of jealousy, when she'd been afforded a passionate kiss from him, but denied the rest of that pleasure.

'What about you? Surely there was someone back in England?' He was teasing her, but Inés found herself wanting to open up about Marty. She'd kept the details of the relationship secret for years, as though it was something she should be ashamed of. It had been a big part of her life. Made her who she was now and she wanted to exorcise herself of that particular demon so she could forget about him.

'I was in a long-term relationship up until recently.'

'It must have been difficult for you to leave and come back here. Is that what caused the break up?'

Inés inhaled a shaky breath. This was the moment she thought she'd never come to, when she opened up about what she'd been through. But Ángelo felt like a safe space. Hopefully he wouldn't blame, or shame, her for the circumstances she'd let herself get into.

'No, but it was a good reason for me to leave. I'm not sure I would've found the courage to do so otherwise.' She gulped her wine.

'That bad?' Ángelo's eyes were full of concern and it encouraged her to tell him everything and get it off her chest once and for all.

She nodded, willing the tears to stay at bay when she was trying to be strong. 'Not at first, of course. Marty was very charming and attentive when we met. I suppose I was naive. I hadn't been allowed to date here, so when I moved to London I was easily flattered by the attention I received. The men I dated turned out to be immature and only interested in partying. I thought Marty was different. He was older, a handsome, successful surgeon, and he had his own place in the city.'

'I can see why your head was turned. I might have dated him myself at that age.' Ángelo was trying to make her feel better about her choices, but they both knew he was more careful than that when it came to relationships.

'I rushed into things. Who knows, maybe I was just trying to find some stability in my life. I wanted the happy ever after, but it turned into a nightmare. Marty gradually took control of everything. Of me and my life. To the point where I wasn't allowed to do anything without his say so. I was afraid to do anything in case it upset him. Basically, I swapped one control freak for another. So you see, I'm not the strong, independent woman you've mistaken me for.'

'You broke away, didn't you? I see no mistake.' He took a sip of wine and didn't bat an eyelid at her big reveal.

'I was weak.'

'You were conditioned, Inés. In some ways, so was I. We repeat the patterns we've grown up with. In your case it was having someone control you. With me, I couldn't let go of the fact my father was my family. Regardless of how he treated me. We're both survivors and probably better people for what we've come through. I don't suspect either of us would ever cause the same pain to anyone else that our parents caused us.'

It was an angle she'd never explored before. Ángelo's insight certainly gave her something to think about. She didn't see him as weak, or stupid, for looking after his father. Clearly, it wasn't how he saw her either.

'You're right about that. Nor will I ever again be with someone who tries to clip my wings. What about you? No horror dating stories?'

Ángelo swallowed his wine with a gulp and she got the impression there was more to his story than a troubled childhood too.

'I was with someone for a couple of years. Camila. I thought we would settle down and raise a family.'

'And she didn't?'

He shook his head. 'We were young. I was still living with my father and studying medicine. In hindsight, I didn't have much to offer. She ended things when she realised I couldn't put her first. I suppose that helped spur me on to be a success, to have that stability in place that I never had as a child.'

Inés could tell he'd been hurt deeply by the rejection when he hadn't seemed to have had a serious relationship since. Believing that no one would have him unless he could provide them with material things.

'If she'd really loved you, she would've wanted to be with you no matter what. The right person wouldn't care how much you earned, or where you lived. You only hurt yourself by staying too long with the wrong person. I'm sure you'll find the right one some day.' Her heart ached at the fact that it wasn't going to be her.

Ángelo held her gaze. 'I hope so.'

Inés's heart started pounding loudly. They were sitting so close. He was so understanding. She was so lonely.

'I should get these dishes done before Mama insists on doing them herself.' There were only a couple of glasses and plates, but she needed to breathe some air which wasn't filled with Ángelo's spicy cologne.

She got up to take the glasses into the kitchen and put some distance between them, but her plan was thwarted when he followed her into the kitchen. Barefoot, she padded across the tiled floor, not thinking anything of it until she felt a sharp stabbing pain in the sole of her foot and cried out. She crumpled to the floor, with a concerned Ángelo standing over her.

'What's wrong?'

Showing off her flexibility, Inés managed to bring her foot up to inspect it and found the culprit. 'I've stood on a tiny sliver of broken glass. I must've missed it when I was sweeping up.'

Ángelo crouched down and inspected the puncture wound where the blood had begun to pool. 'We need to get that out before it disappears beneath the skin. Sit still.'

He grabbed the first-aid kit from earlier which had been left on the kitchen worktop and rummaged around inside. With a pair of tweezers, he held her foot in one hand and carefully extracted the glass. Inés watched the concentration on his face, thinking more about the warmth of his touch than her injury.

'Sorry for causing more drama.' It was second nature for her to apologise for virtually everything, but this one was on her. She should have cleaned up properly and should not have been walking about barefoot.

Ángelo frowned at her and her heart gave that extra beat it always used to do when she thought she'd upset Marty and was about to be subjected to one of his rages.

'You don't need to apologise for anything, Inés. It was an accident.'

'I should have been more thorough when I cleaned up. I'm lucky it wasn't Mama who stood on it.' She sat still while he cleaned the small wound and placed a plaster over the area.

His jaw clenched. 'Listen to me. These things happen. You're not going to be punished for a mistake. You're safe here.'

She had no idea she was still in victim mode until he'd pointed it out. He was right. She had become conditioned to always accepting blame. It was disturbing that even away from Marty's influence, she was still acting as though he had control over her. The frustration of that brought tears burning her eyes.

'I hate that he can still do this to me.'

'Don't let him,' Ángelo said softly. 'From now on you're free to do whatever you want, express however you feel. Without having to worry about the repercussions. At least with me.'

Inés wished that were true. Because she'd be acting on those very feelings right now when he was cradling her foot, being all thoughtful and looking as gorgeous as ever.

She pondered over that for a moment, saw the way he was looking at her, too, and threw caution to the wind. Inés leaned in, stroked his cheek with her palm and kissed him gently on the lips. When they broke apart, it seemed like for ever as she waited for his reaction. Then he yanked her leg, pulling her towards him, her backside sliding across the smooth tiles, until she was flush against him. Her legs wrapped around his hips.

Before she could even register what was happening, his mouth was crushing hers, passionate and demanding. She melted into him. This was exactly what she wanted and she wasn't going to let anyone take this moment away.

Ángelo knew he shouldn't be doing this, but how could he lecture Inés on not letting the voice of the past ruin her present when he was guilty of doing the same? Kissing Inés was what he wanted, but he kept letting old insecurities hold him back. As he'd told her, he wasn't a monk. He had needs and wants, and recently they were all wrapped up in her. They didn't have to promise each other for ever, but they could enjoy this for what it was without overthinking everything. It was clear they had chemistry and they couldn't fight it for ever. Perhaps it was about time they stopped living their lives without thinking about future consequences and simply enjoyed the moment.

Inés was straddling his lap now, her arms around her neck, her curves pressed tightly against his body, kissing him with a fervour which was setting his whole body on fire for her. He wanted her and the feeling was clearly mutual. So why deny themselves?

'What about your mother?' That was one reason they probably shouldn't get too carried away.

'She'll be out for the count now. She won't hear us.' Inés was kissing him all over, making his brain fuzzy and his body hard.

'Bedroom?' he asked, knowing exactly what was on both of their minds.

'First door on the right,' Inés mumbled into his neck between kisses.

With the last hurdle seemingly not a problem at all, Ángelo's restraint completely snapped. He didn't have to hold back any more. No more pretending he didn't want this to happen. This had all he'd been thinking about. He scooped her up and carried her the short distance to her room and closed the door tightly behind them. Shutting out the rest of the world, so all they had to think about was what they wanted to do to each other.

He stripped Inés's top over her head, revealing her full breasts encased in ivory satin. Ángelo cupped them in his hands, kissing the tanned globes, worshipping them with his mouth and tongue as he peeled away the underwear. Inés gasped when he caught her nipple, grazed it with his teeth and tugged until she was writhing against him.

He set her down on to the floor and helped her strip away the rest of her clothes until she was standing gloriously naked before him. Brave. Bold. And sexy as hell.

They stood facing one another and Inés began to unbutton his shirt. Her shaking hands giving away her nerves. Ángelo shrugged the half-opened shirt over his head and she covered his chest with her hands. Trailing her fingers over his torso, electrifying his skin everywhere she touched him. He sucked in a sharp breath when she undid his trousers and let them fall to the ground, along with the rest of his clothes.

Inés glanced up and down his body, biting her lip as she did so. Only increasing Ángelo's arousal. He took her in his arms and kissed her until she relaxed against him. Then he laid her down on the small bed a young Inés had likely only ever slept in alone.

He kissed her neck, her throat, her pert breasts, watching the pleasure on her face as he did so. The pride he took in seeing her so undone, spurring him on in his quest to completely unravel her. He drew his hand along her inner thigh and dipped a finger into her molten core, eliciting a gasp from her in response.

As he drew her nipple into his mouth, he slipped his finger inside her, feeling her wet heat beneath his touch. Teasing, pleasing, he increased the pace of his attentions until she was panting with anticipation. Then he felt her tighten around him, she lifted up off the bed, and tried to stifle the cry of her release with her head buried in his chest. He matched her satisfied grin.

'Was it good for you, too?'

She laughed. 'I didn't realise how much I needed that. Needed you.'

'You haven't had me yet.' Ángelo wiggled his eyebrows and made her laugh again, her body rubbing dangerously against his as she did so.

'What about contraception?'

He left her briefly to retrieve his wallet from his trousers and pulled out the emergency condom he kept there.

'I always come prepared,' he said, covering her body again with his.

He kissed her with renewed desire and positioned himself between her legs, thrusting when he was sure they were both ready. Inés's eyes flew open as she gasped and he waited for her to adjust to him before he moved again. She kissed him and, arms braced on either side of her, he began to rock his body to hers.

As he'd told her, sex wasn't something he denied himself, but there was definitely something different about being with Inés. She wasn't a meaningless encounter fuelled by lust, but someone he had a connection with. Not only did they see each other every day at work, but they'd shared a lot with each other about their pasts and the scars they'd been left with. That emotional connection only seemed to heighten his passion and arousal.

They both knew how it felt to be hurt, to be found wanting in some way. Tonight it was clear that they were enough for one another and that was a powerful aphrodisiac in itself.

Joining their bodies together, feeling that euphoria of physical satisfaction, made him forget all the pain of the past. He wanted to have this all the time. Wanted Inés all the time.

With every thrust of his hips he brought them closer and closer to that final burst of bliss. Her little groans of pleasure urging him harder, faster, until all he could hear was the rush of blood in his ears. Everything in his body attuned to reaching that ultimate release for both of them. Ángelo wanted Inés to feel as good as he did. It had been hard to listen to how her ex had treated her, knowing this beautiful, strong woman deserved so much more. Even if it was just for one night he wanted her to be worshipped the way she always should have been.

'Ángelo—' When she gasped his name he was completely undone, barely holding back his needs until he knew for sure she was equally as satisfied.

Then her breathing changed into rapid pants, a whimper, her body contracting around his and the rush of her orgasm enveloping them both. Ángelo finally allowed himself to give in to his own pleasure, roaring his release into the crook of Inés's neck.

He was happy, he was exhausted, and he knew in that moment everything between them had changed for ever.

CHAPTER EIGHT

FIGHTING TO GET her breath back and regain control of both her brain and her body, Inés was stuck under the weight of Ángelo's body. And there was nowhere else she would rather be. Except somewhere they would have had more time and privacy to recover from their exertions without worrying about her mother discovering them. There was nothing she would have liked more than to simply curl up beside him for the rest of the night and let this fantasy play out a little longer.

Neither of them had anticipated this happening tonight, but it had probably been on the cards for a while. The kind of passion they'd shared was never going to have stayed bottled up for long. Instead, it had coming fizzing to the surface and exploded everything around her.

Ángelo, too, was panting, wiped out by the energetic, unexpected and extremely erotic encounter. Unfortunately they couldn't chance lying here naked any longer. They'd already taken a risk, blinded by desire. Now common sense had kicked in, the implications of being caught like this were too great to ignore a second longer.

'I don't know how we're going to explain this away if my mother catches us.' Despite current appearances, there was no way she was going to let her mother get carried away with the idea that they were going to be a couple. Inés didn't know what the future held, but she was sure that wasn't in their plans. Apart from anything else, she wasn't going to be railroaded into anything she wasn't ready for.

'I know. Just give me a second.' Ángelo didn't make any attempt to move as he mumbled against her neck, making her laugh.

'I'm serious. I don't want to feel like some shamed horny teen. We took the risk and got away with it until now. Let's not spoil things.' Though it was inevitable. Once they left this little bubble, reality would kick in, along with common sense, and they'd both try to distance themselves from what had just happened.

The only thing worse than trying to forget, would be her mother there to constantly remind her. Inés didn't need that when she was always going to have her own memory, along with the way her body reacted to him every time she saw him, to remind her of what they'd shared.

'Okay.' He stirred momentarily, then flopped back down.

'Ángelo.' She slapped his back, trying not to laugh and encourage him to stay where he was. It would be easy to simply give in to the urge to stay here for as long as possible, but she'd learned not to jump into relationships. If they stayed here much longer, she had a feeling they'd end up drifting into one and she wasn't ready for that. Ángelo wanted a wife, children, a family. She needed to explore her independence before she even thought of that kind of serious commitment.

A groan, a shift of position, and Ángelo finally moved away. Inés immediately felt the loss. Not only of his body heat, but also of the connection they'd had. That moment when they'd been the only two people in the world, totally lost in the feelings they'd aroused in one another, was gone. Probably for ever. There was a certain kind of grief washing over her naked body at the realisation. Sadder still, as they dressed in silence.

'Do you want me to go?' Ángelo asked, as he put his shoes on.

'Yes. Sorry. I don't mean to sound harsh, but I don't relish the idea of sharing an awkward post-sex breakfast with my mother.' There were more reasons than that to put some distance between them, but this was one that would keep things simple between them. He didn't need to know she was afraid of getting too close, too quickly, and living to regret it as she had with Marty. Something told her he wouldn't appreciate being likened to her manipulative ex.

'No problem.' He made his way hastily to the door, probably relieved that she wasn't going to read too much into the fact they'd had sex. It had been obvious how much he'd regretted their kiss, so sleeping together was bound to give him heart palpitations once reality set in.

They both knew she wasn't the wife and mother he'd pictured when he'd been putting everything into place for his future family. This was a one off. A much-needed release which would hopefully put an end to the fizzing chemistry that kept testing her vow not to get involved with anyone for a long time to come.

He kissed her hard on the mouth, almost knocking her off her feet with surprise so that he had to sling an arm around her waist to keep her upright. Pulling her close to him and jumpstarting all of those feelings that got her into trouble in the first place. The taste, smell and feel of him so very moreish she was tempted to forget those red flags all over again. Especially when the rewards were so great.

Although they'd had such a short time together, wary to some degree that they weren't alone in the villa, Inés had experienced an awakening. Sex with Ángelo hadn't been something expected of her, or that she'd felt obliged to engage in to avoid an argument or ill feeling. It had been an expression of her passion and desire, too. A feeling of freedom in simply doing as she pleased, giving in to those urges, and to hell with the consequences. As long as it never happened again and put her in danger of making more mistakes.

'Next time we'll got to my place where there's no worry about being interrupted.' Ángelo gave her a wink and walked away.

Devastating her attempt to convince herself this wasn't going to happen again. Because right now all she wanted was a repeat performance. Somewhere private where they had the freedom to explore one another completely for as long as they wanted. Where the new Inés had the same control of what happened in the bedroom as in every other part of her life. Denying herself the pleasure of sleeping with Ángelo again was letting Marty still have control, wasn't it?

By the time Ángelo had disappeared out of sight and Inés was closing the door, she was already planning on buying herself some new sexy underwear for their next rendezvous.

Sex didn't have to mean a serious commitment, or a lifetime of handing over control. It could just be having fun, exploring and enjoying a passion she'd never felt before. If she told herself that sleeping with Ángelo was simply another facet of her life as an independent woman, then she didn't have to worry about getting trapped with a man who wanted to change everything about her. She could walk away at any moment. Couldn't she?

It was the first time Ángelo was heading into work with knots in his stomach. A fluttering inside which grew faster and made him more nauseous with every step closer to work. Rising early and unable to even eat breakfast, he'd chosen to go on foot rather than by bicycle. Partly so he could have time to think, but also in case he caused an accident when he was so distracted.

He had no idea what he was facing this morning, or how he even felt about last night with Inés. The sex had been amazing. Passionate, powerful and all consuming. It was the implications of what they'd shared which had caused him concern. He knew there was no future for them as a couple, yet he wanted to do it all over again. Something he'd let her know as he left.

Now he had to face her in the cold light of day he'd find if it was something she was interested in, or would rather forget all about. He knew which one he'd prefer, otherwise it was going to make life very difficult at work. Seeing her, working with her and knowing how it felt to be with her.

Though getting romantically involved would bring its own problems, too, when she wasn't guaranteed to be in his life permanently. They both had some decisions to make—if last night was anything to go by, their libidos were leading the way instead of their heads.

The door to the clinic was already open when he got there, with Inés inside talking to the woman the agency had sent to cover her mother's absence.

'Morning.' He hovered in reception, waiting for some sign of how she felt about last night.

Her bright smile was a good sign. 'Morning. This is Giselle. I'm just giving her a rundown of how the place works.'

'Hello. I'm Ángelo.' He shook hands with the middle-aged blonde woman he was hoping wouldn't be around too long. As much as he wanted Marie to have a rest, he was looking forward to having her back so the place felt normal again. Regardless that things between him and Inés were now very different.

'I'll come and see you in your office once we're set up here.' Inés let him know her plan and he headed to his office with anticipation swirling in his belly.

There was no way of knowing what her decision would be regarding continuing what they'd started last night, but he was simply looking forward to spending time alone with her again.

When the brief knock came on his door he could stop pretending he was focusing on the paperwork on his desk. 'Come in.'

'Hey.' Inés entered, closing the door behind her, but not moving away from it to come closer to him.

'How's your mother today?' He thought they needed

an ice breaker before they got to the serious stuff. Besides, he was genuinely concerned for both of her parents.

'I took her breakfast in bed and she's under strict instructions not to do anything strenuous. I think she just needs some rest.'

'Good. Oh, I took some stuff to the hospital for your dad and left it with the staff.'

'Thanks for that. At least that will put Mama's mind at ease that he got what he was looking for.'

'Yes. All under control.' Unlike his current emotions. 'So…'

'So…' He echoed her foray towards the elephant in the room, exchanging coy grins with one another over their shared secret.

'About last night…'

'Hmm?' It seemed she was as unsure of the next move as he was and he couldn't resist teasing her a little bit.

He watched her eyes sparkle and her cheeks redden. 'Don't make me spell it out.'

Unable to keep up the charade, or resist her any longer, Ángelo got up from his office chair and walked towards her. She bit her lip as she waited for him to come to her and telling him everything he needed to know about how she felt.

Ángelo brushed the soft curls away from her face so he could study her closer. 'You're so beautiful.'

The words slipped easily from his lips when he was this close to her, seeing her pupils dilate and her teeth worry her full lips. Whatever spell she'd cast over him was clearly still working when he was casting aside all of those doubts he'd fretted about this morning in favour of giving in to temptation all over again.

Then she tilted her chin up and drew him towards those lips he'd been dreaming about all night. He gripped her arms and kissed her hard, as though he was fighting the attraction and succumbing to it all at the same time. When he was with Inés it felt as though he had no control over his body, or his mind. Exactly what made her so dangerous. He didn't want to fall for someone who didn't have the same vision for the future as he did. Not when he'd been there before and still bore the scars.

Yet it seemed as though he was doomed to repeat the mistake when Inés was all he wanted in this moment.

Hands wound in her hair now, he drank her in. Sipping from her lips and savouring her sweetness. Inés draped herself around his body and it was clear that she was in as much trouble as he was.

Then the sound of patients congregating in reception, chatting to their temp, filtered through their passionate haze. Reminding Ángelo they both had jobs to do and his career was something he couldn't afford to be distracted from.

He gave her one last kiss before he took a step back so he could think clearly again. 'The clinic is open.'

'Right. Yes. We have work to do.' Inés sounded uncharacteristically flustered. She brushed down her clothes and patted down her hair where Ángelo's fingers had been entwined in her soft tresses.

'We can pick this up again later if you'd like?' He wasn't ready to put a permanent end to things just yet.

'I'd like.' Her smile made him want to take her back in his arms and forget work even existed.

'I have a couple of errands to run, so it might have to be a late one. Unless you'd like to come with me?' He hadn't expected to invite her into another area of his life he didn't usually share with anyone, but he wanted to spend more time with her. Even if it meant opening up even more to someone he knew was probably all wrong for him.

'I'd like.' Inés's agreement seemed to stun them both into silence. It was a knock on the door from his first patient which spurred them back into action, both going their separate ways to concentrate on the job at hand.

The end of the day couldn't come quick enough for Ángelo.

'I thought you didn't drive?' Inés wasn't sure whether to be impressed or horrified when Ángelo turned up outside the family home in a battered old van.

'I don't drive. It doesn't mean I can't drive. I've borrowed this to transport some things. That's why I told you to put something old on. In case you get dirty.' He leaned out the window and waved her round to the other side of the van.

Inés was beginning to wonder about her clothing choice now. When he'd told her he'd pick her up, and for her to wear old clothes, she thought it was just his way of telling her they weren't going anywhere fancy. Still wanting to make a good impression, she'd donned a floral embroidered, white linen shirt with her jeans. As she climbed into the van and saw the stack of bags and boxes in the back, she suspected it wasn't the correct attire for manual labour.

'So where are we going?' She noted his holey charcoal-grey T-shirt and faded jeans frayed at the knees and found it just as arousing as his pristine work wear.

It was another side to him. More in keeping with the wild side he'd shown last night in the throes of passion. Rough and rugged, and extremely sexy.

She had to give herself a mental shake. If they were going to sleep together tonight, it would be a long way off. After he completed whatever task apparently took priority over everything else. She was going to have to learn to keep her libido in check if she was ever going to survive whatever this was between them. It wouldn't do her any favours to lose herself in either the romance, or sex, and fail to keep herself protected a second time.

'To see a few friends of mine. I do some fundraising from time to time to get them some supplies.' Ángelo was doing his best to keep her in the dark, but Inés had a feeling she was about to see a whole other side to him. He had a habit of surprising her.

'I'm sure they appreciate it.' She had no idea who these friends were, but the fact that he took time out of his work schedule to help them said they were important to him.

They drove in comfortable silence down the motorway before he turned off down a dusty track. A large white building came into view and Ángelo pulled up around the back.

'Okay. So, I need you to know before we go in…this is a shelter for victims of domestic abuse. I know you'll be discreet and compassionate, but some of the people here will be wary of you until they get to know you.'

She shouldn't have been shocked by the revelation given what she knew about his background, and his kindness, but she felt a wave of affection towards him for doing this. For being there for people who otherwise did not have any support. She was lucky she'd never experienced physical violence in the home, but she knew how it felt to be alone and not have anyone to turn to. Being unhappy at home was an awful position to be in and it took a lot of courage to walk away from the situation. As Ángelo kept telling her…

'Of course. Just tell me what you want me to do.' She didn't want to upset anyone, including Ángelo, but she was glad she had the opportunity to help, too, in some way. To assist someone who'd struggled to leave a toxic relationship as she had and simply needed some reassurance that things would work out.

'I have some toiletries and essentials to hand out, but if anyone needs a medical check, perhaps you could help? Some of the residents are naturally hesitant to leave the place to seek medical treatment and wary of a man coming into the building at all. Most of them know me and I've built up enough trust to engage with them, but the most recent inhabitants might prefer to deal with a woman.'

'I completely understand. Though if you'd told me I would have brought my medical bag,' she chided him, wondering if he'd been afraid to tell her all the details in case she declined the opportunity to attend with him.

'No problem. I've got plenty of medical supplies in the back, too.' He jumped out, opened her door for her, then unlocked the back door.

The scale of his fundraising efforts immediately became apparent, with the boxes stacked floor to ceiling. In typical Ángelo fashion, he'd downplayed the strength of his conviction to help these people.

'How did you fund all of this?'

Ángelo shrugged, then began lifting boxes out on to the ground. She couldn't help but stare, mesmerised by the flex of his biceps. Made all the more attractive by his altruistic gesture she was sure everyone beyond this place was oblivious to. She was certain if her parents had known she would definitely have heard them singing his praises for it.

The fact he did all this without the expectation of praise, and simply because he wanted to, wasn't helping her keep those emotional defences in place. Inviting her here to be a part of it should have set off alarm bells that this was already going beyond the casual relationship she told herself they were venturing into, but her inner swooning romantic didn't want to hear them.

'The usual...sponsored cycles, begging businesses to help, shaking a charity tin in every establishment within a hundred kilometres. It's not just me contributing. The whole community has helped make this happen.' Though not without a nudge from Ángelo.

'*Hola*, Ángelo!' A woman Inés guessed to be in her fifties, dressed in a polka dot jumpsuit and sporting a pink pixie haircut, greeted him with a kiss on each cheek.

She was irrationally jealous by the display until Ángelo introduced her and the woman displayed the same affection to her, too. Daniela apparently ran the shelter and called the others out from the house to help. One by one, anxious faces appeared at the windows and doors, making sure it was safe to come out before setting foot over the doorstep.

Inés couldn't blame them. For the first few days after she'd left Marty, she'd expected him to turn up. Jumping at every knock on the door, looking inside every car that passed in case he was watching her. There was a certain level of paranoia which followed long after that kind of relationship ended. She didn't know if she'd been more afraid of him making a scene and forcing her to go back with him, or that she'd convince herself he was the only person in her life that loved her. That perhaps she would be better off staying with him. Thankfully, coming out here gave her that space to realise she'd made the right decision in leaving.

'Take the boxes into the front room and we'll sort the distribution from there.' Daniela organised the troops, with Ángelo and Inés following the conga line all carrying boxes.

It wasn't long before they'd emptied the van and the front room of the house looked like a budget Santa's grotto. Though those in receipt of the basic supplies were every bit as overjoyed as a child on Christmas morning.

'It's funny how much the little things can mean when you have nothing.' Ángelo was standing beside her, watching the residents clutching on to bars of soap and bottles of shampoo, as though they were precious jewels.

'I suppose I was fortunate in that way when I had my income at least to buy the essentials after I left Marty.' If she'd given up her job, there was no way she would ever have been able to get away from him. Perhaps that had been his plan.

'A lot of these women leave with nothing. They're lucky just to get away with their lives in some cases.'

It made this set up all the more remarkable. That these women had somewhere to go knowing they would receive this help when they had nothing. It enabled them to take that giant leap and make the break. She was sure the children would be grateful for it, their haunted faces telling of the horror they'd gone through just to get here. Hopefully they'd find some peace here, as well as having a new future to look forward to.

'I don't think we'd be able to take in as many women if Ángelo wasn't on board. The donations mean we don't have to divert funds into basic essentials and can focus on supporting our residents.' Daniela sang Ángelo's praises for him, highlighting exactly how much his contribution meant to the shelter.

He flushed pink, clearly not used to receiving such effusive gratitude. 'Speaking of which, Inés is a doctor, too. We thought we could both offer our services today if anyone needs us?'

Although he was clearly trying to divert attention away from himself, Inés was keen to do something equally useful to the people here. 'Yes, I'm on hand for any medical queries. Just point me in the right direction.'

'I have a new mother and son who just arrived. They're still in their room, but I think they've had a particularly tough time, if you wouldn't mind having a chat with them? I think they're both harbouring some superficial injuries, but they weren't willing to go to the hospital when they first arrived.'

Inés and Ángelo agreed to see them and followed Daniela to a small room at the top of the stairs.

Daniela knocked on the door and went into the room first to make sure the new arrivals were comfortable speaking to them. Once they got the go ahead, they ventured into the darkened room.

'Hi. I'm Ángelo. I'm a doctor. Is it okay if I open the

curtains so we can see a little better in here?' Ángelo's soft tone came across as non-threatening and the woman huddled up to her small son nodded. Though she kept her wide eyes on him at all times as he let some light into the room.

'I'm Inés. I'm a doctor, too. Daniela said you might need some medical treatment? We're here to help.'

The woman was watching Ángelo with some suspicion. Unsurprising if she'd been a victim of domestic abuse and saw men as a potential threat. Inés could relate to some extent when she was still wary of getting too close to anyone who might hurt her again too. Albeit in a different way.

When there was no response, she tried again. 'What's your name?'

'Sofia. This is Emiliano.' The woman stroked her son's hair as he huddled close. It was clear they were afraid to be separated, but Inés and Ángelo needed to assess them properly.

'Well, Sofia, if it's okay with you we want to give you both a check over? Ángelo could take a look at your son over there. We don't have to leave the room.' When Inés left Marty she only had herself to worry about. She could understand the woman's reluctance to let her son out of her sight when she was responsible for his safety, too. It was important that they didn't make them feel any more afraid than they already were so they knew they were safe here.

'Why don't you take a seat over here, Emiliano, and we can have a chat?' Ángelo patted the mattress on the other single bed across the room.

The boy looked at his mother for permission and she nodded, bringing a sigh of relief to Inés.

'I understand you've had a difficult time. I'm just here to help you, okay? Can you show me where you're hurt?' The woman cast an eye over to where her son and Ángelo were chatting about football. Once she was sure he wasn't watching, she carefully lifted her shirt at the side. Revealing very vivid purple bruising.

The sight made Inés clench her jaw in anger at the man who'd inflicted such awful injuries, but held her tongue.

'I'm just going to have a feel to make sure there's nothing broken. I'll be as careful as I can. Just let me know where it hurts.' Inés positioned herself so she was blocking the child's view and kept her voice low so he wouldn't hear their conversation.

She carefully felt around the injury, felt the woman tense and suck in a sharp breath.

'Sorry. I don't think anything's broken, but your ribs are very badly bruised. I'm going to sound your chest so this might be a bit cold.' Inés pulled out the stethoscope from Ángelo's medical bag and breathed on the end of it to try to heat it before positioning it under the woman's shirt.

If she had missed a rib fracture there was a possibility of it puncturing a lung, but everything sounded clear. It was just going to be painful for a while.

'You need to rest and give the bruising time to heal. I'll leave you some painkillers. Is there anything else you want me to take a look at?' Inés didn't want to cross any boundaries, and would only treat any injuries Sofia was comfortable sharing with her.

The woman parted her hair to reveal a gash at her

temple. Blood had congealed in her hair, and it had obviously been a traumatic injury.

'Have you experienced any headaches, dizziness or nausea?' Inés didn't know exactly what had happened, but if she'd had a significant impact there was a possibility of concussion or worse.

Sofia shook her head.

'I'd prefer you to have it checked at the hospital. Promise me if you develop any of those symptoms you'll go immediately to A&E.' Inés didn't like to leave her here unchecked, but she was also aware the woman wasn't actually her patient. She could only advise and ask Daniela to keep an eye on her.

'I promise,' Sofia said meekly.

Inés's heart went out to the woman. She'd been through such a horrendous event and had no idea what the future held for her or her son. That level of uncertainty was stress in itself without the constant fear of her abusive ex turning up again. All she really wanted to do was give the woman a hug.

Instead she asked her to accompany her to the bathroom so she could get the wound properly cleaned.

She filled the sink with warm water and took some cotton pads and began to clean the area, wiping away the blood and grime. It took a lot to prevent a sob escaping not only for this woman and her child, but for the same scared Inés who'd been through something similar.

'Everything will be okay, you know. I know it might not seem like it right now, when everything is so frightening and overwhelming, but you have good support here.'

Sofia nodded, tears silently dripping down her cheeks.

Even that was something she recognised, crying without making a sound. Doing it somewhere Marty wouldn't see or hear in case she incurred his temper. He hadn't had to use his fists on her when words had always been enough to control her. That thought that she was only lovable if she did as she was told. Not enough for her parents, or her partner, just the way she was. It dawned on her that so far, Ángelo hadn't asked her to change. Even when she'd been rude and abrupt to him, he hadn't chastised her. He accepted her, faults and all.

'I was in a bad relationship myself until recently.' Inés's words caused the woman to look at her with wide eyes.

'But you're a doctor.'

'I'm still human. Still capable of falling for the wrong man. I know how it feels to be trapped in a toxic relationship. You keep telling yourself that they'll change, or that you'll be better so you don't anger them. But it's not you and it wasn't me.' She took Sofia gently by the shoulders, wishing someone had given her this talk when she'd first made the break. It had taken her a while to understand she wasn't the one at fault.

'No…' Sofia said softly. 'I didn't hurt anyone. I had to protect my son.'

'Exactly. You've done the right thing for you and Emiliano. This is the start of your new life.'

A knock on the bathroom door interrupted their heart to heart.

'Inés? Is everything all right? Emiliano was getting worried about his mother.' Ángelo sounded concerned, too, and she realised she'd broken her promise not to leave the room.

Inés opened the door. 'I was just dressing a cut on Sofia's head.'

Ángelo hovered as she covered the wound with some paper stitches and a dressing and Emiliano was standing behind him.

'See, your mother's fine.' Ángelo moved aside so he could see for himself.

'Everything's okay. We're going to be okay,' Sofia said through a watery smile, giving Inés hope that her talk had helped in some way. It wasn't easy opening up about her own experiences, but it was important she knew she wasn't on her own.

'Well, Emiliano is fighting fit. He has a few scrapes and bruises, but nothing he won't shake off.' Ángelo and the boy exchanged a high five, with Emiliano already looking brighter and happier.

It occurred to Inés that the two might have shared a similar conversation. After all, Ángelo had been brought up in a similar environment and seeing the man he'd become would surely make him a positive role model for anyone.

'If there's anything you need, I'm sure Daniela has our contact details. I think you and Emiliano should both have counselling to help you move on. You've been through a lot. We can help you access whatever services you need.' Inés didn't want to overwhelm them all at once. The next steps should be down to Sofia, but she wanted her to know there were resources available for her.

'Yes. Anything you or Emiliano need, don't hesitate to get in touch. We want to get you back on your feet as soon as possible.' Ángelo held out his hand and Sofia shook it.

'Thank you both,' she said quietly, folding her son back in the safety of her arms.

Inés suddenly had to get out before she burst into loud messy tears and caused a scene, making them all uncomfortable. It so easily could've been her in this situation if she'd waited any longer to leave. If they'd had a child, he or she would've been subjected to the same life, or worse.

She *was* brave and so was Sofia.

'We'll see you again soon,' Ángelo promised as he hurried Inés out the door and out of the building.

He'd seen the wobble in her usually strong countenance and knew he had to get her out of the very emotive situation. They'd done everything they had to do and now he had to make sure she was okay.

He called their goodbyes and helped Inés into the van. Leaving a trail of dust as he drove away at speed, wanting to put some space between them and the shelter. Once he thought they were a safe distance away, he abruptly pulled the van over to the side of the road, undid his seat belt, and reached over to hug her tight.

'I'm so sorry. I should have realised it was too soon to put you through that.' He'd only been thinking about what an asset she would be. Never imagining the horrors that were going on behind her strong exterior.

He'd overheard her in the bathroom sharing something of her experiences with Sofia. It was clear the relationship had been traumatic and still had a lasting impact on her, but she'd been so brave it was easy to forget how fragile she still was. And no wonder. It said a lot about her strength of character that she'd been able to come out here and work so soon. Especially to help her parents who she'd had a troubled relationship with, too.

It was about time someone took care of her for a change.

'It's okay,' she mumbled into his chest. 'I didn't expect to get so emotional either. It was just the thought of how I could have ended up, too. If I'd stayed. If we'd had children.'

Ángelo let go of her so he could tilt her chin up to face him. 'But you didn't. You were strong. You left. You're the bravest woman I've ever met.'

'Take me home,' she said firmly.

'Okay. I'm sorry. I shouldn't have brought you here. I'll take you home.' He buckled his seatbelt and started the van, sorry that he'd put her through this when he'd simply intended to share a part of his life with her he thought she'd relate to. Far too well it turned out.

Inés turned to him, jaw set with determination. 'No. I meant take me to your home.'

Ángelo hit the brakes. 'What do you mean?'

'You know what I mean. Tonight has reminded me that I wasn't to blame for what happened to me and I shouldn't let Marty dictate my life any more. I want to be with you, Ángelo, and I don't want my past stopping me from being happy.' She was back to being the direct Inés he knew, but he didn't want to take advantage of her when he knew she was emotionally vulnerable.

'As much as I want that, too, Inés, perhaps you need some space before you make any rash decisions you might come to regret.'

'Please don't tell me what I need. I've had enough of that for one lifetime. Unless you don't want me…'

Ángelo hated that he'd caused that little waver in her new-found confidence and reached out to grab her hand. 'Of course I do. I just want you to be sure it's what you want.'

Inés fixed him with those intense blue eyes. 'It is.'

With the strength of her response, there was no denying that going home with him was exactly what she wanted. He'd hoped that was where they'd end up tonight, Inés was simply taking the lead. Something he understood she needed to do after everything she'd been through.

Now the pressure was on Ángelo to make sure it wasn't something she'd come to regret.

CHAPTER NINE

Inés's bravado was gradually ebbing away, the closer they got to Ángelo's place. When he pulled up outside his modest villa, her heart was pounding so loudly she was sure he'd be able to hear it too.

'Nice place,' she said, admiring the ochre-coloured, one-storey building with white-shuttered windows and roof terrace.

'Thanks. It's home. And I'm hoping I'll never have to move again.' He opened the gates and drove into the small driveway at the side of the house. With the gates closed again, and the high surrounding walls, it gave that feeling of being in their own bubble again. Of safety.

Inés tried not to think about the fact he'd probably bought the place with the idea of raising a family in mind. This was a home for someone intent on settling down with a wife and children. A long-term commitment with an eye on the future. Not a casual fling with someone who wasn't sure where she would be in a few months' time.

She fought the doubt demons threatening to spoil the evening and tried to recapture the warrior spirit which had brought her here in the first place. The Inés who knew exactly who and what she wanted and wasn't going to let anyone take it away from her.

There was tension in the air as they made their way inside. Anticipation for the evening ahead bouncing off the whitewashed walls. For a bachelor pad, it was well furnished—for comfort rather than aesthetic—with oversized sofas and plump cushions. The open-plan layout let her see the modern kitchen with the farmhouse-style dining room table dominating the room. All set up for the family he was expecting to have in the near future, no doubt.

She consoled herself with the fact that he'd known about her issues before they'd gone to bed together the first time. He'd been well aware of the sort of person she was, so she wasn't under pressure to pretend to be someone she wasn't. They'd both apparently decided that they still wanted a casual sexual relationship for whatever time they'd have together. Because she wasn't promising either of them any more than that. Even if she was beginning to long for more.

At this moment in time she was questioning her plans to leave as soon as possible. She couldn't imagine going now and never seeing Ángelo again. Although the idea of getting into another relationship terrified her, the future he'd painted for himself with a partner and children was bringing out the green-eyed monster inside her for the woman who'd get to share that with him. If she was brave enough, perhaps there was a chance to have that for herself.

'I had hoped to have my own home some day, too.' Inés had never really had the chance of living independently. She'd left her father's home and rules, flat shared for a while in London, then moved into Marty's place.

Although her parents' villa was home for now, it was really only because of her financial circumstances. Once she'd put enough money by, she'd hoped she'd be able to rent a small place. Not caring where, or what it looked like, as long as it was hers and she didn't have to rely on anyone else to have a place to stay. Now, being here with Ángelo, she wasn't sure that was still what she wanted. She'd been frightened to want more. Trying to protect herself from getting hurt again by isolating herself. But, if Ángelo was the man she thought he was, running away from her feelings could mean she was punishing herself by denying them a chance to be together.

Ángelo Caballero had well and truly stuffed up her plans for a quick getaway.

'It took a while for me to get to this point in my life and a lot of hard work. There's no feeling like it, though.' Ángelo looked understandably pleased with himself and Inés hoped that somewhere down the line she could be proud of herself, too. So far, she didn't think she'd done a lot to cover herself in glory.

When she said as much to Ángelo, he frowned and stalked across the floor towards her, increasing her heart rate just a little bit more.

'I don't care how many times I have to say it. In fact, I'll keep telling you until you believe it, but you are one of the most amazing people I've ever met in my life.' He wrapped his arms around her waist and pulled her close, his fierce scowl melting into a soft smile.

At least this little interaction managed to ease some of the awkwardness between them since walking into the house together. There was no need to try to fill the air with small talk when it was crackling with that sexual awareness again. Looking into one another's eyes, seeing that desire reflected back, and knowing where it was going to lead.

And she wasn't disappointed. Ángelo ducked his head and captured her mouth with his in a tender kiss. Inés's insides immediately turned molten, her body draped around his. In his embrace was the one place she felt content and safe.

He let his hands drift down to her backside, giving her a territorial squeeze, eliciting a little thrill for her in the process. She didn't mind being treated as a possession as long it was only Ángelo taking ownership and it didn't go beyond the confines of the bedroom.

Seemingly with the same idea in mind, he released her and took her by the hand. He led her towards the bedroom at the far end of the villa. Inés followed at his behest into the masculine bedroom. The cream walls and deep red rugs spread on the wooden floor gave the feeling of warmth and intimacy. Rich earthy colours from the tapestries on the walls, to the covering on the huge bed, all contributed to the feeling of a cosy oasis. Somewhere they could get lost in one another and forget about the outside world. All the heat and passion she'd come to associate with Ángelo's touch was there in the decor.

And in his ensuing kisses. He backed her up against the bed until they both tumbled down on to the mattress, tearing at one another's clothes in a lust-fuelled frenzy. Impatiently tugging and unbuttoning, the sound of fabric giving way didn't stop their hurry to have that skin-to-skin contact. It wasn't long before they were both naked and wanting.

The strength of Inés's need for him still came as a surprise to her. Her body responding quickly and fully to his touch until she was aching for him. A throbbing, desperate need which could only be satisfied by Ángelo.

She wrapped her arms and legs around him, pulling him flush to her body, communicating exactly what she wanted. But he seemed determined to drive her to the brink of madness before she found any release.

He dotted barely there kisses along her collarbone and along that sensitive part of her neck which sent shivers all over her skin. The gasps and moans of pleasure and frustration coming from her body were almost alien to her. She couldn't remember a partner ever showing so much consideration, giving her body such thorough attention that she didn't know whether to laugh or cry.

In the past, she'd been the one eager to please, afraid of doing something wrong. Her pleasure had never really come into things. If it happened, it was by accident, not design, and she'd always thought sex was purely for the man's benefit. How wrong she'd been!

If she'd known this was how it was supposed to feel, as though she was the most cherished woman on the earth whose satisfaction was all that mattered, she might have realised Marty was not the man for her before she'd even moved in with him. She was grateful now at least that she knew sex could be something enjoyable for both partners and was an important, intimate part of a relationship. No matter how casual.

Ángelo dipped lower, his hands kneading and caressing her breasts, his tongue licking and flicking around her ever-hardening nipples. That throbbing need for him now like a second heartbeat reverberating throughout her body. And when he tugged on her nipple with his mouth and rolled his tongue around it, she thought she might orgasm there and then.

Lower, deeper, he tended to what seemed like all of her erogenous zones, until he was positioned between her thighs. He lifted her legs on to his shoulders and she held her breath, exhaling loudly when he plunged his tongue inside her. Arousal consumed her, rendered her almost immobile. A slave to everything Ángelo was doing to her.

He showed her exactly how much he wanted to please her. Didn't stop until she was completely satisfied and felt as though she was having an out-of-body experience she was on such a high.

When she finally drifted back and opened her eyes, it was to see him lying beside her with a smug grin all over his face.

'That was…' She had no words to explain what he'd just done to, and for, her.

'I aim to please,' he said with a deep laugh that went straight to her erogenous zones.

'Well, you definitely did that.' She stretched and sighed, rolling over to give him a kiss.

It was nice to share a bed again. Nicer still not to be full of anxiety and worry, completely relaxed and fully satisfied. She traced abstract patterns on his taut chest with her fingertip, enjoying the smooth warmth of his skin on hers.

'Good.' He lifted her hand to his mouth and kissed her. If he hadn't just done what he'd done to her, she might've said he was a gentleman. Thankfully, the bedroom brought out his wild side, even if he still insisted that the lady came first.

'What about you?' Inés slid her hand between their naked bodies and took a firm hold of his arousal, making him gasp for a change.

'Don't worry, I know exactly what I want.' His voice was so deep and gravelly, he practically growled the words. The sound of his heavy desire calling directly to her libido.

Ángelo left her briefly to sheath himself with a condom he took from his bedside unit. Then he was back, kissing her, anchoring her legs around her waist and… *oh!*

That full feeling of having him inside her was satisfying all on its own, but when he moved, she was in heaven. Ángelo was the whole package, in more ways than one. Not only was he handsome, successful and compassionate, but he was a fabulous lover, too. The fact that he wanted to settle down, too, made him the ideal man for anyone who hadn't been scarred by an emotionally abusive relationship.

For the first time, Inés wished she'd never left Spain. Then she might have met him earlier and they could have stood a chance of both having that happy ever after which had eluded them both so far. Unfortunately, her bad experience meant she didn't want to think beyond the present. She couldn't commit when she was so afraid of losing her identity again. Even though Ángelo made her feel more and more like the Inés she knew she was deep down with every second she spent with him.

Especially when he'd awakened the wanton inside

her with such ferocity. She'd gone from someone who thought she could live in celibacy quite happily for the rest of her life to now she couldn't get enough of him.

It made her wonder if there was a possibility they could take the next step beyond the casual nature of their arrangement. He wasn't frightening, or threatening. Ángelo was sexy and loving, and always mindful of what she needed. The sort of person she needed in her life.

So why was she punishing herself by denying there was a future with him? That was letting Marty keep control of her in some way. Keeping a huge part of a normal life on lockdown, afraid that she'd let someone else like him sneak into her life. Except she knew Ángelo was nothing like her ex. He would never undermine her, or make her feel anything less than she was. Especially in the bedroom where he made her feel like a goddess.

He thrust with a grunt. She cried out with pleasure. They could have this every day.

Their bodies rocked together. Once. Twice. Three times. Inés tightened her body around him. Clenched her inner muscles. And Ángelo cried out. She watched the ecstasy on his face. Saw him finally lose control. Finally felt the power she had over him. He was hers as much as she was his. No matter how hard they fought it, they were in this together. Completely and utterly lost to one another. And she realised she was no longer terrified at the prospect.

Wrung out by her emotions and the physical release Ángelo commanded time and time again, her body was limp. All she wanted to do was roll over and sleep. Preferably with a naked Ángelo spooning her from behind. But that hadn't been the plan. She didn't want to push him into something he didn't want. So, with some reluctance, she swung her legs over the edge of the bed and groped around the floor for her discarded clothes.

'Where are you going?' Ángelo was watching her, his head propped up on one bent arm, the bed covers draped tantalisingly across the middle of his body. She didn't have to use her imagination to picture exactly what was underneath when she had intimate knowledge of every part of him. It didn't make it any easier to leave him.

'Home. I can order a taxi if you prefer?' She could understand if he was too exhausted to get her back home when her legs didn't want to work either.

'Stay.' His quiet plea and the cute head tilt would've been enough to convince her to get back into bed, but Inés wanted some clarification about what that meant.

'Why?'

'Because I want you to.' His lazy smile completely seduced her so she didn't care about his motives any more and simply wanted to lie back down beside him.

She sighed at her own weakness. 'What are we doing, Ángelo?'

'Enjoying ourselves, I hope.' He nuzzled into her neck, completely eroding what was left of her willpower.

'You know what I mean. You've made it clear you want the whole wife and two kids and I'm terrified of getting into anything serious. So where does that leave us if we can't keep our hands off each other?' It was clear abstinence wasn't going to be the answer when she was rewarded time and time again for giving in to temptation where Ángelo was concerned.

He rolled on to his side and fixed her with his deep brown gaze. 'I'm not asking anything of you that you're not ready, or willing, to give, Inés. I just like being with you. Yes, I would like more, but I'm not going to put any pressure on you. That has to be your decision.'

It was clear he was taking her feelings into consideration, knowing the issues she had around relationships. At this point in time she was more afraid of her own feelings than anything she believed Ángelo might be capable of.

'Thanks.'

'Maybe we just need to enjoy this for what it is. Who knows, maybe our next relationships will be better for it?' Ángelo was trying to make this an easier decision for her. Keeping the idea that being together was nothing more than a casual arrangement, even though deep down she knew it had become more than that for her. Especially when the thought of him moving on with someone else, setting up that cosy family environment which didn't include her, was painfully squeezing her heart.

As Inés cuddled into him, relished the warmth of his arm around her holding her close to his naked body, she realised how much she did want this on more than a temporary basis. It would be nice to stay with someone that was making her happy and she had her job, too. Life was beginning to look up for her, but there was a black shadow on the happy scene which she couldn't ignore for ever.

If she was going to ever be able to move on, she had to confront the past first. She didn't want to hide from it, or let it dominate her life any more. It was time to see her father and get some closure before it was too late. Then perhaps she might be able to fully enjoy a life with Ángelo in it, without thinking that he was hiding something from her, and the minute she committed to him he was going to show her a side of him she didn't like. And break her heart all over again.

'I'll see you later tonight. I just have a couple of things to do first.' Inés gave Ángelo a lingering kiss which only made him pull her back for more when she tried to leave.

'I have to go,' she laughed through the kisses.

'Okay. I'll see you later.' He didn't like to push too far in case he scared her away when she was still trying to rid herself of past demons. As much as he wanted something more than the casual arrangement they'd fallen into, he'd rather have her on her own terms than not at all.

Despite her previous protest that she didn't want to get involved so soon after Marty, they'd got into a routine of working and sleeping together. Going out for meals and walks on the beach. They were a couple without the actual label. He was hoping some day she'd feel safe enough to commit to him, but for now he was content to simply have her in his life. There had been no mention of moving away, or looking for work elsewhere, and he got the impression she was happy with things the way they were, too.

Marie was back at work and even she knew better than to comment on whatever was going on in case it upset Inés. Though she must have known when her daughter was spending most nights away from home and the lingering looks Ángelo and Inés exchanged through the working day, when they were waiting to be alone in private, were probably a dead giveaway.

He knew, though, that there was an issue that they all

needed to deal with if they were ever going to be able to be together in any significant way. Inés's father.

Ángelo was worried that if Juan died without ever having reconciled with Inés, that the guilt and regret might force her to move away from the area. After all, she had a history of leaving when she was in pain. Rightly so, but for his own selfish benefit, he wanted her to be content where she was. To have some closure and be able to live her life freely. Preferably with him.

For now, he was simply going to try to keep the peace. Helping out where he could, while still trying to maintain a relationship with Inés and her estranged father. Though he knew she didn't like to hear when he was visiting the hospital. He got the impression it made her feel guilty that he was going to see her father, when it should have been her. But that was a decision he'd learned to leave entirely to her.

It was also the reason he hadn't told her he was journeying to the hospital tonight after work. He'd promised to take some things over for Marie, still trying to prevent her from doing too much in the process. The last thing anyone needed was for both of Inés's parents to end up in the hospital.

When he walked into Juan's hospital room, he was once again struck with sympathy for the man who'd given him a job and friends at a time when he'd needed them most. Pale, arms bruised from having bloods repeatedly taken, and his usually neat hair, dishevelled against his pillow, he looked nothing like the man Ángelo had known for years.

Still, Ángelo plastered a smile on his face and walked

towards the bed. '*Hola*, Juan. I thought I'd come and see how you were today.'

'You're the only one who bothers,' he grunted.

Ángelo knew that lying here, knowing his days were limited, he was likely to dwell on all the negatives of his life, and he wanted to do his best to make him feel a little better at least.

'As you know, Marie is under strict instructions to take it easy. She's been doing too much. She's on the mend now, but I said I'd pop in and see you today to save her the journey.' Ángelo deposited the clean clothes he'd been tasked with bringing into Juan's bedside locker and left the sweet treats Marie had made on the table across the bed.

'It's too much trouble to come and see a dying man,' Juan grumbled, clearly having a bad day.

'She has been here twice a day ever since you were admitted. I just thought she needed to rest.' Ángelo wasn't going to mention Inés. With the mood her father was in, he doubted anything good would come of it when she had made no mention of coming to see him.

'You've looked after the business, you're making sure my wife is okay and you're here when I need you. You're the only one who cares, Ángelo. The only one who has ever been there for me.'

'You know that's not true, Juan. Inés and Marie are running the clinic, too. If no one cared, we wouldn't all be running ourselves ragged. Marie will be up to see you tomorrow, on her day off.' Ángelo knew it was difficult for Juan being here, not knowing how long he had left and likely scared that he'd die alone. However, he also knew that Marie needed a break. They were all doing their best.

'And my daughter? She's living in my house, working in my practice and knows I haven't long left. Yet she won't come and see me.'

'It's not easy for her, Juan. She's still hurting.' He didn't want to upset his friend, but he wasn't going to stand back and let Inés take all of the blame.

'Ten years and she won't even come and see me before I'm gone for ever. She's never going to forgive me for the past,' he sighed. 'I only wanted to do what was right for her. Make sure she had a job for life. Perhaps I didn't go about things the right way...' It was clearly something weighing heavily on the man's mind and no wonder when his daughter was so hesitant to see him. However, now having all of the facts, Ángelo could understand her reluctance. She still bore the scars from her past relationships with controlling men who included her father.

'She just needs time, Juan. Maybe if she knew you had some regrets she might be persuaded to see you.' He was torn between two of the most important people in his life. Although Inés didn't want to discuss her father with him any more, Ángelo thought she needed to get that closure for herself.

He also wanted to pacify Juan, too. He needed some reassurance that there was still a chance to make amends with his daughter. Perhaps he could clear his conscience by apologising to her for what had gone on in the past and, at the same time, give Inés some sense of peace, too.

'All I did was push her away. Now she's been forced to come back.'

'It shows you at least that she still cares about you and Marie.' Ángelo knew that her own circumstances had come into play, but it was obvious that Inés loved her parents in some form or she wouldn't have entertained the idea of coming back at all.

'Nevertheless, I've spoken to my solicitor. When I die, the practice will go to you, Ángelo. You're like the son I never had.'

Though he was stunned by the generous gesture, and the sentiment behind it, Ángelo knew he couldn't accept it. Inés was the one who deserved to inherit, not him. Regardless that this was the opportunity for the financial stability he'd been searching for, she needed it, too. This could be her chance to start her new life properly. And it meant she would have a reason to stay. Not only would that be for his benefit, but it could also help her relationship with her mother.

Ángelo had a home and a job—the only other thing he needed was Inés. His feelings were becoming stronger for her and her happiness meant more to him than a boost to his bank account.

'I appreciate the offer, Juan, but I can't accept it. You have a daughter who deserves it more than I do. Inés is a wonderful doctor and she's a great asset to the practice. I couldn't think of anyone better to continue your legacy.'

'I wasn't sure Inés would want to be tied to the clinic when she'd fought so hard against being part of it in the first place…' It was obvious Juan had given the matter some thought, which was evidence enough for Ángelo that this was the right thing to do. He wanted his daughter to take over the family business and Inés would see it was in her best interests, too.

'Inés doesn't always make the right decisions for herself. She might need a little nudge in the right direction on this one, but trust me, this is what she needs.' Ángelo knew she was scared to commit herself to anything after the rough time she'd had with her ex. This was one way they could help her make the right decision.

'If you're sure, I'll contact my solicitor and instruct him to leave the practice to Inés.' Juan closed his eyes as he spoke, clearly exhausted by the conversation, but also looking as though he'd found some peace in making the decision. The one Ángelo was sure he'd wanted to make all along.

'I'll let you get some rest.' Ángelo made to take his leave and caught sight of Inés in the corridor, the expression on her face one of total horror.

Ángelo rushed out after her as she turned away, apparently having decided not to see her father after all.

'Inés, wait!'

She spun around to face him, unshed tears sparkling in her eyes. 'I can't believe I fell for it again. You're just another man who wants to control my life.'

'What are you talking about?' Ángelo had thought he was doing the right thing, sacrificing his own secure future to provide Inés with one. She was acting as though he'd stolen her inheritance from her instead of making sure it went to the right person.

'I went to England ten years ago because my father had been trying to force me into joining the practice. Now you're conspiring with him to tie me to the place for ever, making decisions about my life without even consulting me. You know what I've been through with Marty and I told you I would never put myself in that position again. I guess you decided you'd do it for me. I thought you were better than that, Ángelo, but I always was a bad judge of character.' Even if she hadn't said a word, it was the tears now streaming down her face that gave away how utterly devastated she'd been by the conversation she'd apparently just overheard.

Ángelo cursed himself for not thinking things through properly before opening his mouth to Juan. He'd been so carried away with securing a stable future here for Inés, he hadn't stopped to consider her feelings about it. Or how it would seem to someone who'd been controlled by men her entire life. He hadn't asked her what she wanted, or let her make the decision whether or not she wanted to stay, and that did make him guilty of trying to control her in some way. Even if he hadn't meant to.

In trying to give her a reason to stay, perhaps make her think about having a future here with him, all he'd succeeded in doing was push her away.

Blinded by tears, Inés couldn't see where she was going, but she hurried down the corridor regardless, pushing open every set of double doors until she was outside. Inhaling gulps of air through her sobs. The sense of betrayal she felt literally stealing the oxygen from her lungs. She'd come to the hospital with some trepidation, half expecting to incur her father's wrath. Willing to at least try to talk, rather than live with regret for the rest of her life. What she hadn't anticipated was finding out the man she'd given her heart to was as calculating as every other man in her life who'd tried to control her.

They weren't even a couple and he was already making plans on her behalf. After a decade estranged from her father she'd never expected to inherit anything—now Ángelo appeared to have taken control to ensure she did. Deciding that her future was in the practice here in Spain without any consultation, or consideration of how that would make her feel. Tying her to the place she'd run from forever.

Ángelo had made no secret of the fact he wanted to settle down and though he'd been making her wonder if she wanted the same thing, red flags were waving all around. If he was planning her life out like this for her already, just like her father and Marty had, what would it be like for her to be in a relationship with him? She hadn't fled from Marty just to end up in a similar situation, with another man telling her what she could, or couldn't, do. Making decisions on her behalf and not caring about what she wanted. As far as she could see, the only thing Ángelo would get out of this arrangement was having control of the situation once her father passed away. Having control of her.

'Stupid. Stupid. Stupid.' She hit her forehead with the palm of her hand, punishing herself for falling for it again. For getting drawn in with a few kisses and kind words, only to find out the truth once she'd lost her heart. That's why it hurt so much. She'd fallen for Ángelo and convinced herself he could never hurt her the way Marty had.

It seemed she was doomed to go through this time and time again. Falling for the wrong man and discovering when it was too late to do anything.

Someone grabbed her hand before she could hit herself again for being so gullible.

'Stop it, Inés.' Ángelo's voice, calm and quiet, sounded at her ear.

She hated that it still made her weak at the knees.

'Why? I'm so stupid I need some way of making it sink in that I shouldn't get involved with anyone because it always ends in tears. Mine.' Inés rounded on him, fired up by anger and heartache.

He wrenched her hand away before she could do any more damage. 'What is so bad about making sure you have a secure future in the family business?'

Inés couldn't believe he was being so obtuse when she'd literally just caught him conspiring with her father to keep her here, knowing the control issues she'd had with Marty. 'You made that decision without consulting me, without asking me what I want.'

'I'm sorry. I thought I was doing the right thing for you.' He was very good at playing the wounded party when she was the one in pain. Just like Marty. Somehow everything was always turned around so it was her fault. Then she was the one who ended up trying to placate him, knowing she hadn't done anything in the first place.

Well, those days were long gone. She hadn't moved here to make exactly the same mistakes. At least she wasn't living with him and the sooner she found somewhere else to work, the better.

'No, you were doing what you wanted, with no consideration of my feelings. If you'd thought about me at all, you would've known this was exactly what I didn't want. I left the country ten years ago rather than take on my father's role. Now you've made sure I can't leave. I'm trapped.' That familiar sensation of suffocation, of struggling to breathe, threatened to overwhelm her. The same way she'd felt every time Marty took control of her plans and told her what was happening rather than let her choose for herself.

'I'll tell Juan I spoke out of turn. You two need to work things out between you. I'll stay out of it the way I should have done from the start. I just wanted to be with you, Inés, and hadn't thought about the consequences of interfering.' Therein lay the problem. Ángelo's natural instinct had been to take control and railroad her into what he wanted.

Whether he'd intended to manipulate her, or not, Inés wasn't going to take the chance of getting involved with someone else who might try to control her. It had taken her too long just to get to this point in her life where she had a say in what happened to her. For once, she was taking the lead and making the decisions about her own future.

'It's too late, Ángelo. I can't afford the risk of getting trapped with another control freak, thanks. Papa can do what he wants with the practice, but I won't be a part of it. Goodbye, Ángelo.' Inés didn't wait to hear any more excuses, or attempts to gaslight her. She'd made the call and she wasn't going to be persuaded otherwise. For once in her life she was making herself a priority and that meant no more men in her life. No more giving her heart away to the wrong people. No more Ángelo.

CHAPTER TEN

'Mrs Alvarez?' Ángelo called out into the waiting room.

There was no response. When he glanced up from his notes he realised why. The room was empty.

He turned to Marie behind the reception desk. 'Shouldn't she be here by now?'

'Oh, yes. She called about twenty minutes ago to say she couldn't make her appointment, so I think you're done for the day.' Marie smiled at him as though she was doing him a favour by cutting short his working day, when it would only give him extra moping time.

'Somebody else could have had that appointment. It's about time we started charging for time wasters.' He couldn't seem to stop the outburst even though it wasn't Marie's fault. It didn't take much for him to get upset these days. He'd been in a constant bad mood since the day at the hospital. Not least because he hadn't seen Inés from the moment she'd walked away from him. She'd even called in a locum to cover her at work.

Marie took off her glasses and set the pen she'd been making notes with down on her desk. 'Ángelo, I don't know exactly what went on with you and my daughter, but it's clear you're both unhappy. You're both acting so out of character.'

So, Inés hadn't told her about their relationship, or what she'd overheard, it seemed. He didn't know if that was a good thing, or simply a sign that she'd internalised everything. If she was in as much pain as he was, he'd prefer she confided in her mother. Even if it did paint him as the bad guy here. He knew how it looked with him convincing her father that Inés should be the one to inherit the business, but he hadn't meant to come across as controlling. His only thoughts had been providing her with the security he thought she needed. And yeah, if he was honest, he wanted to give her a reason to stay. Selfish, perhaps, but he would never have treated her the way her ex had.

It was Inés's fiery nature which had drawn him to her and he would never have wanted to extinguish that fire inside of her. However, she'd made it clear that whatever they had between them was over and he had to respect that. Otherwise he was guilty of everything she'd accused him of.

'Inés made some decisions and I'm doing my best to respect them.' No matter how painful.

Marie sighed. 'It must've been something serious when she's talking about going back to England to look for another job. I thought when she came back it would be for good. It would make things easier for me when Juan goes to have my daughter around, but she seems determined to go. I had hoped she and her father would make peace, too. We have no way of knowing how long he has left, but it won't be long.'

Ángelo could see her starting to get upset. So was he. If Inés left now without making amends with her father, he doubted she'd ever come back. There would be too much guilt and grief involved for everyone, including him.

She'd come to the hospital that day of her own accord to see her father and Ángelo's interference had likely ruined any chance of a reconciliation. A stain which could never be removed from his conscience if Juan died and he hadn't reunited with his daughter. It also meant that Ángelo would never see her again either and it had been difficult enough without her just for a few days.

He knew they weren't right for each other. That had been apparent from the moment they'd met. Yet, neither of them could deny the chemistry that had sparked between them. The bond they'd forged outside of that with their shared pasts had been a bonus. Despite all attempts to the contrary, there had been an emotional connection between them. They understood one another.

Deep down he supposed he'd been hoping that Inés was the one. That he'd be enough for her to stay, to want a family with him. Instead, it seemed as though she'd been waiting for an excuse to end things. Unwilling to hear him out, or give him a second chance to prove himself that he wasn't like her ex. All he was guilty of was falling for her and wanting her to stay.

Perhaps he could have tried harder to explain that. Waited until she'd calmed down. Told her he loved her. In the end he'd let his own fear keep him from trying.

He'd convinced himself she would have left him eventually, because she wasn't the settling down type. Then again, he wasn't supposed to be the emotionally involved type and look what had happened. He was simply afraid that he'd lost his heart to someone who wasn't going to give him that safe, secure, family environment he'd always wanted. Now he realised he just wanted Inés. Nothing else was as important than still having her in his life and he might just be about to lose her.

'Where is she now?' he demanded, sick of brooding and wallowing in his own misery when it was of his own making. At least if he knew he'd tried to win Inés back he might be able to live with himself. One thing was sure—if he didn't, he'd never forgive himself. He'd always done his best to make sure he had no regrets in his life. Not following his heart would be the greatest.

Marie blinked at him in surprise. 'I don't know. She's been making arrangements to go back as soon as possible. You know Inés, she's impulsive. She could already be on her way for all I know.'

He hoped not. It was doubtful she'd leave any forwarding address if this was the end.

'Where did you last see her?' He dumped his paperwork on the desk and grabbed his jacket, wishing he had the van with him today instead of his bike.

'At the villa getting her things together. She wouldn't tell me what happened between you two, but I could tell she'd been crying. I know my daughter well enough to know that she wouldn't be upset if she didn't care about you.'

There was a silent plea beneath Marie's concern. *Make her stay.*

He was going to do everything in his power to make that happen. It didn't matter if he had a family, a business, or anything else in his life. All that mattered was Inés and the love he had for her which scared him senseless.

Inés mentally ticked everything off her to-do list. She'd registered with an agency in the hope she'd get some work by the time she got back to London. With no other option, she'd had to book herself into a hostel. It would do until she found a job and an income, then hopefully she'd find somewhere else to stay. For now, a bed in a shared dorm was all she could afford. Her flight was booked, as was her taxi to the airport. She just had one last thing to do, then she could start yet another new chapter of her life.

A deep breath and she stepped into the hospital room. 'Hello, Papa.'

It had been difficult enough to find the courage to come the first time around, only to have her heart broken by an overheard conversation. She'd debated long and hard about coming today, but in the end, she knew she needed closure. Whatever worries she had that he would reject her, or be disappointed in her life choices again, she would have to set aside for the next few minutes. He was still her father and she didn't want to live with the guilt and regret if she didn't say goodbye to him at least.

'Inés?' Her father tried to lift his head off the pillow to see her, but it was taking him so much effort, she moved closer.

The speech she'd planned for years to tell him exactly how he'd made her feel, and what a terrible parent he'd been to her, suddenly felt too cruel to say aloud. It was apparent that this was a dying man and the only thing she felt for him was sympathy.

For years she'd been eaten up with anger at her father, picturing the wagging finger, hearing the raised voice and the commands he issued. Now all she saw was her parent clearly in pain and more vulnerable and fragile than she could ever have imagined.

She'd wondered how she would react to seeing him again. Would she cry? Freeze? Instinctively, she found herself reaching out and taking his hand. 'I came to say goodbye.'

'I'm not going anywhere yet.' He pulled off his oxygen mask to speak.

'No, but I am. I'm going back to England.'

She saw the same pain in his eyes as she'd seen in her mother's when she'd told her the news, too. It surprised Inés and she supposed it was a sign of how ill he really was when the anger she'd anticipated was noticeably absent.

He closed his eyes and sighed, as though all the fight had simply gone out of him. 'I had hoped you'd stay. For your mother's sake. And Ángelo's. He's going to miss you, too.'

Inés bristled at the mention of him and she knew she had to say what was on her mind or else this visit was pointless. It was important to get it off her chest when she'd had a lifetime of holding back how she really felt through fear of upsetting someone else.

'I think he can manage perfectly well without me. After all, you said he was the son you'd never had.' Her voice caught on the words, surprisingly upsetting to someone who thought she hadn't even needed to see her father again. Perhaps it had simply been a defence mechanism because she'd known all along he'd only hurt her again, when she only wanted him to love her.

He squeezed her hand. 'I'm sorry, Inés. I'm in pain and frightened and I thought you weren't going to come and see me. That I wouldn't have the chance to ask for your forgiveness. I thought Ángelo was the only one who cared about me.'

Inés hadn't been expecting that at all. 'I just needed time. We never had an easy relationship, Papa.'

'I know. I only wanted what was best for you, Inés, but I didn't go about things the right way. I wasn't always a good father to you and I'm sorry for that. I don't want to die knowing that you hate me.' Tears clouded his eyes. Something she'd never witnessed before and it clutched at her heart. He was trying to clear his conscience and, suddenly, the past didn't matter. Already in so much pain, she didn't want him to carry the guilt of their troubled relationship to his grave, too. It was the one thing she could do to ease his suffering.

'I don't hate you, Papa. I love you. That's why it hurt so much when I could never seem to please you.' Probably why she'd adopted that role again with Marty, desperate to please and always failing.

'I was... I am very proud of you. I just wasn't very good at expressing that. I expected too much. Liked to get my own way. And I didn't know how to deal with it when I didn't get what I wanted. I should never have taken it out on you, or your mother. I thought I was doing the right thing leaving the practice to Ángelo. You never wanted to work there and I didn't want to tie you to it for ever. I wanted to show you I was finally listening to what you wanted.'

The revelation that he'd acted in her interests for once was overwhelming. In his own way, her father was trying to show her he cared.

'I appreciate that, Papa. Mama always said we were too alike. Perhaps I was too impulsive, leaving the way

I did ten years ago, cutting off all contact. I should have come to see you sooner.' Seeing how little time he had now, realising that she'd had a huge part in the breakdown of their relationship, Inés regretted that they hadn't reconciled before now.

'You're here now. That's all that matters. I hope you can forgive me, Inés.' That desperation to wipe the slate clean was there in his small voice and the compassion she had for him in that moment wouldn't allow anything else.

'It's all in the past.' She meant it. Being here with him, seeing how frightened he was facing death, she wanted to give him that peace. She didn't care about the practice, or the years she'd held on to her anger. Inés was ready to set it all aside, when she knew this was the moment she'd remember for the rest of her life. That she'd been able to give him some sense of relief in his dying days. In the process, she could forgive herself, too, for the mistakes she'd made along the way.

'Thank you.' He closed his eyes, apparently exhausted by the emotional confrontation.

'I'll let you get some sleep, Papa.' She did something she'd never done before, and leaned in to give him a hug, not knowing if she'd ever see him again.

The feel of his clammy skin beneath her fingers stole away the last of her strength, leaving tears streaming down her face as she rushed out of the ward. Straight into Ángelo.

'Hey. What's wrong, Inés?'

She wished the hands holding her would pull her close, hug her tight and make her feel as though everything was going to be all right. Even though she knew nothing was ever going to be the same again.

Inés swiped away the tears that had fallen and swallowed the ones threatening to show themselves. 'I was just saying goodbye.'

'Are you okay?' Worried eyes searched her face and it would be easy to believe he genuinely cared. But she'd let her guard down too soon and found herself falling for someone else she apparently couldn't trust. Hadn't known as well as she'd thought.

'I'm fine. I have to go.' She attempted to push past him, wishing she'd taken that earlier flight after all. It was going to be harder leaving when the last memory she had was Ángelo being nice to her.

He released her from his grasp, but followed her down the hallway regardless. 'You just saw your dying father and apparently you're leaving the country. I know you aren't fine.'

Inés wished everyone was as transparent as she obviously was. 'We made our peace, now I'm leaving.'

'And you're okay with that? With never seeing anyone again?' Still Ángelo followed her out the exit and into the carpark. He was probably going to sit with her at the bus stop, too, if she didn't tell him everything now.

'He apologised and I forgave him. I think that's more than either of us expected to happen. What are *you* doing here?' It occurred to her that if it was her father he'd come to see he was going the wrong way.

'I've been looking for you. This was a last resort. I didn't actually expect you to be here.' There was that little smile again that made her heart skip a beat. Damn him.

'Not for long. I have a flight to catch.' She didn't

know what he wanted to say, but she wanted to get it over with so she could leave. Goodbyes had never been her speciality. Probably because she'd always been afraid she'd be convinced to stay somewhere she needed to get away from.

'Then I'll say what I have to say quickly. Please, hear me out.'

When she reached the bus stop, Inés had no choice but to wait and listen to whatever he had to say. She checked the timetable, then her watch.

'You've got three minutes.' If the bus was on time, which was always doubtful.

'I swear I had no intention of hurting you, or trying to take control of your life. I just wanted to find a reason for you to stay.' It was apparent Ángelo didn't realise the strength of her feelings for him, when all he would have needed to do to keep her here was tell her how he felt about her.

Given that she'd been able to make amends with her father and the life she'd already begun here in Spain, she suspected Ángelo's interference had simply given her an excuse to call things off. Because she was scared of how she felt about him. Because that meant leaving herself vulnerable to getting hurt again.

'I was afraid of getting myself into an all-too-familiar situation with a man who was going to take away my new-found freedom. Hearing you make that decision on my future for me made me question if I really knew you at all.' She bit her tongue so she wouldn't say how hard she'd fallen for him and the pain it was causing her to leave.

'Of course you know me, Inés. You know me better than anyone else in my life ever has. I've told you things

I've never shared with anyone. I know Marty hurt you, but I'm not him. I love you, Inés. And I'm not saying that to emotionally blackmail you into staying. If you want to go, that's your choice. But I want you to know how I feel about you regardless.'

Inés tried to stop her battered little heart from soaring, but it was impossible when he was saying those words she never expected to hear from him. Ángelo wouldn't bandy the 'L' word about lightly. This was a man who'd avoided relationships until he was sure he could provide a stable home for his future family. Something he was aware she wasn't ready for.

Surely he wouldn't put that dream he had at risk unless he truly loved her? He wasn't trying to impose his will on her, forcing her back home and telling her she was in the wrong here, the way Marty would have. Instead, he was sitting waiting with her for the bus that could potentially take her out of his life for ever.

Inés wanted to believe that she wouldn't find out somewhere down the line that she had got him completely wrong after all and he was the kind, considerate person she'd taken him for all along. She thought of the patients she'd seen him treat, his rapport with her parents and the women at the shelter he helped. Surely they couldn't all be mistaken about his strength of character? Yet she was still afraid to stay in case she was wrong. She couldn't go through another living hell with a man who tried to control her. The only thing that would persuade her to stay and admit her feelings was if he truly put her first.

'I'm sorry, Ángelo. I just can't take the chance of getting hurt again.'

'I understand. I know what you've been through and how my actions must have seemed to you. But I swear I would never do anything to cause you pain. I don't want the clinic, I don't care about a family. I just want you, Inés. I love you. And, if you don't feel the same way, I'll respect that. I'll resign from the practice. I don't want to interfere while you are working things out with your parents, or start your life out here. I won't get in the way of whatever it is you want.'

The plea was there in his eyes. Ángelo didn't have to raise his voice or get physical to make her question herself. All he'd had to do was tell her he loved her, and show her he meant it.

The sacrifices he was apparently willing to make were proof of the extent of his feelings for her. Ángelo was prepared to give up that future he'd been working towards for her to believe in him. All Inés had to do was give him a chance. Give herself a chance to be happy.

'I love you, too, Ángelo. Why do you think I'm so terrified of getting this wrong?' Her words put a big dopey smile on his face, as though he'd never let himself believe that she might feel the same way about him.

He took her hands and made her turn and look at him. 'If you give us a chance, I promise I will prove to you every day that you made the right choice. Please stay.'

It was a plea, not a command, and Inés could almost feel the love radiating from his body to hers. No man had ever laid himself bare to her the way Ángelo was doing now. The only reason she was at the hospital was that she didn't want to live with any regrets and if she walked away now she might be left wondering for ever if she'd thrown away real love for the first time.

'I suppose I could book a later flight if I needed to…' She already knew everything she wanted was here in Spain. Her family, her job and the love of her life she couldn't imagine being without right now.

Then Ángelo kissed her and she knew for once she'd made the right decision. She'd finally taken control of her own life.

EPILOGUE

'Is that all you have?' Ángelo eyed up the couple of bags Inés had sitting waiting at the door of the villa.

'I travel light in case I have to make a quick getaway,' Inés teased, waiting for a thin-lipped response.

'That's not even funny.' He wrapped his arms around her and pulled her in for a kiss. They both knew she wasn't going anywhere but to his place.

'If I'd known, I wouldn't have bothered borrowing the van and just brought my bike.' Once he was done kissing her so thoroughly she would have followed him anywhere, he lifted her bags from the step.

'I guess I'll have to get myself one, too. I don't fancy having to get a lift on yours, or chasing you every morning to work. Maybe we should get a tandem…'

'I will happily walk with you every day if it means we get to spend more time together.' Ángelo put her bags in the back of the van before coming back for another lingering embrace.

It had been six months since she'd made the decision to stay and give their relationship a chance and the novelty hadn't worn off for either of them. That was why she was moving in with him. They'd taken things slowly so they both knew for sure that this was what they wanted.

When he'd asked her to live with him she hadn't needed to think twice about saying yes. He'd been there for her through her grief for her father when he'd died not long after she'd had her heart to heart with him.

In those last few days of his life, she and Ángelo had visited every day and even told him they were a couple. Which seemed to make both of her parents very happy. Before he passed, her father had made the decision to leave the practice to both Inés and Ángelo, so they were enjoying a whole new chapter together.

Her mother, who'd inherited the villa and enough money to live comfortably, was still working part time at the practice, but had decided to go to college to study ceramics. Although she'd mourned for the loss of her husband, Inés thought she also had a renewed self-confidence. Doing things that she wanted to do without having to get permission from anyone. She was even talking about setting up her own studio.

'I hope you weren't going to leave without saying goodbye.' Her mother appeared behind them, arms outstretched for a hug.

'Of course not.' Inés immediately went to her. They'd grown close over these past months and she was glad they had a good relationship. It gave her a sense of belonging and security to have family she could turn to, as well as Ángelo.

'You know you're welcome at our place any time. We're only a few streets away,' Ángelo reminded them, as Inés and her mother clung to each other as though they were never going to see one another again.

'"Our place". I like the sound of that.' It made her smile that Ángelo was already thinking of it as their home, regardless of how long he'd been living there and paying the bills. Marty had always made a point of saying she was lucky to be living under his roof. Making sure she was aware of the threat he could throw her out on the streets at any time. She knew Ángelo would never do that.

'Well, it is. It only feels like home when you're in it.'

'It might feel even more like that in another six months…' She smiled, unable to keep the secret to herself any longer.

Ángelo frowned, clearly bewildered by her comment. 'What's happening in six months?'

'You know, for a doctor I'm surprised you haven't noticed my symptoms. Nausea, weight gain…'

'I've put a few pounds on myself. I thought we were just comfortable together.'

Inés was really going to have to spell it out, though by the teary gasp her mother just gave, she had at least figured it out. 'I'm pregnant, Ángelo.'

She waited, watching the realisation on his face, before sheer joy took over. 'Pregnant? We're going to have a baby?'

'I know it wasn't something we'd planned, but I'm sure we can deal with whatever is thrown at us. We have so far.' It had taken her a while to get used to the idea herself. There was no greater commitment than becoming a mother and no greater worry. She hoped she would be the parent neither of them had growing up. With Ángelo by her side, she was sure they could provide a safe, loving home to raise their child. They even had a doting grandmother nearby.

'Congratulations. I'm going to be an *abuela*!' her mother said through her happy tears.

Without warning, Ángelo scooped her up and twirled her around. 'I can't believe it. We're going to be the best parents ever. I love you, Inés.'

'I love you, too, Ángelo.' She'd never been so happy, so content.

They were both finally going to have the family they'd always wanted.

* * * * *

*If you enjoyed this story,
check out these other great reads
from Karin Baine*

Temptation in a Tiara
Tempted by Her Off-Limits Boss
Nurse's New Year with the Billionaire
Festive Fling with the Surgeon

All available now!

MILLS & BOON®

Coming next month

HAWAIIAN KISS WITH THE BROODING DOC
Scarlet Wilson

'You can sometimes be a little grumpy at work.'

For a moment, Jamie looked tense, but then Piper noticed his shoulders relax as he sank back further into the chair. 'And you think you'll win me around by telling me this?'

There was a hint of amusement in his voice. She kept things light. 'Well, I figured you already knew anyway.'

He let that hang for a few moments. 'Maybe. I just don't like to get too friendly with people at work.'

Wow. How to sting. She tilted her head and contemplated him for a few minutes. 'You spend more than eight hours a day at work. Sometimes you can be there for more than twenty-four hours. Why would you want to have no friends?'

'It's complicated.'

He didn't expand. But she wasn't going to let it go.

'You're not grumpy all the time. At least not around me.'

She met his blue gaze straight on. It was a challenge. They were out of work now. And she had to know if the flirtations, glances, and that touch the other day, was all just a figment of her imagination. This—whatever it was between them—seemed like a two-way thing to her. If she was wrong, she wanted to know. Before she became the talk of the hospital again. And before she started to get her hopes up.

Continue reading

HAWAIIAN KISS WITH THE BROODING DOC
Scarlet Wilson

Available next month
millsandboon.co.uk

Copyright © 2025 Scarlet Wilson

COMING SOON!

We really hope you enjoyed reading this book. If you're looking for more romance be sure to head to the shops when new books are available on

Thursday 17th July

To see which titles are coming soon, please visit
millsandboon.co.uk/nextmonth

MILLS & BOON

FOUR BRAND NEW BOOKS FROM
MILLS & BOON MODERN

The same great stories you love, a stylish new look!

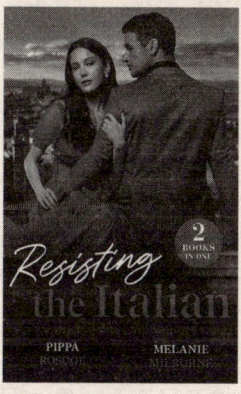

OUT NOW

Eight Modern stories published every month, find them all at:
millsandboon.co.uk

afterglow BOOKS

Afterglow Books is a trend-led, trope-filled list of books with diverse, authentic and relatable characters, a wide array of voices and representations, plus real world trials and tribulations. Featuring all the tropes you could possibly want (think small-town settings, fake relationships, grumpy vs sunshine, enemies to lovers) and all with a generous dose of spice in every story.

♪ @millsandboonuk
◉ @millsandboonuk
afterglowbooks.co.uk
#AfterglowBooks

For all the latest book news, exclusive content and giveaways scan the QR code below to sign up to the Afterglow newsletter:

SCAN ME

afterglow BOOKS

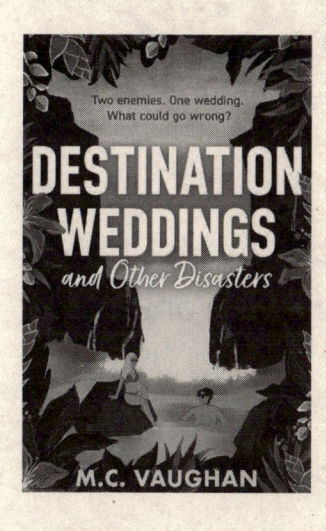

DESTINATION WEDDINGS and Other Disasters
M.C. VAUGHAN

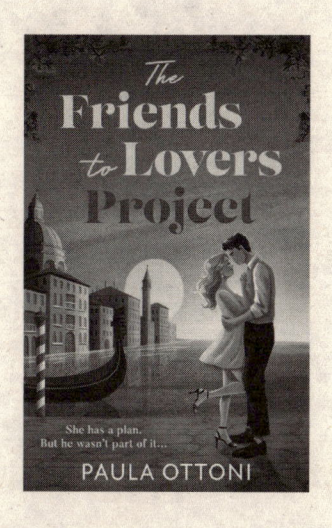

Two enemies. One wedding. What could go wrong?

The Friends to Lovers Project
PAULA OTTONI

She has a plan. But he wasn't part of it...

- ✈ International
- ♥ Enemies to lovers
- (♥) Forced proximity

- 👥 Friends to lovers
- ✈ International
- ▲ Love triangle

OUT NOW

Two stories published every month. Discover more at:
Afterglowbooks.co.uk

LET'S TALK
Romance

For exclusive extracts, competitions and special offers, find us online:

- **f** MillsandBoon
- **X** @MillsandBoon
- **◉** @MillsandBoonUK
- **♪** @MillsandBoonUK

Get in touch on 01413 063 232

For all the latest titles coming soon, visit
millsandboon.co.uk/nextmonth

OUT NOW!

Opposites Attract: Workplace Temptation

3 BOOKS IN ONE

CHRISTY McKELLEN · BARBARA WALLACE · STEFANIE LONDON

Available at
millsandboon.co.uk

MILLS & BOON

OUT NOW!

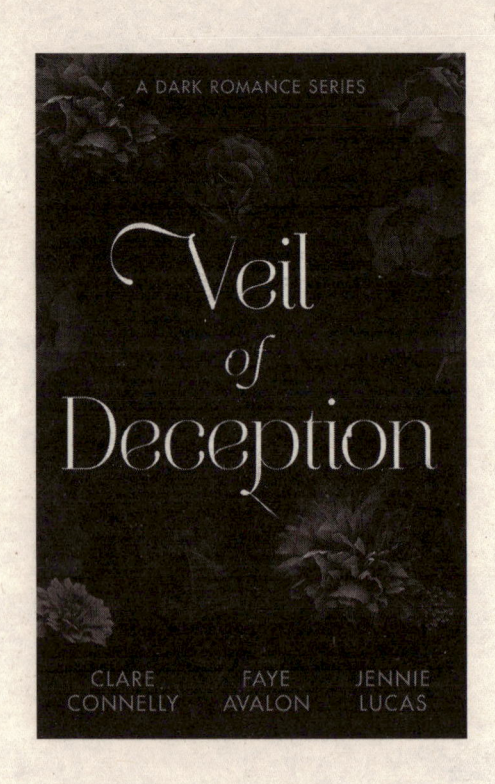

A DARK ROMANCE SERIES

Veil of Deception

CLARE CONNELLY · FAYE AVALON · JENNIE LUCAS

Available at
millsandboon.co.uk

MILLS & BOON

OUT NOW!

SECOND Chance

HIS UNEXPECTED HEIR

3 BOOKS IN ONE

LOUISE FULLER — AMANDA CINELLI — HEIDI RICE

Available at
millsandboon.co.uk

MILLS & BOON

OUT NOW!

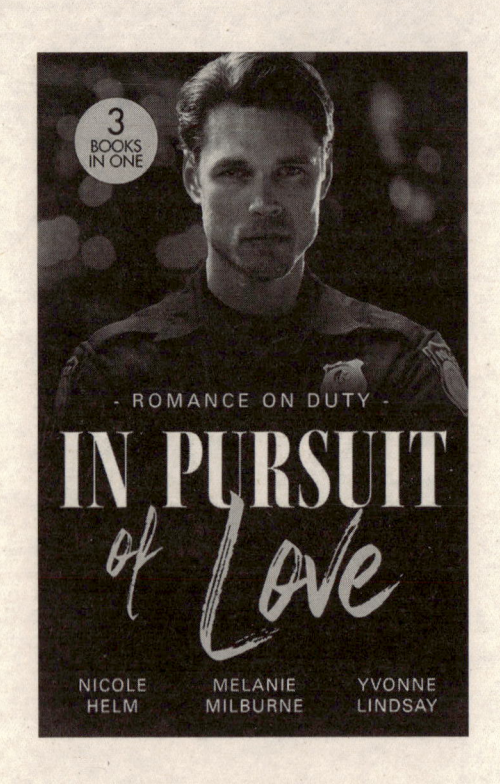

ROMANCE ON DUTY

IN PURSUIT of Love

3 BOOKS IN ONE

NICOLE HELM • MELANIE MILBURNE • YVONNE LINDSAY

Available at
millsandboon.co.uk

MILLS & BOON